# STAR WARS™

## THE COMPLETE
### VISUAL DICTIONARY

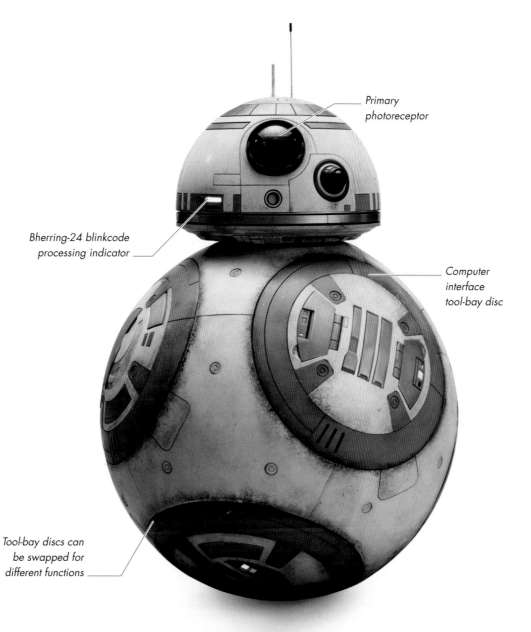

Primary photoreceptor

Bherring-24 blinkcode processing indicator

Computer interface tool-bay disc

Tool-bay discs can be swapped for different functions

BB-8

# STAR WARS™

## THE COMPLETE
## VISUAL DICTIONARY

Written by JAMES LUCENO, DAVID WEST REYNOLDS,
RYDER WINDHAM, JASON FRY, & PABLO HIDALGO

Special fabrications by ROBERT E. BARNES, DON BIES,
JOHN GOODSON, NELSON HALL, & MIKE VERTA

New photography by ALEX IVANOV

ANAKIN SKYWALKER'S
LIGHTSABER

LUKE SKYWALKER'S
SECOND LIGHTSABER

OBI-WAN'S
LIGHTSABER

DARTH VADER'S
FIRST RED LIGHTSABER

MACE WINDU'S
LIGHTSABER

# CONTENTS

Targeting rangefinder
(retracted)

Macrobinocular
viewplate

Utility
pouch

Kneepad
rocket dart
launchers

Boot spikes
(spring loaded)

**BOBA FETT**

Goggles are
stormtrooper
helmet lenses

Salvaged
quarterstaff

Salvaged
gauze
wrap

Survival
equipment
stored
inside

Mesh-
windowed
salvage sack

Govath-wool
traveler's
boots

**REY**

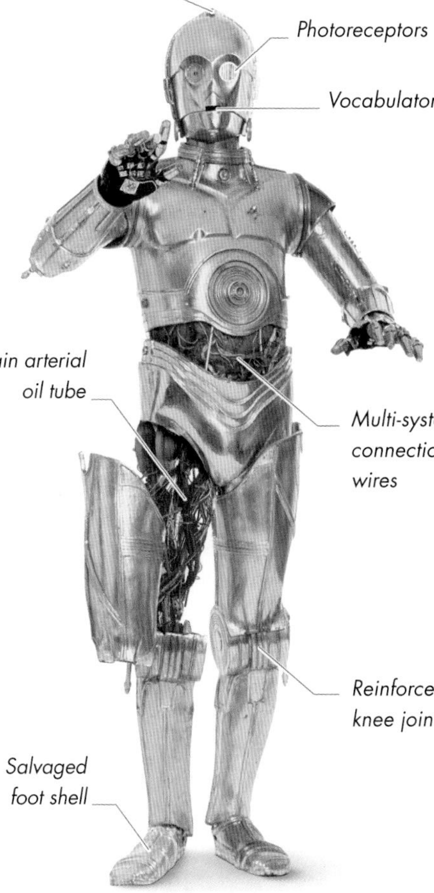

Microwave emitter/sensor
Photoreceptors
Vocabulator
Main arterial oil tube
Multi-system connection wires
Reinforced knee joint
Salvaged foot shell

C-3PO

Short Naylian-style haircut
Draped fibercord livery collar
Chandrilan medal of freedom
Simple robe of office

MON MOTHMA

# CONTENTS CONT.

Reinforced helmet

Broadband communications antenna

Energy sinks absorb blast energy

Energy ration

Suit systems power cells

STORMTROOPER

Cowl is a remnant from Ren's early training

Battered combat helmet

Unstable plasma blade matrix

KYLO REN

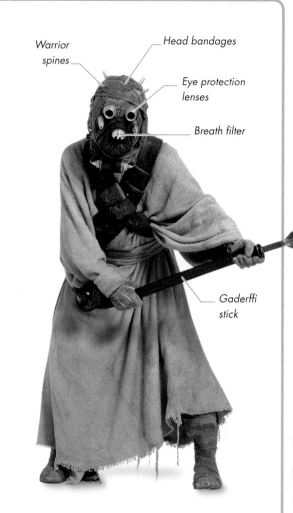

Warrior spines
Head bandages
Eye protection lenses
Breath filter
Gaderffi stick

**TUSKEN RAIDER**

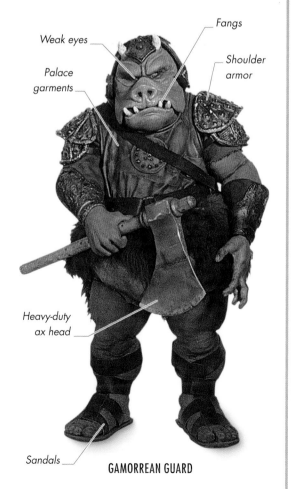

Weak eyes
Fangs
Palace garments
Shoulder armor
Heavy-duty ax head
Sandals

**GAMORREAN GUARD**

# INTRODUCTION

Except for a brief moment of darkness that conveys a former Jedi's final transformation into a cybernetic Sith Lord, nearly every scene in the *Star Wars* movies displays a wealth of visual information. Heroes and villains ride in instrument-laden starships, aliens wield uniquely crafted weapons, and the histories of various cultures are indicated by distinctive architecture on numerous worlds. Although many background characters, devices, vehicles, and structures were not identified by name on screen, most have acquired names and backstories by way of *Star Wars* novels, reference books, comics, toys, and games. Much has transpired since the publication of the first *Star Wars Visual Dictionary*, and this revised and expanded guidebook illuminates even more nooks and crannies of that far away galaxy....

# GALAXY OVERVIEW

**THE GALAXY HAS SEEN** many changes over the years. Governments, leaders, and Empires rise and fall—as do the rebellious organizations that oppose them. There are those who are devoted to serving and protecting the galaxy, and there are those who seek only to rule it. These constant power struggles lead to war and conflict, which inevitably alters the fate of many planets and those living on them.

## THE EMPIRE

In contrast to the democratic Republic, the Empire is a dictatorship with ultimate power resting in the hands of the Emperor. On a regional level, sector governors, called Moffs, oversee different areas. They exploit these planets for resources to construct Imperial vehicles and weapons.

## THE REPUBLIC

The Republic exists for over a thousand years and is the dominant political institution in the galaxy. It is a representative parliament that governs the galaxy from Coruscant. The Chancellor is the Republic's leader and is elected by the senators.

## THE REBEL ALLIANCE

Formed by Mon Mothma and Bail Organa in secret, the Rebel Alliance is an organization dedicated to restoring democracy to the galaxy. Not only do they wage a civil war against the Empire, they also assist civilian populations suffering under Imperial oppression.

## THE SEPARATISTS

Following the Naboo Crisis, a number of planets declare their independence from the Republic. Known as the Separatists, they object to excessive taxes and rampant corruption in the Senate. The Separatists' cause is funded by massive corporations, including the Trade Federation.

## THE NEW REPUBLIC

Following its great victory against the Empire at the Battle of Endor, the Alliance to Restore the Republic rebrands itself as the New Republic, and shortly afterward a peace treaty—the Galactic Concordance—is signed with the remnants of the Empire. Believing that the Empire was no longer a threat, the New Republic turns its attention to reshaping galactic politics.

## THE JEDI ORDER

The Jedi Order is a group of Force-sensitives that follow the light side of the Force and have existed for thousands of years. They uphold peace and democracy in the galaxy primarily through diplomacy, but will occasionally resort to lightsabers.

## THE FIRST ORDER

The Galactic Concordance defangs the Empire's ability to wage war, with strict disarmament treaties and punishing reparations. The Old Empire withers away, becoming a remnant of political hardliners locked in a cold war with the New Republic. The faction eventually breaks away to reform in the Unknown Regions as the mysterious First Order.

## THE SITH

The Force-sensitive Sith are the Jedi's ancient enemies. They are fuelled by anger and hatred, and follow the dark side of the Force. The Sith have two main aims: rule the galaxy and wipe out the Jedi.

## THE RESISTANCE

The Resistance is a small, private force created by Princess Leia Organa to keep watch on the movements of the First Order. With the loss of the New Republic Senate and fleet, the Resistance becomes the first line of defense against the military faction.

## CORUSCANT

Coruscant is the captial of the galaxy, and during the time of the Republic, it is the base for both the Galactic Senate and the Jedi Council. The entire planet is made up of one incredible city, and as such it is a hub for business, politics, and culture. Coruscant's glittering skyline makes an impressive sight, but beneath the towering skyscrapers lies a dark underworld. When the Republic is transformed into the Empire, Emperor Palpatine establishes himself in Coruscant's Jedi Temple, turning into an Imperial Palace.

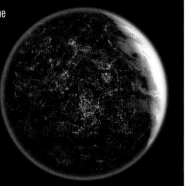

## JAKKU

Jakku is a striking example of a world shaped by the aftermath of the Galactic Civil War. The barely settled desert world becomes a rallying point for retreating Imperial forces. A fleet of New Republic warships engages Imperial vessels in the upper atmosphere, and the crippled Imperial ships use their tractor beams to drag Republic vessels into the sands below. The end result is a vast graveyard of warships, waiting to be plundered.

## NABOO

Naboo is a small, idyllic planet, filled with both dazzling cities and lush scenery. Humans live on land, while the underwater realms are inhabited by the native Gungans. During the time of the Republic, the Naboo live peacefully under the rule of democratically-elected leaders, and their small military generally serves a ceremonial purpose. This quiet existence comes to an abrupt end when Naboo is invaded by the Trade Federation—a battle which would ultimately lead to the galaxy-wide Clone Wars.

## STARKILLER BASE
Located in the Unknown Regions, this forested ice planet is transformed into the First Order's base of operations—and their deadly secret weapon.

## TATOOINE

Home to both a young Anakin Skywalker, and later his son, Luke Skywalker, Tatooine is a scorching-hot desert planet. Inhabitants include poor moisture farmers, market traders, dangerous Tusken Raiders, and scavenging Jawas. Life is extremely tough for those living and working on this harsh, sand-covered world, and the planet is rife with gambling, crime, and slavery.

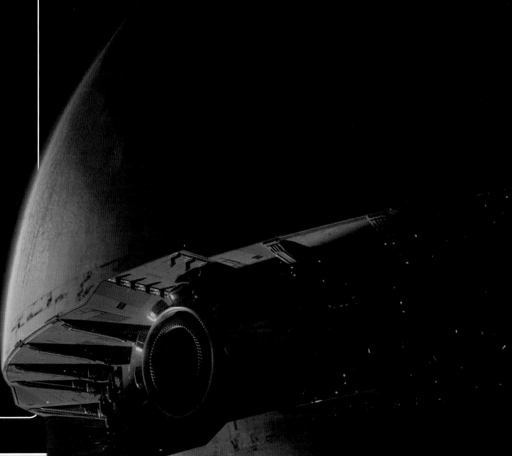

# SPECIAL TECHNOLOGY

**FOR THOUSANDS OF YEARS,** high technology has existed throughout the galaxy, ebbing and flowing with the rise and fall of civilizations. The development of technology has taken many different paths, and what is a natural extension to one culture may be overlooked by another. Traditional technology such as the Jedi lightsaber may remain constant for centuries. Alternatively, military pressures may bring new innovations in areas which have remained unchanged for millennia. As cultures meet and interact, advanced devices fall into the hands of otherwise primitive groups, and many creatures use technology of which they have no real understanding.

*Reinforced stock*

**ION BLASTERS**
Electronic components can be disrupted by ion blasts. Ion cannons can disable spacecraft without damaging them, while custom-built Jawa ionization blasters stun droids in the same way.

**DARTH VADER'S LIGHTSABER**
Lightsaber designs often relate to personal histories. Darth Vader's lightsaber looks much like the one he used as a Jedi learner, only darker. Luke Skywalker's lightsaber, on the other hand, follows the type used by Luke's mentor Ben Kenobi.

**OBI-WAN KENOBI'S LIGHTSABER**

**LUKE SKYWALKER'S SECOND LIGHTSABER**

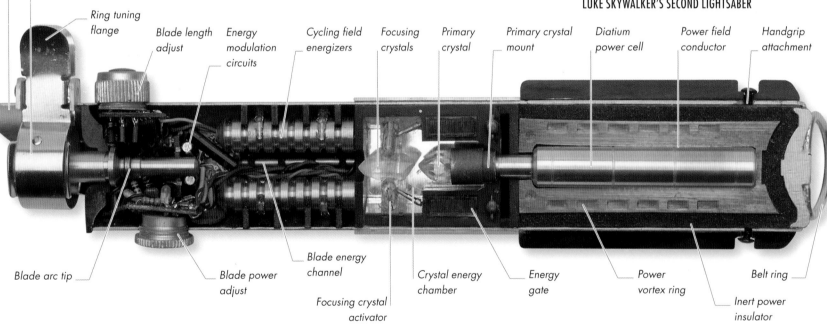

*Blade emitter shroud*

*Magnetic stabilizing ring*

*Ring tuning flange*

*Blade length adjust*

*Energy modulation circuits*

*Cycling field energizers*

*Focusing crystals*

*Primary crystal*

*Primary crystal mount*

*Diatium power cell*

*Power field conductor*

*Handgrip attachment*

*Blade arc tip*

*Blade power adjust*

*Blade energy channel*

*Focusing crystal activator*

*Crystal energy chamber*

*Energy gate*

*Power vortex ring*

*Belt ring*

*Inert power insulator*

## LIGHTSABERS

Lightsabers tend to follow a similar basic structure, although many are very individualized by their Jedi builders. While the pure energy blade has no mass, the electromagnetically generated arc wave creates a strong gyroscopic effect that makes the lightsaber a challenge to handle. Operating on the principle of tightly controlled arc-wave energy, it requires focusing elements made from kyber crystals. A lightsaber must be assembled by hand, as there is no exact formula for the crucial alignment of the irregular crystals. The slightest misalignment will cause the weapon to detonate on activation.

**LUKE SKYWALKER AND DARTH VADER DUEL IN CLOUD CITY**
The legendary lightsaber is the ancient traditional weapon of the Jedi Knight, guardians of justice for so many generations. Building a working lightsaber is one of the tests for Jedi in training—accomplishing the impossibly fine alignment task proves their Force sensitivity.

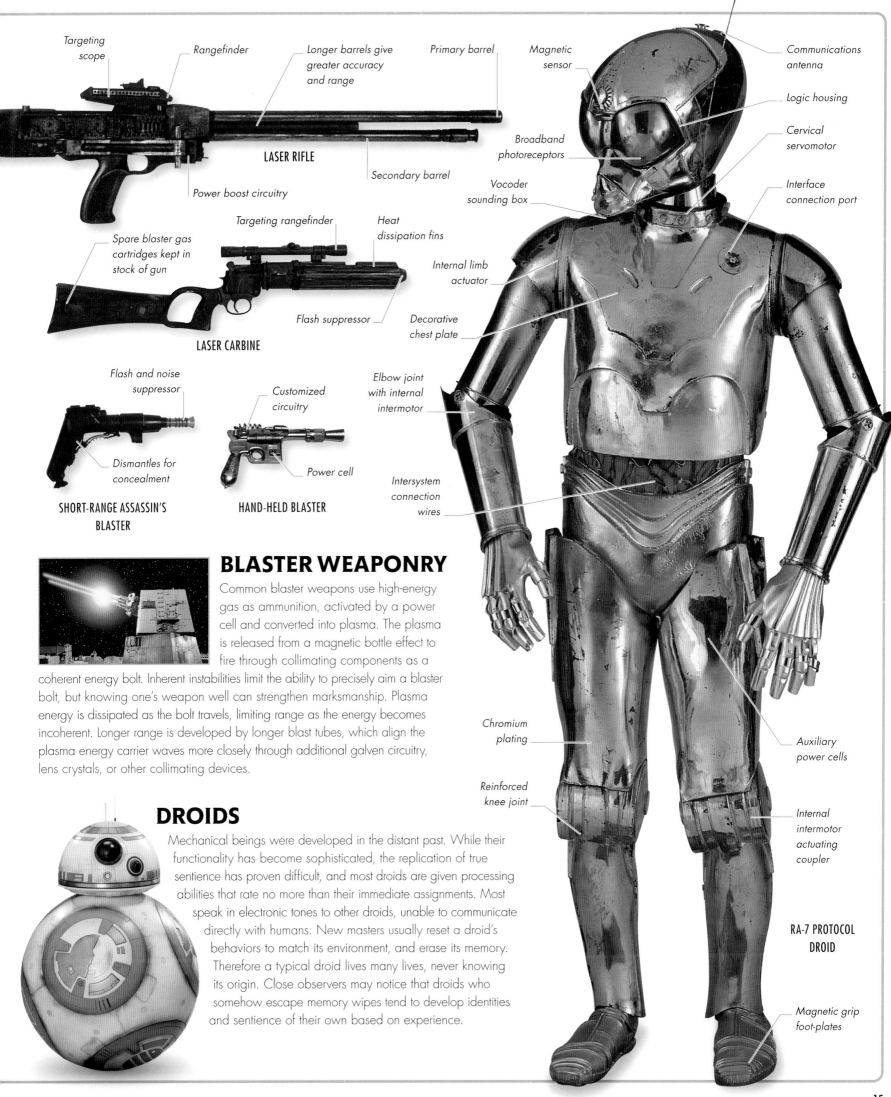

**LASER RIFLE**

Targeting scope

Rangefinder

Longer barrels give greater accuracy and range

Primary barrel

Power boost circuitry

Secondary barrel

**LASER CARBINE**

Spare blaster gas cartridges kept in stock of gun

Targeting rangefinder

Heat dissipation fins

Flash suppressor

**SHORT-RANGE ASSASSIN'S BLASTER**

Flash and noise suppressor

Dismantles for concealment

**HAND-HELD BLASTER**

Customized circuitry

Power cell

# BLASTER WEAPONRY

Common blaster weapons use high-energy gas as ammunition, activated by a power cell and converted into plasma. The plasma is released from a magnetic bottle effect to fire through collimating components as a coherent energy bolt. Inherent instabilities limit the ability to precisely aim a blaster bolt, but knowing one's weapon well can strengthen marksmanship. Plasma energy is dissipated as the bolt travels, limiting range as the energy becomes incoherent. Longer range is developed by longer blast tubes, which align the plasma energy carrier waves more closely through additional galven circuitry, lens crystals, or other collimating devices.

# DROIDS

Mechanical beings were developed in the distant past. While their functionality has become sophisticated, the replication of true sentience has proven difficult, and most droids are given processing abilities that rate no more than their immediate assignments. Most speak in electronic tones to other droids, unable to communicate directly with humans. New masters usually reset a droid's behaviors to match its environment, and erase its memory. Therefore a typical droid lives many lives, never knowing its origin. Close observers may notice that droids who somehow escape memory wipes tend to develop identities and sentience of their own based on experience.

Magnetic sensor

Communications antenna

Logic housing

Cervical servomotor

Broadband photoreceptors

Interface connection port

Vocoder sounding box

Internal limb actuator

Decorative chest plate

Elbow joint with internal intermotor

Intersystem connection wires

Chromium plating

Auxiliary power cells

Reinforced knee joint

Internal intermotor actuating coupler

**RA-7 PROTOCOL DROID**

Magnetic grip foot-plates

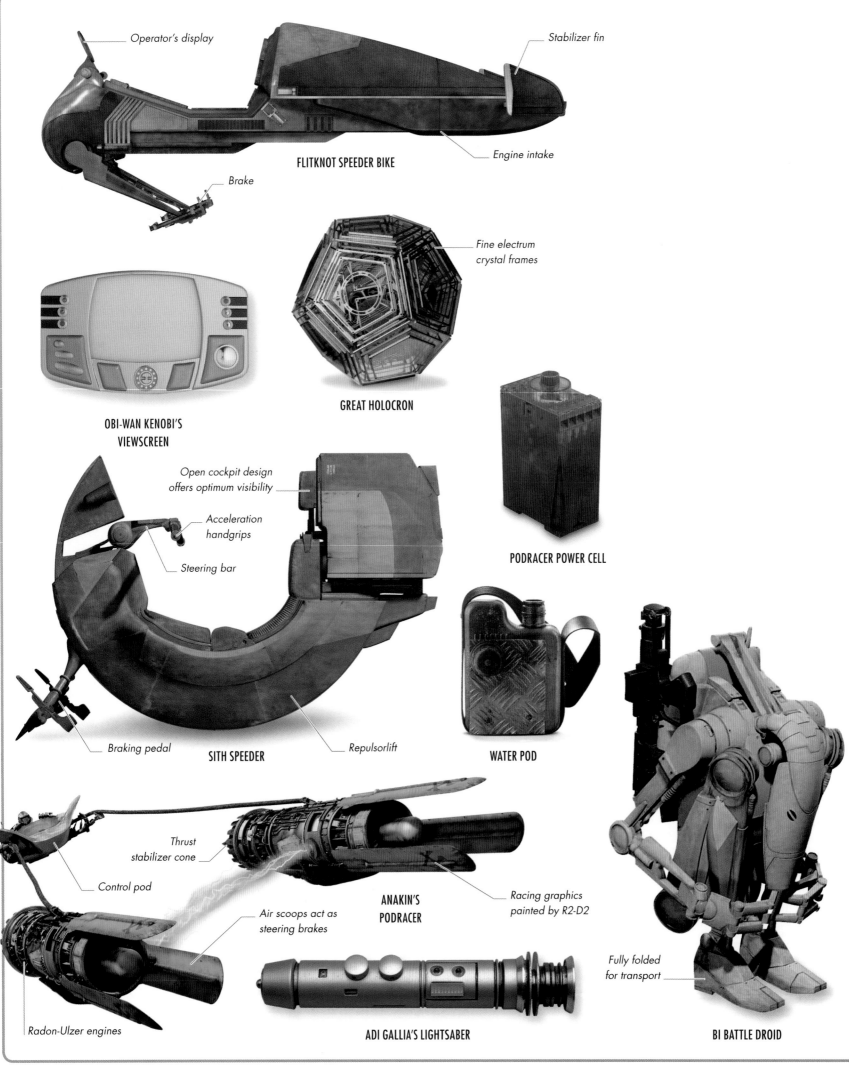

Operator's display

Stabilizer fin

FLITKNOT SPEEDER BIKE

Engine intake

Brake

Fine electrum
crystal frames

GREAT HOLOCRON

OBI-WAN KENOBI'S
VIEWSCREEN

Open cockpit design
offers optimum visibility

Acceleration
handgrips

Steering bar

PODRACER POWER CELL

Braking pedal

SITH SPEEDER

Repulsorlift

WATER POD

Thrust
stabilizer cone

Control pod

ANAKIN'S
PODRACER

Racing graphics
painted by R2-D2

Air scoops act as
steering brakes

Fully folded
for transport

Radon-Ulzer engines

ADI GALLIA'S LIGHTSABER

B1 BATTLE DROID

# THE PREQUEL TRILOGY ERA

Travel back to the beginning of the *Star Wars* saga, a generation before Luke Skywalker meets Ben Kenobi and sets out on his path to his destiny. In this era, Luke's father Anakin Skywalker is nine years old; the great Galactic Republic and its noble protectors the Jedi still stand, although they are both under threat from the machinations of the dark side of the Force. This time is populated with new characters, whose worlds are replete with gleaming spacecraft, intricate clothing, and exotic-looking droids. Just as in the real world, these artifacts tell a story. They are clues to identity. From the ferocious visage of Darth Maul to the famous sliders served at Dexter's Diner, and the lava fleas of Mustafar, discover the dazzling worlds explored in this initial trilogy of the *Star Wars* fantasy.

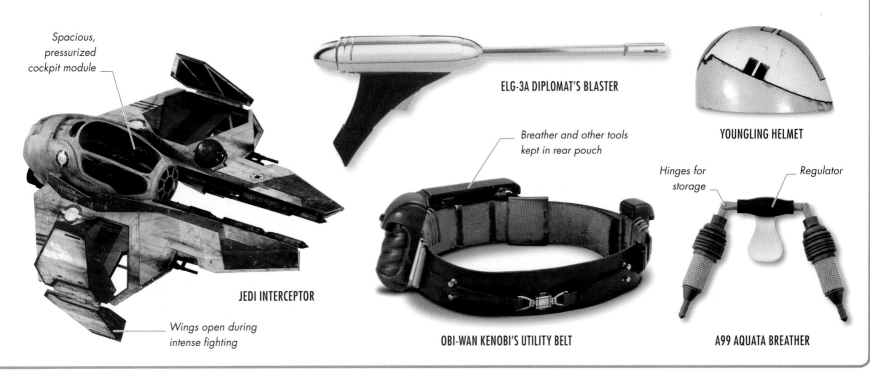

Spacious, pressurized cockpit module

ELG-3A DIPLOMAT'S BLASTER

YOUNGLING HELMET

Breather and other tools kept in rear pouch

Hinges for storage

Regulator

JEDI INTERCEPTOR

Wings open during intense fighting

OBI-WAN KENOBI'S UTILITY BELT

A99 AQUATA BREATHER

# THE JEDI

**FOR THOUSANDS OF YEARS,** the Jedi Temple on Coruscant serves as the training ground and home base of the Jedi Knights, the peacekeeping defenders of justice throughout the galaxy. It is here that Jedi initiates learn the ways of the Force—a mystical energy field created by all living things. Hundreds of other individuals who are not Jedi Knights provide vital support in everything from operations management to technical analysis. The galaxy is so large that complete law enforcement is impossible, so most Jedi rove through assigned regions on "journey missions," empowered to support justice as they see fit. Jedi based at the Temple travel on special assignments.

The Jedi eschew materialism as they do any attachments that could cloud their judgment. Mace's years of dedication have raised him to power and influence, but he meets his colleagues in a simple cell.

**STATUE FROM THE JEDI TEMPLE MAIN HALLWAY**

## ACTIVE JEDI

Jedi begin their lifelong training when they are recognized as gifted children. They become "younglings," accepting a life of total dedication and self-sacrifice to become diplomat-warriors. As initiates, they train together until they are accepted as Padawans. They must then face the Trials to become Jedi Knights, who are allowed in turn to take on an apprentice and earn the title of Master.

*Jedi Padawan with learner braid*

*Gesture of patience*

*Traditional Jedi robes*

*Diplomatic boots are less rugged than field-agent boots*

**BAIRDON JACE**

**KHAAT QIYN**

The Jedi Temple on Coruscant occupies hallowed ground sanctified by the noble efforts of Jedi dating back many thousands of years into remote antiquity.

**BEAR CLAN YOUNGLINGS**

**J.K. BURTOLA**   **MARI AMITHEST**   **SAYLIND DONELS**   **LEXA TCHEIL**

Ready stance

## CIN DRALLIG

Jedi Master Cin Drallig is head of Temple Guard at the Jedi Temple. The talented Drallig was personally trained by Jedi Master Yoda, and goes on to teach lightsaber combat to many students, including Obi-Wan Kenobi and Anakin Skywalker. Despite being the Temple's finest swordmaster at the time of Darth Vader's raid on the Jedi Temple, even the esteemed Cin Drallig is unable to defeat a raging Sith Lord in combat.

Scaly skin

The Jedi Temple's elegant halls and chambers are meant to encourage contemplation. Here, at the heart of the Order, Masters consider galactic crises and ponder the Force's will.

Two-handed grip for control

Mirialan tattoos

### J'OOPI SHÉ

Jedi Master J'oopi Shé is a Kadas'sa'Nikto from the planet Kintan. He is stationed at the Temple and is a member of the Technical division, which is responsible for maintaining and repairing all craft.

Hooded robe

Attack stance

Lekku (head tails) can express emotions

Ruttian skin color

## AAYLA SECURA

Aayla Secura is a talented Twi'lek Jedi, whose quick thinking has saved many lives. As one of the Jedi Order's bravest and most skilled lightsaber combatants, Aayla is greatly admired by many Padawans. Ahsoka Tano in particular looks up to her as a mentor.

Belt made of rycrit hide

## BARRISS OFFEE

Padawan Barriss Offee is a thoughtful, daring, and studious Jedi. She is the loyal Padawan learner of Master Luminara Unduli, and she adheres closely to the Jedi Code—until the trials of the Clone Wars change her point of view.

Fitted clothing allows complete freedom of movement

Belt contains secret compartment

Combat boots

# JEDI ARCHIVES

**EVER SINCE THE ANCIENT ORIGINS** of the Jedi Order, knowledge has been vital to the Jedi mission of supporting peace and justice throughout the Republic. The great Archives Library in the Jedi Temple safeguards the accumulated knowledge gathered by millions of individuals over hundreds of generations. It is a repository of seemingly infinite information on every part of the known galaxy and on billions upon billions of its inhabitants. The Archives is the greatest library in the Republic, and an incomparable asset to the Jedi, whether they are acting as diplomats, counselors, or fighters.

## HOLOCRONS

The Jedi Holocrons stored in the Archives transcend the capabilities of traditional data files and holobooks. They are imbued with perpetual, subtle power and can be used only by Force-sensitives with extrasensory abilities. Holocrons are repositories of knowledge and wisdom, holding the teachings and mentalities of great Jedi Knights and Masters. To those disciplined enough to bear power with responsibility, they serve as a unique form of living instruction.

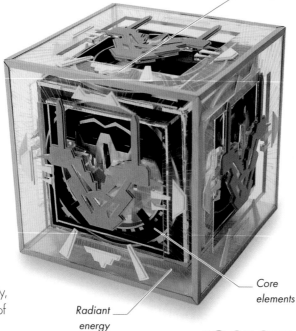

*Activator panel for simple Holocron*

*Core elements*

*Radiant energy*

*Chon Actrion, "Architect of Freedom"*

The Archives offer many opportunities for reflection. Statues remind those walking past of the Jedi who have gone before them.

*Simple plinth*

## JOCASTA NU

Master Jocasta Nu is the Chief Librarian of the Jedi Archives. Her astonishing memory seems to rival the Archives itself, but her pride in the Archives sometimes blinds her to its limitations. Nu survives Order 66 and is determined to protect the Jedi's legacy. She is a potent threat to the new Empire, so Palpatine orders Darth Vader and the Inquisitors to hunt her down.

*Twin Ansata hair sticks*

*Traditional Ansata pattern symbolizing knowledge*

*Full robe worn by Nu in elder years*

## DATA FILE

> Knowledge has been a key source of Jedi power for centuries. It is considered one of the three pillars of Jedi strength, along with the Force and self-discipline.

> Holobooks are an ancient self-contained technology requiring only small amounts of energy. They are easy to use and offer many modes of interaction with their users.

# LIGHTSABER COMBAT

**THE LIGHTSABER IS** a powerful symbol of discipline as well as a weapon. In the hands of the untrained, it is worse than useless against modern blasters, and may even injure its user. But in the hands of a Jedi, the lightsaber can become as powerful as any weapon turned against it, deflecting energy bolts back at attackers in a deadly hail and leaving the Jedi wielder untouched. Lightsaber combat is a subtle and intricate art that takes years of practice to master.

1 HEAD

2 RIGHT ARM AND SIDE

3 LEFT ARM AND SIDE

5 RIGHT LEG

6 LEFT LEG

4 BACK

## BODY ZONES

Attacks and parries are described in terms of the body zone they concern. "Attack 1" is a blow to the opponent's head, "parry 2" the block of an attack to your right arm or side, and so on. Attack zones are those you see on your opponent, while parry zones are those of your own body. So to go from attack 3 to parry 3, your blade must move from your right side to your left.

### LIGHTSABER PRACTICE

After learning the basics, Jedi in training run lightsaber drills, named velocities, to increase their key skills and physical stamina. A Padawan also practices dulon: solo sequences of moves in which the opponents are only envisioned. The patterns of velocities and dulon prepare a Jedi for the unpredictable realm of live combat. They help Jedi to go beyond what is physically possible by allowing the Force to flow through them.

YOUNGLING HELMET

TRAINING LIGHTSABER

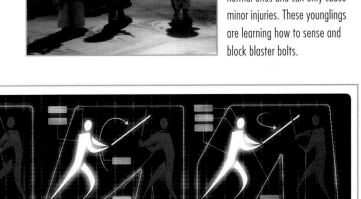

Jedi younglings begin training with a lightsaber at a young age. They wear helmets that mask their vision, training them to see using the Force rather than their bodily senses alone. They wield training lightsabers that are smaller than normal ones and can only cause minor injuries. These younglings are learning how to sense and block blaster bolts.

| ATTACK 1/PARRY 1 | ATTACK 6/PARRY 6 | ATTACK 5/PARRY 5 | ATTACK 3/PARRY 3 | ATTACK 2/PARRY 2 |

### LIVE COMBAT

In contrast to practice, blade attitude for attack in live combat is often angled downward to minimize body movement and increase speed. Knowing the ideal distinction between attack and defense attitudes improves a Jedi's precision.

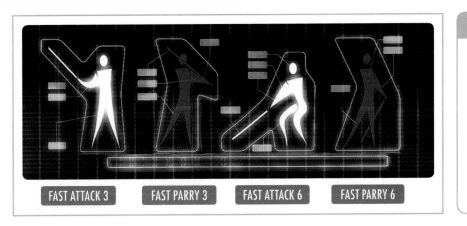

| FAST ATTACK 3 | FAST PARRY 3 | FAST ATTACK 6 | FAST PARRY 6 |

## DATA FILE

> Some Jedi, like Ahsoka Tano, prefer to wield two lightsabers in battle. Other Jedi resort to this tactic only in specific situations. General Grievous, neither a Jedi nor a Force-user, can wield up to four lightsabers during combat, due to his augmented and enhanced physique.

# THE JEDI HIGH COUNCIL

Tholothian tendrils

**THE TWELVE MEMBERS** of the Jedi High Council represent a gathering of great minds who have proven themselves and their abilities in the service of peace and justice. Confident in their attunement to the Force, the Council members work together in trust, free from the petty constraints of ego and jealousy. Their Council Chamber is a place of open thought and speech, a realm of mutual respect, and a haven of shared noble purpose. Jedi Council Members tend to serve for life, but they can be removed for unconventional viewpoints, or choose to step down.

Gallia's second lightsaber replaces her first, which was destroyed on a mission

### ADI GALLIA

Born into a highly placed diplomatic family stationed on Coruscant, the intuitive Adi Gallia often seems to know what people are about to say. Gallia has many contacts throughout the Coruscant political machine, making her one of the Supreme Chancellor's most valuable sources of intelligence.

The Council Chambers top each of the spires atop the Jedi Temple on the galactic capital planet, Coruscant. The 12 members sit in a ring of chairs that are spaced equally around the chamber.

**KI-ADI-MUNDI'S LIGHTSABER**      **ADI GALLIA'S LIGHTSABER**

**BUST OF KI-ADI-MUNDI**

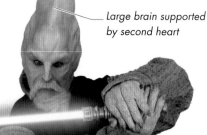

Large brain supported by second heart

Hollow montrals sense space

Visually disruptive patterning

Cerean cuffs

Surcoat adapted from ancient Cerean garb

## KI-ADI-MUNDI

A Jedi from the largely unspoiled paradise world of Cerea, Ki-Adi-Mundi's high-domed head holds a complex binary brain. Joining the Jedi Council before the Battle of Naboo, Ki-Adi-Mundi is known for his wisdom. He has a tendency to refute unlikely events—such as Qui-Gon Jinn's encounter with a Sith Lord. Ki-Adi-Mundi is given the rank of General in the Clone Wars and leads the Galactic Marines—a relentless clone trooper unit.

Plain trousers

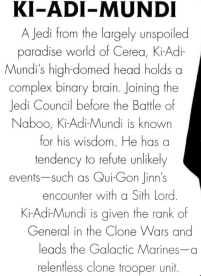

## SHAAK TI

Jedi Master Shaak Ti is a Togruta, a species which lives in dense tribes on the planet Shili, where the disruptive coloration of their long lekku (head-tails) serves to confuse predators. Unlike most of her kind, Ti is a highly-independent spirit. Ti serves upon the Council during the Clone Wars, and is frequently stationed at Kamino, overseeing the development of the clone troopers for the Republic.

Natural Togruta skin colors

Jedi robes

Tough skin impervious to high winds of Iktotchon

Well-developed horns

Customary humanoid Jedi robes

## SAESEE TIIN

Saesee Tiin is a reserved Jedi Master, but his piloting skills are legendary. This Iktotchi Jedi Master provides aerial cover during the Battle of Lola Sayu and Battle of Umbara. He also joins Mace Windu's task force on their mission to imprison Darth Sidious, but he falls to the Sith Lord's blade.

Mark of illumination

Jedi robes cover practical fighting tunic

Lightsaber worn on utility belt under robes

## DEPA BILLABA

Dutifully serving the Council, Depa Billaba offers a considered viewpoint in any discussions. She takes an apprentice named Caleb Dume and sacrifices her life to save him during Order 66. Caleb, later known as Kanan Jarrus, joins a rebel cell and fights the Empire.

Protective goggles

Highly developed extrasensory organs

Mask patterns are unique to Kel Dor clans

## PLO KOON

Jedi Master Plo Koon is very strong with the Force and provides an analytical and calm voice on the Council. This Kel Dor leads a clone trooper unit named Wolf Pack and is devoted to protecting them. Plo is also particularly close to Jedi Padawan Ahsoka Tano as he discovered and recruited Ahsoka as an infant into the Jedi Order.

### PLO KOON'S GOGGLES & MASK

Oxygen is poisonous for Kel Dor like Plo Koon. Plo must protect his eyes and nostrils from the oxygen-rich atmosphere of Coruscant with special devices.

Unblinking, big eyes give excellent night vision

## KIT FISTO

As a Nautolan from Glee Anselm, Kit Fisto is amphibious and can live in air or water. His head tentacles are highly sensitive olfactory organs that precisely detect subconscious pheromonal expressions of emotion. This ability allows him to take instant advantage of an opponent's uncertainty.

### DATA FILE

> The 12 High Council members reflect a mere hint of the diversity within the Jedi ranks, which include members of hundreds of species and cultures.

# YODA

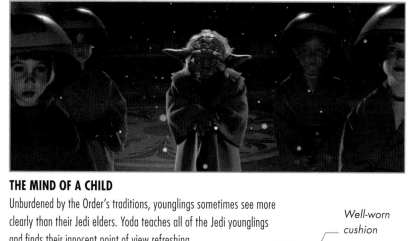

**WISE AFTER CENTURIES** of service to the ways of the Jedi, Grand Master Yoda leads the Order during the twilight years of the Galactic Republic. He has come to believe the galaxy is in grave peril, and the Jedi Order itself is threatened by the complacency of its members. There are strange stirrings in the Force, and Yoda senses the dark side behind what many Jedi dismiss as schemes of politicians.

### THE MIND OF A CHILD
Unburdened by the Order's traditions, younglings sometimes see more clearly than their Jedi elders. Yoda teaches all of the Jedi younglings and finds their innocent point of view refreshing.

### ON THE COUNCIL
As head of the Jedi Council, Yoda seeks an understanding of the will of the Force. But the shroud of the dark side has left the Council blind and fumbling for enlightenment.

*Well-worn cushion*

*Highly sensitive ears*

*Hand gestures help focus mental use of the Force*

## SAGE LEADER
Yoda is a well-respected voice of reason outside the Jedi Council's chamber. He is a natural and persuasive diplomat and has quelled many galactic disuputes with his wise words. Yoda was even given the prestigious title of "Defender of the Home Tree" by the Wookiees of Kashyyyk, for his assistance during their negotiations with the Trandoshans.

*Simple robe is a sincere expression of humility*

### DUEL WITH DOOKU
Forced to battle his former Padawan, Dooku, Yoda relies upon his acrobatic style of fighting to overcome the limitations of his size. Dooku endangers Anakin and Obi-Wan's lives, forcing Yoda to save them and allowing Dooku's escape.

### DATA FILE

> Yoda meets frequently with Chancellor Palpatine and other key Republic ministers, helping them with his wisdom and experience.

> Yoda has never revealed his homeworld, and his species is rarely seen anywhere in the galaxy.

# LIVING LEGEND

As a member of a long-living species, Yoda has had to face the sadness of seeing many friends grow old and pass into the Force. These losses have taught him the value of detachment: One must celebrate life rather than mourn its inevitable end.

Bust sculpted when Yoda had more hair

Sculptor worked in bronzium, guided by the Force

Blade emitter shroud

Blade power control

Yoda's eyes seek vision through the Force

Activator matrix

Worn handgrip

Old comfortable robes

## YODA'S HOVERCHAIR

As most Jedi have a longer stride than Yoda, he relies upon his hoverchair to keep up with them in the corridors of the Jedi Temple.

Yoda's staff is a gift from the Wookiees

**GIMER STICK**

## YODA'S SABER

Yoda's strength with the Force gives him incredible power and speed, and he remains a master of lightsaber combat. This Jedi Master prefers peaceful solutions and only relies upon his combat skills as a last resort.

Control probe

Power cell

## TESTING SCREEN

The Jedi High Council uses multi-function viewscreens to test Jedi apprentices. These screens are built without buttons and are operated by Jedi mind powers. Only Force-attuned individuals can follow the high-speed series of images generated on screen. Testing screens keep the Jedi Council members in constant practice with their Force abilities.

Standard tests stored in memory cell

**REVERSE VIEW**

Testing screen displays transmitted or recorded information

Handgrip

Test results are recorded in removable memory cell

Through the Force, Yoda senses the terrible annihilation of the Jedi Order. Palpatine initiates Order 66, activating a pre-programmed command in all clones to turn on their Jedi comrades. A handful of Jedi survive the treachery. Thanks to his heightened awareness, Yoda easily overcomes his clone attackers.

## ESCAPE POD

An escape pod, crafted by the Wookiees, lifts Yoda to safety from the traitorous clones on Kashyyyk. He is picked up by sympathetic Senator Bail Organa, who witnessed the attack on the Jedi Temple, and they rendezvous with Obi-Wan. The Jedi decide to split up to defeat each Sith separately.

# MACE WINDU

**THE GRIM JEDI MASTER** Mace Windu is a senior member of the Jedi Council, renowned as a warrior, tough negotiator, and ardent defender of the Order and its place in the galaxy. Windu is suspicious of politicians, whom he regards as ruled by their passions, and has little patience for dissent from fellow members of the Jedi Order. He warily eyes the current crises facing the Republic, sensing the hand of the Sith at work behind the scenes.

Under tunic

Tunic

Jedi robe

Even as a senior
Council member,
Windu wears
standard robes

## JEDI DEFENDER

Master Windu is an insightful and decisive Jedi leader who does his utmost to protect the Order. He opposes Qui-Gon Jinn's plea to train Anakin Skywalker, whom he regards as dangerous and reckless. Mace even convinces the Council to sanction an assassination of the Sith Lord Count Dooku—an action that contradicts the Jedi way and could lead to the dark side.

Lightsaber emits
rare purple blade

### JEDI GENERAL
Mace Windu is prepared to leave the Council Chamber and take on a mission to protect the Republic. Notably, he leads the mission to investigate the Separatist presence on Hissrich. He joins Cham Syndulla to liberate Ryloth, and prevents the evil Mother Talzin's return to a corporeal form on Zardossa Stix.

Viewscreen

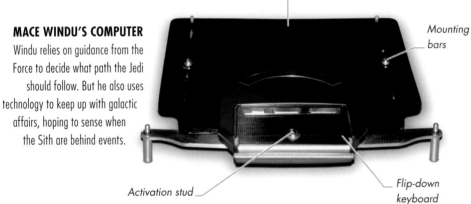

### MACE WINDU'S COMPUTER
Windu relies on guidance from the Force to decide what path the Jedi should follow. But he also uses technology to keep up with galactic affairs, hoping to sense when the Sith are behind events.

Mounting
bars

Activation stud

Flip-down
keyboard

Energy
capsule

Dispenser
track

Travel clip

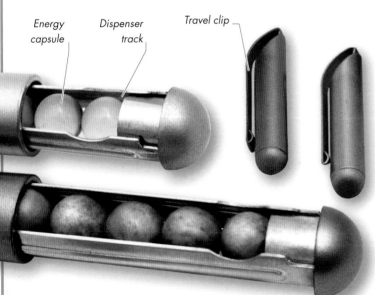

### FOOD AND ENERGY CAPSULES
Jedi are encouraged to sample local cuisine, as many cultures share food as a sign of good fellowship. However, on some missions it is simpler to get sustenance from concentrated capsules.

Food capsule

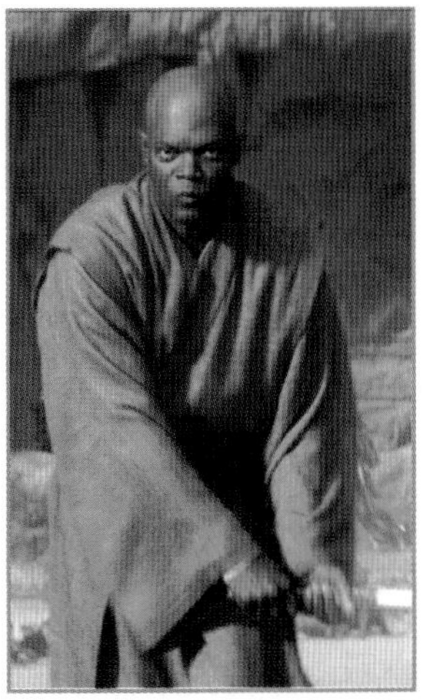

**TAKING ACTION**

When Mace realizes that Count Dooku endangers galactic peace, he leads a 212-strong Jedi task force to Geonosis, intending to rescue Obi-Wan and destroy the Separatist armies. A surgical strike might thwart the Separatist plot and prevent a wider war, but the Jedi fail and take heavy casualties.

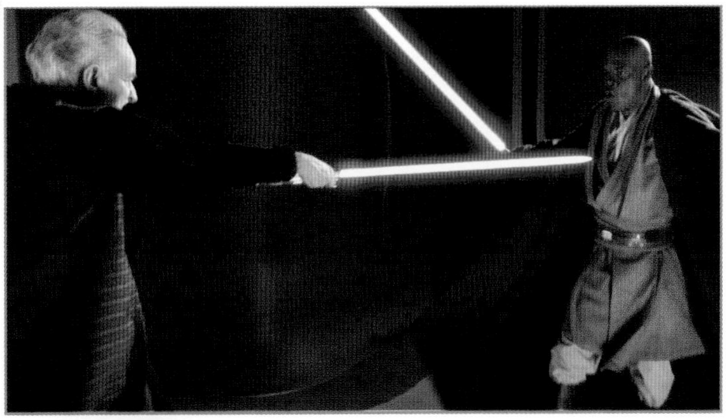

**SITH REVEALED**

Upon discovering that Palpatine was a Sith, Mace forms a Jedi strike team to arrest him. While his comrades fall, Mace is nearly successful. However, Anakin arrives and defends Palpatine, allowing an opening for Palpatine to kill Mace.

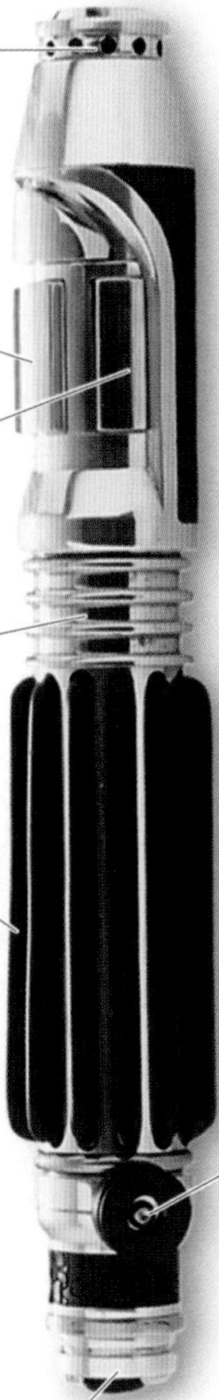

Blade projection plate
Power indicator
Rare electrum finish
Crystal chamber
Handgrip
Blade length adjuster
Power cell access cap

**MACE WINDU'S LIGHTSABER**

After his appointment as a senior member of the Jedi Council, Mace constructs a new lightsaber. Displaying the highest standards of precision, it represents Mace's mature abilities as a Jedi leader.

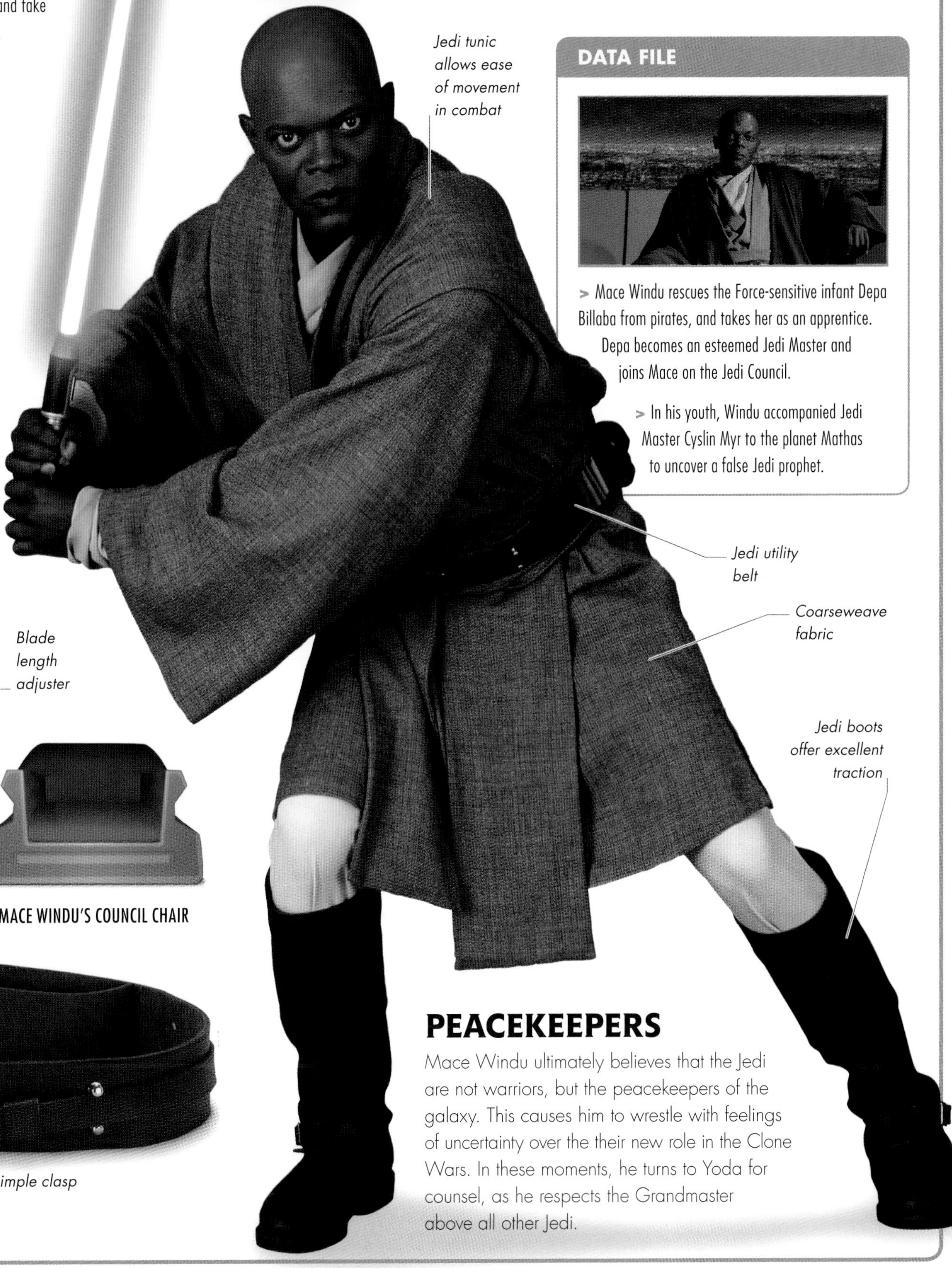

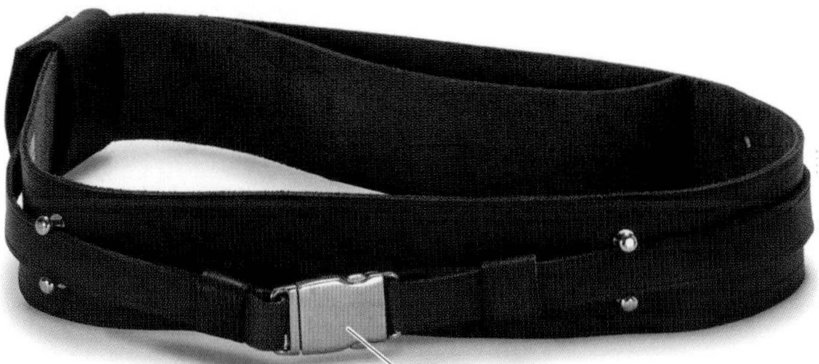

Jedi tunic allows ease of movement in combat
Jedi utility belt
Coarseweave fabric
Jedi boots offer excellent traction

**DATA FILE**

> Mace Windu rescues the Force-sensitive infant Depa Billaba from pirates, and takes her as an apprentice. Depa becomes an esteemed Jedi Master and joins Mace on the Jedi Council.

> In his youth, Windu accompanied Jedi Master Cyslin Myr to the planet Mathas to uncover a false Jedi prophet.

MACE WINDU'S COUNCIL CHAIR

Simple clasp

MACE WINDU'S UTILITY BELT

## PEACEKEEPERS

Mace Windu ultimately believes that the Jedi are not warriors, but the peacekeepers of the galaxy. This causes him to wrestle with feelings of uncertainty over the their new role in the Clone Wars. In these moments, he turns to Yoda for counsel, as he respects the Grandmaster above all other Jedi.

# QUI-GON JINN

**MASTER QUI-GON JINN IS** an experienced Jedi who has proven his value to the leadership of the Jedi Order in many important missions and difficult negotiations. In his maturity, however, he remains as restless as he was in his youth. When Qui-Gon encounters young Anakin Skywalker on the Outer Rim desert world of Tatooine, the Jedi is deeply struck by an unshakeable sense that the boy is part of the galaxy's destiny. In boldly championing the cause of Anakin, Qui-Gon sets in motion momentous events that will ultimately bring balance to the Force—but not without great cost.

Long hair worn back to keep vision clear

Jedi robe

Blade projection plate

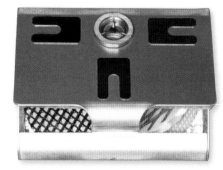

Jedi test kits employ swabs treated with a chemical that reacts to midi-chlorians. A being's midi-chlorian count indicates his or her Force potential.

**JEDI BLOOD TEST KIT**

## QUI-GON JINN'S LIGHTSABER

Following personal taste, Qui-Gon has built a lightsaber with a highly elaborate internal design. Multiple small power cells are stored in the scalloped handgrip and microscopic circuitry governs the nature of the green energy blade.

Jedi tunic

Activator

Series of micro-cells

Charging port

Qui-Gon is a capable diplomat and is respectful of those on the other side. He doesn't, however, hesitate to use his reputation as a warrior to great effect, or drop the diplomatic niceties for blunt talk. Supreme Chancellor Valorum secretly sends Qui-Gon to Naboo to strong-arm the Trade Federation into dropping its blockade of the planet.

## LOYAL TO THE FORCE

Qui-Gon is an unusual Jedi Master. He has a bold, headstrong nature, nurtured in him when he was a Padawan by his Jedi Master Dooku. Qui-Gon also insists on knowing and heeding the will of the Force in all situations, even when that causes him to defy his Jedi peers to follow his own path. While Qui-Gon is a prominent Jedi with an outstanding record, he has been passed over for a seat on the Council, perhaps due to his maverick nature.

Rugged travel boots

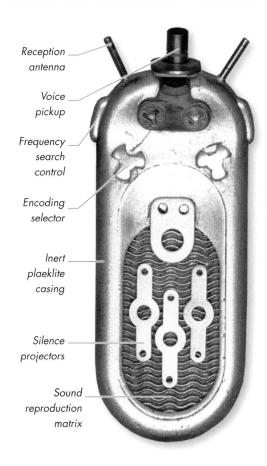

- Reception antenna
- Voice pickup
- Frequency search control
- Encoding selector
- Inert plaeklite casing
- Silence projectors
- Sound reproduction matrix

## HOLOPROJECTOR

One of the utility devices that Qui-Gon carries is a small holoprojector. This can be tuned with a comlink to carry a hologram transmission for face-to-face contact, or it can be used as an independent image recorder and projector.

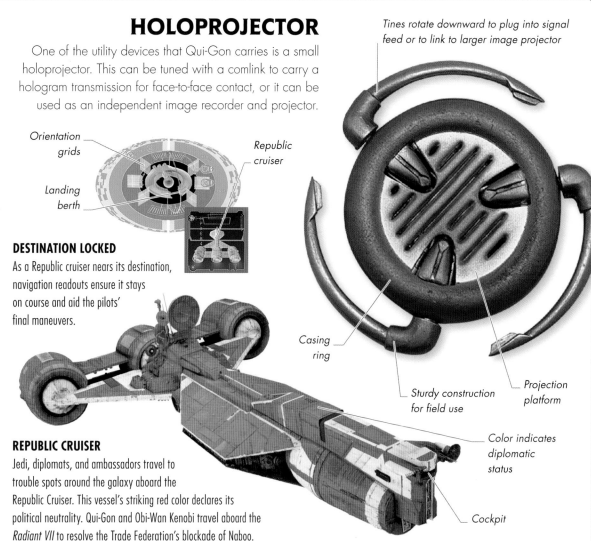

- Orientation grids
- Landing berth
- Republic cruiser

*Tines rotate downward to plug into signal feed or to link to larger image projector*

- Casing ring
- Sturdy construction for field use
- Projection platform
- Color indicates diplomatic status

### DESTINATION LOCKED

As a Republic cruiser nears its destination, navigation readouts ensure it stays on course and aid the pilots' final maneuvers.

### REPUBLIC CRUISER

Jedi, diplomats, and ambassadors travel to trouble spots around the galaxy aboard the Republic Cruiser. This vessel's striking red color declares its political neutrality. Qui-Gon and Obi-Wan Kenobi travel aboard the *Radiant VII* to resolve the Trade Federation's blockade of Naboo.

- Cockpit

## COMLINK

Qui-Gon's comlink allows him to keep in touch with Obi-Wan Kenobi when the two operate separately. It features complex security devices to prevent unauthorized interception and is unlabeled to thwart use by non-Jedi. A silence projector lends privacy to conversations and helps Qui-Gon maintain stealth in the field.

**REVERSE VIEW**

On meeting Anakin, Qui-Gon believes he has recognized the prophesied individual who will restore balance and harmony to the Force. The Jedi feels so strongly that he has recognized this individual that he is not persuaded otherwise by Jedi High Council members, including the influential Yoda, who sense danger in the boy.

Prior to the Naboo Blockade, Qui-Gon selects Obi-Wan Kenobi as his Padawan. During a civil war on Mandalore, they had to defend a Mandalorian Duchess from her enemies. Qui-Gon speaks highly of Obi-Wan, who is a worthy student of his wisdom and skill.

On Tatooine, Qui-Gon battles a Sith warrior wielding a deadly lightsaber. Since lightsabers are seldom handled by non-Jedi, the order primarily uses them as defense against blaster bolts rather than other lightsabers. However, lightsaber dueling is still taught as part of Jedi training.

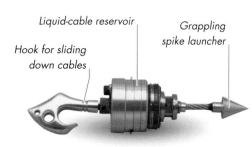

- Liquid-cable reservoir
- Grappling spike launcher
- Hook for sliding down cables
- Spinner tip
- Dual-strand liquid-cable rotator

**JEDI FIELD GEAR**

### DATA FILE

> Qui-Gon underwent a spiritual journey where he learned incomplete knowledge of how to retain his consciousness in the Force after death.

> Years after his passing, Qui-Gon appears as a spirit to Obi-Wan and Anakin. He warns them that the powerful Force-users they have encountered on Mortis will attempt to use Anakin's power for their own goals.

# OBI-WAN KENOBI

**OBI-WAN KENOBI HAS FOLLOWED** a responsible path on his journey toward Jedi knighthood as the Padawan apprentice to Jedi Master Qui-Gon Jinn. Strongly influenced by other leading Jedi as well as by Qui-Gon, Obi-Wan is more brooding and cautious than his teacher. He is careful to weigh the consequences of his actions and is reluctant to entangle himself unnecessarily in transgressions against the will of the Jedi High Council. A serious, quiet man possessed of a dry sense of humor, Obi-Wan strives to be worthy of his order and feels honored to be Qui-Gon's student, although he worries about his Master's tendency to take risks in defiance of the Council. Nevertheless, Obi-Wan follows Qui-Gon Jinn's example and develops an independent spirit of his own.

Tunic

Hooded robe

Apprentice's long braid

Breather and other tools kept in rear pouch

## A99 AQUATA BREATHER
In this era, Jedi Knights usually carry various high-tech devices concealed in their robes or in belt pouches. On their mission to Naboo, Obi-Wan and Qui-Gon Jinn carry A99 Aquata breathers, knowing that much of the planet's surface is water. Breathers allow the Jedi to survive underwater for up to two hours. In other times, Jedi have avoided such technological devices in order to minimize their dependence on anything but their own resourcefulness.

## UTILITY BELT
Obi-Wan's utility belt carries a minimal amount of gear: A Jedi is expected to solve problems through self-reliance, not technology. Still, a few necessities make missions go more smoothly. In the field, Obi-Wan is never without credit chips, food and energy capsules, and an assortment of tools.

R4-P17

**TRACER BEACON**

## JEDI GEAR
The basic Jedi clothing of belted tunic, travel boots, and robe speaks of the simplicity vested in Jedi philosophy and carries overtones of their mission as travelers. Individual Jedi keep utility belt field gear to a minimum. As initiates are taught in the great Temple, Jedi reputations are based on their spirits and not on material trappings.

Engine duct outlet

## JEDI STARFIGHTER
The Delta-7 *Aethersprite* light interceptor is a state-of-the-art fighter, customized by the Jedi for their unique mission profiles. The nimble fighter's slim profile makes it hard to detect on scanners, and its powerful engines and responsive steering are a good match for the uncanny reflexes of Jedi pilots calling upon the Force.

Communications and scanning suite

Rugged travel boots

# LIGHTSABER

Lightsabers follow a common design. Optional elements, like blade power and length modulators, are small and unobtrusive. Accordingly, Jedi lightsabers appear similar at first glance. A closer inspection, however, reveals that lightsabers rarely look exactly alike. All are hand-built by the initiates themselves, making design details a matter of individual choice. Most Padawan apprentices build their lightsabers to resemble those of their teachers as a mark of respect.

Blade modulation circuitry

Blade length and intensity control

Activator

Single main internal power cell

Handgrip

Power cell reverse cap

After his capture on Geonosis, Obi-Wan is sentenced to death, but finds he has no shortage of rescuers, from his Padawan to a strike force of 212 Jedi, led by Mace Windu. Count Dooku counters with waves of battle droids. The Republic's political turmoil has exploded into full-scale war, and the Jedi must fight to preserve the Republic.

## SCANNER MONITOR

The quartermasters in the Jedi Temple issue Obi-Wan with field equipment, such as this scanner monitor.

Wide-band sensor scan

Sensor select monitor

Graphic damage monitor

Systems impedance monitors

## STARFIGHTER DISPLAYS

Pilots can't afford to divert attention from their surroundings, so the Jedi starfighter's tactical display sits just below eye level. Most pilots let their astromech droids control the display, but the readouts also respond to the pilot's voice commands or direct input via touchscreen.

## JEDI IN BATTLE

Obi-Wan is a highly skilled swordsman. The Jedi generally favors a nonaggressive, defensive style of lightsaber combat. He uses his weapon to protect himself by deflecting oncoming assaults from his opponents and projectiles from weapons, such as blasters.

## CONFRONTING DOOKU

Facing off against Count Dooku, Obi-Wan wisely exercises restraint only to see his Padawan rush in headlong. Though he is a Jedi of powerful inner focus, Obi-Wan finds himself unprepared for the elegant precision of the Count's specialized techniques.

Brace-ready stance

Rugged well-worn travel boots

### DATA FILE

> Jedi robes are virtually indistinguishable from the simple robes worn by many species throughout the galaxy. This signifies the Jedi pledge to the service and protection of even the most humble galactic citizen.

> Obi-Wan remains loyal to Qui-Gon even when this puts him at odds with the Jedi High Council.

# OBI-WAN KENOBI:
## JEDI GENERAL

Unusually grave
expression

**IMPERTURBABLE IN BATTLE,** in deep space, or planetside, General Obi-Wan Kenobi still prefers negotiation to conflict. However, the Clone Wars have pushed him to become more forceful. Where even his lightsaber technique once reflected an affinity for deflection, his style has since become more lethal. Many say this is due to the influence of Anakin Skywalker, and indeed Obi-Wan has become Anakin's champion to those on the Council who dread the power of the Chosen One. As a result of his military successes in the Outer Rim, General Kenobi has been granted the title "Master," and named to the Council. Even so, he feels that his education in the Force is just beginning.

**OBI-WAN KENOBI'S
SCANNER**

Obi-Wan and Anakin's friendship and mutual trust makes them a great team in battle. They attack Count Dooku aboard the Separatist command cruiser, lulling him into a false sense of confidence by using standard lightsaber tactics, only to shift to advanced forms. This forces a confused Dooku to retreat.

Rangefinder
lock

Cushioned
eyecup

**JEDI MACROBINOCULARS**

Traditional
blue blade

Fabric looks
heavier than it is

## JEDI TRADITION

Honoring the wishes of his former Master, Qui-Gon Jinn, Obi-Wan makes Anakin his life's focus, instilling in him the belief that the dark side can be defeated and the Force brought back into balance. Yet Obi-Wan worries about Anakin's refusal to surrender the past, especially his fixation with his mother's death.

Despite his failure to take Dooku into captivity, Obi-Wan is held in great esteem by the members of the Jedi Council. They conclude that Obi-Wan is the only person skilled enough to capture the elusive and dangerous General Grievous on Utapau.

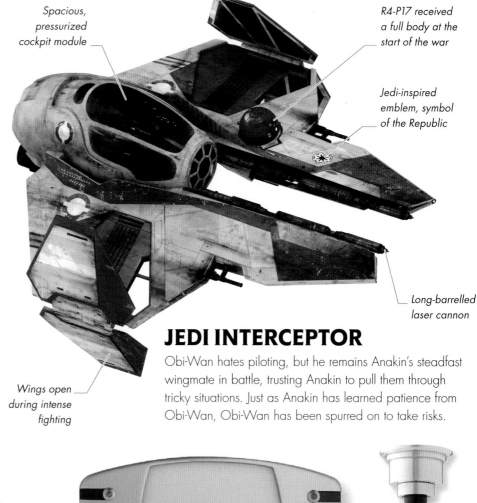

Spacious, pressurized cockpit module

R4-P17 received a full body at the start of the war

Jedi-inspired emblem, symbol of the Republic

Long-barrelled laser cannon

Wings open during intense fighting

Obi-Wan's worst fears for Anakin are realized when he views a Jedi Temple security recording. It proves that Anakin has turned to the dark side, pledged himself to the Sith, and has been responsible for the murder of many Jedi Knights and younglings.

# JEDI INTERCEPTOR

Obi-Wan hates piloting, but he remains Anakin's steadfast wingmate in battle, trusting Anakin to pull them through tricky situations. Just as Anakin has learned patience from Obi-Wan, Obi-Wan has been spurred on to take risks.

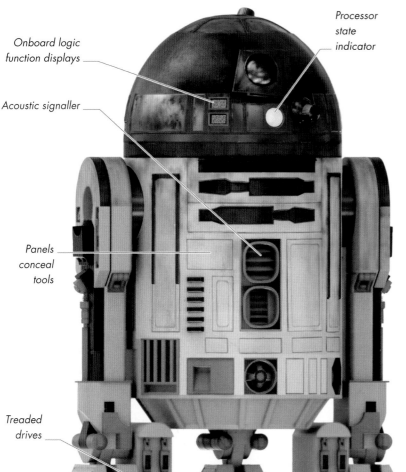

Onboard logic function displays

Processor state indicator

Acoustic signaller

Panels conceal tools

Treaded drives

**OBI-WAN KENOBI'S VIEWSCREEN**

# R4-P17

R4-P17 is Obi-Wan Kenobi's trusty astromech droid, used in his red starfighter. Before the Clone Wars, she was copilot when Kenobi chased Jango Fett through the asteroid rings above Geonosis. R4-P17 continued to assist Obi-Wan during the Clone Wars and participated in the Battle of Teth among others.

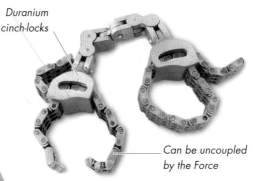

Duranium cinch-locks

Can be uncoupled by the Force

**SEPARATIST BINDERS**

**OBI-WAN'S LIGHTSABER**

Though it often slips from his grip, Obi-Wan's lightsaber will remain in his possession for his 19 years of self-exile on Tatooine, watching over young Luke Skywalker.

# ANAKIN SKYWALKER

**ALTHOUGH HE LOOKS** like any other nine-year-old boy living on the planet Tatooine, Anakin Skywalker is far from ordinary. He lives with his mother in the spaceport city of Mos Espa, and is a slave to the junk dealer, Watto. Anakin has a natural ability with mechanical devices, and repairs and builds machines in his spare time, including podracer engines and a working droid. The Jedi Knight Qui-Gon Jinn notices his keen perception and unnaturally fast reflexes, and recognizes that the Force is extraordinarily strong in Anakin. This leads to Anakin being accepted into the Jedi Order at the age of 10—unusally late for a Padawan.

*Connection plate*

**PODRACER POWER CELL**

**WUPIUPI (TATOOINE COINS)**

Anakin thinks he simply has faster reflexes than normal humans, but the truth is stranger—he uses the Force to react to events before they happen.

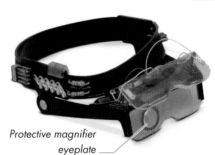
*Protective magnifier eyeplate*

**WELDING GOGGLES**

*Adjustable goggles*

*Leather neck wrap*

## SLAVE AND DREAMER

Anakin's mother, Shmi, has raised him to believe in himself and his dreams, in spite of their humble situation as slaves. Anakin looks forward to the day when he will be free to pilot starships of the mainline through the spacelanes of the galaxy. He soon finds that belief in one's dreams can have powerful results.

*Rough work clothing*

*Leg wraps keep out sand*

*Tool pouch*

*Survival flares for use in sandstorms*

**TRAVEL LUGGAGE**

*Headphones*

**PODRACING HELMET**

*Retriver shaft*

*Electromagnet tuned to polarity of control cable*

**CABLE RETRIEVER**

34

## JEDI PILOT

When Anakin commanders an airspeeder to pursue Zam Wesell, his abilities prove phenomenal. He violates Jedi policies on speed and risk—guidelines intended to safeguard other craft, but not designed with so gifted a pilot in mind. His antics prompt Obi-Wan to ask, "Why do I get the feeling you're going to be the death of me?"

## SECRET PODRACER

Anakin has secretly restored and rebuilt a junked podracer using parts Watto didn't think could be salvaged, and others obtained from Jawa traders. Anakin and Qui-Gon convince Watto that the podracer belongs to Qui-Gon, and enter it in the notorious Boonta Eve Classic Podrace.

**PODRACER DISPLAYS**

Short hairstyle with learner braid

Standard Jedi tunic style

Communications antennae

Narrow-beam headlight

Heavy-duty capacitors

Exposed turbojets

Widebeam headlight and anti-collision scanner

**UTILITY BELT**

Anno here

When Anakin senses his mother in pain, he returns to Tatooine in search of her—but is too late to save her from the Tusken Raiders. His guilt and sorrow drive him into a rage fueled by the dark side of the Force.

At the Varykino lake retreat on Naboo, Anakin confesses his love for Padmé. The young senator is drawn to the passionate Jedi, but tries to resist her feelings: Love is a complication neither of them can afford.

## ANAKIN'S LIGHTSABER

Most Jedi Padawans build their lightsabers to resemble those of their masters as a gesture of respect. Anakin's construction of his own lightsaber results in a design that favors maximum strength.

Heavy duty body cylinder

Activator and power indicator

Power-cell housing

# JEDI APPRENTICE

Anakin grows up to be a gifted Padawan. His talents make him impatient with Jedi traditions that seem to hold him back, and he often disagrees with his Master, Obi-Wan Kenobi. The Jedi Council suspects Anakin of being the prophesied One who can bring balance to the Force. But Anakin must face ever greater challenges to master the dangerous force that is himself.

Field boots weighted for training

# ANAKIN SKYWALKER:
## FALLEN JEDI

**AS THE CLONE TROOPER** becomes the emblem for the Grand Army of the Republic, Anakin Skywalker—dashing pilot and brave Jedi Knight—becomes the symbol of the Jedi Order. Praised by Supreme Chancellor Palpatine, applauded by the Senate, glorified on the HoloNet News, the "Hero With No Fear" is held by many to be the warrior-savior of the Republic. However, Anakin increasingly finds himself torn between his duties and a desire to accomplish great things.

**DOUBLE AGENT**

When Palpatine appoints Anakin to serve as his voice in the Jedi High Council, the Council orders Anakin to spy on the Chancellor. They also refuse to make Anakin a Master, despite his accomplishments. Discouraged to learn that the Jedi are not above duplicity, Anakin no longer feels guilty about keeping secrets from them.

Gauntlet worn
in combat

Synthleather
surcoat

Tunic apron

Utility pouch for
emergency rations

Military grade
trousers

Durable
grip-sole boots

HEADSET
COMLINK

**JEDI STARFIGHTER**

Anakin asks that his starfighter be painted yellow, allegedly in tribute to the podracer he flew as a youth, but perhaps to call attention to himself in battle.

Electrostatic fingertips
allow some feeling

**CYBORG LIMB**

Some Jedi Council members believe that when Anakin lost his right arm to Count Dooku, he lost some of his humanity. The result has been a chip on his shoulder to go with the prosthesis. In fact, Anakin has always been at ease with technology, and tinkers with his arm as he does his starfighter.

Armored shielding protects
electromotive lines

Alloy ligaments provide
pronation and supination

Electrodrivers
for pistons

Interface modules link
prosthesis to surviving nerves

**UTILITY POUCH**

## CHOSEN ONE?

Anakin is fearful of change, and of losing control. While he is believed to be the Chosen One, he frequently finds his hands tied, in the same way that the Senate binds the hands of Supreme Chancellor Palpatine. Nevertheless, Anakin is determined to honor Obi-Wan, and to live up to the title the Jedi have bestowed upon him.

DATA FILE

> Anakin trains a Padawan named Ahsoka Tano. She leaves the Jedi Order shortly before the end of the Clone Wars.

> After Anakin is gravely wounded on Mustafar, he is given life-saving surgery by a Tripedal Med droid and an FX-9 Surgical Assistant.

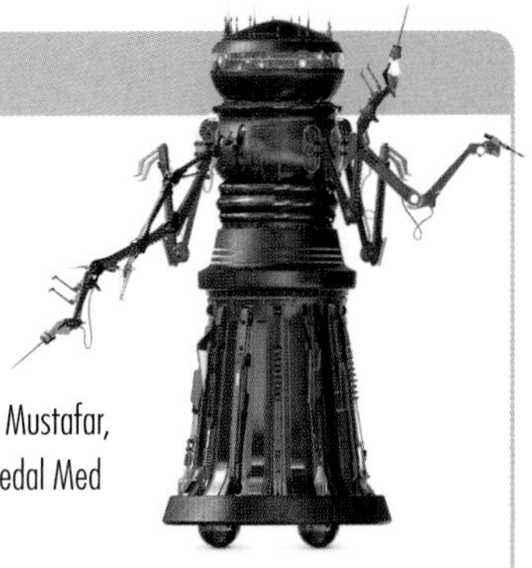

On the fiery planet Mustafar, Anakin's love for Padmé and Obi-Wan mutates to hatred when he convinces himself that his wife and his former Master have betrayed him. Now that he has embraced the dark side, Anakin shows no remorse in Force-choking Padmé, and engaging Obi-Wan in a duel to the death.

Function indicators

Locking helmet

Vision enhancement receptors

Voice projector/ respiratory intake

**SYSTEMS STATUS BELT**

Blast-dampening armor

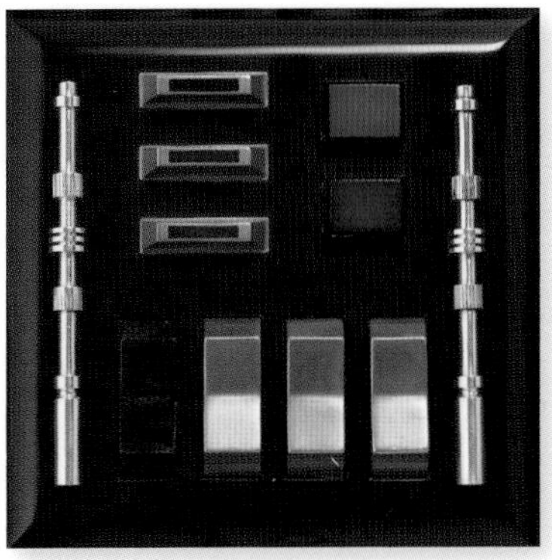

**COMPUTERIZED CONTROL PANEL**

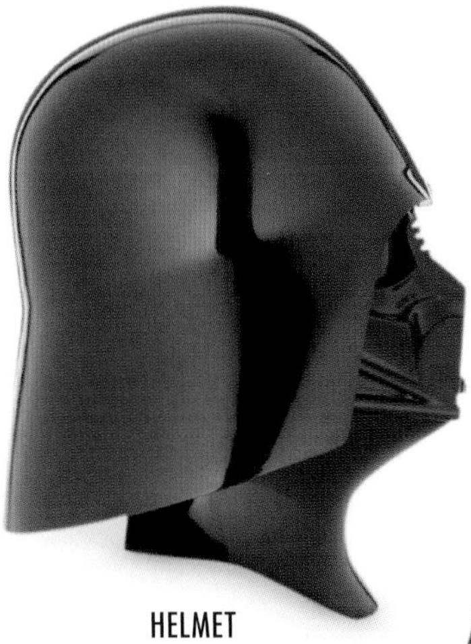

**HELMET**

Crystal chamber

Activator

**SITH LIGHTSABER**

Power indicator

Blade power adjuster

# DARTH VADER

Anakin falls to the dark side, accepting Darth Sidious as his new Master and taking a new identity as the Sith lord, Darth Vader. After committing terrible atrocities on Courscant and Mustafar, Anakin loses his lightsaber battle with Obi-Wan. The only way Sidious can save his new apprentice is with extreme surgical reconstruction. When Vader awakes, he learns that Padmé is dead—most likely by his own hand. The realization that he has killed the person he loved most will haunt him for the rest of his life.

# THE SITH

**WHEN QUI-GON JINN** is killed by Darth Maul, the Jedi discover that the Sith have not been destroyed, but merely driven into hiding, with only one master and one apprentice existing at any one time. But they are no closer to knowing whether Darth Maul was the master or the apprentice. Now the Jedi fear a Sith plot has been set in motion, shrouding the Force. They are correct, but have failed to realize that the Sith plot is nearing fruition, or that the Order and the Republic are on the edge of ruin.

## DARTH TYRANUS

The galaxy knows Count Dooku as the idealistic leader of the Separatists. But in truth he is now Darth Tyranus, apprentice to the hidden Sith Lord. He dreams of ruling the new Sith Empire at his Master's side, unaware that he will soon be replaced by another.

**CLOSE TO HOME**
The Jedi have found clues that the Sith have infiltrated Coruscant and the upper ranks of the Republic's government. However, they have not found the hidden Sith lair in the bleak precinct of Coruscant known as the Works. Nor has anyone guessed the terrifying truth about just how high in the establishment Sith corruption reaches.

## HIS MASTER'S LESSONS

After he leaves the Jedi Order, Dooku no longer has access to the Sith Holocrons in the Jedi Archives. But his lessons in the dark side of the Force are not over. After Dooku pledges himself to the Sith and becomes Darth Tyranus, Darth Sidious supplies him with a holoprojector and cells containing mystic teachings of shadowy power.

*Black crystal*

*Sith incantation hieroglyphs*

*Sith inscriptions*

*Duelist's stance*

## A SECRET ARMY

Troubled by visions of ruin, the Jedi Master Sifo-Dyas ordered the Kaminoans to create a clone army. The Kaminoans never heard from Sifo-Dyas again, but the army was paid for—by Darth Tyranus, the same man who erased Kamino from the Jedi Archives.

## THE PUBLIC THREAT

Tyranus rallies new worlds to the Separatist cause, while securing the secret loyalty of the galaxy's great corporations—and their private armies. Thanks to Dooku's machinations, in the Republic's greatest hour of need, the clone army will become available to counter this threat.

Face known to only a few

## THE CLONE WARS BEGIN

From the royal box on Geonosis, Tyranus watches Jedi lead clones into battle and allows himself a moment of satisfaction. The Sith plan is unfolding exactly as he and his hidden Master planned.

Concealed lightsaber

### DATA FILE

> Darth Bane reshaped the Sith Order, declaring the Rule of Two: one master and one apprentice preserving Sith teachings.

> The Geonosians have created plans for a weapon to ensure the Sith will rule the galaxy unopposed: a space station with enough firepower to destroy a planet.

## SECRET LORD

The secret ruler of the Sith is Darth Sidious, whose plot to rule the galaxy now nears actualization. Sidious's war has begun—a war that will destroy the Republic's wealth, its Jedi guardians, and its democratic ideals. When the Republic falls, the Sith Empire will rise.

## HIDDEN IN PLAIN SIGHT

Dooku tells a captive Obi-Wan that the Republic is controlled by a Sith named Darth Sidious. It is the truth, but a truth so ludicrous that Obi-Wan dismisses it as a lie, just as Dooku hoped he would.

Rough, simple robes

# SHEEV PALPATINE

**THE SITH HAVE WAITED** centuries for the birth of one who is powerful enough to return them from hiding. Darth Sidious is that one—the Sith's revenge on the Jedi Order for having nearly eradicated the practitioners of the dark side of the Force. Trained by Darth Plagueis, Sidious takes the guise of Naboo Senator, and later Supreme Chancellor, Sheev Palpatine. He understands that the corrupt Republic and the subservient Jedi Order can be brought down by playing to the weaknesses of the former: its mindless bureaucracy and attachment to power. Sidious meticulously plans his actions and is willing to ruthlessly discard his apprentices in order to eliminate the Republic and its Jedi protectors.

## SEAT OF OFFICE
Palpatine has bowed to the concerns of his aides by accepting a chair that affords him secret shielding. It also provides direct, secure communication with his aides and the Red Guard.

*Ultra-dense lanthanide alloy armor*

## UNASSUMING DISGUISE

Palpatine is careful to protest the limits of his abilities and present himself as a mild-mannered public servant. However, always citing the best interests of the Republic, he has consistently increased his own power, from his legal authority to his institution of the Chancellor's Red Guard, whose members now attend every committee meeting. For some, his true intentions remain unclear.

*Sleeves of ancient design*

*Subdued color and simple style convey gravity without pompous exhibitionism*

The Jedi Council regularly discusses political opinions with Supreme Chancellor Palpatine in his impressive audience chambers. The support of the great Jedi reassures many in the Republic who might otherwise doubt the Chancellor's motives.

**SITH CHALICE**

**FRIEZE FROM SUPREME CHANCELLOR PALPATINE'S OFFICE**

## DATA FILE

> A powerful practitioner of the dark side of the Force, Sidious uses Sith lightning to attack his enemies.

> After the destruction of the Jedi Order, Sidious has no need to reveal his Sith identity, for he is now the beloved Emperor Palpatine, who has restored peace to the galaxy.

**OFFICE IDOLS**
Palpatine's statues honor obscure figures from the past who possessed much arcane wisdom and law, but whose actions are shrouded in controversy.

**BLUE GUARD RIFLE**

## SITH LORD

For Sidious, everything is proceeding according to plan. Soon the Jedi will be remembered only as archaic warriors, practicing a sad religion, and memories of the Republic will disappear. The Sith Lord founds a group of Force-sensitive beings called the Inquisitorius. These agents hunt down and eradicate any remaining survivors.

*Precious aurodium cap and blade emitter*

*Face has turned yellow in anger*

*Dark robes hide Sidious's identity*

*Blade-length adjust*

**SIDIOUS'S LIGHTSABER**
Sidious has two identical lightsabers. They are usually concealed within a neuranium sculpture that adorns his chambers in the Senate Office Building.

*Sith lightsaber*

*Phrik alloy casing*

**MAS AMEDDA**
Senate Speaker, Mas Amedda, is one of the select few who understands that Palpatine is more than he appears. He knows that the Chancellor's look of practiced humility belies that of a cunning manipulator of political power.

"Always two there are"—not only master and apprentice, but persona and true face. When the Sith Lord is unmasked by deflected lightning during his duel with Mace Windu, his true face is revealed to the world. However, the Jedi cannot damage Palpatine's reputation in the Senate.

*Vials of injectable bacta and bota*

*Filtration transpirators*

Jedi Master Yoda discovers that Palpatine has been the Sith Lord all along. Palpatine gleefully duels Yoda but is unable to defeat him, as both are equally matched. Yoda retreats into exile.

**MEDICAL KIT**
Sidious plucks Darth Vader from death on the black-sand bank of one of Mustafar's lava rivers, and has him placed in a medical capsule that will keep him alive. On the way to Coruscant, Sidious uses special potions and implements to begin transforming Darth Vader into a cyborg.

# DARTH MAUL

**DATA FILE**

> After Obi-Wan defeats Maul, the Jedi believe he is dead, but Maul's brother finds him broken on a junk planet. Once healed, Maul forms a rival Sith order with his sibling that threatens Sidious.

> During the Empire's reign, Maul, still bitter about his defeat by Obi-Wan, learns that the Jedi is hiding on Tatooine. Maul duels the Jedi one last time.

**FUELED BY THE AGGRESSIVE** energies of the dark side, Darth Maul is one of the most highly trained Sith in the order's history. Darth Sidious stole Maul as a child from his mother—a powerful Nightsister witch named Talzin—and transformed him into a vicious warrior. Maul serves his master obediently and participates in the first recorded duel between a Sith and a Jedi in centuries. Maul believes that his own time for strategic wisdom and eventual domination will come.

## THE *SCIMITAR*

Darth Maul's Sith Infiltrator is a heavily customized Star Courier produced by the brilliant engineer Raith Sienar. It incorporates an experimental ion engine system and a rare cloaking device which renders Maul's ship invisible to organic eyes as well as mechanical sensors when activated.

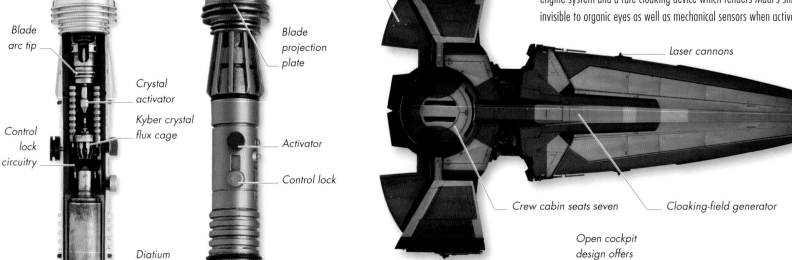

Bat-like wings fold inwards

Blade projection plate

Blade arc tip

Crystal activator

Kyber crystal flux cage

Control lock circuitry

Activator

Control lock

Diatium power cell

Blade modulation control

Bi-directional power circuitry

Control lock

Laser cannons

Crew cabin seats seven

Cloaking-field generator

Flange coupler

Blade modulation circuitry

Thin layer of power insulation

Primary crystal

Cycling field energizers

Ribbed handgrip

Open cockpit design offers optimum visibility

Acceleration handgrips

Steering bar

Braking pedal

Repulsorlift

## SITH SPEEDER

Maul's speeder carries no weapons, since he prefers the direct assault of blade weapons or the treachery of bombs to the use of blasters.

## PROBE DROID

One of Maul's most useful tools is the "dark eye" probe droid, a hovering reconnaissance device that can be programmed to seek out individuals or information.

Scan-absorbing stealth shell

Primary photoreceptor

External weapons mount

Levitator

## MAUL'S LIGHTSABER

Pushing his physical and Force-assisted abilities to the utmost, Darth Maul uses a double-bladed lightsaber as his primary weapon. In untrained hands, Maul's saber can be much more dangerous to its wielder than an enemy. In the hands of Darth Maul, however, it becomes a whirling vortex of lethal energy.

## JEDI KILLER

Qui-Gon Jinn is not the first Jedi to fall to Maul's blade. Darth Sidious instils in Maul an intense hunger to kill Jedi, but forbids him from doing so until the time is right. Needing to satiate his desire, Maul learns that Jedi Padawan Eldra Kaitis is being auctioned off by a criminal. He captures Eldra, and they start dueling. Eldra is a worthy opponent, but Maul kills her. He is surprised to find that killing a Jedi leaves his bloodlust undiminished.

Vestigial horns

Hairless skull

Gleaming yellow eyes

Maul's natural markings are augmented with tattoos.

Gauntlets

Field cloak cut to allow fighting movement

Lightsaber blades are red due to corrupted kyber crystals

Heavy-action boots

**WRIST LINK**

With his double-bladed lightsaber, Maul is equal to two Jedi who are unprepared for his powers. Since the Sith disappeared almost 1,000 years ago, Jedi are not used to facing opponents armed with lightsabers.

Light-gathering lens

Multi-scan controls

Power cells

## ELECTROBINOCULARS

On Tatooine, Maul uses electrobinoculars to search for the Jedi. These electrobinoculars are equipped with radiation sensors for night vision and powerful light-gathering components for long-distance scanning.

Filters screen out atmospheric interference

Memory stores 360° horizon view

Alarm signals energy sources or visual targets

Mode indicator

Nav-grid can be projected onto landscape

Range to target

Magnification

### ELECTROBINOCULAR VIEWSCREEN

Tied to global mapping scanners in his starship, Maul's electrobinocular viewscreen displays the precise location of targets and indicates life signals or power frequencies. Specific shapes, colors, or energy types can be set as targets, and even invisible defensive fields can be detected.

# COUNT DOOKU

**DATA FILE**

> Count Dooku is one of the wealthiest individuals in the galaxy. He could field an army on his own resources.

> Even though Sith doctrine forbids it, Dooku has trained three apprentices of his own—Asajj Ventress, Savage Opress, and fellow fallen Jedi, Quinlan Vos.

**THE DANGEROUS AND ELEGANT** Count Dooku was once a renowned Jedi Master, but he is now a Sith Lord and the leader of the Separatists—a group of planets that wants to secede from the Republic. By protesting the failure of the Republic, Dooku has swayed many systems to the Separatist side, but his real motives lurk in darkness. This double-dealing master of the Force has assumed a place at the heart of galactic events and threatens the very survival of the Republic.

*Belt made of rare rancor leather*

*Count's gaze immobilizes weak-minded individuals*

*Cape enlarges Count's silhouette to intimidating effect*

*Cape is emblem of Count of Serenno*

**COUNT DOOKU'S BELT**

## DARK ALIGNMENT

Although Dooku joins the Order at a young age, he never fully gives it his inmost allegiance. He maintains a streak of independence, which he transmits to his pupils, including Qui-Gon Jinn. Dooku's considerable strength in the Force makes him enigmatic even to Yoda, and the Council sadly underestimates Dooku's hunger for power. He leaves the Order, taking up his hereditary title as Count of Serenno, and secretly becoming Darth Tyranus—Darth Sidious' second Sith apprentice. During the Clone Wars, Dooku is the public face of the Separatists, but follows Sidious' orders.

*Curved lightsaber hilt allows precise crossparry moves*

Battling Anakin and Obi-Wan, Dooku reveals how far he has fallen when he casts legendary Sith lightning. Sith lightning causes excruciating pain and weakens life—a terrifying and evil use of the Force.

*Underlayer made of costly, fine-grade armorweave fabric*

## DOOKU'S LIGHTSABER

As a Jedi Master, Count Dooku sets aside the lightsaber he built as a young Padawan to create a superior one, as Jedi sometimes do. In creating his personalized design, he choses a configuration that had no connection to that of his master, Yoda, nor to the style in fashion at the time. Instead, he studies Jedi Archive records to create a lightsaber that suits his technique, which favors long, elegant moves and incredible deftness of hand.

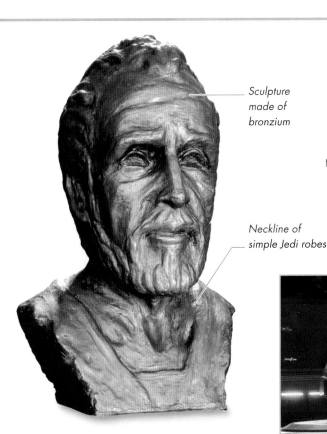

*Sculpture made of bronzium*

*Neckline of simple Jedi robes*

### STATUE REMINDER
Those entering the Jedi Archives will see a bronzium bust of Count Dooku, along with statues of several other former Jedi.

A shackled Palpatine watches Dooku and Anakin duel aboard the Separatist flagship. In fact, the abduction is an elaborate ruse, engineered to ensnare Anakin and test him to determine whether he can be turned to the dark side. Dooku realizes too late that the test involves Anakin taking his life.

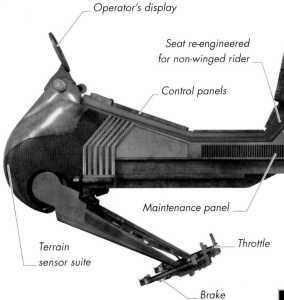

*Operator's display*

*Seat re-engineered for non-winged rider*

*Control panels*

*Engine housing*

*Stabilizer fin*

*Maintenance panel*

*Terrain sensor suite*

*Throttle*

*Brake*

*Engine intake*

### FLITKNOT SPEEDER BIKE
Deciding to escape from the fighting on Geonosis, Dooku flees on his open-cockpit *Flitknot* speeder, which has been modified for non-Geonosians.

## GALACTIC TREASURES

When he was a Jedi, Dooku chafed at the Order's disdain for technology, seeing it as another example of the Jedi favoring the tedious study of ancient texts over engaging with the galaxy and its people. Free of the Order's fussy rules, Dooku uses his wealth and power to experiment with machinery. He seeks better warcraft and weapons, and indulges his own curiosity about the limits of technological ingenuity.

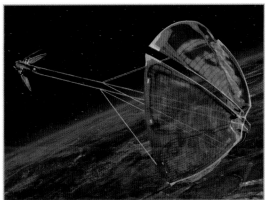

Dooku's solar sailer combines a Geonosian-built sloop with a sail of unknown manufacture that catches mysterious supralight energies, propelling the craft through hyperspace.

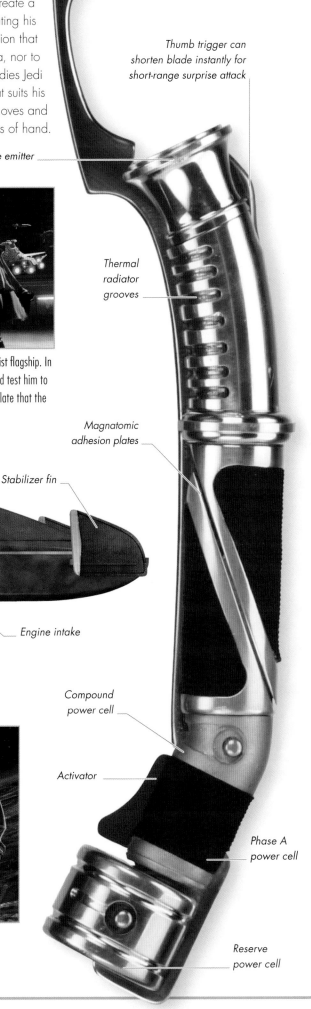

*Emitter guard*

*Thumb trigger can shorten blade instantly for short-range surprise attack*

*Blade emitter*

*Thermal radiator grooves*

*Magnatomic adhesion plates*

*Compound power cell*

*Activator*

*Phase A power cell*

*Reserve power cell*

# THE NEIMOIDIANS

**BORN AS MAGGOT-LIKE GRUBS,** Neimoidians spend the first seven years of their lives competing for food in enormous hives. The most acquisitive grow strong by hoarding more than they can eat, causing their rivals to weaken and die. As a result, those Neimoidians that survive into adulthood are naturally greedy and pathologically selfish. This makes them gifted and ruthless merchants, well suited to ruling positions in the Trade Federation—an interplanetary guild designed to promote commerce above all other concerns. The Neimoidians will happily use slave labor to advance their interests, and have been known to invade whole worlds for profit.

### NEIMOIDIAN SHUTTLE

Neimoidian dignitaries use *Sheathipede*-class transport shuttles for short-distance travel on Trade Federation business. The vessels are far from spacious, and usually unarmed, but they can be upgraded with laser cannons and automatic pilots. The latter enhancement allows for the passenger compartment to extend into the cockpit area.

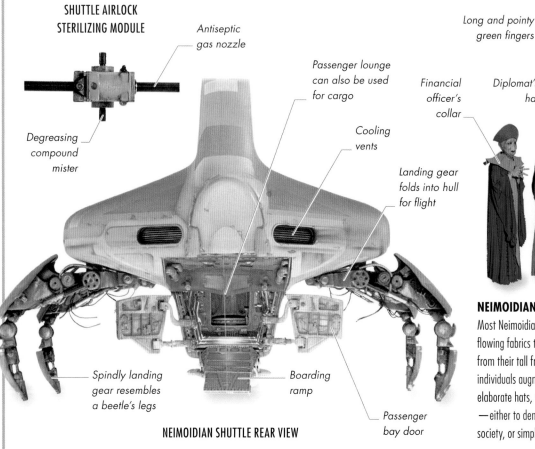

SHUTTLE AIRLOCK STERILIZING MODULE

Antiseptic gas nozzle

Degreasing compound mister

Passenger lounge can also be used for cargo

Cooling vents

Landing gear folds into hull for flight

Spindly landing gear resembles a beetle's legs

Boarding ramp

Passenger bay door

**NEIMOIDIAN SHUTTLE REAR VIEW**

Neimoidian senatorial miter

Dod, like all Neimoidians, has no nose

Neimoidian senatorial mantle

### LOTT DOD

Neimoidian politician Lott Dod is the Trade Federation's representative in the Galactic Senate. His voice in the law-making assembly makes the Trade Federation as powerful as a planet. Dod uses his influence to disrupt and delay the Senate's attempts to hold the rapacious Trade Federation to account for its actions.

Long and pointy green fingers

Financial officer's collar

Diplomat's hat

### NEIMOIDIAN DRESS

Most Neimoidians dress in long, flowing fabrics that hang elegantly from their tall frames. High-status individuals augment their robes with elaborate hats, collars, and jewelry —either to denote specific roles in society, or simply to indicate wealth.

# RUNE HAAKO

Rune Haako may be cautious to the point of cowardice, but he has still risen to high office within the Trade Federation. As Settlements Officer, he serves as Nute Gunray's right hand, offering counsel while the Viceroy plots with his Sith masters, Darth Sidious and Darth Tyranus.

Neimoidians are a naturally guarded species, and the Trade Federation goes to great lengths to hide its aggressive business practices. Nute Gunray and Rune Haako are more than a little uneasy when the Sith Lord Darth Sidious convinces them to launch an all-out battle droid invasion of the peaceful planet Naboo.

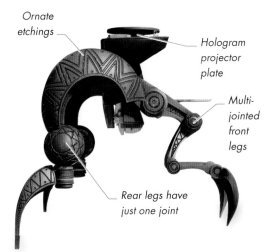

Ornate etchings

Hologram projector plate

Multi-jointed front legs

Rear legs have just one joint

### MECHNO-CHAIR
Walking mechno-chairs are neither comfortable nor practical. They are, however, hugely expensive, making them popular with high-ranking Neimoidians. They can also be used as mobile platforms for projecting holograms.

# NUTE GUNRAY

As Viceroy of the Trade Federation, Nute Gunray is one of the most powerful businessman in the galaxy. This scheming leader will go to any lengths to enrich himself—even if it means starting a war! His ruthless nature helps him to become a senior figure in the Separatist Alliance by the outbreak of the Clone Wars.

Two-pronged cowl denotes status

Crested fabric tiara

Viceroy's collar

## DATA FILE

> The Neimoidians are native to Cato Neimoidia, but have colonized several neighboring planets, which are known as the Neimoidian purse-worlds.

> The Neimoidian leadership uses vast Trade Federation cargo freighters to deploy and control its enormous armies of battle droids.

# THE INVASION FORCE

LANDING CRAFT UNDERSIDE VIEW

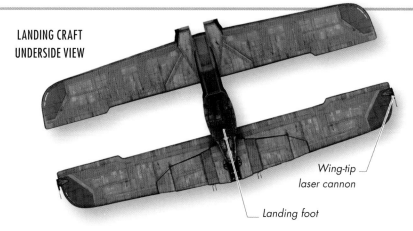

Wing-tip laser cannon

Landing foot

**AFTER JAMMING ALL COMMUNICATIONS** on Naboo, the Trade Federation begins its invasion of the peaceful planet. Massive landing ships descend into the forests, their bellies filled with powerful war machines. They open up to deploy hulking Multi Troop Transports—which smash through the trees to deliver battle droids into combat—and smaller Armored Assault Tanks, armed with powerful laser cannons. In the sky above, vast Droid Control Ships coordinate the troops, while flying vulture droids defend the Trade Federation leaders from any counterattack.

## LANDING CRAFT

The C-9979 landing craft is designed to ferry cargo in peacetime, but it also makes for an effective troop transport. Its single landing foot allows it to land in Naboo's dense forests, while its 270 m (885 ft) wingspan stretches above the treetops. Each landing craft carries 11 MTTs, plus other battle droids and armaments.

## MTT

The Multi-Troop Transport glides above the ground using powerful repulsorlift engines, battering its way past any obstacle to reach a battlefield. On arrival, its large front hatch opens and a troop deployment rack slides out. This holds up to 112 battle droids, all of which quickly unfold from their space-saving configuration.

Designed by Haor Chall Engineering for the Trade Federation's merchant fleet, the C-9979's huge wings are, in fact, long cargo bays. Repulsorlifts built into the ends of the wings allow the vessels to stay airborne when they enter a planet's gravity.

Hydraulic deployment rack

Folded B1 battle droids

Twin blaster cannon

Command bridge

Main deployment hatch

Lower deployment hatch

Armored hull

Repulsorlift impellor

Each MTT is armed with a pair of twin blaster cannons for defense, but they are not designed for combat. Instead, they rely on AATs to provide an escort in the thick of battle.

Repulsorlift exhaust vents

**MTT SIDE VIEW**

MTTs thunder along programmed routes with no regard for what might be in their path! On Naboo, Jedi Master Qui-Gon Jinn has to run for his life to avoid being crushed by one.

# DROID CONTROL SHIP

The Trade Federation modifies the *Lucrehulk*-class LH-3210 cargo freighter *Saak'ak* to control its battle droids during the invasion of Naboo. Captained by the Neimoidian Daultay Dofine, this vessel beams orders to troops on the ground while keeping Dofine and his fellow officers well away from the firing line.

Control bridge tower

Command centersphere

Droid signal receiver station

Can carry 1,500 droid starfighters

Docking claw

**VULTURE DROID
SIDE VIEW**

As the flagship of the Trade Federation's invading force, the *Saak'ak* is heavily shielded against attack, and armed with 42 quad turbolaser cannons spread across its 3.11 km (1.93 mi) diameter.

If battle droids lose contact with their control ship, they will shut down. This makes the *Saak'ak* a key target for the bright yellow starfighters of the Royal Naboo Security Forces—one of which is flown by a young Anakin Skywalker.

Vulture droids use just a few simple attack patterns, and so rely on sheer numbers to defeat more imaginative foes.

Photoreceptor "eyes" glow red when active

Cooling vents

Torpedo tube

Walking gear

Twin blaster cannon

## VULTURE DROID

The Variable Geometry Self-Propelled Battle Droid, Mark I—also known as the vulture droid—is a starfighter that has a computer brain instead of a living pilot. It is extremely maneuverable and heavily armed for its size, just 3.5 m (11 ft 6 in) long. It can use its wings as legs in order to walk on a planetary surface.

### AAT
Droid-controlled Armored Assault Tanks are the Trade Federation's main artillery on Naboo. Each AAT is armed with six energy shell launchers, four lateral lasers, and a heavy laser cannon.

WALK MODE

# BATTLE DROIDS

**THE GALACTIC REPUBLIC** has no army of its own, relying instead on the Jedi Knights to maintain law and order in a largely peaceful galaxy. The worlds that do retain a military force do so purely for internal security, or for ceremonial purposes. So when the power-hungry Trade Federation turns its manufacturing might to the secret production of a vast droid army, there is little to stand between it and galactic supremacy. The droids are first deployed in the invasion of Naboo—alerting the Republic's leaders to a major change in the galactic status quo.

Battle droids are built in the image of the Geonosians, the insect-like species that designed them for the Trade Federation. However, standing 1.93 m (6 ft 4 in) tall, they are taller than the average Geonosian.

Command ship signal receiver

Optical sensor

Comlink booster pack

E-5 blaster rifle

Pistons function like muscles

Motorized joints

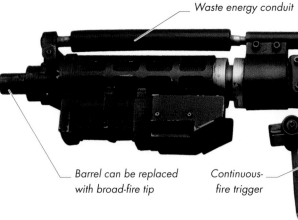

Waste energy conduit

Blaster gas cartridge

Barrel can be replaced with broad-fire tip

Continuous-fire trigger

Power cell

## E-5 BLASTER RIFLE

The E-5 is the standard issue blaster rifle for battle droids, built by Baktoid Armor Workshop. It is a powerful weapon, but the droids themselves are mostly poor shots, despite being programmed with moves from highly trained organic soldiers.

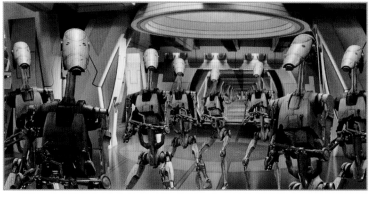

### OOM-SERIES BATTLE DROIDS

Before the Trade Federation built its army of B1 battle droids, small numbers of identical OOM-series battle droids were already a familiar sight on Trade Federation vessels.

The command droid OOM-9 leads an army of B1 battle droids in the invasion of Naboo.

Blue indicates a pilot droid

Security droids are red

## DROID DESIGNATIONS

OOM-series battle droids can perform more functions than their B1 battle droid successors, thanks to the level of independent reasoning that is included with their programming. Color-coding is used to indicate a droid's specialist function, with yellow-colored OOM command battle droids, for example, serving as officers that can give orders to other battle droids.

# B1 BATTLE DROID

B1 battle droids are mass produced quickly and cheaply. They have thin armor, limited capabilities, and rely on commands received from a Droid Control Ship, to save on the cost of individual brains. But these weaknesses mean little when the droids are deployed *en masse*. Programmed to obey orders without question and never surrender, they are relentless and endlessly replaceable.

### UNFOLDING DROID

B1 battle droids are designed to fold up tightly for transit on board Multi-Troop Transports. They are stored on racks and can deploy in seconds when activated.

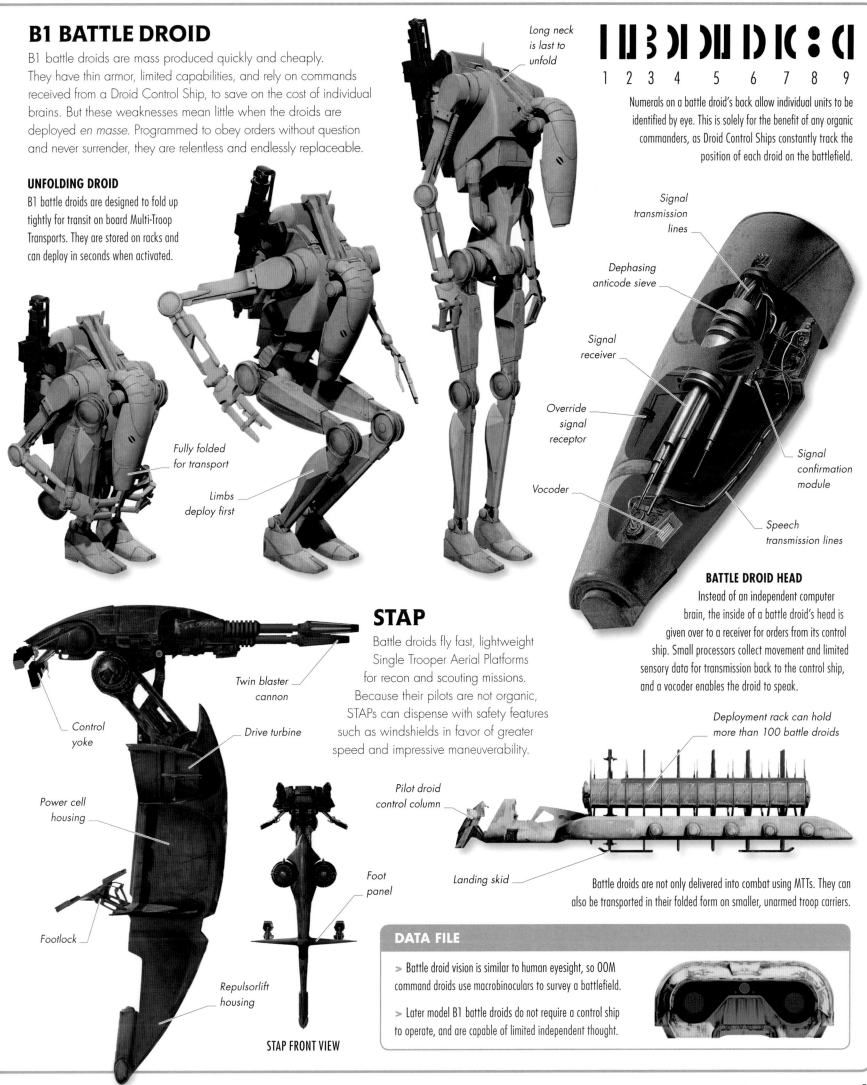

Long neck is last to unfold

Numerals on a battle droid's back allow individual units to be identified by eye. This is solely for the benefit of any organic commanders, as Droid Control Ships constantly track the position of each droid on the battlefield.

Fully folded for transport

Limbs deploy first

Signal transmission lines

Dephasing anticode sieve

Signal receiver

Override signal receptor

Vocoder

Signal confirmation module

Speech transmission lines

### BATTLE DROID HEAD

Instead of an independent computer brain, the inside of a battle droid's head is given over to a receiver for orders from its control ship. Small processors collect movement and limited sensory data for transmission back to the control ship, and a vocoder enables the droid to speak.

## STAP

Battle droids fly fast, lightweight Single Trooper Aerial Platforms for recon and scouting missions. Because their pilots are not organic, STAPs can dispense with safety features such as windshields in favor of greater speed and impressive maneuverability.

Twin blaster cannon

Control yoke

Drive turbine

Power cell housing

Footlock

Repulsorlift housing

Foot panel

Pilot droid control column

Deployment rack can hold more than 100 battle droids

Landing skid

Battle droids are not only delivered into combat using MTTs. They can also be transported in their folded form on smaller, unarmed troop carriers.

**STAP FRONT VIEW**

### DATA FILE

> Battle droid vision is similar to human eyesight, so OOM command droids use macrobinoculars to survey a battlefield.

> Later model B1 battle droids do not require a control ship to operate, and are capable of limited independent thought.

# DROIDEKAS

**DROIDEKAS ARE FAR MORE** deadly than standard battle droids. Designed by a murderous insectoid species called the Colicoids, these war machines are literally armed with built-in blasters, and spring into action from a fast-moving wheel mode. They are just what the Trade Federation needs as it ramps up its aggressive presence in the galaxy, so they are bought in exchange for exotic meats that the bloodthirsty Colicoids can feast on. The droidekas are then effectively deployed in the invasion of Naboo.

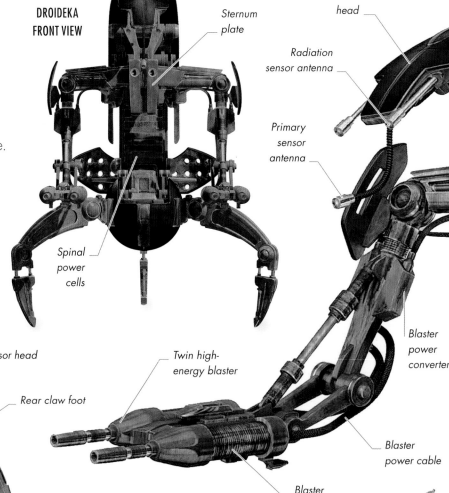

DROIDEKA
FRONT VIEW

Sternum plate

Sensor head

Radiation sensor antenna

Primary sensor antenna

Spinal power cells

Blaster power converter

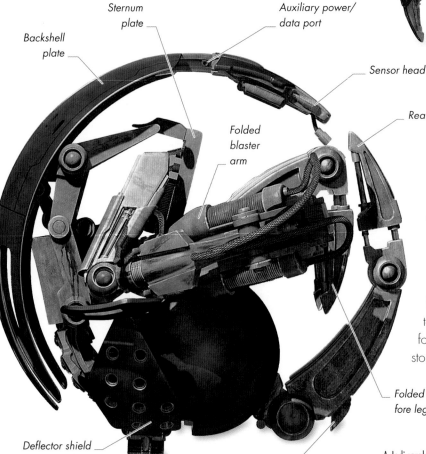

Backshell plate

Sternum plate

Auxiliary power/ data port

Sensor head

Folded blaster arm

Rear claw foot

Twin high-energy blaster

Blaster power cable

Blaster energizer

Deflector shield projector plates do not function in wheel mode

Flanges stop limbs from overextending

Folded fore legs

Hip joint

Claw foot designed for hard surfaces

## WHEEL MODE

Droidekas walk on three spindly legs, but they are designed to move fastest in wheel mode. Curled into a tight ball, a droideka rolls into battle at high speed. This makes it a difficult target, while also shielding vital systems. This formation is also used when droidekas are stored onboard troop transports.

A Jedi rarely runs from danger, but Qui-Gon Jinn and his Padawan, Obi-Wan Kenobi, have little choice when they are faced with a pair of droidekas on a Trade Federation ship.

Each droideka has a pair of twin blasters, which it fires in quick succession. While one blaster fires, the other recharges from the spinal power cells. This allows for a continuous stream of left-right fire.

## ATTACK SEQUENCE
Racing toward a target at up to 75kph (47mph), a droideka senses when it is in firing range. It unfurls its legs first, using the front two to come to an almost instant halt. It then swiftly rises to its full height and activates its deflector shield.

In wheel mode

Coming to a halt

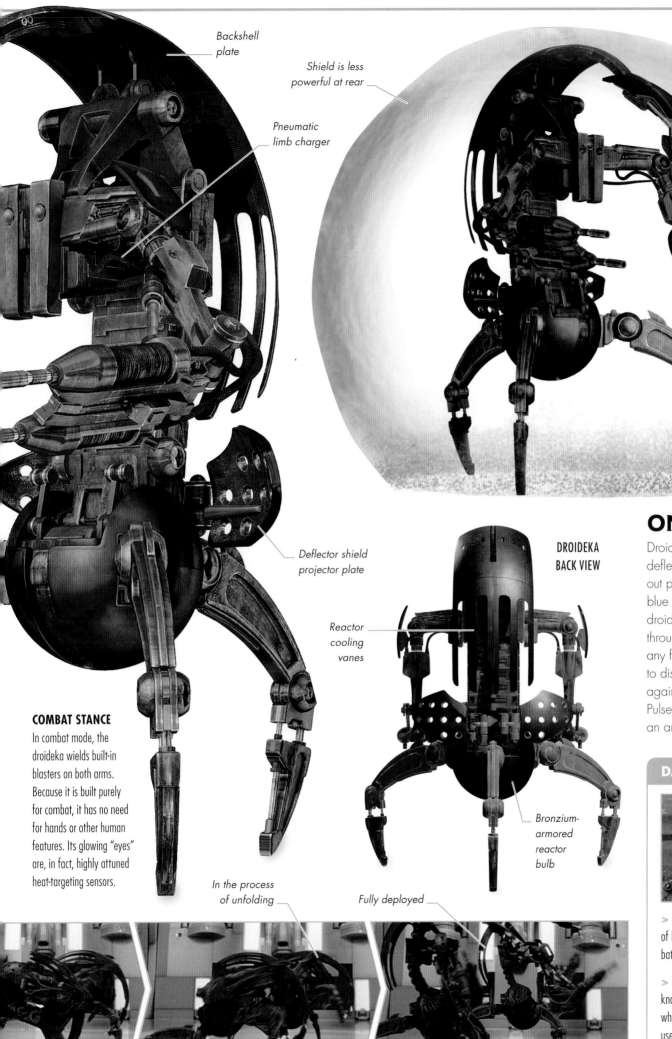

Backshell
plate

Shield is less
powerful at rear

Blaster fire
can pass
outward but
not inward

Pneumatic
limb charger

Deflector shield
projector plate

DROIDEKA
BACK VIEW

Reactor
cooling
vanes

Bronzium-
armored
reactor
bulb

## ONE-WAY SHIELD

Droidekas are equipped with personal deflector shields, projected from fold-out plates on their sides. The translucent blue shields are polarized to allow the droidekas' own blaster pulses to pass through to the outside, while causing any fire coming from the other direction to dissipate. Hand weapons are useless against droidekas, but Electro Magnetic Pulse grenades are effective if used in an ambush from the rear.

### COMBAT STANCE

In combat mode, the droideka wields built-in blasters on both arms. Because it is built purely for combat, it has no need for hands or other human features. Its glowing "eyes" are, in fact, highly attuned heat-targeting sensors.

In the process
of unfolding

Fully deployed

# THE NABOO

**LONG AGO, A GROUP** of humans from the planet Grizmallt crashed on Naboo and set up a small colony there. In time, they established a great society—entirely separate from that of the native Gungans—and began to refer to themselves as the Naboo. Today, the Naboo thrive as artists and scholars, living under the rule of democratically elected leaders. They are active on the fringes of interplanetary affairs via their voice in the Galactic Senate, Senator Palpatine. However, despite their technological advances, they are ill-prepared for an attack on their world by the powerful Trade Federation.

Naboo is a small, lush planet, criss-crossed by a vast network of tunnels and caves created by underground plasma deposits. It is noted across the galaxy for its natural beauty.

*Finely manicured beard*

*Formal collar*

**FUTHARK SCRIPT** The Naboo alphabet has a formal handwritten form called the futhark, and a day-to-day form known as the futhork. The formal script is used for most official purposes, such as labeling on government spacecraft.

*Subtly but ornately patterned fabrics*

*Fashionable sleeves and cuffs*

When the Trade Federation blockades Naboo, Governor Bibble implores Queen Amidala to flee the planet with Captain Panaka, while he stays behind to speak for their people.

## SIO BIBBLE

As the elected Governor of Naboo, Sio Bibble oversees the planet's day-to-day administration on behalf of the monarch. He first served under King Veruna, and remains in post throughout Queen Amidala's reign. He is the main point of contact in the Royal Palace for regional representatives and officials.

### NABOO ROYAL ADVISORY COUNCIL

The Governor of Naboo chairs a council of ministers that advises the monarch. The council is made up of luminaries from the arts and sciences, who guide public policy all over the planet.

**HELA BRANDES**
MUSIC ADVISOR

**GRAF ZAPALO**
MASTER OF SCIENCES

**HUGO ECKENER**
CHIEF ARCHITECT

**LUFTA SHIF**
EDUCATION REGENT

# THEED

The jewel in the crown of Naboo civilization is the capital city, Theed. Soaring high above the Solleu River, its stunning towers and domes are surrounded by waterfalls, the most impressive of which is the Virdugo Plunge. Beneath the city is a rich source of plasma, which is mined to meet the Naboo's power needs.

### CULTURAL CAPITAL

Theed is home to the greatest museums, theaters, and libraries on Naboo. It is also the site of the celebrated Royal Academy, where gifted youngsters train to become public servants. Queen Amidala is a former student.

### THEED ROYAL PALACE

Reached along the wide boulevard known as Palace Plaza, Theed Royal Palace is the grand seat of power on Naboo. In its lavish chambers, the monarch consults with advisors, receives dignitaries, and hosts cultural events. The palace is stormed by battle droids when the Trade Federation invades Naboo.

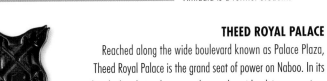

*Zoorif feather motif*

*Organic chif stone*

Elegant rings of polished marble hide a holoprojector set into the palace throne room floor.

### THEED HANGAR

The palace is connected to the Theed Hangar, home of the Royal Naboo Security Forces. The hangar is also linked to the Theed power generator, by means of a blast-proof door.

### FUNERAL TEMPLE

The Funeral Temple is an ancient place of cremation, located on the outskirts of Theed. Naboo mourners gather around a central pyre, before the ashes of the deceased are collected and scattered into the Solleu River below.

**EXAMPLES OF NABOO JEWELRY**

# QUEEN AMIDALA

**PADMÉ NABERRIE IS JUST** 14 years old when she becomes queen of Naboo, taking the royal name Amidala. A gifted child from a modest background, she devotes herself to public service, becoming an apprentice legislator at the age of eight, and then a junior senatorial advisor. After serving for two years as supervisor of Theed—the capital city of Naboo—she is elected Queen of the entire planet. Just a short time later, her world gains new galactic significance when the Trade Federation invades.

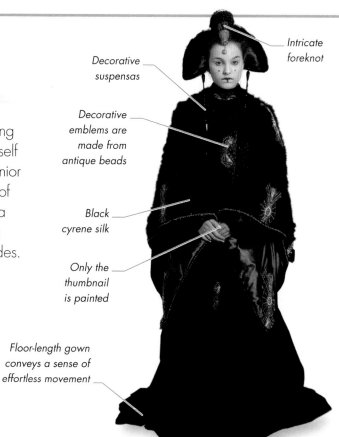

Intricate foreknot

Decorative suspensas

Decorative emblems are made from antique beads

Black cyrene silk

Only the thumbnail is painted

Floor-length gown conveys a sense of effortless movement

Jewel of Zenda

Gold faceframes

Hair sculpted over a padded frame

Hand-stitched gold embroidery

Fur trim made from shed potolli hair

## THRONE ROOM GOWN

As Queen of Naboo, Padmé is a symbol of hope and tradition for her people. She wears elaborate gowns to convey this status, with a change of costume to suit every occasion and duty. Her throne room gown is among the most lavish, designed to delight and impress visiting dignitaries from other worlds.

### FOREIGN RESIDENCE GOWN
On the planet Coruscant, Amidala wears a dark foreign residence gown. It is designed to acknowledge the sadness of being parted from Naboo.

Mauve chersilk hair veil

Antique tiara

Drapa bindings

Cerlin sleeves

Queen Amidala governs from the luxuroius throne room of Theed Royal Palace. She is flanked by loyal handmaidens and guided in her decisions by the Royal Advisory Council.

When the Queen is off-world, she holds court in a throne room on the Naboo Royal Starship. A holoprojector allows her to keep in contact with her advisors back on Naboo.

Self-illuminating sein jewel

Hem fitted to a circular frame

### TRAVELING GOWN
When Amidala leaves Coruscant to return to her besieged homeworld, she wears a somber outfit in recognition of her people's plight.

**GOLD BEADS**

The Queen's gowns are set off by many fine details, such as beads and suspensa ornaments. Many of these come from the Royal Palace treasure rooms.

The Queen's stylized makeup draws upon ancient Naboo customs. The red "scar of remembrance" on her lower lip honors Naboo's years of suffering before the Great Time of Peace.

**NABOO VICTORY PARADE**

*Royal Sovereign of Naboo medal*

*Escoffiate headpiece*

*Golden hairbands*

*Orichalc finework suspensas*

*Grand finial hairtip ornaments*

*Embroidered rosette design*

*Gold, triple-braided soutache*

## SENATE GOWN

When Amidala calls on the Galactic Senate to come to her planet's aid, she wears a magnificent gown and hairstyle. Her finery pays respect to the assembled senators and expresses the majesty of Naboo and its people. The regal trappings also help the young Queen to remain calm and aloof.

*Royal diadem*

*Jeweled finials*

*Petaled cape*

## JUBILATION DRESS

The people of Naboo celebrate the defeat of the Trade Federation's invading army with a lavish victory parade. For this joyous occasion, Padmé wears a traditional outfit favored by past Queens of Naboo during times of great happiness.

*Symbol of the Royal House of Naboo*

### DATA FILE

> Queen Amidala is not Naboo's youngest ever monarch. The planet often chooses young females as rulers, owing to their unspoiled wisdom.

> Amidala serves two terms as Queen before stepping down.

# SENATOR AMIDALA

**AFTER TWO TERMS** as Queen of Naboo, Padmé Amidala makes way for her successor, Queen Jamillia. When the new monarch asks Padmé to serve as Naboo's representative in the Galactic Senate, she accepts. Padmé travels widely to build support for her causes, returning to the capital of Coruscant when necessary. As a senator, she sees firsthand the political chaos caused by the Separatist movement, which threatens to undermine the entire Galactic Republic as more planetary systems break away. But when the Senate debates a Military Creation Act that would allow the Republic to meet the Separatist threat with force, Padme opposes it, believing that war is never the answer.

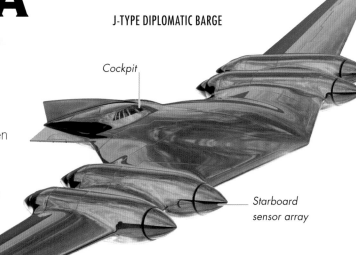

Cockpit

Starboard sensor array

*Severe hairstyle conforms to diplomatic etiquette*

*Choker is a gift from the Naboo Royal Advisory Council*

*Starfighter recharge socket*

## FLYING INTO DANGER

Senator Amidala has made many enemies over the years. The Trade Federation and the Separatists still bear a grudge over her part in thwarting the Invasion of Naboo, while her opposition to the Military Creation Act makes her a controversial figure within the Senate. When she arrives on Coruscant to vote on the Act, she travels alongside her diplomatic barge as part of its security escort, in order to evade would-be attackers.

*Comlink pouch*

## SENATOR'S QUARTERS

On Coruscant, Senator Amidala lives atop a grand apartment block. Though lavish by most standards, it is modest compared to many senatorial homes, and lacks advanced security features.

*Blaster holster*

*Gown blends sober colors with rich fabrics and ornate detailing*

## LOVE ON NABOO

After two attempts on her life, Padmé returns to Naboo for her own safety. She is happy to be accompanied by Anakin Skywalker, who serves as part of her security detail. As the pair grow closer, the Jedi Padawan confesses his love for Padmé.

## SERVING IN THE SENATE

In her role as senator for Naboo, Padmé continues to project the image of decorum and elegance she perfected as its queen. However, she is no mere figurehead, as she works tirelessly in the name of peace and freedom. She is a member of the Senate's Loyalist Committee, which advises Supreme Chancellor Palpatine on the Separatist crisis. As the situation worsens, she and her fellow committee members come into conflict with Palpatine, whom they suspect of using the Clone Wars as an excuse to tighten his grip on power.

Intricately looped hairstyle

E-5 blaster rifle taken from a fallen battle droid

Narrow-fire tip for close quarters combat

Overheating makes the grip uncomfortable for humans

Collimating tube and heat radiators

## READY FOR ACTION

Padmé is the driving force behind an attempt to rescue Obi-Wan Kenobi when he is held prisoner by Separatists on Geonosis. When she and Anakin are captured too, all three of them are sentenced to death in the Geonosis Arena, and must fight their way out.

### SECRET WEDDING

After escaping Geonosis, Padmé and Anakin get married on Naboo. They keep their union secret, as such personal attachments are strictly against the Jedi Code. But when Padmé becomes pregnant three years later, both husband and wife know that the truth must come out.

Padmé is in the Senate chamber when Chancellor Palpatine declares that the Galactic Republic will become an Empire. As other senators applaud, she mourns the death of democracy in the galaxy.

### H-TYPE NUBIAN YACHT

Padmé and Anakin travel to Geonosis on the senator's H-type Nubian yacht. It is chromium-plated to indicate her status as a former queen of Naboo.

Cockpit

Simple outfit allows for easy movement in combat

Lightweight shin armor

### LIFE IN DEATH

Obi-Wan rescues Padmé from Mustafar and takes her to a medical facility on Polis Massa. She gives birth to twins—Luke and Leia—before dying of her injuries and a broken heart.

Practical boots with good grip

## MEETING ON MUSTAFAR

A heavily-pregnant Padmé refuses to believe Obi-Wan when he tells her that Anakin has turned to the dark side. She takes a ship to the planet Mustafar to see her husband, only to find that he has become a megalomaniacal Sith Lord. She backs away from him in horror, and in his anger he chokes her with the Force.

# QUEEN AMIDALA'S HANDMAIDENS

**THE NABOO ROYAL HANDMAIDANS** are an elite group of highly trained young women who act as constant companions and secret bodyguards to Queen Amidala. Handpicked for their intelligence, courage, and fitness, they are also required to bear a close resemblance to the Queen, so they can pose as decoys should the monarch find herself under attack. When Padmé becomes Queen, she gains five handmaidens: Sabé, Rabé, Eirtaé, Saché, and Yané.

Sabé wears a royal gown and headdress as she performs her decoy duties on Naboo. Her entourage of fellow handmaidens, Palace Guards, and Governer Sio Bibble all take part in the charade.

*Traditional royal makeup helps Sabé to pass as Queen Amidala*

## SABÉ

Queen Amidala's most trusted handmaiden is Sabé. She serves as the Royal Decoy during the Trade Federation's blockade and subsequent invasion of Naboo, wearing the stylized makeup and garments of the monarch, while Padmé poses as a handmaiden. The two women use secret signals to exchange messages when their roles are reversed.

*Handmaiden outfits vary to complement the Queen's ensembles*

*On peaceful Naboo, this royal "battle dress" is largely ceremonial*

## EIRTAÉ

Eirtaé learned the niceties of royal etiquette from an early age. She assists the Queen and her fellow handmaidens with questions of protocol. She is the only one of Amidala's royal handmaidens to have blond hair.

**ROYAL PISTOL**
Each handmaiden is trained by the Royal Naboo Security Forces in sharpshooting and self-defense, and carries a small blaster pistol to protect the Queen.

*Medium-range barrel*

*Power cell in grip*

## RABÉ

Rabé has learned to exercise great patience in her role as handmaiden. She counsels the Queen while working on her exotic hairstyles, which can take several hours to perfect.

*Queen Amidala in shiraya fan headdress*

*Eirtaé*

*Rabé*

# THE ROYAL NABOO SECURITY FORCES

ALSO KNOWN AS THE Naboo Royal Guards, the Royal Naboo Security Forces are made up of three distinct branches: the Palace Guard; the Security Guard; and the Space Fighter Corps. All three divisions are mostly made up of volunteers. They are highly trained in security functions, but primarily serve as a police force, rather than a standing army. The Forces perform various ceremonial roles on Naboo, and are traditionally responsible for protecting the monarch. As a result, they come under the collective command of the head of security for the Royal House of Naboo, Captain Panaka, who takes personal responsibility for Queen Amidala's safety.

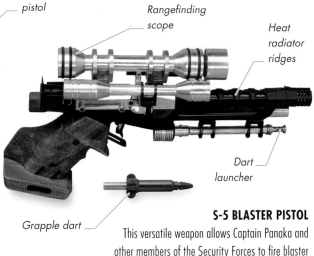

## CAPTAIN PANAKA

Quarsh Panaka is Queen Amidala's most senior bodyguard. As head of security for the Royal House of Naboo, he provides protection for the monarch, and oversees the broader strategic functions of Naboo's defense. He fights bravely when the planet is invaded by the Trade Federation, but is forced to concede that his forces are no match for an entire droid army.

### PALACE GUARD
Members of the Palace Guard are mostly seen in and around the grounds of Theed Royal Palace. They protect the Queen and other dignitaries.

Palace Guardsman

Security Guard officer

Leather jerkin covers anti-blast armor

Security Guard trooper

Armor plating

CR-2 blaster pistol

Rangefinding scope

Heat radiator ridges

S-5 blaster pistol

Blast-damping armor

Full-cut pants for mobility

Blaster strap

Dart launcher

Grapple dart

### S-5 BLASTER PISTOL
This versatile weapon allows Captain Panaka and other members of the Security Forces to fire blaster bolts, microdarts, and even a grappling-hook cable.

Transmitter

Speaker

**ROYAL NABOO SECURITY FORCES COMLINK**

### SECURITY GUARD
The Security Guard is made up of troopers in mustard-colored uniforms and officers clad in red and blue. Charged with keeping the peace across Naboo, it is the closest thing that the planet has to an army, but has rarely had to face any real danger.

## DATA FILE

> The Royal Naboo Security Forces patrol in Gian speeders equipped with side-mounted lasers and, in some cases, a hood-mounted heavy cannon.

# THE NABOO ROYAL SPACE FIGHTER CORPS

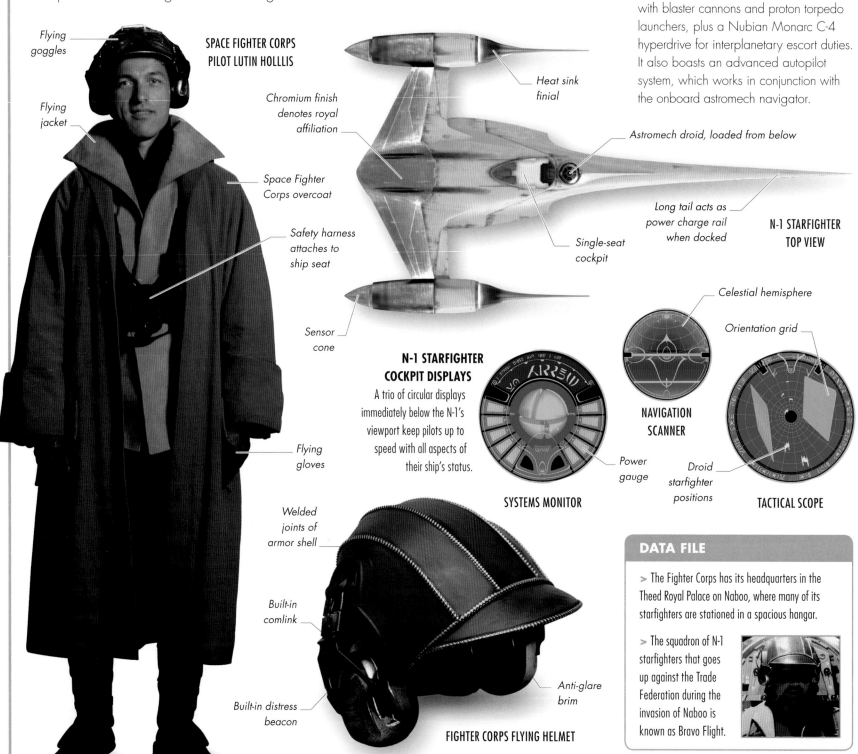

**JUST LIKE THEIR COMPATRIOTS** in the Palace Guard and Security Guard, the Naboo Royal Space Fighter Corps are part of the Royal Naboo Security Forces. While their ground-based colleagues carry out policing work, the pilots of the volunteer Fighter Corps must content themselves with a largely ceremonial role, serving under Captain Panaka. They are experts at fly-bys and formation displays, and they provide an honorguard for Queen Amidala when she travels off-world. However, the Corps stands ready for an attack on its peaceful planet, and proves its mettle against droid starfighters when the Trade Federation invades.

## N-1 STARFIGHTER

The N-1 is the main starfighter in the Fighter Corps fleet, which blends form and function to create an eye-catching but effective strike ship. It is equipped with blaster cannons and proton torpedo launchers, plus a Nubian Monarc C-4 hyperdrive for interplanetary escort duties. It also boasts an advanced autopilot system, which works in conjunction with the onboard astromech navigator.

Flying goggles

Flying jacket

SPACE FIGHTER CORPS PILOT LUTIN HOLLLIS

Chromium finish denotes royal affiliation

Space Fighter Corps overcoat

Safety harness attaches to ship seat

Heat sink finial

Astromech droid, loaded from below

Long tail acts as power charge rail when docked

Single-seat cockpit

Sensor cone

N-1 STARFIGHTER TOP VIEW

Flying gloves

Welded joints of armor shell

Built-in comlink

Built-in distress beacon

Anti-glare brim

FIGHTER CORPS FLYING HELMET

### N-1 STARFIGHTER COCKPIT DISPLAYS

A trio of circular displays immediately below the N-1's viewport keep pilots up to speed with all aspects of their ship's status.

ARREW

Power gauge

SYSTEMS MONITOR

Celestial hemisphere

NAVIGATION SCANNER

Orientation grid

Droid starfighter positions

TACTICAL SCOPE

### DATA FILE

> The Fighter Corps has its headquarters in the Theed Royal Palace on Naboo, where many of its starfighters are stationed in a spacious hangar.

> The squadron of N-1 starfighters that goes up against the Trade Federation during the invasion of Naboo is known as Bravo Flight.

# NABOO ROYAL STARSHIP

Queen Amidala's personal transport is a gleaming work of art, modified from a standard J-type 327 Nubian starship. Naboo artisans hand-crafted its royal chromium finish, and equipped the interior with a sumptuous throne room. The ship has no weapons, as a statement of peaceful intent.

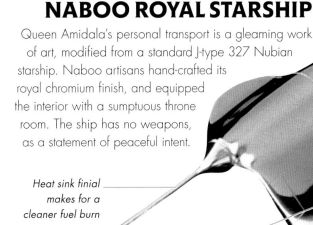

Navigation light recess

Sensor cone

Command bridge viewports

Heat sink finial makes for a cleaner fuel burn

Throne room located at rear

Hand-polished chromium finish

Sublight engine

### ROYAL REFINEMENT

Elegant curves and refined detailing characterize the Royal Starship inside and out. Even functional spaces such as cargo holds are designed to look beautiful while also serving a purpose.

# RIC OLIÉ

The commander of the Space Fighter Corps is Ric Olié, a veteran pilot who answers directly to Naboo's head of security, Captain Panaka. As well as being an ace starfighter pilot, Olié also has the honor of captaining the Naboo Royal Starship. His piloting skills are tested to the limit when he flies the royal ship through the Trade Federation's blockade of Naboo, in order to get Queen Amidala away from the planet.

Naboo script

Starship overview

Enlargement of damaged area

View mode indicator

### ENGINEERING ANALYSIS BOARD

Power cells send energy pulses through equipment to test its functionality

High-resolution eyepiece

**MESON TALOSCOPE**

Diagnostic block

Talo-effect lens for subatomic analysis

Touch control

### PRECISION INSTRUMENTS

The Royal Starship is a technological feat inside and out. It is outfitted with state-of-the-art scientific instruments that can anticipate problems before they occur.

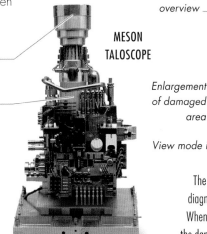

### DAMAGE MONITOR

The crew of the Royal Starship constantly monitors a range of diagnostic displays for real-time updates on the vessel's status. When the ship comes under attack from Trade Federation lasers, the damage monitor instantly shows where the weapons have hit.

**HYPERDRIVE MONITOR**

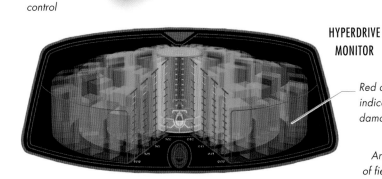

Red areas indicate damage

Area of field leakage

Overload burnout scarring

# HYPERDRIVE GENERATOR

Built by the Nubian Design Collective, the T-14 hyperdrive generator enables the Naboo Royal Starship to travel at faster-than-light speeds. Housed within an intricate maze of charge planes and effect channels, its core is prone to damage and fails when the Trade Federation fires on the ship, forcing an unscheduled landing on Tatooine.

Charge plane

Generator core

**T-14 HYPERDRIVE**

Effect channels improve supralight performance

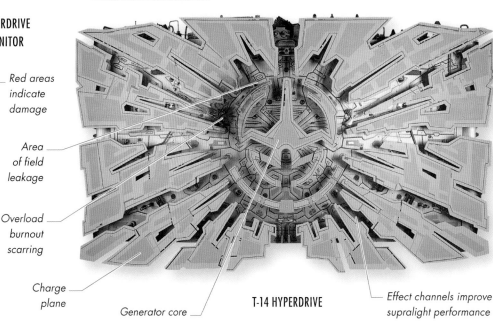

# R2-D2

**R2-D2 LOOKS MUCH LIKE** any other astromech droid, but he has developed a unique personality and a daring spirit over the course of his adventures. Originally based on Naboo, he gets his first taste of interstellar adventure when the planet comes under attack from the Trade Federation. He becomes an inseparable ally of the Jedi during the Clone Wars, and is never far from momentous galactic affairs.

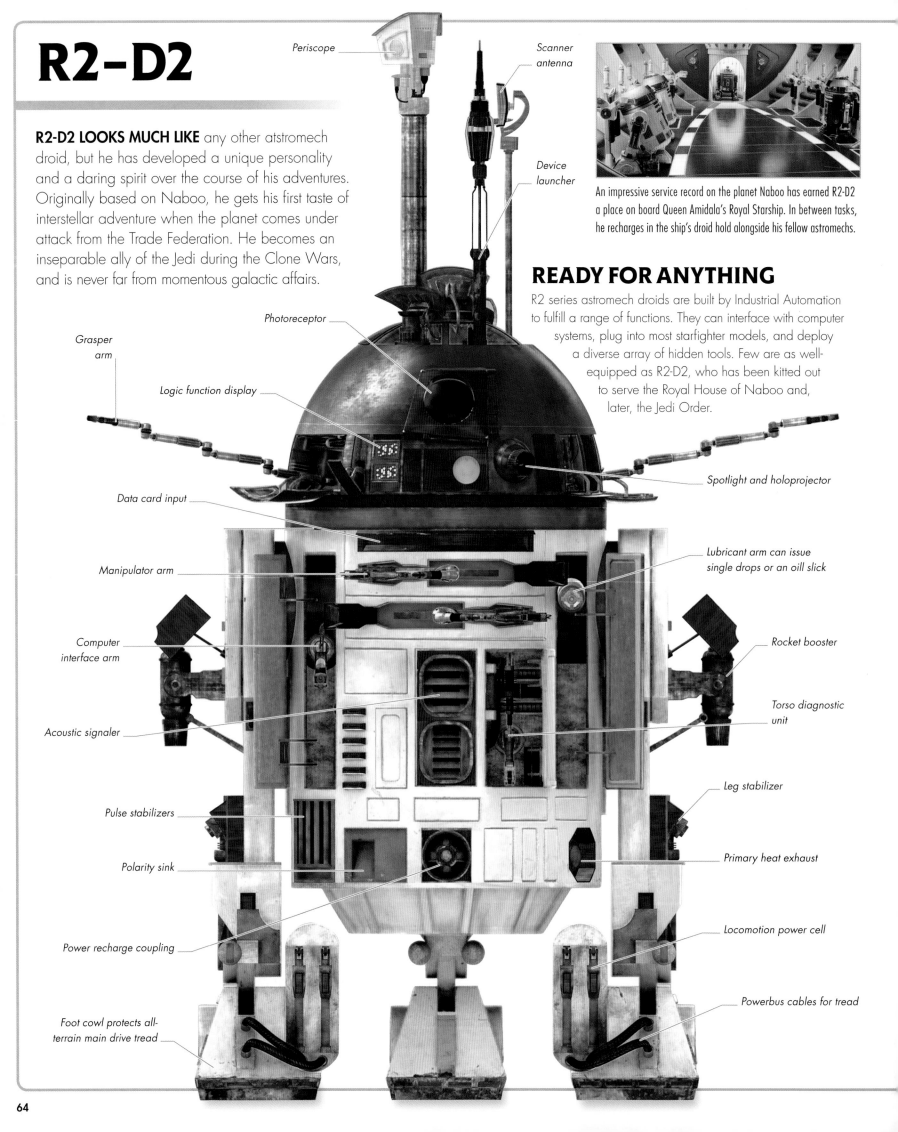

Periscope

Scanner antenna

Device launcher

An impressive service record on the planet Naboo has earned R2-D2 a place on board Queen Amidala's Royal Starship. In between tasks, he recharges in the ship's droid hold alongside his fellow astromechs.

## READY FOR ANYTHING

R2 series astromech droids are built by Industrial Automation to fulfill a range of functions. They can interface with computer systems, plug into most starfighter models, and deploy a diverse array of hidden tools. Few are as well-equipped as R2-D2, who has been kitted out to serve the Royal House of Naboo and, later, the Jedi Order.

Grasper arm

Photoreceptor

Logic function display

Spotlight and holoprojector

Data card input

Lubricant arm can issue single drops or an oill slick

Manipulator arm

Computer interface arm

Rocket booster

Acoustic signaler

Torso diagnostic unit

Pulse stabilizers

Leg stabilizer

Polarity sink

Primary heat exhaust

Power recharge coupling

Locomotion power cell

Foot cowl protects all-terrain main drive tread

Powerbus cables for tread

## TEAM ASTROMECH

Queen Amidala's Naboo Royal Starship is serviced by several R-series astro-droids. When the ship comes under fire from the Trade Federation during the invasion of Naboo, the droids venture on to its outer hull to carry out repairs. When the Trade Federation continues its attack, the unlucky droids are picked off one by one until only R2-D2 remains.

Status indicator

Sensor hatch

Diagnostic input receptors

R2-M5

R2-B1

R2-R9

Recharge coupling

Polarity sink

R2-D2 at work on the hull

Captain Ric Olié uses the Royal Starship's display screens to monitor the progress of the astromech droids as they work to repair its damaged shield generator.

Damaged deflector shield generator

Naboo script readout

R2-D2 succeeds in restoring the shields by bypassing the main power drive. This ingenious solution saves the life of Queen Amidala and everyone else on board her Royal Starship.

# R2-D2 IS MY CO-PILOT

R2-D2 finds himself plugged into the astromech socket of an N-1 starfighter during the Battle of Naboo, and is soon in space with Anakin Skywalker in the pilot's seat. Together they fly inside the Trade Federation's droid control ship, destroying it from within.

When the Queen's ship is forced to stop for repairs on the planet Tatooine, R2-D2 meets Anakin Skywalker and his home-made droid C-3PO. All three bond as they work on young Anakin's podracer.

In a Separatist battle droid factory on the planet Geonosis, R2-D2 gets a rare opportunity to use his rocket boosters. By flying above the production line to access its computer interface, he once again saves the life of Padmé Amidala.

### DATA FILE

> R2-D2 can use his scanner antenna to detect everything from lifeforms to ships and even bombs.

> The beeps and whistles made by R2-D2 and other astromech droids is a complex language known as binary or droidspeak. It can be learned by organics, but most people rely on Basic-speaking protocol droids to translate for them.

# R2-D2:
## JEDI DROID

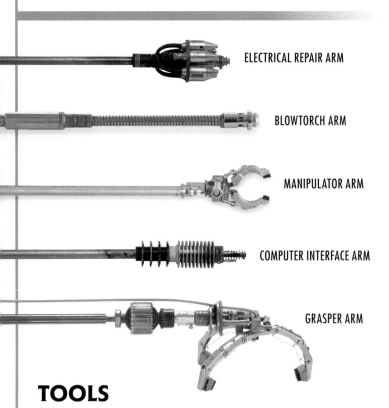

**ELECTRICAL REPAIR ARM**

**BLOWTORCH ARM**

**MANIPULATOR ARM**

**COMPUTER INTERFACE ARM**

**GRASPER ARM**

Secondary holoprojector

Luminescent diagnostic display

Lubrication fitting

Hydraulic arm shaft

Secondary heat exhaust

Lubricant reservoir

Sealed joint

Photoreceptor "eye"

Actuating coupler

Pulse stabilizers

Retractable third leg

## TOOLS

R2-D2's many extending tools are designed for performing mundane tasks, but the little droid has found ways to use them for espionage, misdirection, and even self-defense. His full range of devices includes a circular saw, a lubricator arm, and a fire extinguisher.

Over the course of the Clone Wars, R2-D2 becomes Anakin Skywalker's faithful co-pilot in starfighter battles. He offers vital navigation and tactical data from the astromech socket of Anakin's Jedi interceptor.

Poor R2-D2 is much smaller than the two hulking super battle droids who seize him on board the Separatist flagship. However, their might is no match for his quick-thinking. He deals with the brutish pair by squirting them with his internal supply of oil and setting it ablaze with his rocket boosters.

R2-D2 saves his Jedi masters' lives when they and the Supreme Chancellor are brought before General Grievous. The resourceful droid activates all his loudest, most eye-catching systems at once, distracting Grievous long enough for Obi-Wan to retrieve his lightsaber from their captor.

## R4-G9

Toward the end of the Clone Wars, Obi-Wan Kenobi flies to the planet Utapau with a bronze-colored droid called R4-G9. On the Jedi's orders, the droid flies their ship away from Utapau alone, making it seem like Obi-Wan has departed.

## LOYAL TO THE END

When Anakin Skywalker becomes Darth Vader, R2-D2's loyalty compels him not to abandon his master. He accompanies the Sith Lord when he leaves Coruscant in his Jedi interceptor, and sees him attack Padmé and duel Obi-Wan Kenobi on Mustafar. He leaves the fiery planet with Obi-Wan, believing that his master is now dead.

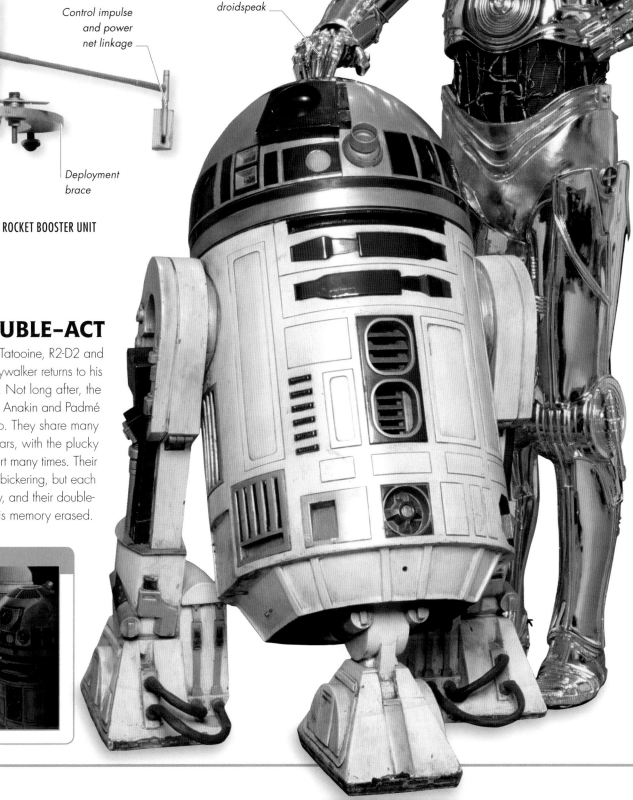

Protocol droid C-3PO

C-3PO is fluent in R2-D2's binary droidspeak

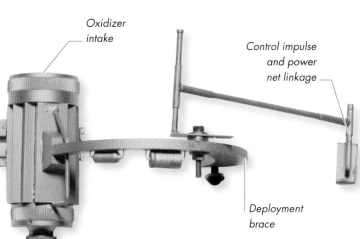

Oxidizer intake

Control impulse and power net linkage

Deployment brace

Thrust nozzle

**ROCKET BOOSTER UNIT**

## DROID DOUBLE–ACT

Ten years after their first meeting on Tatooine, R2-D2 and C-3PO are reunited when Anakin Skywalker returns to his homeworld looking for his mother. Not long after, the two droids are the only witnesses to Anakin and Padmé Amidala's wedding on Naboo. They share many adventures during the Clone Wars, with the plucky astromech saving his nervy counterpart many times. Their partnership may be characterized by bickering, but each is the other's best friend in the galaxy, and their double-act endures even after C-3PO has his memory erased.

# THE GUNGANS

**THE NATIVE INHABITANTS** of Naboo, the Gungans, are born as tadpoles and develop limbs in their first few months of life. These amphibious beings are proud warriors, but mostly live peacefully in advanced underwater cities with breathable atmospheres. Some of their most impressive technology is grown organically rather than built, and the species as a whole strives to live in harmony with the natural world. The Gungangs have little to do with the human population of Naboo—until a Trade Federation invasion brings both civilizations together.

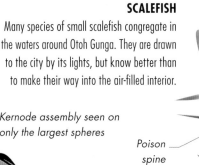

## HYDROSTASIS

The force fields that keep air inside each Gungan sphere is a form of hydrostatic membrane. Its complex structure allows the Gungans and their visitors to move through the barrier in either direction, while resisting any water ingress. It is far more efficient than an airlock.

### SCALEFISH

Many species of small scalefish congregate in the waters around Otoh Gunga. They are drawn to the city by its lights, but know better than to make their way into the air-filled interior.

 FAA

 MEE

Poison spine

 TEE

 LAA

 RAY

 SEE

Atmospheric purifiers

Kernode assembly seen on only the largest spheres

Utanodes contains hydrostatic force-field

Utanode assembly brace

Root counterphase array

## OTOH GUNGA

Deep beneath the surface of Lake Paonga, the Gungans' capital city is made up of linked spherical structures that are grown out of plasma and bubble wort extract. The Gungans, who can live on land or underwater, built the city when the human settlers known as the Naboo started to spread more widely across the planet's surface.

Habitation level

No two spheres in Otoh Gunga are identical. They gleam like lanterns at a depth where sunlight cannot penetrate.

Hydrostatic force-field generators

Field-wave stabilizing vane

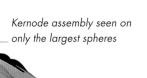

In times of crisis, the Gungans of Otoh Gunga abandon the city and head for their sacred place. Here, north of the Lianorm Swamp, they take refuge amid the ruined statues and buildings of a long-lost civilization known only as the Elders.

# BOSS NASS

The Gungan leader, Rugor Nass, rules his people from the High Board Room in Otoh Gunga. He is no fan of Naboo's human population, believing them to be arrogant pacifists who look down on the Gungans and their warrior culture. He also bears a grudge against his fellow Gungan Jar Jar Binks, whom he personally banished from Otoh Gunga. Boss Nass is a loud and charismatic leader, and is prepared to admit when he is wrong. In time, he comes to respect both Jar Jar and Naboo's human monarch, Padmé Amidala.

Mangana aqua jewel

Ruler's crown

Chain of office

Design style known as "Otoh swirls"

Comfy pants under robe

Gungan sandals

Rep hood

Rep robe

**REP TEERS**

Older Gungans grow hair-like finlets

Whiskers indicate maturity

## CAPTAIN TARPALS

As the captain of a security patrol in Otoh Gunga, Roos Tarpals is well acquainted with local troublemakers, such as Jar Jar Binks. He saves Jar Jar's life during the Battle of Naboo, and is at his side when the Trade Federation's droid army is defeated. He goes on to serve as a general in the Gungan Grand Army during the Clone Wars.

**GUNGAN HIGH COUNCIL**

Chaired by Boss Nass, the Gungan High Council is made up of officials known as Reps. Clothed in hoods and ornate robes of office, they govern Gungan society and grant audiences to outsiders such as the Jedi Qui-Gon Jinn and his Padawan Obi-Wan Kenobi. Notable Reps include Teers, an important female voice on the Council, and Rish Loo, who betrays Naboo during the Clone Wars.

### DATA FILE

> Other semi-aquatic creatures that share the waters with the Gungans include reptavian pikobis and waterfowl including pelikki.

> As a gesture of faith and good relations with the Gungans, Queen Amidala presents a relic known as the Globe of Peace to Boss Nass.

69

# JAR JAR BINKS

**JAR JAR BINKS** is an amphibious native of Naboo, and is a luckless exile from the underwater city of Otoh Gunga when the Trade Federation invades his world. Living as an outcast in Naboo's swamps, he is overwhelmed when the Jedi Qui-Gon Jinn rescues him from the path of a Trade Federation transport, and pledges a life-debt to his savior. From then on, he insists on accompanying Qui-Gon wherever he goes, whether the Jedi likes it or not.

Port cargo bubble

Cockpit bubble

Electromotive tentacles

Organically grown hull

## TRIBUBBLE BONGO

When Qui-Gon Jinn pleads to Boss Nass on Jar Jar's behalf, the Gungan leader entrusts his wayward subject with a tribubble bongo submarine, so that he can escort the Jedi to Naboo's human capital, Theed. It is a perilous journey through flooded caverns in the planet's core, and the bongo only narrowly escapes being eaten by huge sea creatures!

Four digits on each hand

Navigation sensor field

Yaw steer

Yaw thrust

Main thrust

**TRIBUBBLE BONGO COCKPIT MONITORS**

Jar Jar's first trip away from Naboo takes him to the planet Tatooine, where he meets and befriends young Anakin Skywalker.

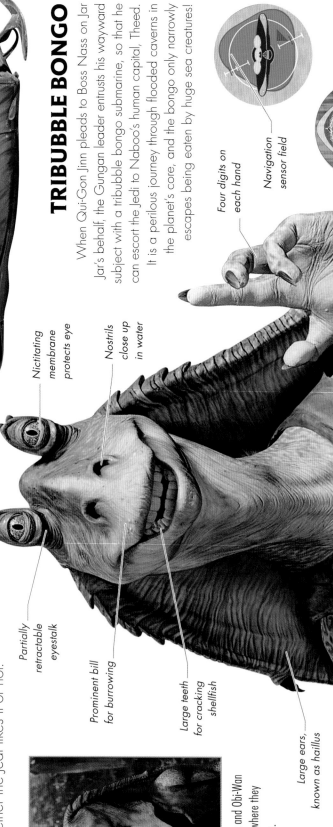

Nictitating membrane protects eye

Nostrils close up in water

Partially retractable eyestalk

Prominent bill for burrowing

Large teeth for cracking shellfish

Large ears, known as haillus

Long, flexible limbs

Jar Jar quickly proves his usefulness to Qui-Gon Jinn and Obi-Wan Kenobi, telling them about the city of Otoh Gunga, where they can seek refuge from the Trade Federation's attacks.

### RETURN FROM EXILE

On arrival at Otoh Gunga, Jar Jar is put under arrest by his old "friend" Captain Tarpals. He is reluctant to tell Qui-Gon and Obi-Wan why he is unwelcome in his home city, but eventually admits to them that he was sent into exile after he crashed the prized heyblibber submarine of Gungan leader, Boss Nass!

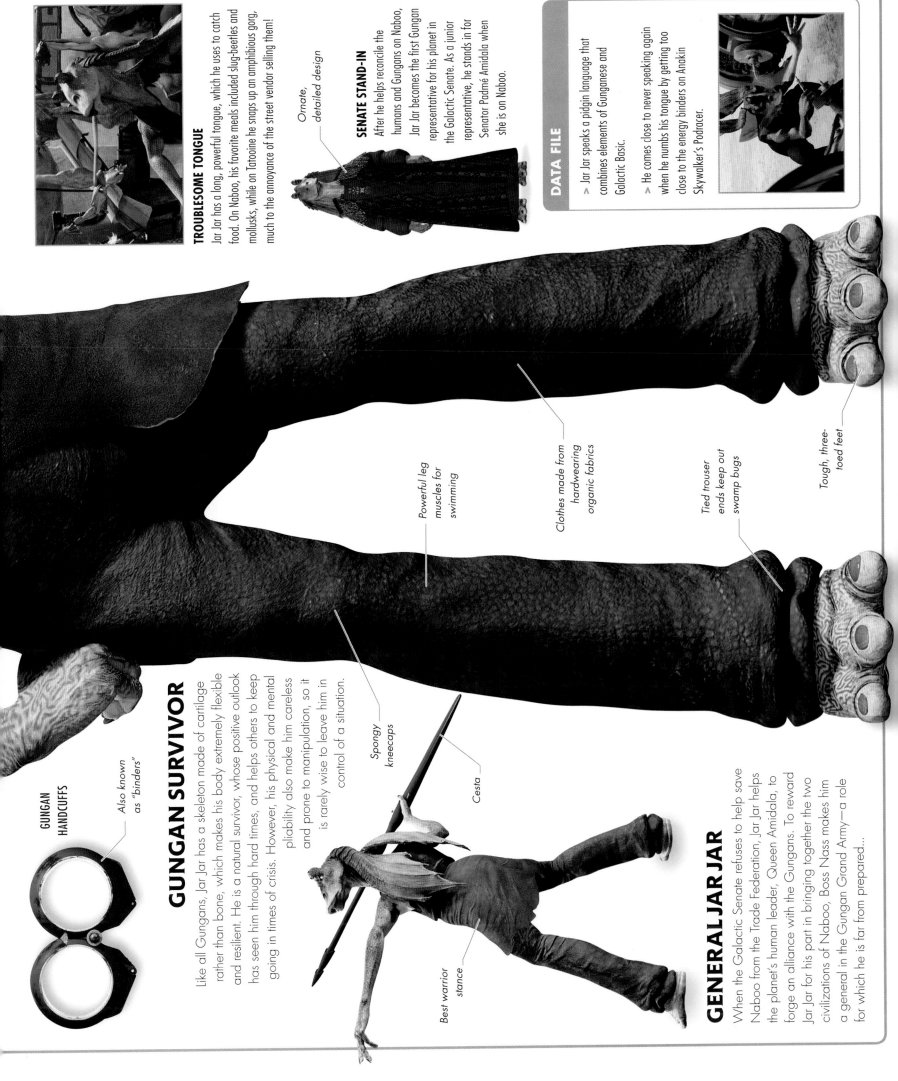

## TROUBLESOME TONGUE

Jar Jar has a long, powerful tongue, which he uses to catch food. On Naboo, his favorite meals included slug-beetles and mollusks, while on Tatooine he snaps up an amphibious gorg, much to the annoyance of the street vendor selling them!

*Ornate, detailed design*

### SENATE STAND-IN

After he helps reconcile the humans and Gungans on Naboo, Jar Jar becomes the first Gungan representative for his planet in the Galactic Senate. As a junior representative, he stands in for Senator Padmé Amidala when she is on Naboo.

*Powerful leg muscles for swimming*

*Clothes made from hardwearing organic fabrics*

*Tied trouser ends keep out swamp bugs*

*Tough, three-toed feet*

## GUNGAN SURVIVOR

Like all Gungans, Jar Jar has a skeleton made of cartilage rather than bone, which makes his body extremely flexible and resilient. He is a natural survivor, whose positive outlook has seen him through hard times, and helps others to keep going in times of crisis. However, his physical and mental pliability also make him careless and prone to manipulation, so it is rarely wise to leave him in control of a situation.

*Spongy kneecaps*

*Cesta*

*Best warrior stance*

### GUNGAN HANDCUFFS

*Also known as "binders"*

## GENERAL JAR JAR

When the Galactic Senate refuses to help save Naboo from the Trade Federation, Jar Jar helps the planet's human leader, Queen Amidala, to forge an alliance with the Gungans. To reward Jar Jar for his part in bringing together the two civilizations of Naboo, Boss Nass makes him a general in the Gungan Grand Army—a role for which he is far from prepared...

# SEA MONSTERS OF NABOO

**THE WAY THROUGH THE WATER**
The Gungan inhabitants of Otoh Gunga use bongo submarines to traverse the labyrinthine passages that riddle Naboo's core. Though the vessels are not impervious to attack by sea monsters, they are fast and maneuverable enough to evade most predators for just long enough to survive.

**THE WATERS OF NABOO** are rich with life, as the balance of sunlight and nutrients is ideal for many life forms. Microscopic plankton flourish in prodigious numbers, supporting a food chain that reaches its peak in giant predators. The sea monsters of Naboo are primarily lurkers of the deep, haunting the most out-of-the-way caverns and passages that make up the planet's honeycombed core. But from time to time, some of these megabeasts do drift closer to the surface, where sightings earn them their place in the planet's folklore.

Baby colo are born with fangs

Long, powerful tail provides propulsion

Bioluminescent markings help to attract prey in the dark

Eyes extend from flexible stalks

Poisonous fangs

## JUVENILE COLO CLAW FISH

Female colo claw fish chase away males after mating to prevent them from eating their eggs and hatchlings. Young colos also face other predators, as they are eaten by Gungans and the Naboo.

Defensive spines

Stretchy stomach

Distensible jaw

Angling lures

Tail section is highly sensitive to movement

Articulated claw

## COLO CLAW FISH

This serpentine predator has evolved to swallow food bigger than its own head, with jaws that distend and skin that stretches to engulf astonishingly large creatures. It disorients its prey with a terrifying shriek, before seizing it in the huge pectoral claws from which it gets its name. The colo digests its meals slowly, so must be certain to stun live food with its venomous fangs, to be sure the swallowed creature doesn't eat its way out again.

SCALE:
1CM = 10M

OPEE SEA KILLER

COLO CLAW FISH

SANDO AQUA MONSTER

GUNGAN BONGO SUBMARINE

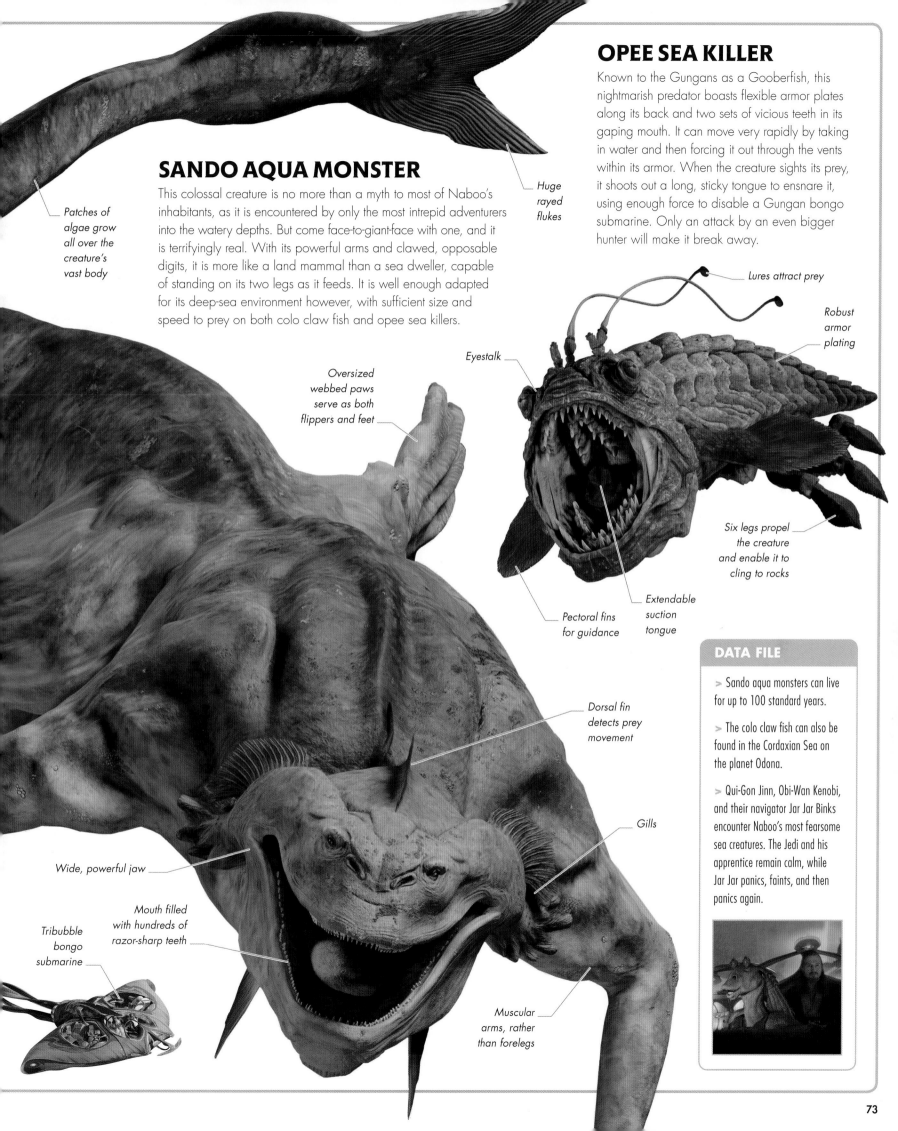

## SANDO AQUA MONSTER

This colossal creature is no more than a myth to most of Naboo's inhabitants, as it is encountered by only the most intrepid adventurers into the watery depths. But come face-to-giant-face with one, and it is terrifyingly real. With its powerful arms and clawed, opposable digits, it is more like a land mammal than a sea dweller, capable of standing on its two legs as it feeds. It is well enough adapted for its deep-sea environment however, with sufficient size and speed to prey on both colo claw fish and opee sea killers.

Patches of algae grow all over the creature's vast body

Huge rayed flukes

Oversized webbed paws serve as both flippers and feet

Eyestalk

Dorsal fin detects prey movement

Wide, powerful jaw

Gills

Mouth filled with hundreds of razor-sharp teeth

Tribubble bongo submarine

Muscular arms, rather than forelegs

## OPEE SEA KILLER

Known to the Gungans as a Gooberfish, this nightmarish predator boasts flexible armor plates along its back and two sets of vicious teeth in its gaping mouth. It can move very rapidly by taking in water and then forcing it out through the vents within its armor. When the creature sights its prey, it shoots out a long, sticky tongue to ensnare it, using enough force to disable a Gungan bongo submarine. Only an attack by an even bigger hunter will make it break away.

Lures attract prey

Robust armor plating

Six legs propel the creature and enable it to cling to rocks

Pectoral fins for guidance

Extendable suction tongue

### DATA FILE

> Sando aqua monsters can live for up to 100 standard years.

> The colo claw fish can also be found in the Cordaxian Sea on the planet Odona.

> Qui-Gon Jinn, Obi-Wan Kenobi, and their navigator Jar Jar Binks encounter Naboo's most fearsome sea creatures. The Jedi and his apprentice remain calm, while Jar Jar panics, faints, and then panics again.

# THE GUNGAN GRAND ARMY

**THE GUNGAN GRAND ARMY** is born of ancient warrior traditions, but now survives as a purely defensive force on peaceful Naboo. Its weaponry comprises simple but effective hand-held tools—some of which harness plasma technology—and around a thousand well-trained animals. The Grand Army's finest hour comes during a seemingly unwinnable battle against the Trade Federation's droid army, in which the Gungans prevail, against all odds.

Tensioner brace

Tensioner coil

Missile firing arm

Strong hornweed fiber structure

Transportation wheel

Militiagung operator

Booma cradle

## CATAPULT

The Gungan Grand Army mostly favors close-quarters fighting, but also employs some long-range artillery. Its huge, wheeled catapults fire large boomas and are pulled along by large mammals called falumpasets.

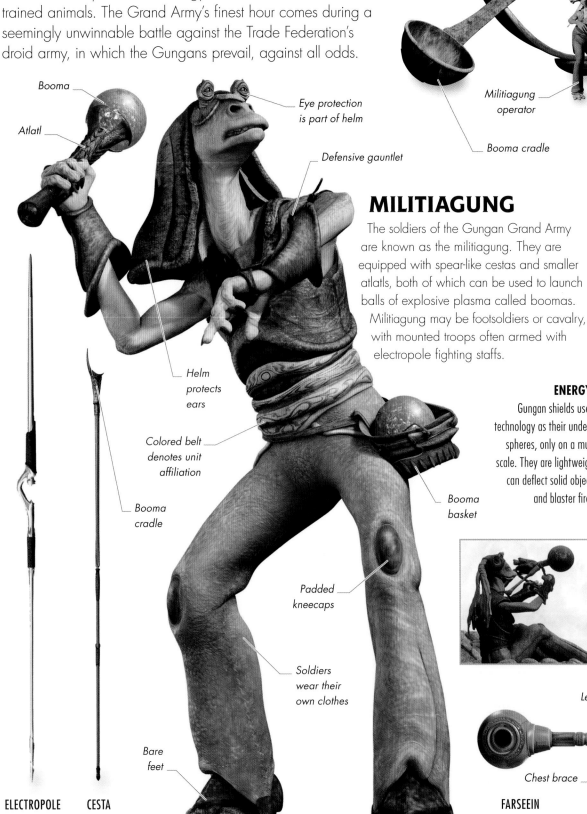

Booma

Atlatl

Eye protection is part of helm

Defensive gauntlet

## MILITIAGUNG

The soldiers of the Gungan Grand Army are known as the militiagung. They are equipped with spear-like cestas and smaller atlatls, both of which can be used to launch balls of explosive plasma called boomas. Militiagung may be footsoldiers or cavalry, with mounted troops often armed with electropole fighting staffs.

Good visibility through shield

Hydrostatic bubble can be switched on or off

Helm protects ears

Colored belt denotes unit affiliation

Booma cradle

Booma basket

## ENERGY SHIELD

Gungan shields use the same technology as their underwater city spheres, only on a much smaller scale. They are lightweight and can deflect solid objects and blaster fire.

Center handle

Padded kneecaps

## FARSEEIN

Militiagung lookouts use magnifiers called farseein to observe their enemies. The large devices use oil lenses and feature built-in braces to ensure a steady image.

Soldiers wear their own clothes

Bare feet

**ELECTROPOLE**    **CESTA**

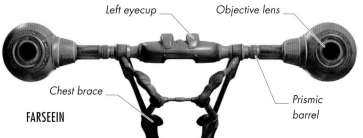

Left eyecup

Objective lens

Chest brace

**FARSEEIN**

Prismic barrel

Drum assembly receives beam from emitter

Overload discharge spine

Saddle distributes weight of assembly

Energy distributor

Reins

## DRUM FAMBAA

Scaly lizard hide

Ion feed sostor

Shield energy emitter

Overload discharge prongs

Static energy accumulation vanes

Cockpit

Bridle harness

Sturdy, pillar-like legs

## FAMBAA SHIELD

Pairs of giant fambaas carry the Gungans' main shield generators. An emitter mounted on the foremost fambaa fires into the projector on the fambaa at the rear, producing a large, dome-shaped energy shield that can resist almost any bombardment.

## BEAM FAMBAA

Gungan for scale

Giant goff bird feathers

Electropole

Saddlehorn

HORN

DRUM AND DRUMSTICKS

WHISTLE

Fambaa horn

Stirrups

The Gungans deploy fambaa shields in the Battle of Naboo, but the Trade Federation's droid army steps through the barrier with ease.

## KAADU

Bird-like, but with no wings, the duck-billed Kaadu are domesticated by the Gungans to serve as mounts. Their bouncy gait can give them a comical appearance, but they are capable of beating a hasty retreat when the situation demands it. Many Gungans decorate their kaadus with feathers from giant birds.

## COMMUNICATION

The Gungan Grand Army favors traditional methods of communication that cannot be jammed electronically, such as horn signals, drummed messages, and hand gestures.

## BATTLE WAGON

Gungan battle wagons are supply transports rather than combat vehicles. Pulled by falumpasets and rolling on two huge wheels, they carry large boomas onto the battlefield for deployment by catapult.

Grand Army General Jar Jar Binks pioneers a new way of deploying boomas during the Battle of Naboo. Racing to jump on a battle wagon, he accidentally opens its tailgate, releasing its entire cargo into the path of pursuing battle droids.

Saddle platform

Long neck for grazing on grassy plains

Electropoles

Bridle harness

Reins

Long legs for crossing swamps and grasslands

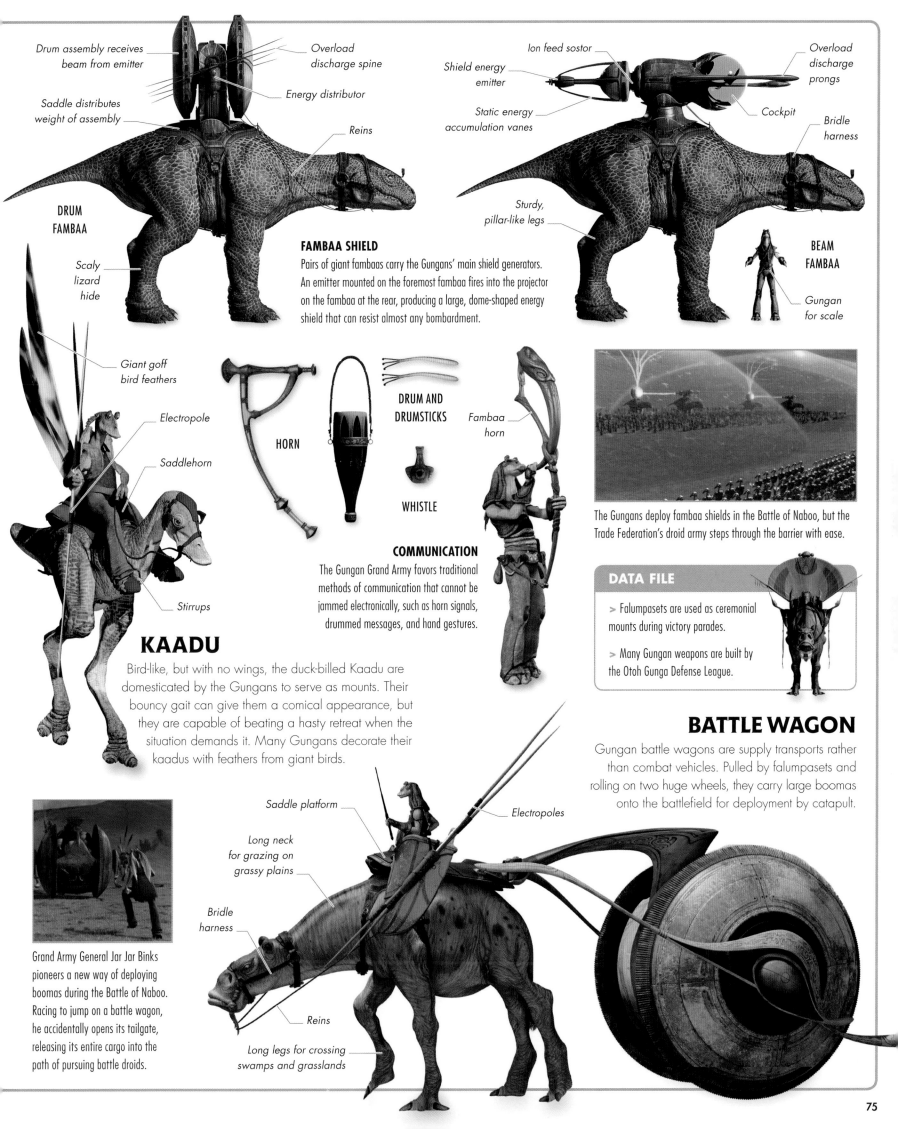

# TATOOINE

**SCORCHED BY TWIN SUNS,** the desert world of Tatooine is an inhospitable place, barely capable of supporting life. Its native inhabitants live a nomadic life in the desert, while humans and other colonists have established settlements, drawing water from the air to survive. Located in the Outer Rim, far from the rule of galactic law, Tatooine attracts smugglers and other criminals, such as the gangster Jabba the Hutt—the closest thing to a ruler on the planet. But others here are just down on their luck, trying to get by as best they can.

Player one or "drann" home

Marker box

Player two or "sett" home

**TRIGA BOARD**

**EYE OF MESRA**

### RECREATION
The biggest draw in Mos Espa is the thrilling Podracing scene, but pilots waiting for work find simpler pleasures in a game of triga. Children, meanwhile, play in the alleyways with "Eyes of Mesra" fortune-telling toys.

## MOS ESPA

The most significant city on Tatooine, Mos Espa, is a bustling but down-at-heel spaceport. Under the control of criminal Hutts, it is home to a thriving market in everything from starship spare parts to human slaves. Pirates, bounty hunters, and black-marketeers all pass through, but no one wants to stay for long.

**HUMAN MOS ESPA SETTLERS**

### MOISTURE FARMING
There is no surface water on Tatooine, so most settlers beyond the main cities work as moisture farmers. By using dozens, or even hundreds, of tall vaporator devices, they can harvest enough precious water from the atmosphere to sell it on, or use it for hydroponic gardening.

Resilient, scaly hide

The towering Erdan is a slave in Mos Espa. His face is patterned as a mark of ownership.

Gragra sells food in the Mos Espa marketplace. A member of the Swokes Swokes species, she is unimpressed when Jar Jar Binks helps himself to a gorg from her street stall.

Long, sweeping tail can cover a dewback's tracks in sand

Pale underside

Handle

Intake

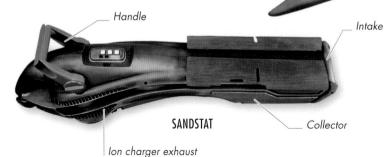

**SANDSTAT**

Collector

Ion charger exhaust

Sand blows into every corner of Mos Espa. Most inhabitants are resigned to it, but the fastidious do their best to clean up with electrostatic tools called sandstats.

### JAWAS
The indigenous Jawas have learned to live alongside humans and other space travelers. In Mos Espa, their short, robed figures are a familiar sight as they go about their business selling desert salvage.

# EOPIE

Tatooine's heat, dust, and sandstorms can damage mechanical transport, but domesticated desert animals such as eopies and dewbacks make ideal beasts of burden. Though they can be stubborn and bad-tempered, eopies are also strong and dependable, and can live for up to 90 standard years.

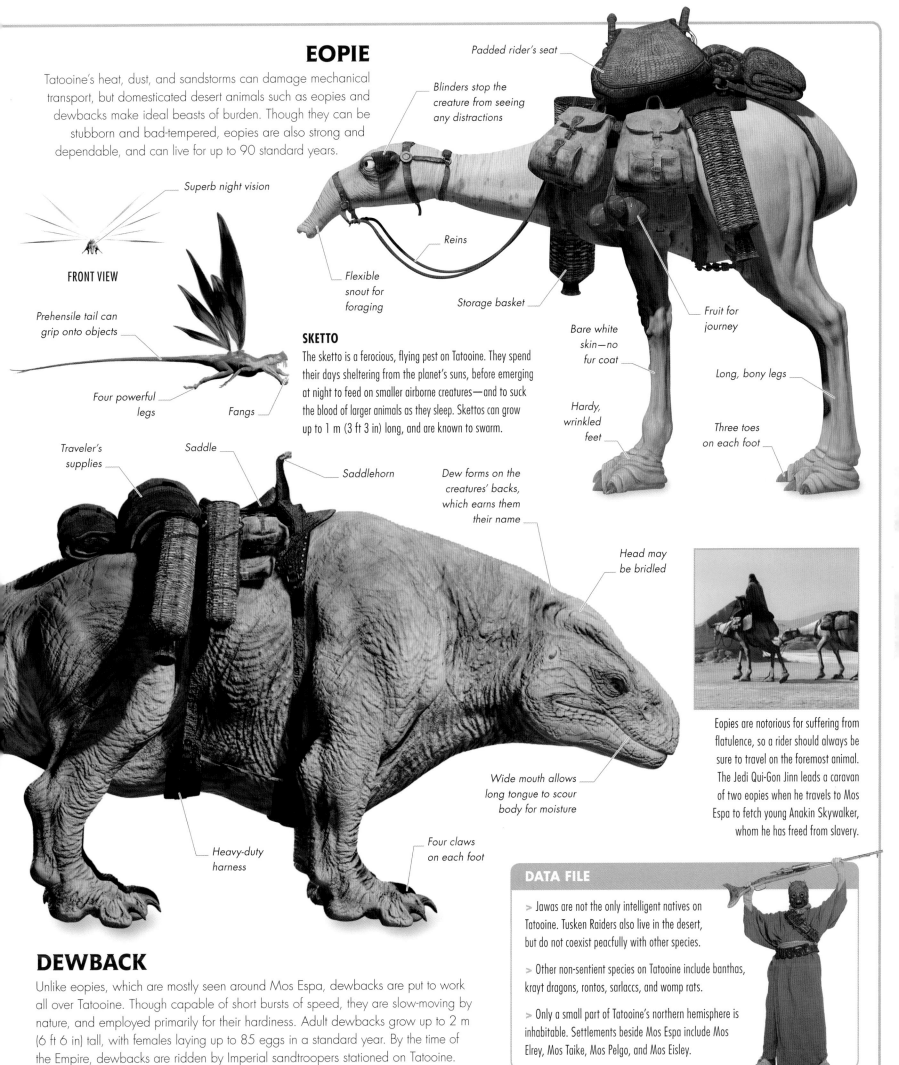

Padded rider's seat

Blinders stop the creature from seeing any distractions

Superb night vision

FRONT VIEW

Prehensile tail can grip onto objects

Four powerful legs

Fangs

Reins

Flexible snout for foraging

Storage basket

Bare white skin—no fur coat

Fruit for journey

Hardy, wrinkled feet

Long, bony legs

Three toes on each foot

## SKETTO

The sketto is a ferocious, flying pest on Tatooine. They spend their days sheltering from the planet's suns, before emerging at night to feed on smaller airborne creatures—and to suck the blood of larger animals as they sleep. Skettos can grow up to 1 m (3 ft 3 in) long, and are known to swarm.

Traveler's supplies

Saddle

Saddlehorn

Dew forms on the creatures' backs, which earns them their name

Head may be bridled

Wide mouth allows long tongue to scour body for moisture

Heavy-duty harness

Four claws on each foot

Eopies are notorious for suffering from flatulence, so a rider should always be sure to travel on the foremost animal. The Jedi Qui-Gon Jinn leads a caravan of two eopies when he travels to Mos Espa to fetch young Anakin Skywalker, whom he has freed from slavery.

# DEWBACK

Unlike eopies, which are mostly seen around Mos Espa, dewbacks are put to work all over Tatooine. Though capable of short bursts of speed, they are slow-moving by nature, and employed primarily for their hardiness. Adult dewbacks grow up to 2 m (6 ft 6 in) tall, with females laying up to 85 eggs in a standard year. By the time of the Empire, dewbacks are ridden by Imperial sandtroopers stationed on Tatooine.

## DATA FILE

> Jawas are not the only intelligent natives on Tatooine. Tusken Raiders also live in the desert, but do not coexist peacfully with other species.

> Other non-sentient species on Tatooine include banthas, krayt dragons, rontos, sarlaccs, and womp rats.

> Only a small part of Tatooine's northern hemisphere is inhabitable. Settlements beside Mos Espa include Mos Elrey, Mos Taike, Mos Pelgo, and Mos Eisley.

# WATTO

**WATTO IS THE OWNER** of a spare parts store in Mos Espa on Tatooine. He is shrewd and possessive, with a sharp eye for a deal. His business acumen enables him to indulge his passion for gambling, which he does with some degree of success. Among his winnings are Shmi Skywalker and her young son Anakin, a pair of slaves whom he puts to work in his home and store. Having spotted Anakin's natural talent, he has helped the boy take part in several Podraces, but always bets against him because of his inexperience.

**WATTO'S JUNKSHOP**
Although Watto insists that his establishment is a parts dealership, everyone calls it a junk shop. The range of merchandise runs from desirable rare parts and working droids to unusable scrap that he would have a hard time unloading even on desperate Jawas. Watto's droids and slaves perform repairs, obtain parts needed by clients, and do custom work with a wide range of mechanical devices.

Flexible, trunklike nose

Fast-beating wings for flying or hovering

**AT THE RACES**
Watto loves to bet on the Podraces at the Mos Espa Grand Arena—but he hates to lose! At the Boonta Eve Classic Podrace, he is just as shocked as his fellow gamblers when his wager on the favorite—Sebulba—turns out to be a bad bet, and his own slave Anakin Skywalker wins the race at astronomical odds.

Keycodes for main safe and slave keepers

Heavy-looking belly is actually gas-filled

## TOYDARIAN TRADER

Watto was born amid the muck lakes of the planet Toydaria, where he grew up to be a soldier. When an injury ended that career, he came to Tatooine and set up as a shopkeeper. Many useful items can be found among the junk he sells—such as the hyperdrive unit he loses to the Jedi Qui-Gon Jinn in a bet.

Datapad

Bizarre, improvised equipment can be found in Watto's shop, such as the modified R1-series astromech droid that helps out with the shopkeeping.

Welding torch power cord

Webbed feet

Portable welding torch

Watto is an inveterate gambler, using chance cubes to make his business deals a little more interesting.

### DATA FILE

> When Watto first arrives on Tatooine, it is the Jawas' success in selling old technology that inspires him to launch his own business.

> Watto sometimes carries a walking stick, even though he mostly gets about by flying. He may not need it for mobility, but it does help inspire sympathy when he is making deals.

Security codeout

Credit algorithm memory stripes

REPUBLIC CREDIT CHIP

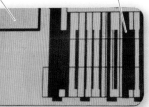

Watto scoffs at Qui-Gon Jinn when the Jedi offers to trade with him using Republic credits rather than hard cash. Like all Toydarians, he also proves impervious to Jedi mind tricks when Qui-Gon does his best to insist.

# SHMI SKYWALKER

**ANAKIN SKYWALKER'S MOTHER** lives on Tatooine as a slave, caring for her son as best she can in her straitened circumstances. Formerly in the service of the crime lord Gardalla the Hutt, she is the property of the junk dealer Watto when the Jedi Qui-Gon Jinn comes to Tatooine and recognizes her son's extraordinary talents. After Qui-Gon wins custody of Anakin from Watto, Shmi is torn between letting him fulfill his potential and giving up the one thing she truly loves. Although it breaks her heart, she finally chooses to let him go in search of a better life.

*Practical servant's hairstyle*

*Rough-spun tunic*

*Natural colors are far more affordable than dyed fabrics*

## SHMI'S KITCHEN

In spite of their poverty, Shmi's tireless efforts have made a good home for herself and her son. Their simple kitchen boasts some labor-saving devices, but none of the essential moisture-collecting technology that most inhabitants of Tatooine use to gain access to precious water.

*Repulsor hood*

*Illuminator rings*

*Magnifier*

## WORKSTATION

When Watto has no need of Shmi, he permits her to earn a modest income cleaning computer memory devices. She has turned a small area of her home into a workstation where she keeps just enough tools and equipment to do the job properly.

### AEROMAGNIFIER

Among the tools at Shmi's workstation is a repulsor-powered floating magnifier. It was given to her by Watto, in a rare show of kindness, as recognition for all her hard work in his service.

## SLAVE AND MOTHER

Though she has not lost hope that she will one day be freed, Shmi Skywalker accepts her lot in life and finds joy through her relationship with her son. She does not question how he came to be conceived without a father, and cherishes their modest life together in Mos Espa's Slave Quarter.

*Lamta*

*Spicy ahrisa*

*Haroun bread*

*Sidi gourd*

*Tezirett seed*

*Driss pod*

MOS ESPA PRODUCE

### DATA FILE

> Watto eventually sells Shmi to the moisture farmer Cliegg Lars, who releases her from bondage. The pair fall in love and are married soon after.

> Shmi dies in her teenage son's arms when Anakin returns to Tatooine in an attempt to save her from Tusken Raiders.

# C-3PO

## YOUNG ANAKIN SKYWALKER finds C-3PO's key

components discarded as junk and sets about rebuilding him. He scavenges the parts he doesn't have, and upgrades those he does to make the droid better suited to Tatooine's harsh conditions. Before long, the only elements he lacks are the body plates that give a protocol droid its finished look, and so Anakin sets his creation to work. With none of his young master's appetite for adventure, C-3PO is very happy helping Anakin and his mother around their simple family home, but fate has another path in store for him—whether he likes it or not!

## ANOTHER LIFE

C-3PO was originally manufactured by Cybot Galactica, and he retains many of his original components and memories. His TranLang III communication module gives him fluency in more than six million forms of language, and he is an expert in diplomacy.

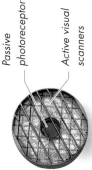

## PHOTORECEPTORS

A droid's photoreceptors not only enable it to see the world like a human, but also in a number of other ways, too. The pair of photoreceptors that Anakin finds for C-3PO in the Mos Espa marketplace allow him to see in infrared, and scan for heat signatures and specific gases using his Myriad Visual System.

### EYES ARE THE PRIZE

Anakin almost misses out on photoreceptors for C3PO when a greedy Gran at the Mos Espa marketplace refuses to accept that the youngster saw them first. He chases Anakin through the market to get his hands on the precious merchandise, and the future Jedi has to topple an Ithorian trader's stall to stop the Gran from catching him.

*Image signal transmitter*

*Image component lines*

*Modulation impulse carrier*

*Composite image integrator*

*Signal component collector pins*

*Mount frame*

*Balance gyro*

*Movement sensor wiring*

*Flexible mid-body section*

*Passive photoreceptor*

*Active visual scanners*

**PHOTORECEPTOR FRONT VIEW**

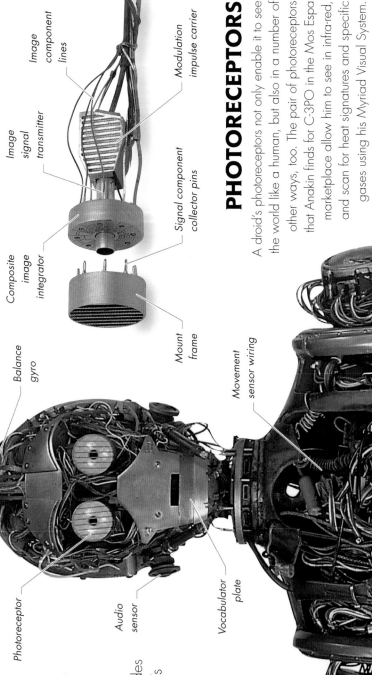

*Photoreceptor*

*Audio sensor*

*Vocabulator plate*

*Main power recharge socket*

*Pelvic joint*

*Fingers and thumbs are some of C-3PO's few plated parts.*

Most people wouldn't know where to begin when assembling a protocol droid, but Anakin is an exceptionally gifted engineer. He rebuilds C3PO partly for the challenge, but mainly as a gift for his overworked mom.

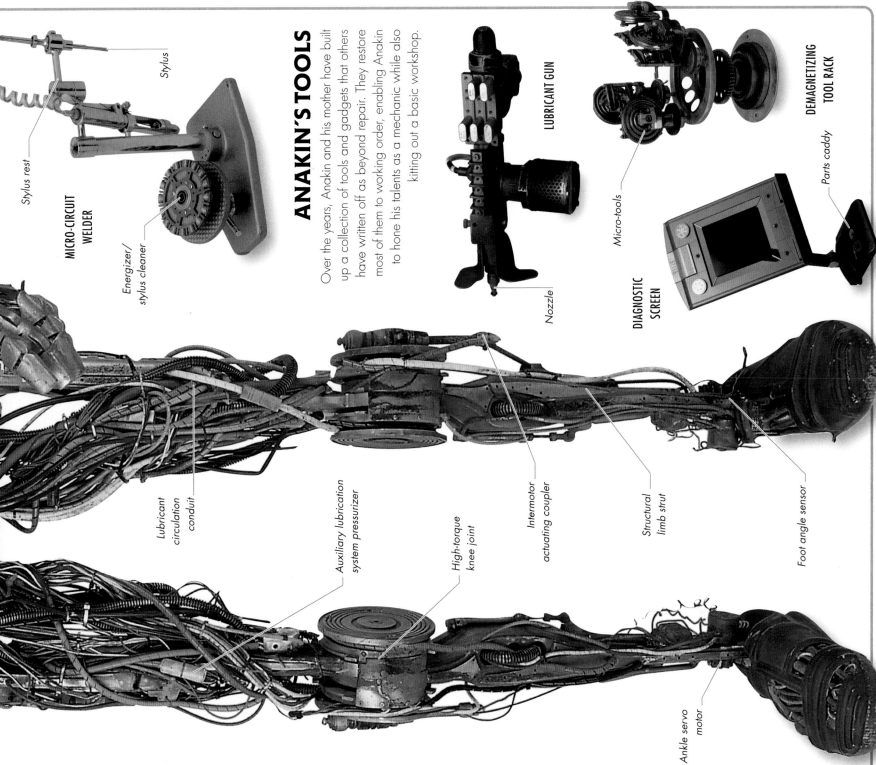

## ANAKIN'S TOOLS

Over the years, Anakin and his mother have built up a collection of tools and gadgets that others have written off as beyond repair. They restore most of them to working order, enabling Anakin to hone his talents as a mechanic while also kitting out a basic workshop.

**MICRO-CIRCUIT WELDER**

Stylus

Stylus rest

Energizer/stylus cleaner

**LUBRICANT GUN**

Nozzle

**DEMAGNETIZING TOOL RACK**

Micro-tools

Parts caddy

**DIAGNOSTIC SCREEN**

Lubricant circulation conduit

Auxiliary lubrication system pressurizer

High-torque knee joint

Intermotor actuating coupler

Structural limb strut

Foot angle sensor

Ankle servo motor

C-3PO first meets R2-D2 when he arrives on Tatooine as part of Queen Amidala's retinue. The smaller droid makes an immediate impression, telling C-3PO that he is naked without any plating! Before long, the two are working together to help Anakin win the Boonta Eve podrace.

Magnetic rotation assembly links to actuating coupler

Rotating pin anchors into limb

### HIGH-TORQUE MOTOR

C-3PO's arms and legs are powered by high-torque motors and attached to his torso using anchor pins. They are secure, but also allow him to be taken apart and reassembled easily. If one of his limbs is lost or damaged, the standard fitting can be replaced in an instant.

### DATA FILE

> In a galaxy populated by many thousands of sentient beings with their own customs, protocol droids exist to help different species interact politely and peacefully.

> When Anakin activates C-3PO in the Skywalker's workshop, he does so by pressing a small on/off button on the right-hand side of the droid's chest. The button is designed to be hidden by body plates.

# C-3PO:
## HANDY HELPER

Microwave
sensor/emitter

Digits are
badly worn

Restraining
bolt scar

Main power
socket

### MEET THE MAKER

After 10 years apart, C-3PO doesn't recognize Anakin Skywalker when he and Padmé return to Tatooine in search of Anakin's mother, Shmi. When Shmi dies in her son's arms, C-3PO attends a funeral service for the woman he has known ever since Anakin activated him as a child. He then leaves Tatooine with his maker.

Left shoulder missing

Badly
rusted
joints

LEFT ARM
PLATES

FOOT
SHELLS

Power and
impulse wiring

Remnants of an
old paint job

### BREASTPLATE

### FINALLY FINISHED

In the years since Anakin left C-3PO unfinished on Tatooine, his mother has completed the droid using rusted secondhand plating she acquired in Mos Espa. When the rust is cleaned off, the plates are a dull gray color.

Droid foot shells
are especially prone
to wear and tear

Secondhand
plating is pitted
and scarred

Joints are
relatively
sandproof

### FADED FARM DROID

After Anakin leaves to train as a Jedi, his mother, Shmi, marries Cliegg Lars and goes to live with him on his moisture farm. She takes C-3PO with her, and thereafter he spends his time repairing broken vaporators and carrying out other agricultural chores. He often thanks his maker that he has been upgraded to withstand the heat and sandstorms, but he never expects to meet Anakin again—or to see any more of the galaxy.

One leg is
rustier than
the other

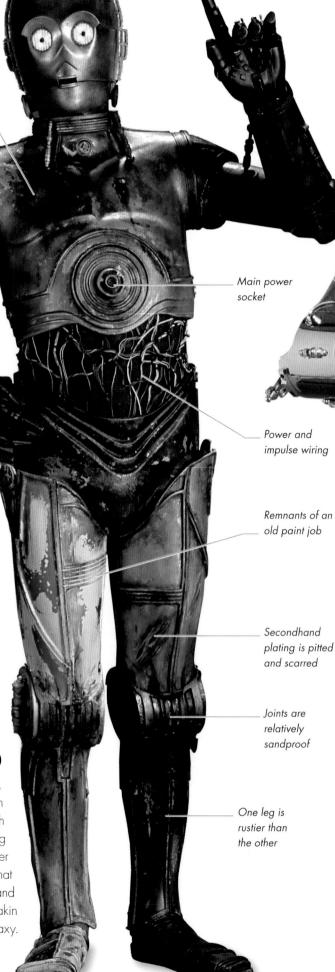

On Tatooine, C-3PO is reunited with R2-D2, the plucky astromech he met when Padmé first visited the planet a decade before. In the coming years, they will team up again and again, eventually returning to Tatooine.

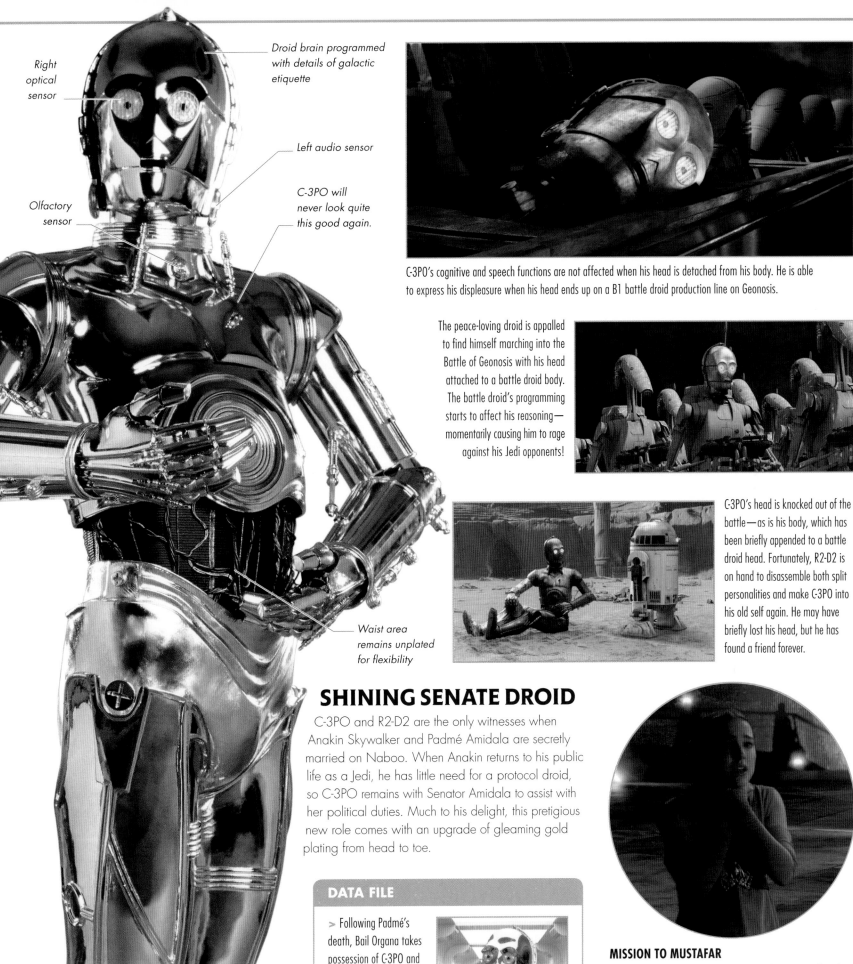

Right optical sensor

Droid brain programmed with details of galactic etiquette

Left audio sensor

C-3PO will never look quite this good again.

Olfactory sensor

Waist area remains unplated for flexibility

C-3PO's cognitive and speech functions are not affected when his head is detached from his body. He is able to express his displeasure when his head ends up on a B1 battle droid production line on Geonosis.

The peace-loving droid is appalled to find himself marching into the Battle of Geonosis with his head attached to a battle droid body. The battle droid's programming starts to affect his reasoning—momentarily causing him to rage against his Jedi opponents!

C-3PO's head is knocked out of the battle—as is his body, which has been briefly appended to a battle droid head. Fortunately, R2-D2 is on hand to disassemble both split personalities and make C-3PO into his old self again. He may have briefly lost his head, but he has found a friend forever.

## SHINING SENATE DROID

C-3PO and R2-D2 are the only witnesses when Anakin Skywalker and Padmé Amidala are secretly married on Naboo. When Anakin returns to his public life as a Jedi, he has little need for a protocol droid, so C-3PO remains with Senator Amidala to assist with her political duties. Much to his delight, this pretigious new role comes with an upgrade of gleaming gold plating from head to toe.

### MISSION TO MUSTAFAR

When Padmé races to Mustafar to see Anakin, C-3PO pilots the ship on behalf of the heavily pregnant senator. On arrival, she is Force-choked by her husband, who has turned to the dark side and is now more interested in dueling Obi-Wan. While the Jedi and his former apprentice fight, C-3PO brings Padmé back on board the ship and tends to her until Obi-Wan returns.

# PODRACERS

**THE EXTREME SPORT** of podracing attracts daredevil pilots from all over the galaxy. Each competitor flies a small, custom pod and risks life and limb to complete a perilous course at breakneck speed. Cheating and sabotage are accepted tactics, and races do not stop in the case of fatalities. The biggest podrace on Tatooine is the Boonta Eve Classic—an annual event hosted by Jabba the Hutt. When young Anakin Skywalker enters the race, he finds himself up against some stiff competition.

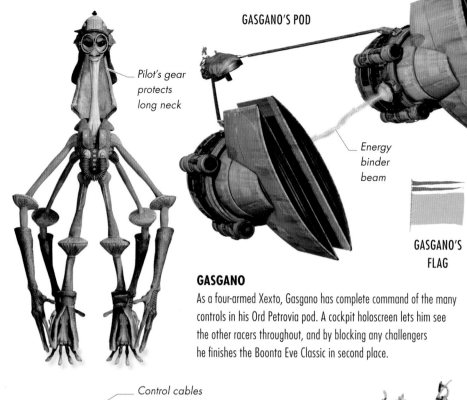

GASGANO'S POD

Pilot's gear protects long neck

Energy binder beam

GASGANO'S FLAG

## GASGANO

As a four-armed Xexto, Gasgano has complete command of the many controls in his Ord Petrovia pod. A cockpit holoscreen lets him see the other racers throughout, and by blocking any challengers he finishes the Boonta Eve Classic in second place.

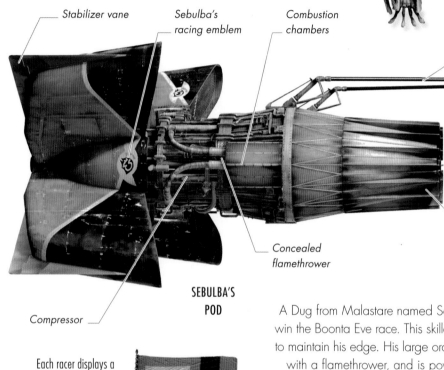

Stabilizer vane

Sebulba's racing emblem

Combustion chambers

Control cables

Repulsor threader helps pod avoid obstacles

Custom control seat

Exhaust nozzle

Concealed flamethrower

Compressor

**SEBULBA'S POD**

Feet have evolved into dextrous hands

## SEBULBA

A Dug from Malastare named Sebulba is the favorite to win the Boonta Eve race. This skilled racer uses dirty tricks to maintain his edge. His large orange pod is armed with a flamethrower, and is powerful enough to ram opponents out of contention. Sebulba does his best to force Anakin Skywalker off the track, but instead damages his own pod on the final lap, leaving the way clear for Anakin to win.

Each racer displays a personal flag at the start of the Boonta Eve Classic podrace.

Trophy coins

**CLEGG HOLDFAST**
This Nosaurian crashes on the second lap after an encounter with Sebulba's flame-jets.

**ALDAR BEEDO**
This Glymphid from the planet Ploo II finishes a respectable third on Boonta Eve.

**NEVA KEE**
A Xamster from Xagobah, Kee veers off course in search of a shortcut during lap two.

**EBE E. ENDOCOTT**
In fourth place is this veteran of the podracing scene from the planet Triffis.

**ODY MANDRELL**
This Er'Kit has to drop out when a pit droids gets sucked into his pod's engines.

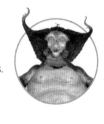

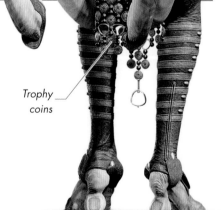

Combined head and torso

BEN QUADINAROS'S POD

**DATA FILE**

> Neva Kee's pod is notable for having its engines mounted to the rear of the cockpit, as part of one rigid structure.

> When he is not racing, Clegg Holdfast is a journalist for *Podracing Quarterly* magazine.

Unusual, four-engine design

# TEEMTO PAGALIES

Teemto Pagalies is an exile from his home planet, Moonus Mandel, who finds fame and acceptance in the dangerous world of podracing. He is forced out of the Boonta Eve Classic when his IPG-X1131 LongTail pod is shot down by a Tusken Raider during the second lap.

BEN QUADINAROS'S FLAG

Rotating cockpit

# BEN QUADINAROS

Ben Quadinaros is an inexperienced podracer from the planet Tund. He fails to make it off the starting grid when his rented BT310 quadra-podracer stalls in the Boonta Eve Classic.

TEEMTO PAGALIES' POD

Energy-binder plate

Pilot's goggles

RATTS TYERELL'S FLAG

Long Veknoid tail

RATTS TYERELL'S POD

Unusually large engines

## RATTS TYERELL

The smallest racer in the Boonta Eve Classic, Rats Tyerell, is killed when his accelerator jams on the first lap, causing his pod to smash into a stalactite. His death is widely marked on his homeworld, Aleen, where he was a big star.

TEEMTO PAGALIES' FLAG

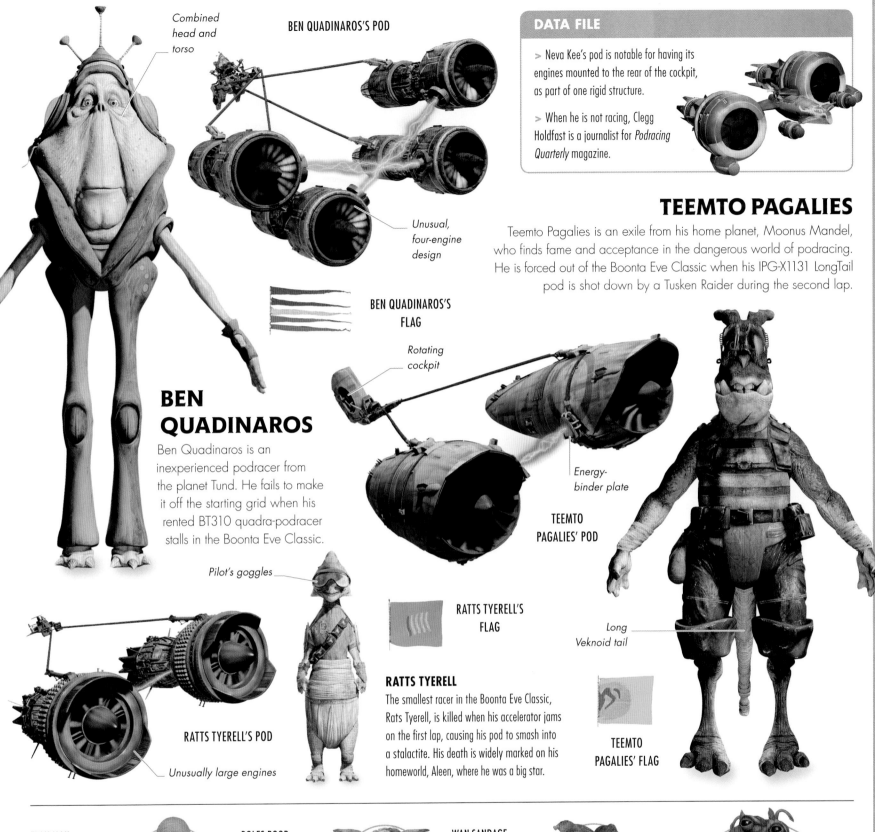

**ELAN MAK**
A Fluggrian from Ploo IV named Mak makes it into fifth place in his outdated KRT 410C pod.

**BOLES ROOR**
Sixth place goes to a two-time Boonta Eve Classic champion from the planet Sneeve.

**WAN SANDAGE**
A Devlikk from the planet Ord Radama named Sandage crashes on the third lap.

**ARK "BUMPY" ROOSE**
This Nuknog from the planet Sump crashes out when he collides with Dug Bolt's pod.

**MARS GUO**
Sebulba causes this Bardottan from the planet Phu to crash out in flames during lap two.

**DUD BOLT**
This Vulptereen crashes his celebrated pod on lap three.

**MAWHONIC**
This Gran from the planet Hok falls on the first lap as Sebulba forces his pod into a cliff face.

# PODRACE CREWS

**KEEPING A PODRACER RUNNING** at speeds in excess of 700 kph (435 mph) is a precision job, calling for specialist teams of organics and droids. In between races, pods are constantly maintained, enhanced, fine-tuned, and tested. In the midst of a contest, pit crews stand by to deal with any eventuality, from overheated engines to blatant sabotage. These crews must also contend with the egos of the racers themselves, and the interference of trackside officials.

Harmonic sensor

**INSTRUMENT CALIBRATOR**

Rectifier scale

Output sampler

**POWER OUTPUT ANALYZER**

Podracing pit crews use a range of specialized instruments to analyze engine performance and to diagnose faults. These tools should be standardized for fairness and safety, but in practice no two crews have—or want—exactly the same gear.

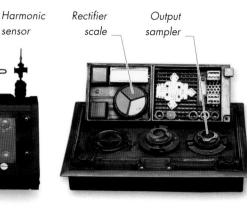

## PIT HANGAR

Podracers are worked on right up until the last minute before a race. Heavy-duty cranes move the oversized engines around in the busy Mos Espa Arena hangar, while dewbacks haul the pods out to their starting positions. The hangar is also a place for pod owners to do deals, bribe drivers, and sabotage their rivals.

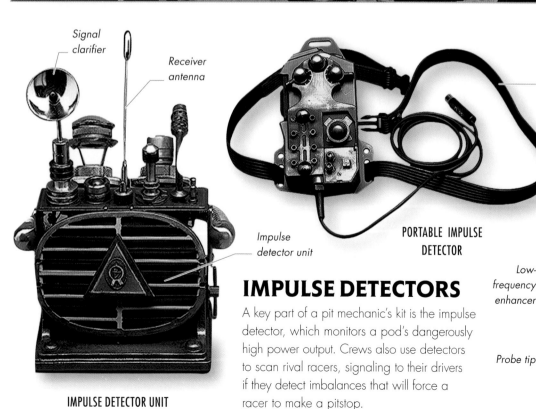

Signal clarifier

Receiver antenna

Carry strap

Handle

Impulse detector unit

**PORTABLE IMPULSE DETECTOR**

## IMPULSE DETECTORS

A key part of a pit mechanic's kit is the impulse detector, which monitors a pod's dangerously high power output. Crews also use detectors to scan rival racers, signaling to their drivers if they detect imbalances that will force a racer to make a pitstop.

**IMPULSE DETECTOR UNIT**

Low-frequency enhancer

Probe tip

**IMPULSE PROBE**

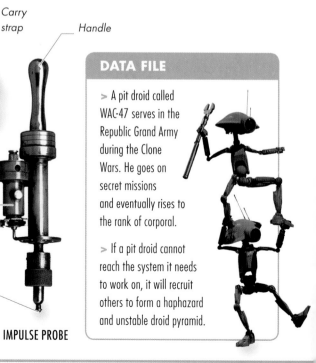

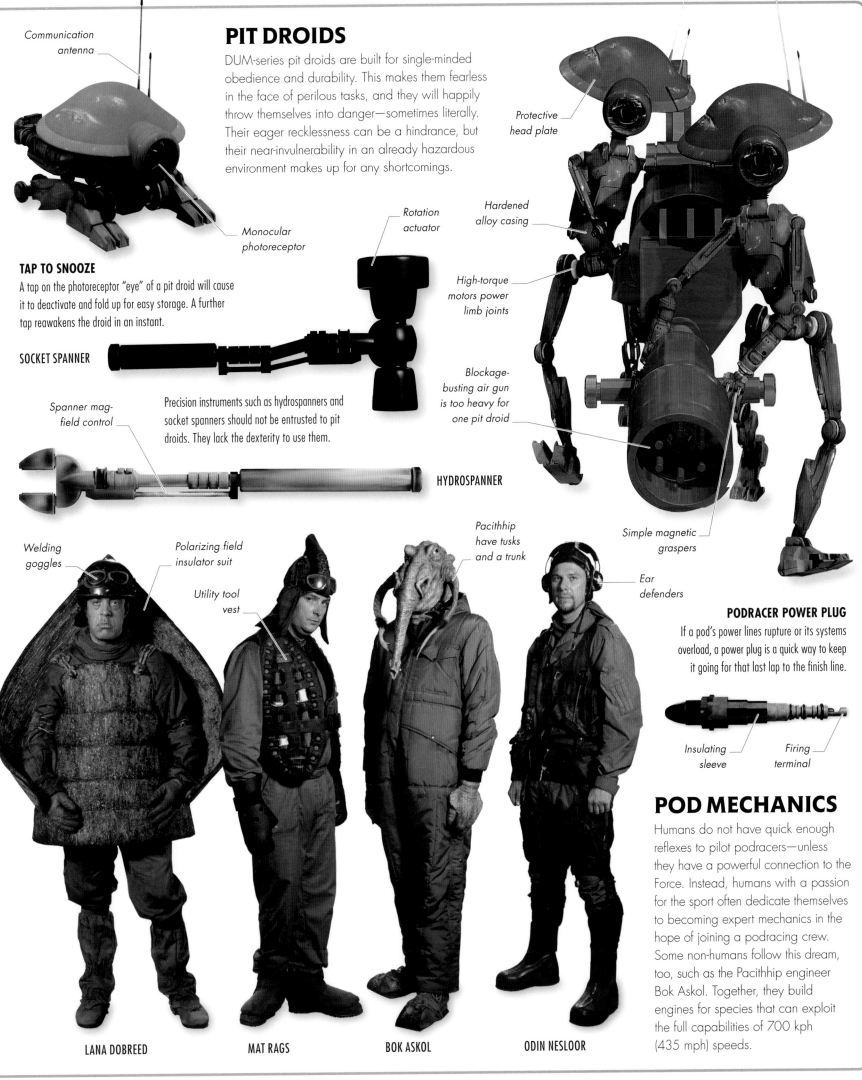

Communication
antenna

# PIT DROIDS

DUM-series pit droids are built for single-minded obedience and durability. This makes them fearless in the face of perilous tasks, and they will happily throw themselves into danger—sometimes literally. Their eager recklessness can be a hindrance, but their near-invulnerability in an already hazardous environment makes up for any shortcomings.

Protective
head plate

Hardened
alloy casing

Rotation
actuator

Monocular
photoreceptor

### TAP TO SNOOZE

A tap on the photoreceptor "eye" of a pit droid will cause it to deactivate and fold up for easy storage. A further tap reawakens the droid in an instant.

High-torque
motors power
limb joints

### SOCKET SPANNER

Spanner mag-
field control

Precision instruments such as hydrospanners and socket spanners should not be entrusted to pit droids. They lack the dexterity to use them.

Blockage-
busting air gun
is too heavy for
one pit droid

**HYDROSPANNER**

Simple magnetic
graspers

Welding
goggles

Polarizing field
insulator suit

Pacithhip
have tusks
and a trunk

Ear
defenders

Utility tool
vest

### PODRACER POWER PLUG

If a pod's power lines rupture or its systems overload, a power plug is a quick way to keep it going for that last lap to the finish line.

Insulating
sleeve

Firing
terminal

# POD MECHANICS

Humans do not have quick enough reflexes to pilot podracers—unless they have a powerful connection to the Force. Instead, humans with a passion for the sport often dedicate themselves to becoming expert mechanics in the hope of joining a podracing crew. Some non-humans follow this dream, too, such as the Pacithhip engineer Bok Askol. Together, they build engines for species that can exploit the full capabilities of 700 kph (435 mph) speeds.

**LANA DOBREED**

**MAT RAGS**

**BOK ASKOL**

**ODIN NESLOOR**

# MOS ESPA ARENA

**THE ATMOSPHERE BEFORE** a podrace is electric. Spectators from hundreds of species crowd into the stands, while the rich and influential file into spacious VIP boxes. At the Mos Espa Arena, all walks of Tatooine society turn out for the Boonta Eve Classic, alongside pod fanatics willing to travel to this galactic backwater just to get a glimpse of their racing heroes. As the pre-race commentary blares out over loudspeakers, bets are placed, cam droids are launched, and the fans prepare their electrobinoculars and personal viewscreens. Nobody wants to miss a crash!

Steering vane

Double balloon for stability

Patches repair damage

High tensile-strength cables

Spectator gondola

Omnicam

### PODRACE BALLOONS
Podrace fans unwilling or unable to pay for official hovercam feeds can take advantage of cheaper, balloon-powered options. A small sum buys access to live coverage from a slow-moving balloon, while brave racegoers can pay more to float over the arena in person.

Hutt skin can dry out quickly under Tatooine's suns

Gorgs make a tasty Hutt snack

Vast mouth

## ARENA GRANDSTAND

The main arena complex is dwarfed by the vast natural canyon in which it sits, yet is capable of holding more than 100,000 spectators. Located at the edge of Tatooine's Northern Dune Sea, its citadel and west stands overlook the start and finish line, while the cheaper west stands face the nearby pit hangar.

### HANDHELD VIEWSCREENS
Giant screens in the sumptuous levels of the Arena Citadel betting floors monitor the views from the race cameras. However, most fans prefer to watch the race in the stands using rented screens or electrobinoculars.

Display mode select

### SPECTATOR SPORT
There is always a party atmosphere in the stands at the Mos Espa Arena. Spectators cheer on their favorite racers and heckle others, while food vendors and buskers move through the crowd. However, fans must stay alert for pickpockets and con artists.

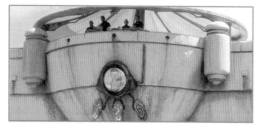

The outside of the starters' box displays the starting light and three lap indicators. Inside, race officials observe procedings.

## FODE AND BEED

Fodesinbeed Annodue is the two-headed Troig sports announcer best known as the one-man double-act, Fode and Beed. His lively commentary is a highlight of the Boonta Eve Classic podrace, with Fode (his red head) speaking in Galactic Basic, while Beed (his green head) does so in Huttese.

### DATA FILE

> The Boonta Eve celebration is named in honor of the Hutt deity Boonta Hestilic Shad'ruu.

> Podracers' friends and family are given preferential seating in the Arena. Anakin's mother and his new friends watch him win his race from atop a viewing tower.

Transmission antenna

Metal pitted by kicked-up grit

SIDE VIEW

Customized DX-13 blaster pistol

Comlink antenna is built into skull

Slugthrower fires solid projectiles

Once-gleaming finish faded from Tatooine's frequent sandstorms

Mini-reactor power feeds

Extra-long thumbs and fingers

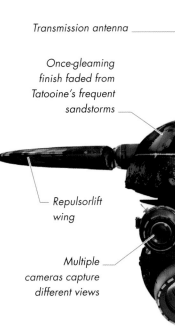

Repulsorlift wing

Multiple cameras capture different views

### HOLOGLIDE J57 CAM DROID

A fleet of hovering camera droids covers the circuit from every angle, feeding the action back to the Hutt-owned podracing channels. Fans in the arena pay to view these live channels on handheld devices, or on big screens inside the citadel building.

Chalk-white skin

### AURRA SING

Bounty hunter Aurra Sing has many enemies, and steers clear of the Mos Espa Arena when she is on Tatooine. However, she does not miss the Boonta Eve Classic, making use of a high viewpoint overlooking isolated Beggar's Canyon to watch the race alone.

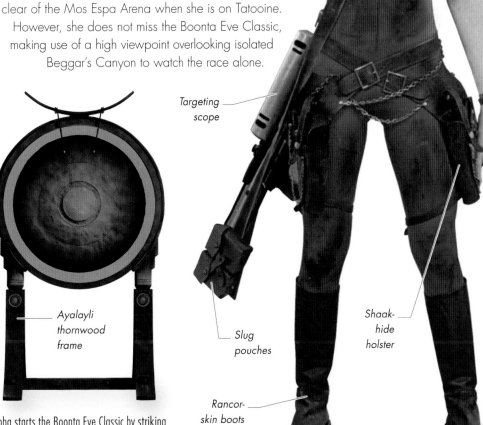

Targeting scope

Slug pouches

Shaak-hide holster

Rancor-skin boots

### JABBA THE HUTT

Crime lord Jabba Desilijic Tiure has no interest in podracing as a sport—failing to even stay awake during the Boonta Eve Classic. His passion is for the money that fans will bet on the race, making huge profits for his gambling rackets. Attending major races is good for business, so he makes a great show of his presence on Boonta Eve (specifically a Hutt day of celebration), starting the race from his executive box.

Powerful, swiping tail

Ayalayli thornwood frame

Jabba starts the Boonta Eve Classic by striking an antique gong—with a spit-out gorg head.

# TUSKEN RAIDERS

**TATOOINE'S NATIVE TUSKEN RAIDERS** are dangerous, nomadic warriors. Highly territorial, and believing that all water is theirs by right, they frequently target the planet's moisture farmers in swift and brutal attacks that have earned them their name. Every Tusken is an expert at blending in to the featureless desert, and knows to cover every inch of his or her flesh in order to survive in its harsh conditions. No outsider ever sees behind a Tusken's mysterious mask and lives to tell the tale.

Bone fastenings

Ancient wood

Urtah carrying pack

## URTYA TENT
Tusken Raiders roam the desert in clans of up to 30 individuals, pitching their urtya tents overnight before moving on the next morning. The tents are made from animal skins stretched over frames of wood or bone.

Male warrior

Female in jeweled mask

Eye slit keeps out sand

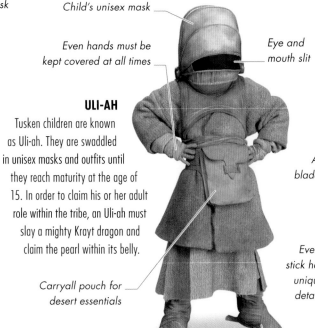

Child's unisex mask

Even hands must be kept covered at all times

Eye and mouth slit

## ULI-AH
Tusken children are known as Uli-ah. They are swaddled in unisex masks and outfits until they reach maturity at the age of 15. In order to claim his or her adult role within the tribe, an Uli-ah must slay a mighty Krayt dragon and claim the pearl within its belly.

Ax blades

Carryall pouch for desert essentials

Every stick has unique details

Sand-shroud covers torso

Bandaged feet

## SHROUDED SOCIETY

Tusken society is strongly divided along gender lines. The males are warriors, distinguished by tight fabric masks with moisture-retaining mouth grilles. Females take on many roles, and are identified by elaborate metal masks that represent the apex of Tusken craft. The Tuskens' need to shield their bodies against the elements has grown into a taboo, meaning that they almost never unmask in front of one another.

Curved "traang" end

### DATA FILE

> As well as gaderffii sticks, Tusken Raiders also use cycler rifles.

> Tuskens harvest milk from the black melons that grow in the Jundland Wastes.

## GADERFFII STICK
Every Tusken warrior fashions his own bladed club, known as a gaderffii stick. Its sharpened tips can be used to kill, or to incapacitate with the addition of paralyzing sandbat venom.

# THE LARS FAMILY

**DATA FILE**

> The Lars' homestead is located on the Great Chott salt flat in the Jundland Wastes, near to the town of Anchorhead.

> Several droids work on the Lars' moisture farm, including a WED-15-XT Treadwell droid, which monitors and repairs the family's numerous vaporators.

FAR AWAY FROM the gamblers and smugglers that drive Tatooine's urban economy, the Lars family live a simple, honest life in the planet's desert. These moisture farmers rely on aging vaporators to collect water from the air, which they use to tend the hydroponic garden that feeds them. It is a hard life, made even more precarious by the threat of sandstorms and attacks by Tusken Raiders. Yet the family members get by in their pourstone underground homestead. Sheltering as best they can from the relentless heat of their world's twin suns, they are sustained by their resourcefulness and their love for one another.

Simple clothing bought in Anchorhead

Practical hairstyle

Close collar keeps out sand

## CLIEGG LARS

As a young man, Cliegg Lars traveled to the Core Worlds, where he fell in love with and married a woman called Aika. She died not long after the birth of their son, Owen, and so Cliegg returned to Tatooine to raise the boy on his family's farm. He marries again after falling in love with the slave Shmi Skywalker, whose freedom he bought from the junk dealer Watto.

The Lars never expected to meet Shmi's son, Anakin, who left Tatooine to train as a Jedi. He returns when he senses that his mother is in danger, and shares in his step-family's grief when she dies in a Tusken camp.

Activator

Control stick

## OWEN AND BERU

Owen Lars is devoted to his family's farm and works hard to make it the very best it can be. His girlfriend, Beru Whitesun, shares his dedication to the desert life, coming from another long-established family of moisture farmers. The pair care very deeply for one another, and for Owen's father and stepmother, Shmi.

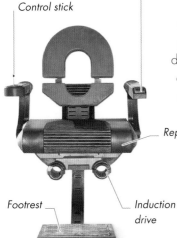

Repulsor unit inside seat

Homemade blaster

Footrest

Induction drive

**REPULSORLIFT CHAIR**

Cliegg Lars uses a repulsor-chair to get around, having lost his right leg in a valiant but doomed attempt to rescue his wife from Tusken Raiders.

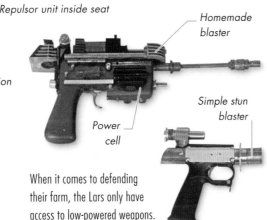

Power cell

Simple stun blaster

When it comes to defending their farm, the Lars only have access to low-powered weapons.

# CORUSCANT

**THE CAPITAL CITY OF** the Galactic Republic spans an entire planet. Coruscant is the center of government, business, technology, and culture in the galaxy, as well as the spiritual home of the Jedi, whose temple stands close to the Galactic Senate. An estimated one trillion people live on the planet, with some of the enormous skyscrapers housing up to a million Coruscanti each. The so-called Galactic City is easy to find, having been given the prestigious coordinates 0-0-0 on all standard navigation star charts.

## DIZZY HEIGHTS

The skies of Coruscant are defined by towering buildings and snaking processions of airspeeders. The tallest structures reach 6 km (3.7 m) into the air—piercing the planet's troposphere and affecting its weather patterns. Luckily, the whole world is covered by an effective climate-control system.

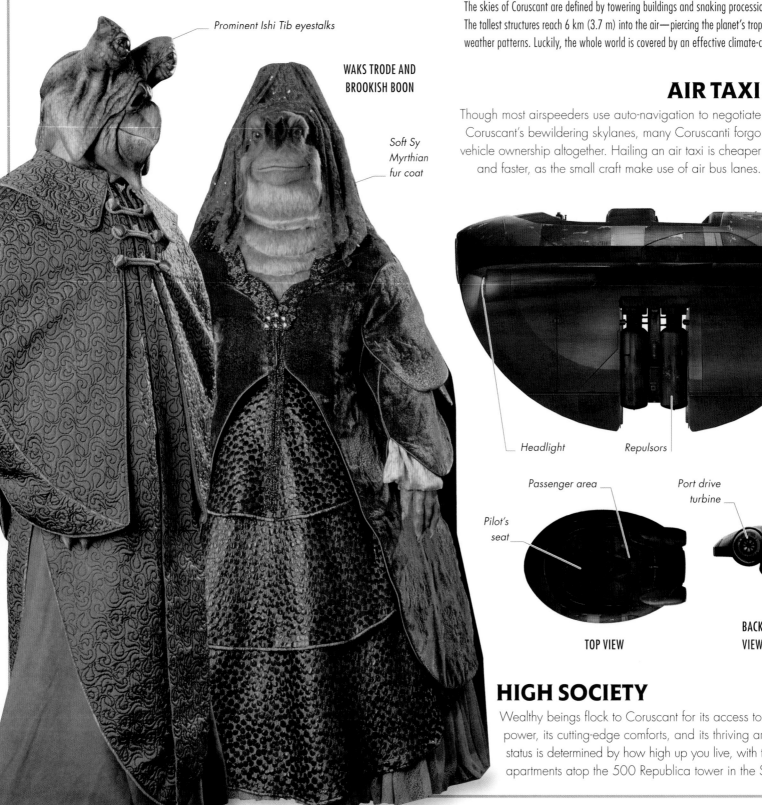

Prominent Ishi Tib eyestalks

WAKS TRODE AND
BROOKISH BOON

Soft Sy Myrthian fur coat

## AIR TAXI

Though most airspeeders use auto-navigation to negotiate Coruscant's bewildering skylanes, many Coruscanti forgo vehicle ownership altogether. Hailing an air taxi is cheaper and faster, as the small craft make use of air bus lanes.

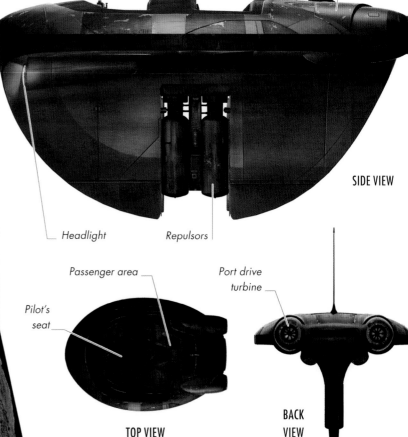

Comlink antenna

Drive engine housing

SIDE VIEW

Headlight

Repulsors

Passenger area

Port drive turbine

Pilot's seat

TOP VIEW

BACK VIEW

## HIGH SOCIETY

Wealthy beings flock to Coruscant for its access to government power, its cutting-edge comforts, and its thriving arts scene. Social status is determined by how high up you live, with the most exclusive apartments atop the 500 Republica tower in the Senate District.

## A NIGHT AT THE OPERA

More than half of Coruscant's population is human, but there are few sentient species that do not have some presence on the planet. On a single night at the Galaxies Opera House, dozens of species turn out to enjoy the likes of *Squid Lake*—and to be seen at the illustrious venue.

Human con artist in fake military gear

Rodian singer and dancer

Theelin/Human hybrid dancer

Rich Twi'lek duchess

Human high-fashion designer

Pantoran political leader

DANNL FAYTONNI        GREEATA JENDOWANIAN        RYSTÁLL SANT        KOYI MATEIL        DELVA RACINE        PAPANOIDA

# THE BATTLE OF CORUSCANT

For most of the Clone Wars, battle rages far away from Coruscant—much to the satisfaction of the planet's rich and comfortable. However, the Separatists eventually launch a surprise attack on the galactic capital. As the Republic Navy engages droid starfighters above the planet, Jedi Anakin Skywalker and Obi-Wan Kenobi race to rescue Supreme Chancellor Palpatine, who is being held captive on the Separatist flagship, *Invisible Hand*.

The Battle of Coruscant ends with the *Invisible Hand* crashing down onto the surface of the planet. Huge loss of life is avoided thanks to Anakin Skywalker's ability to pilot the ship into a controled crash on one a long industrial landing platform.

## DATA FILE

> During the Clone Wars, the enormous Zillo Beast goes on a rampage through Coruscant after breaking out of a science research center.

> There are 24 hours in a Coruscant day, and 365 days in a Coruscant year. Throughout the Galactic Republic, times and dates are often based on these standard increments.

Flame-retardant spray nozzle

Emergency running light

Cockpit

**FIRESPEEDER**
Four emergency fire suppression speeders attend the *Invisible Hand* as it plunges toward Coruscant.

# CORUSCANT UNDERWORLD

**BENEATH THE STUNNING CITYSCAPE** of the surface world lies another Coruscant. What appear from above to be simple ventilation shafts are also entry points to the planet's lower levels—also known as the underworld. This heavily-polluted hidden city is home to a mix of Coruscant's poor and needy, its foolhardy thrill seekers, its dispossessed, and the criminal gangs who prey on them all.

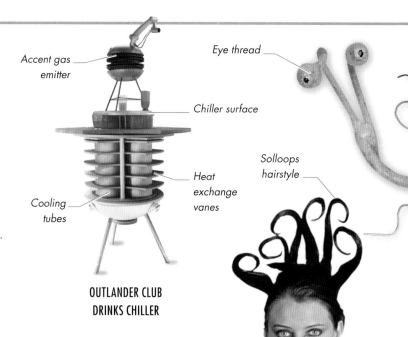

Accent gas emitter

Eye thread

Chiller surface

Solloops hairstyle

Heat exchange vanes

Cooling tubes

**OUTLANDER CLUB DRINKS CHILLER**

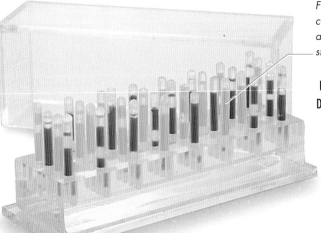

Fluorescent colors are a sick fashion statement

**DEATH STICK DEALER'S BOX**

## THE OUTLANDER CLUB

Sooner or later, everyone comes to the Outlander, a popular nightclub and gambling den in the heart of the underworld. It attracts wealthy pleasure seekers from the upper levels looking to splash their cash incognito, and last-chancers out to bet their last credits on a distant grav-ball game. Its patrons also include cult members such as Agira Nyrat, who trawl the crowd for weak-minded recruits.

A circular bar in the center of the Outlander offers an exotic selection of off-world drinks. But as one species' pleasure is another's poison, patrons place orders at their own risk.

## DEATH STICKS

For the underworld's most unfortunate inhabitants, death can seem like the only way out. That is why many are willing to try their first death stick, before quickly getting addicted to the harmful, fluorescent narcotic. Death stick dealers such as Elan Sleazebaggano are more than happy to take advantage of these addicts, and are known in the underworld as "slythmongers."

**ELAN SLEAZEBAGGANO**

Obi-Wan Kenobi and Anakin Skywalker pay a visit to the Outlander when they are on the tail of the bounty hunter Zam Wesell. Their Jedi robes attract no interest amid the eclectic nightclub crowd.

**AGIRA NYRAT**

### DATA FILE

> Coruscant has 5,127 levels, numbered outward from the planet's core. The very lowest level, Level 1, is uninhabitable.

> Crime families run many of the lower levels, patroling them with hired goons.

The Outlander Club is just one of many drinking dens to be found on Vos Gesal Street in the Uscru Entertainment District. It is located far below the above-ground Galaxies Opera House.

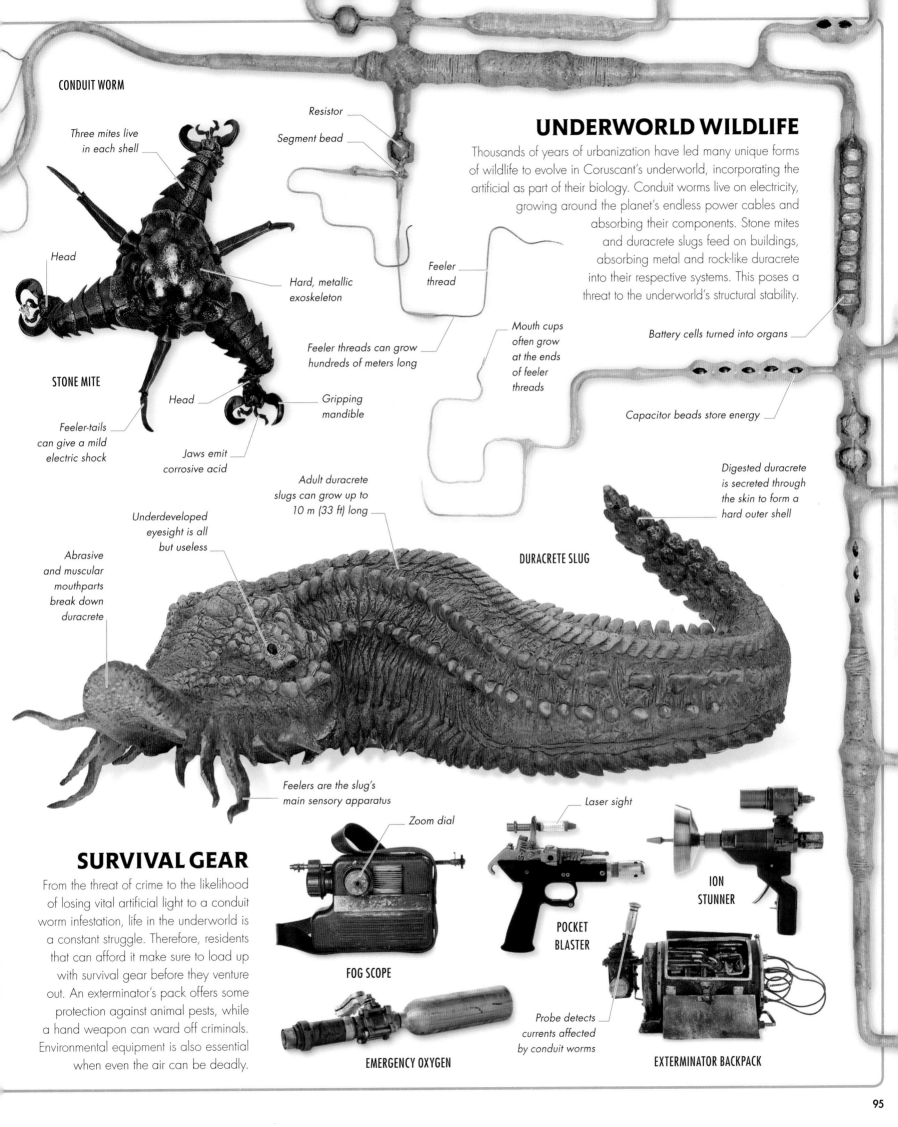

**CONDUIT WORM**

Three mites live in each shell

Head

Resistor

Segment bead

Feeler thread

## UNDERWORLD WILDLIFE

Thousands of years of urbanization have led many unique forms of wildlife to evolve in Coruscant's underworld, incorporating the artificial as part of their biology. Conduit worms live on electricity, growing around the planet's endless power cables and absorbing their components. Stone mites and duracrete slugs feed on buildings, absorbing metal and rock-like duracrete into their respective systems. This poses a threat to the underworld's structural stability.

Hard, metallic exoskeleton

Feeler threads can grow hundreds of meters long

Mouth cups often grow at the ends of feeler threads

Battery cells turned into organs

**STONE MITE**

Head

Feeler-tails can give a mild electric shock

Gripping mandible

Jaws emit corrosive acid

Capacitor beads store energy

Adult duracrete slugs can grow up to 10 m (33 ft) long

Digested duracrete is secreted through the skin to form a hard outer shell

Underdeveloped eyesight is all but useless

**DURACRETE SLUG**

Abrasive and muscular mouthparts break down duracrete

Feelers are the slug's main sensory apparatus

Laser sight

Zoom dial

## SURVIVAL GEAR

From the threat of crime to the likelihood of losing vital artificial light to a conduit worm infestation, life in the underworld is a constant struggle. Therefore, residents that can afford it make sure to load up with survival gear before they venture out. An exterminator's pack offers some protection against animal pests, while a hand weapon can ward off criminals. Environmental equipment is also essential when even the air can be deadly.

**ION STUNNER**

**POCKET BLASTER**

**FOG SCOPE**

Probe detects currents affected by conduit worms

**EMERGENCY OXYGEN**

**EXTERMINATOR BACKPACK**

# DEXTER'S DINER

**AFTER BOUNTY HUNTER ZAM** Wesell is killed by a mysterious toxic saberdart, Obi-Wan Kenobi heads for the haunt of a four-armed Besalisk named Dexter Jettster. The brusque but good-hearted Dex's unassuming diner serves more than hearty food—favored diners can also fill up on information. This small eatery can be found tucked away in a run-down industrial area of Coruscant, known as CoCo Town, and is filled with those on the fringes of the Coruscanti underworld.

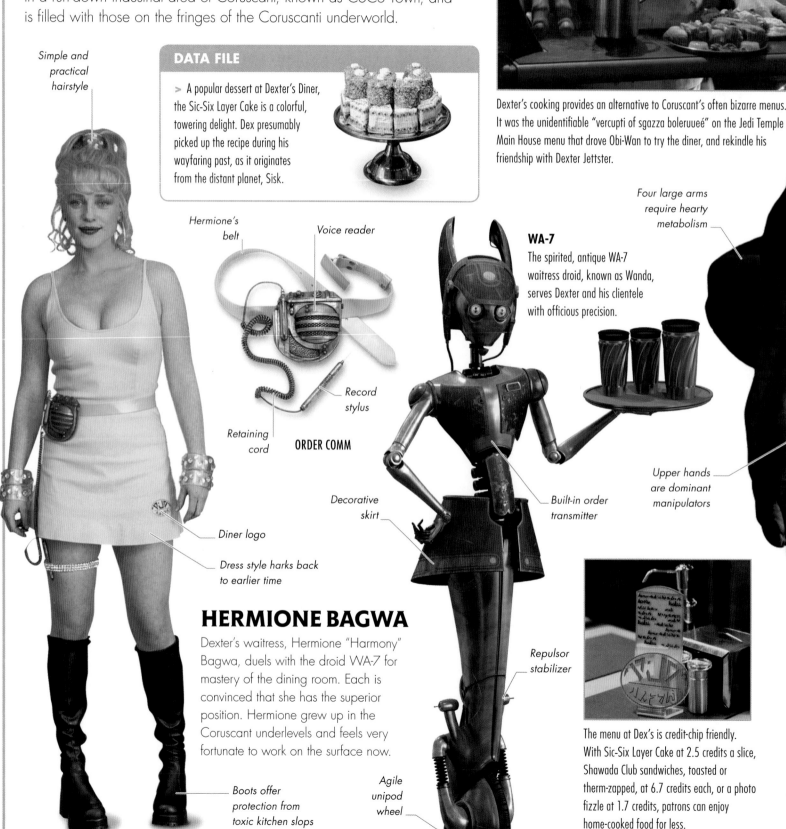

Simple and practical hairstyle

**DATA FILE**

> A popular dessert at Dexter's Diner, the Sic-Six Layer Cake is a colorful, towering delight. Dex presumably picked up the recipe during his wayfaring past, as it originates from the distant planet, Sisk.

Dexter's cooking provides an alternative to Coruscant's often bizarre menus. It was the unidentifiable "vercupti of sgazza boleruueé" on the Jedi Temple Main House menu that drove Obi-Wan to try the diner, and rekindle his friendship with Dexter Jettster.

Hermione's belt

Voice reader

Record stylus

Retaining cord

**ORDER COMM**

Decorative skirt

Diner logo

Dress style harks back to earlier time

Four large arms require hearty metabolism

**WA-7**
The spirited, antique WA-7 waitress droid, known as Wanda, serves Dexter and his clientele with officious precision.

Built-in order transmitter

Upper hands are dominant manipulators

## HERMIONE BAGWA

Dexter's waitress, Hermione "Harmony" Bagwa, duels with the droid WA-7 for mastery of the dining room. Each is convinced that she has the superior position. Hermione grew up in the Coruscant underlevels and feels very fortunate to work on the surface now.

Repulsor stabilizer

Boots offer protection from toxic kitchen slops

Agile unipod wheel

The menu at Dex's is credit-chip friendly. With Sic-Six Layer Cake at 2.5 credits a slice, Shawada Club sandwiches, toasted or therm-zapped, at 6.7 credits each, or a photo fizzle at 1.7 credits, patrons can enjoy home-cooked food for less.

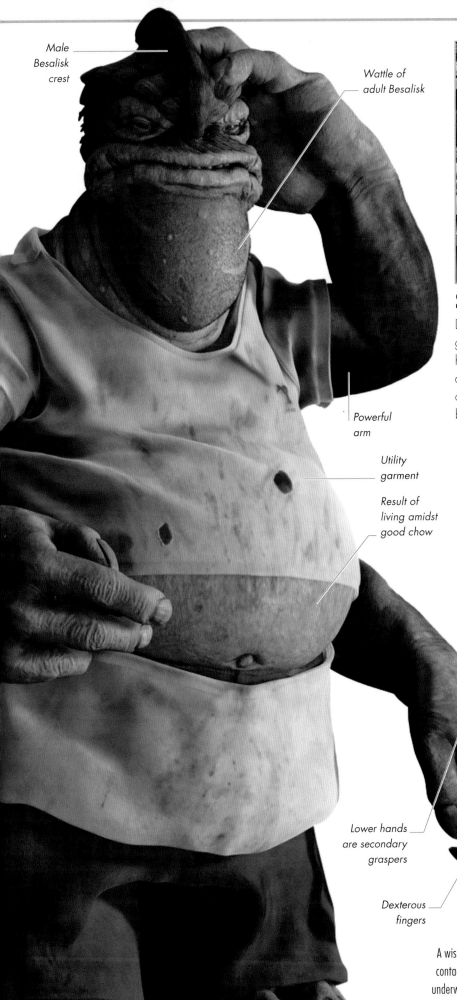

*Male Besalisk crest*

*Wattle of adult Besalisk*

*Powerful arm*

*Utility garment*

*Result of living amidst good chow*

*Lower hands are secondary graspers*

*Dexterous fingers*

## SLIDER FANS

Dexter transforms trans-shipped, medium-density food-board into sliders by griding it, perforating it with five holes, and serving it as a sandwich with his special garnish. There have been accuastions that addictive drugs are added to the square slider's garnish's—which have never been proven, of course. However, customers often take a few gulps of a mild, pink antidote before chowing down, to avoid gastrointestinal distress.

Regulars at the diner travel light-years out of their way just to satisfy cravings for Dexter's small, square sliders, in a comfortable setting. The decor recalls the traditional appearance of diners from the golden days of the Galactic Republic, which stands out from Coruscant's millions of identical food stations.

## SHARP-EYED CHEF

Chief cook and bottle washer, Dexter is an individual of broad experience and diverse connections gathered from stints manning oil-harvesting rigs, tending bars, and dealing in contraband. The diner has let this Besalisk make a fresh start, and he enjoys the stablity of his new life. Trusted by his shady old associates as well as his new crowd of regulars, Dexter is a friend to beings from all walks of life. Hidden within his sloppy exterior, Dexter has a keen sense of observation and a retentive memory that can serve up vital information even to the likes of a Jedi Knight.

A wise field-agent maintains contacts on the fringe of the underworld. Dexter Jettster is glad to help Obi-Wan, knowing he is not a judgmental and pompous creep like so many other elite or high-station Coruscanti.

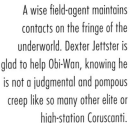

# THE GALACTIC SENATE

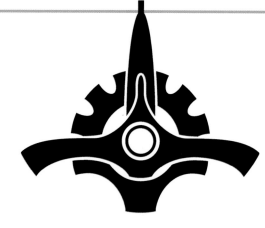

**THOUSANDS OF STAR SYSTEMS** live in peace as part of the Galactic Republic, and the Galactic Senate is the place where their representatives come together. Its purpose is to make the laws that all Republic citizens must live by, and to settle disputes when member worlds disagree. Senators from every corner of the galaxy gather in the Senate Chamber to debate the issues of the day, overseen by a democratically elected Supreme Chancellor and a Vice Chair. These senior roles are designed to keep the business of government moving, while it is the senators' job to stop their leaders from becoming too powerful.

**GREAT GALACTIC SEAL**
The symbol of the Senate is the Great Galactic Seal. It adorns many official locations, including the Chancellor's podium in the Senate Chamber.

*Open-face helmet*

*Robe covers armor*

## THE FEDERAL DISTRICT

The Galactic Senate is located within a huge, domed building in an area of Coruscant known as the Federal District. A smaller dome contains the offices of many senators and the Supreme Chancellor. This is where much of the actual business of government is done.

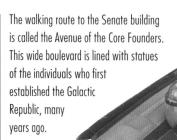

The walking route to the Senate building is called the Avenue of the Core Founders. This wide boulevard is lined with statues of the individuals who first established the Galactic Republic, many years ago.

*Main hatch*

*Guard station*

**VALORUM'S SHUTTLE**
During his time as Supreme Chancellor, Finus Valorum travels to and from the Senate in an *Eddicus*-class planetary shuttle. Just like the ceremonial uniforms of the Senate Guard, it is colored blue to denote its status in service of the Galactic Senate.

## SENATE GUARD

The elite soldiers of the Senate Guard are second only to the Jedi Order as symbols of security in the Galactic Republic. They serve as bodyguards to the Supreme Chancellor and protect Senate buildings, as well as providing a ceremonial flourish with their rich blue robes and elaborate crests.

# THE SENATE CHAMBER

The enormous Senate Chamber comprises 1,024 repulsorpod platforms arranged around the Supreme Chancellor's podium. Senators and other representatives follow Senate proceedings from the platforms, taking their turn to speak when they are given permission to do so by the Vice Chair.

Monitor screen

Central seating

Bench seating

Entry/exit gates

### REPULSORPODS

When a senator's delegation is given leave to speak, its repulsorpod detaches from the Senate Chamber walls and approaches the Chancellor's podium to better address the cavernous space.

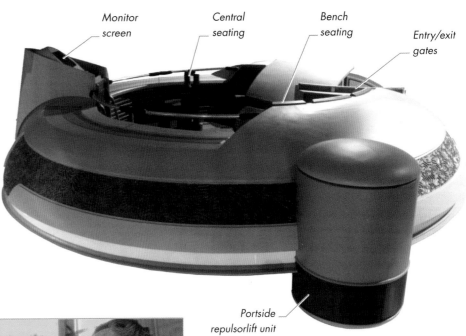

Portside repulsorlift unit

Blue-tipped horns serve to intimidate

Yellow horns hang from tentacles

Mouth conceals a long, black, forked tongue

### THE ROLE OF SUPREME CHANCELLOR

Traditionally, the Supreme Chancellor of the Galactic Senate has limited powers, answering to the senators that elected him for a maximum of two terms of office. However, frustration at the ineffectiveness of the role leads to senators voting to give Supreme Chancellor Palpatine increasing control over decision-making, following a vote of no confidence in the previous postholder, Finis Valorum.

# MAS AMEDDA

A stern Chagrian from the planet Champala named Mas Amedda serves in the Senate as Vice Chair. Having won the role under Chancellor Valorum, he assists and counsels Supreme Chancellor Palpatine on the best ways to get what he wants from the Senate through clever use of protocol and populism.

SIDE VIEW

Wide-angle lens

### CAM DROIDS

A fleet of cam droids patrols the Senate Chamber, recording sessions for posterity and relaying coverage to the screens in each repulsorpod. Audio feeds carry the senators' voices around the chamber, translating languages as required for each pod.

Control antenna

Telefoto lens

FRONT VIEW

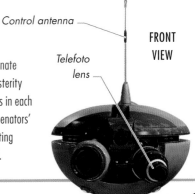

# GALACTIC SENATORS

**THE GALACTIC SENATE** is mired in bureaucracy and rife with corruption. The noble ideas on which it was founded have been chipped away at, as the trappings of high office have attracted greedy frauds over selfless public servants. The few good senators are fighting a losing battle as the Republic's reputation grows more tarnished by the day. Slowly, the Senate splits into two factions: Separatist sympathizers who believe that the only solution is to break up the Republic; and Loyalists who support Supreme Chancellor Palpatine in his efforts to strengthen the government.

Twi'lek head-tails are known as lekku

Bloated features caused by lavish, indulgent lifestyle

**ORN FREE TAA**

**LOYALIST SENATORS**

Elaborate headdress

Three eyes

Opulent, showy outfit

Elegant fabrics

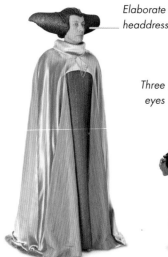

**ISTER PADDIE**

**ASK AAK**

**LEXI DIO**

## THE LOYALIST COMMITTEE

Supreme Chancellor Palpatine establishes the Loyalist Committee to foster support for his own rule. Its members include principled senators, such as Padmé Amidala, but it also attracts corrupt senators who want to protect their own interests. One such individual is Orn Free Taa, the Twi'lek senator for the planet Ryloth. Focused on acquiring riches, rather than working in the interests of his fellow Twi'leks, he represents everything the Separatists say is wrong with the Galactic Senate.

Squid-like beak

Eyes on stalks

Senator Onaconda Farr sides with the Separatists to save his home planet, Rodia, from famine. However, he is a loyalist at heart, and soon renounces his Separatist allies to campaign for peace.

### SEPARATIST SYMPATHIES

Some senators represent corporations rather than planets or systems. The likes of Gume Saam, an Ishi Tib senator for the Techno Union, pretend to uphold Republic values while secretly supporting the Separatist cause.

Koorivar
cranial horn

Aqualish may
have two or
four eyes

SEPARATIST
SENATORS

Quarren
tentacles

Finned
fingers

## SENATORIAL DEFECTORS

Senators whose home planets and systems withdraw from
the Galactic Republic to join the Confederacy of Independent
Systems must stand down from the Galactic Senate. In many
cases, they then take on equivalent roles on the newly formed
Separatist Council. These defections give the Senate's rival body
increased legitimacy in the eyes of the public, as well as the
benefit of many years of political experience.

PASSEL ARGENTE

PO NUDO

TIKKES

MON
MOTHMA

Antique
Chandrilan
headpiece

Daughter of the
powerful Baron
Papanoida

MEMBERS OF THE DELEGATION
OF TWO THOUSAND

MEENA TILLS     GIDDEAN DANU     MALÉ-DEE     FANG-ZAR     TERR TANEEL     CHI EEKWAY PAPANOIDA

## THE DELEGATION OF TWO THOUSAND

Robes of
a senate
representative

Reptilian
Vurk crest

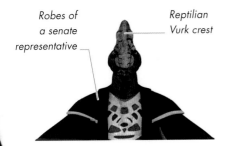

SWEITT CONCORKILL

During the Clone Wars, the Galactic Senate grants Supreme Chancellor
Palpatine emergency powers to combat the Separatist threat. Though many
senators back him completely, others begin to suspect that their leader is
using the conflict to tighten his grip on power. Fearing for the future of
galactic democracy, a delegation of two thousand senators presents the
Chancellor with a petition, insisting that he relinquish his emergency powers.
The main driving forces behind the petition are the Chandrilan senator,
Mon Mothma, and the Alderaanian senator, Bail Organa.

# BAIL ORGANA

**BAIL ORGANA IS** the outspoken senator for the peaceful planet of Alderaan, and is a close ally of Senator Padmé Amidala. During the Separatist crisis, he does his best to avert galactic war. When it proves inevitable, he devotes himself to the relief effort, helping refugees and others civilians affected by the fighting. By the end of the Clone Wars, he is actively campaigning to limit Chancellor Palpatine's powers, but his efforts have little effect.

Outfit is luxurious but not ostentatious

Crest of Alderaan also worn on belt

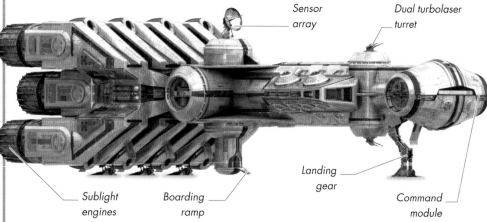

Sensor array

Dual turbolaser turret

Sublight engines

Boarding ramp

Landing gear

Command module

### TANTIVE III

Bail Organa travels onboard a Corellian-built CR70 corvette called the *Tantive III*. It is commanded by Raymus Antilles, a loyal captain who will serve the House of Organa for many years to come.

**BAIL ORGANA'S SENATE IDENTITY PASS**

Organa shares Padmé's disbelief in the Senate chamber as Palpatine declares himself ruler of a new Galactic Empire.

## DATA FILE

> After Padmé Amidala's death, Bail Organa takes possession of the droids R2-D2 and C-3PO.

> Bail's wife is Breha Organa, the Queen of Alderaan. The couple had often spoken about adopting a baby girl before Leia came into their lives.

## FRIEND AND FATHER

When most of the Jedi are wiped out by Order 66, Bail Organa helps Yoda and Obi-Wan Kenobi get to safety aboard the *Tantive III*. However, there is nothing he can do to save his friend Padmé, whom he sees die shortly after giving birth to twins. He promises to raise one of the newborns, Leia, as his own child, and keep her true identity safe from the Empire.

Organa witnesses the attack on the Jedi Temple by Darth Vader and his clone troops from his speeder. He is lucky to escape with his life.

# FREIGHTER TRAMPERS

**FOR HUNDREDS OF YEARS,** Coruscant has attracted workers hoping to make their fortune— or at least a basic living. However, the Separatist crisis has taken its toll on the planet's economy, and now people are being forced to look elsewhere for work. Many cargo ships begin to offer cheap passage off-world, serving economic migrants who feel they have no choice but to abandon the planet that has been their home. Carrying the little they own, they huddle on board these ill-equipped vessels dreaming of a better life. Known as the freighter trampers, they are some of the first victims of what will become the Clone Wars.

*Passenger viewports*

**AA-9 CORUSCANT FREIGHTER**

*Sublight drive*

*Most of the ship is one giant cargo hold*

*Donovian rainmen repair signal towers in all weather conditions*

*Style from the Thousand Moons system*

## SECRET SENATOR

Anakin Skywalker and Senator Padmé Amidala pose as freighter trampers after Padmé is targeted by assassins. They travel on board an AA-9 Coruscant freighter to reach Naboo unnoticed, witnessing firsthand the conditions in which many of the galaxy's inhabitants are forced to live.

*Aqualish waste technician*

### DATA FILE

> When promised work fails to materialize, some trampers find themselves constantly on the move. Over time, their once-pristine work gear becomes more and more battered and improvised.

### TRAMPERS TOGETHER

Freighter trampers come from many different species, and include many talented artisans and technicians. The only thing that unites them is the harsh reality in which they find themselves.

# CAPTAIN TYPHO

**GREGAR TYPHO SERVES AS** Senator Amidala's personal head of security. Just like his uncle, Quarsh Panaka, he is a captain in the Royal Naboo Security Forces, and is fiercely loyal to the former Queen of Naboo. He is at Amidala's side on Coruscant when an assassin tries to murder her, but his security precautions save her life. He remains on Coruscant when the senator returns to Naboo under the protection of Anakin Skywalker, and pledges his service to Padmé's protégé in the Senate: Junior Representative Jar Jar Binks.

Left eye lost in the line of duty

Starfighter pilot's suit

Blaster pistol

Synthetic leather gauntlets for hand-to-hand combat

### SECRET SENATOR
When Senator Amidala travels to Coruscant, Captain Typho insists that she does so disguised as one of his security detail. They travel alongside the senatorial barge as part of its starfighter escort.

### DETONATOR
The Naboo passion for elegance and aesthetics even extends to purely functional objects such as this detonator, which allow the Royal Naboo Security Forces to set off explosives remotely.

## LONG SERVICE
Captain Typho first serves Padmé Amidala during the latter part of her reign as Queen of Naboo. After the outbreak of the Clone Wars, he continues to protect both her and Jar Jar Binks, and helps them to uncover a Separatist cell that is secretly developing a deadly bioweapon on Naboo.

Connection point for optional carry-strap

Activation button

Connection point for optional scope

Extendable antenna

**CR-2 BLASTER**

Power pack in gripstock

**NABOO COMLINK**

Standard-issue military boots

Traction-grip soles

### DATA FILE
> When Typho and Amidala arrive on Coruscant in N-1 starfighters, they are accompanied by Naboo Royal Guards onboard the senator's diplomatic barge.

# PADMÉ'S RETAINERS

**DATA FILE**

> During the Clone Wars, Padmé has a handmaiden called Teckla Minnau, who convinces her to oppose greater military spending.

> As the Clone Wars draw to a close, a handmaiden named Moteé stands alongside Senator Amidala in the Galactic Senate as Palpatine declares himself ruler of a new Galactic Empire.

**AFTER STEPPING DOWN** as Queen to become the senator for Naboo, Padmé Amidala still retains many of the trappings of royalty. As well as traveling in ships that are fully clad in chromium, she also maintains a retinue of handmaidens, who assist her in her day-to-day life and serve as decoy lookalikes to guard against attackers. Though such a lifestyle may at first appear cosseted, it proves to be a vital precaution rather than a privilege as the Republic veers ever closer to all-out war with the breakaway faction known as the Separatists.

*Efficient yet elegant chignon hairstyle*

*Ever watchful gaze*

*Simple gown*

*Belt woven by Naboo artisans*

*Somber colors befit the serious work done in a senator's office*

Dormé is nearly always at Padmé's side, doing everything from keeping her diary to analyzing the body language of Senator Amidala's fellow politicians for subsequent debriefings.

## DORMÉ

Padmé's most devoted retainer serves as an executive assistant, a confidante, and a highly trained bodyguard. She is at Senator Amidala's side when she travels to Coruscant to represent Naboo in the Senate, and stays in the galactic capital to assist Junior Representative Jar Jar Binks in the same role when the senator has to return to Naboo for her own safety.

**AN EYE FOR ROMANCE**
As Padmé's constant companion, Dormé knows the senator very well—sometimes better than Padmé knows herself. Dormé notes Anakin Skywalker's rash words and headstrong nature, but also that Padmé seems drawn to the brash young Jedi apprentice.

## CORDÉ

With tensions running high in the Galactic Republic, Cordé acts as Senator Amidala's decoy when her glistening ship touches down on Coruscant. As she steps out of the diplomatic barge—dressed in the finery of a Naboo senator—she is hit by the full force of an explosive ambush. Mortally wounded, yet devoted to the end, Cordé uses her last few breaths to apologise to the real Amidala for having failed her. Padmé assures her handmaiden that she has done no such thing.

# ZAM WESELL

**AS A CLAWDITE,** Zam Wesell can change her appearance to mimic a range of humanoid forms, giving her a special edge as a hired assassin. Zam learned her trade from an ancient order of warrior-knights named the Mabari on her homeworld, Zolan. Wanting to put her skills to the test, Zam left the order to travel to Denon, where she started her career as a bounty hunter and assassin.

Subdued colors blend into shadows

Natural Clawdite face

Bodysuit stretches to allow shape-shifting

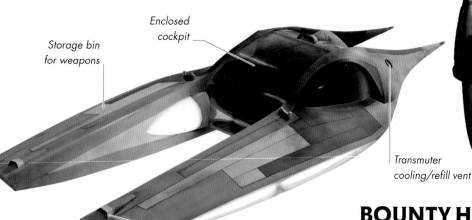

Storage bin for weapons

Enclosed cockpit

Transmuter cooling/refill vent

Forward scanner

## HUNTER'S CRAFT
Built for use on primitive worlds with hostile environments, Zam's Koros-2 airspeeder is completely enclosed, with minimal air intakes and no external thrusters. Rather than using turbojets, the Koros-2 generates thrust through electromagnetism, irradiating the air to ionize it and make it conductive.

## BOUNTY HUNTER
A loner with few close associates, Zam Wesell is typical of bounty hunters. She inhabits a gray zone that extends to both sides of the law. Arrogant and highly skilled, Zam regards bounty hunting as a suitable channel for her superior talent.

Stinger painful but not fatal

Bite delivers lethal nerve poison

## KOUHUN
Zam uses two kouhuns for her senatorial assassination job. Small, deadly arthropods from Indoumodo, kouhuns can evade even tight security and are virtually impossible to trace back to their users. Kouhuns are starved in advance, so they head straight for warm-blooded life forms when released, and use a fast-acting nerve toxin to kill their prey.

Mabari emblem

**CAPE SEAL**

Third-level Mabari fighter markings

Universal key

Blast-energy sink skirt

Shin-guard boots

Boots accept a variety of limb forms

Zam's discipline derives from her Mabari training. She wears Mabari inscriptions and stylized emblems, including a cape seal that is an ancient Mabari artifact.

Cleaning rod

Blaster gas capsule loading port

Igniter pin

Hadrium alloy

Muzzle brake absorbs emitter flash

Electromagnetic pulse barrel

Handle holds power cell

## KYD-21 BLASTER

Although she carries a projectile rifle at Jango Fett's insistence, Zam's primary weapon is a compact, precise KYD-21 pistol. She finds she can hide a pistol more easily when she needs to disguise herself as a non-threatening presence in order to close in on her mark.

ASN-121 ASSASSIN DROID

Embedding prongs

Stabilizing fins

Injector needle

Poison chamber

### SABERDART

Preferring to leave no trace, Zam dislikes projectile weapons. Jango might use a saberdart, which may be silent and highly lethal, but has the potential to lead pursuers back to its source.

Clawdites, or "changelings," evolved on a world inhabited by warring humanoid subspecies. They developed the ability to mimic the appearance of other species in order to blend in and not be killed. As a changeling dies, its ability to shape-shift fades and it returns to a natural Clawdite configuration.

## HIGH STAKES

Zam knows that in accepting a risky assignment from Jango Fett, she is in danger of being used as an expendable pawn. Such are the risks of the high-stakes trade in death, and Zam is prepared to take them… though she will find that she is not equipped to outrun two Jedi.

Visor cuts glare

Light helmet

Comlink system

Scrambled direct comlink pickup to Jango Fett

Flexible armorweave jerkin

Insulated, elasticized gloves

Simple optical scope

Power amplifier circuitry

Recoil-damping stock

Under intense Jedi interrogation, Zam begins to reveal her employer, until she is silenced by an assassin.

KISTEER 1284 PROJECTILE RIFLE

# JANGO FETT

**JANGO FETT IS** widely regarded as the best bounty hunter in the galaxy. He is chosen by the Sith to be the genetic template for an army of clones, and now lives in the cloning facility on the planet Kamino. Here, Fett trains his duplicates in emulation of his physical abilities—but with no hint of his independence.

Energy-shield generator

Variable-opacity viewscreen

Cockpit reorients according to flight mode

Repulsorlift wings for planetary take-off

Laser cannon

Jetpack missile can launch a warhead or a grapple

Targeting rangefinder

Vibroblades deploy from vambrace

## SLAVE I

Jango Fett pilots a modified *Firespray-31*-class patrol and attack craft known as *Slave I*. It boasts a devastating array of weapons, including concussion missiles and seismic charges.

Z-6 Jetpack

WETSAR-34 blaster pistol

ZX miniature flame projector

Boarding ramp

Twin blaster cannon

Whipcord thrower

Mandalorian armor

Thruster

After two attempts on Padmé Amidala's life, the trail of evidence leads Obi-Wan Kenobi to Kamino. He faces Jango Fett in battle, but is unable to stop the expert combatant from getting away.

Utility pouches

Pistol holster

Waterproof flight suit

## ASSASSIN'S ARMOR

While most Mandalorian armor is made from beskar, Jango Fett's is fashioned from a durasteel alloy. In most other respects, however, it conforms to the battle gear designed hundreds of years ago to combat Force users during the Mandalorian-Jedi War. Its key features include wrist-mounted vambraces packed full of powerful weaponry, and a T-shaped, macrobinocular viewplate. The latter goes on to inspire the look of the Galactic Republic's clone trooper armor.

Magnetized boots

Rocket darts

# WESTAR-34 BLASTER PISTOL

Fett carries a pair of expensive blaster pistols that are made to his specification by the arms manufacturer WESTAR. Built from a heat-resistant dallorian alloy, they can emit continuous fire, reaching temperatures that would melt almost any other blaster. Their hollowed-through handles make them lighter to carry and fractionally faster to draw.

*Power cell*

*Trigger*

*Shaped handle for steady grip*

*Overload flash dissipator port*

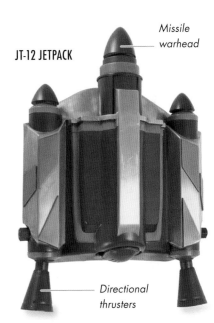

Fett deploys his Z-6 jetpack during his fight with Obi-Wan Kenobi on Kamino. The planet's constant rain does not affect its performance, but a sudden impact with the ground causes the pack to detach and fly out of control.

## LIKE FATHER, LIKE SON

In exchange for his role in creating a modified clone army, Fett demands 20 million credits and a single, unaltered clone that he can raise as his son. He names the boy Boba, and trains him to share his bounty hunting skills. Boba learns to hate the Jedi at a young age when his father is killed by Mace Windu, and he grows up determined to have his revenge.

*Professional fighting stance*

*Boba will grow up to look exactly like his father.*

*Utilitarian garb supplied by the Kaminoans*

### JT-12 JETPACK

*Missile warhead*

*Directional thrusters*

**FINAL FIGHT**
Jedi Master Mace Windu beheads Jango Fett with his lightsaber in battle on the planet Geonosis.

### LOCK BREAKER

*Ultrasonic emitter*

**FIELD SECURITY OVERLOADER**

*Activator*

*Signal projector*

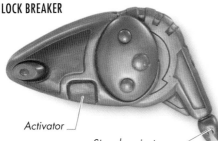

As well as an array of advanced weaponry, Jango relies on a number of gadgets that help him gain access to his targets.

### JANGO'S JETPACKS

Jetpacks are a common feature of Mandalorian battle dress, giving the wearer an advantage of speed and height in battle. Jango switches to the JT-12 jetpack after his favored Z-6 is destroyed in battle with Obi-Wan Kenobi.

*Homing missile*

*Targeting rangefinder*

*Fuel tank*

*Magnetized back*

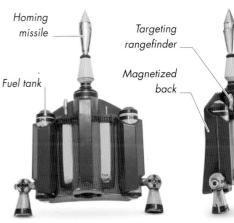

Z-6 JETPACK

SIDE VIEW

## DATA FILE

> When Jango Fett is at the controls of *Slave I*, he swaps his helmet for a comlink headset.

> Fett claims to have been born on the Mandalorian planet Concord Dawn, but his true history remains shrouded in mystery—which is how he likes it.

*Waterproof shinguards*

# KAMINOANS

**BEYOND THE OUTER RIM** territories lies the water-covered world of Kamino. Purged from the Jedi Archives so no one would know of its existence, this planet is home to the native Kaminoans, and the army of human clones they have secretly created for the mysterious Jedi Sifo-Dyas. Obi-Wan Kenobi's investigation into an assassination attempt on Padmé Amidala leads him to Kamino, and before long the Galactic Republic is taking delivery of the new military force it didn't know it had.

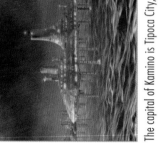

The capital of Kamino is Tipoca City, where the planet's most advanced cloning facilities are located. It is here that the Republic's clone army is created and trained for combat, and the city becomes an important military base during the Clone Wars.

Kaminoan cities are highly advanced structures that rise above the planet's oceans on stilts. With the exception of landing bays, their huge interlinked domes are fully enclosed, to protect against harsh weather conditions.

**KO SAI**

*Elongated neck bones allow for limited flexibility*

*Female Kaminoans have no headcrest*

*Pendant hangs from head-crescent jewelry*

*Long neck made up of seven bones*

*Neck wrap forms part of stylish civilian outfit*

**TAUN WE**

*Scientist's garb*

*Long, dextrous fingers*

*Dome shape withstands constant rain and wind*

*Static discharge towers protect the city during electrical storms*

*Communications tower*

*Slender pylons allow waves to pass with minimal impact*

*Pylons descend into continental shelf*

**TIPOCA CITY (SECTION)**

*Headcrest found on males only*

*Kaminoan eyes can see ultra-violet light*

## A WARM WELCOME

When Obi-Wan Kenobi arrives on Kamino, he is met by Taun We, the administrative aide to her planet's prime minister. She has long been expecting a Jedi visitor to check on the progress of the clone army, and does her best to see to everything that such an important customer could want. Together, they tour the cloning facility, where Kenobi sees clones in various stages of development being monitored by scientists such as supervisor Ko Sai.

Obi-Wan Kenobi is surprised when Taun We says she was expecting his visit.

*Small, hoof-like feet*

*Long, powerful tail*

*Saddle rig and reins*

*Harness*

## AIWHAS

The Kaminoans use huge, winged animals called aiwhas to travel safely through their planet's electrical storms. These impressive creatures can swim and fly, and have been domesticated using the same technology that makes clone troopers so obedient.

*Wings serve as fins in water*

The light-filled chamber where Lama Su meets Obi-Wan Kenobi is the height of Kamino style.

## LAMA SU

The prime minister of Kamino, Lama Su, is very proud of the clone army his people have created for the Galactic Republic. He has no compassion for the individual clones, which he views as nothing more than a satisfactory product. Su was personally commissioned by Sifo-Dyas to create the clone army, and he is eager to show off the results when Obi-Wan Kenobi arrives on Kamino.

*Prime ministerial badge of office*

*Three digits on each hand*

### DATA FILE

> During the Clone Wars, Kamino accepts a place on the Galactic Senate, sending Halle Burtoni to Coruscant as its representative.

> As well as prime minister Lama Su, Kamino's system of government also includes a Ruling Council based in the main hub of Tipoca City.

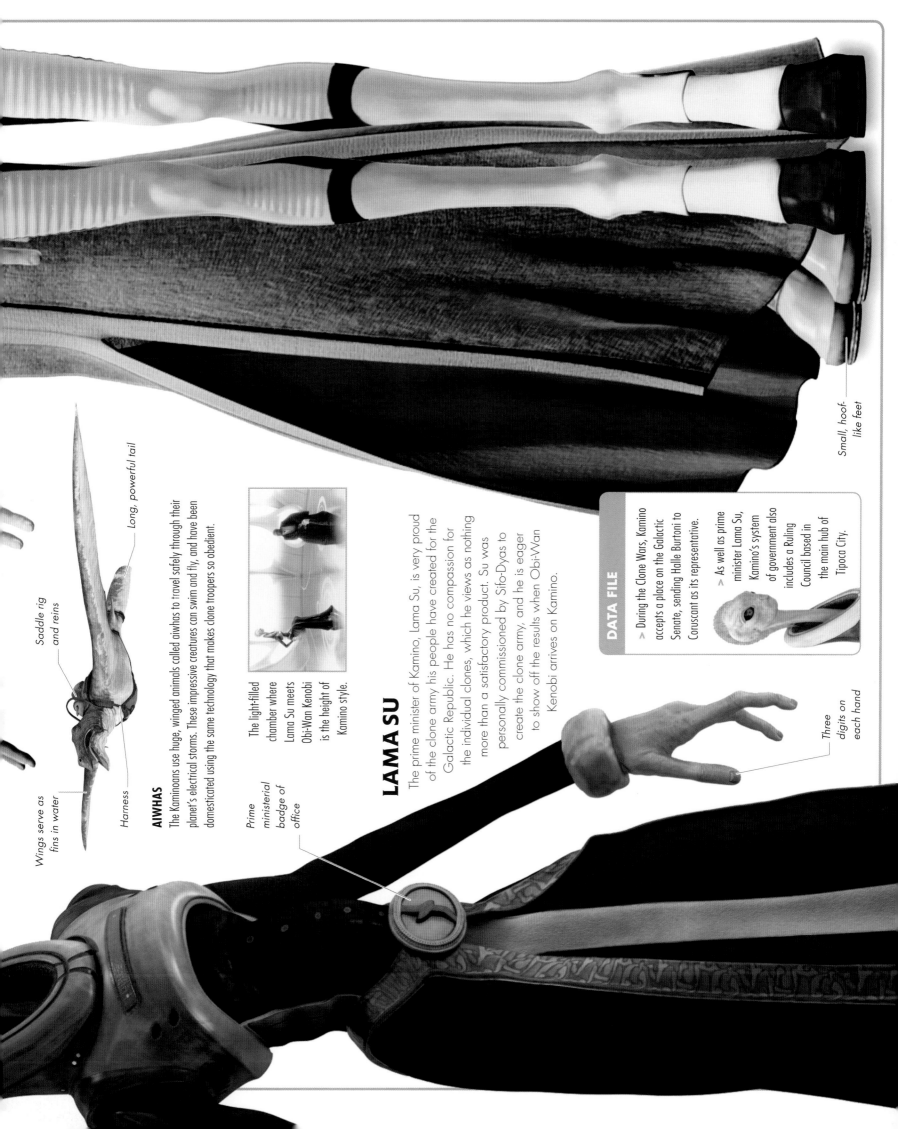

# CLONE TRAINING

**THE CLONES ARE SUPERIOR** to battle droids, owing to their capacity for creative thought. Nevertheless, they are raised to achieve machine-like standards of performance and efficiency. They are genetically modified to retain all the tenacity of their "father," Jango Fett, while also being totally obedient when given orders. This makes them ideal soldiers in the event of a war. Any unwanted characteristics still remaining when a clone emerges from his embryonic development are drilled out in rigorous training. Each clone has a control chip inside his brain, which inhibits volatile behavior. However, it is also the means by which Supreme Chancellor Palpatine will one day compel the clones to obey Clone Protocol 66—the order to destroy all Jedi.

Every clone starts out as an artificially created embryo in the "Egg Lab"—a vast network of maturation chambers within the cloning facility in Kamino's Tipoca City. Visitors to the complex, such as Obi-Wan Kenobi, pass along sealed walkways so as not to contaminate the germ-free environment.

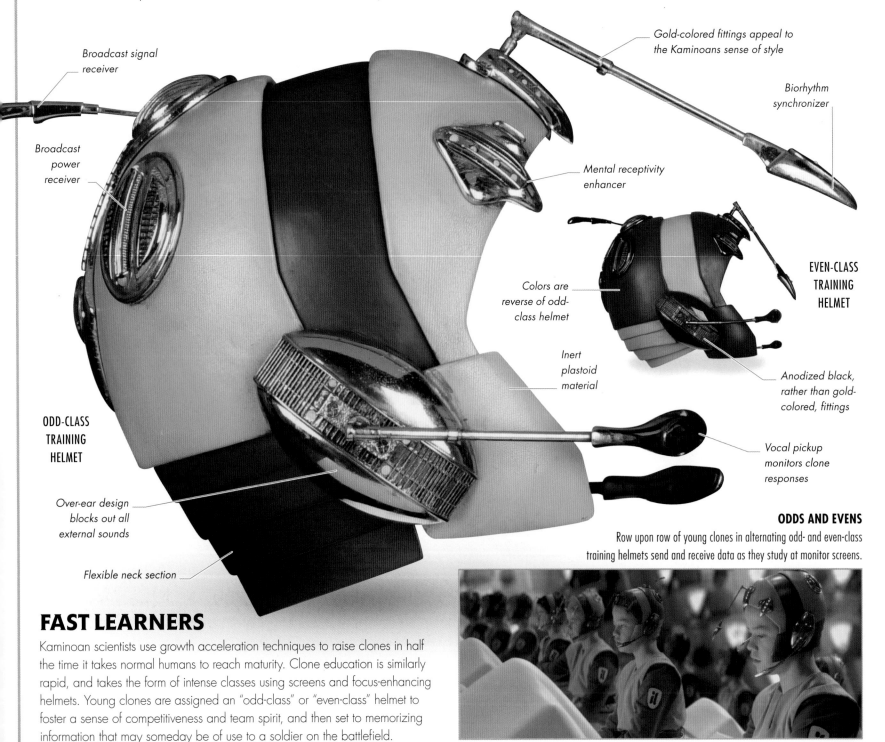

Broadcast signal receiver

Broadcast power receiver

Gold-colored fittings appeal to the Kaminoans sense of style

Biorhythm synchronizer

Mental receptivity enhancer

Colors are reverse of odd-class helmet

**EVEN-CLASS TRAINING HELMET**

Inert plastoid material

Anodized black, rather than gold-colored, fittings

**ODD-CLASS TRAINING HELMET**

Vocal pickup monitors clone responses

Over-ear design blocks out all external sounds

Flexible neck section

**ODDS AND EVENS**

Row upon row of young clones in alternating odd- and even-class training helmets send and receive data as they study at monitor screens.

## FAST LEARNERS

Kaminoan scientists use growth acceleration techniques to raise clones in half the time it takes normal humans to reach maturity. Clone education is similarly rapid, and takes the form of intense classes using screens and focus-enhancing helmets. Young clones are assigned an "odd-class" or "even-class" helmet to foster a sense of competitiveness and team spirit, and then set to memorizing information that may someday be of use to a soldier on the battlefield.

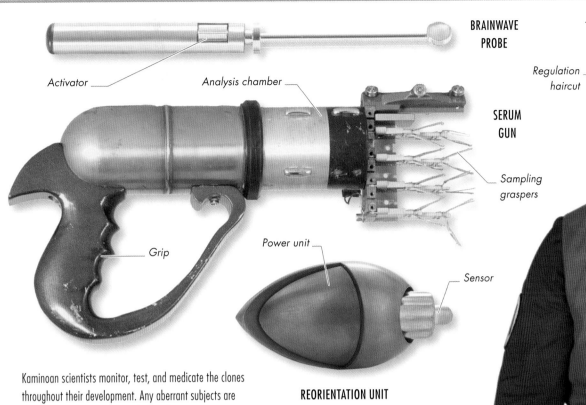

**BRAINWAVE PROBE**

Activator

Analysis chamber

SERUM GUN

Sampling graspers

Grip

Power unit

Sensor

**REORIENTATION UNIT**

Kaminoan scientists monitor, test, and medicate the clones throughout their development. Any aberrant subjects are swiftly reconditioned for complete conformity.

**KAMINOAN EMBLEM WORN BY ALL CLONES**

Regulation haircut

Bone structure is identical to that of Jango Fett, yet 10-year-old clone is more fresh-faced.

Simple, all-purpose outfit

# DEVELOPED CLONE

After just 10 standard years, a clone is a highly trained adult soldier, ready to go into battle for the Republic. Though every clone has the same physique and facial features, each one perceives himself as an individual, and will only grow more distinct once he leaves the training environment. Few clones will retain the regulation haircut worn on Kamino, as each strives to assert his identity within the limited parameters afforded him.

Every clone has an ID tag implanted in his left wrist.

Practical waterproof boots

Clones live and train together in close quarters, preparing them for life in barracks once they leave Kamino. They never become disoriented by the sight of hundreds of faces identical to their own, as it is the only human face that any of them has ever seen. Even Jango Fett, the bounty hunter who supervises their training, is their exact double.

## DATA FILE

> Once they reach adulthood, clones spend much of their time in full clone trooper armor, taking part in combat simulations such as the Citadel Challenge.

> Malformed clones are rare but not unheard of. One defective clone known as 99 was assigned to janitorial work on Kamino. Four other mutated clones, whose abnormalities made them especially effective soldiers, make up the specialist squad Clone Force 99, which is named in honor of the janitor.

# CLONE TROOPER EQUIPMENT

Nonconducting stock

Pressurized gas cartridge

Gas cartridge safety lock

Magnatomic adhesion grip

**CLONE TROOPERS LEAVE** the training facility on Kamino fully equipped with armor, weaponry, and the skills to use them properly. While the armor is custom-designed by the Kaminoans themselves—with input from the bounty hunter Jango Fett—most other equipment is bought from specialist arms manufacturers, such as BlasTech Industries. Far from being just an imposing sight, the complete clone trooper ensemble is an advanced technological marvel, packed full of invisible gadgetry.

Gas refill valve

Push-button trigger

Charge magazine

Extendable stock

## DC-15A BLASTER

The DC-15A blaster features a fold-away stock and weighs just 4.15 kg (9 lbs). It has the same blast capacity as its larger cousin—the DC-15 blaster rifle—but is only effective at a shorter range. It can be set to fire a lethal plasma bolt or lower energy stun charges.

Power pack

Connector pins

## CHARGE MAGAZINE

Power-charge magazines plug into the side of blasters and supply them with the energy they need to create charged plasma from ionized gas.

Comlink antenna in crest

T-shaped viewplate inspired by Mandalorian armor designs

Shoulder bell

Breathing filter

## PHASE I ARMOR

The first clone troopers wear armor made up of 20 form-fitting plates sealed to a pressurized body glove. Magnatomic gription panels hold the armor in place, and the body glove protects against extreme heat and cold. Although the armor is designed for flexibility and made from a lightweight plastoid-alloy composite, Kaminoan armorsmiths' limited knowledge of human ergonomics means it is far from comfortable. As a result of this and other failings, what comes to be known as Phase I clone trooper armor is gradually replaced by a Phase II update during the Clone Wars.

Suit environment controls

Elbow plate

Utility belt carries spare magazines and assault equipment

Knee plate

All clone troopers wear the same size boots and armor

## PHASE I HELMET

Technology found inside every Phase I clone trooper's helmet includes a life-support system, a comlink, a display screen built into the viewplate, and a tracking device to monitor troop movements.

High-traction boots

Armored bootstrap

Gas release valve

Igniter

Power setting adjustor

Electromagnets

Accelerator

Collimating tube

Flip-up optical sight

Ignition chamber

Expansion chamber

Magnetic pulse stabilizers

DC-15 (CUTAWAY)

Radiator fins

Stowed sniper scope doubles as grip

Power amplifier circuitry

Heat-exchange element in muzzle

## DC–15 BLASTER RIFLE

Like all blaster weapons, the DC-15 blaster rifle converts gas into highly charged plasma bolts. A relatively small amount of pressurized gas can generate 500 blasts, freeing troopers from the need to carry heavy reserves of ammunition. However, using the rifle on its highest power setting results in far fewer shots. Built by BlasTech Industries, the DC-15 is the standard-issue weapon for troopers throughout the Clone Wars.

Weighted stock improves rifle balance

Gas pressure indicator

Charge magazine

DC-15 (FULL PROFILE)

### RANK COLORS

All clone trooper helmets are equipped with displays that identify fellow clones, including their rank information. Colored armor helps Jedi generals and other allied forces confirm the command structure.

Each commander leads 16 captains

Each captain commands four lieutenants

Each lieutenant leads four sergeants

Each sergeant commands a squad of nine troopers

COMMANDER

CAPTAIN

LIEUTENANT

SERGEANT

# CLONE SPECIALISTS

**AS THE CLONE WARS** become more entrenched, the need for specialization among clone troopers becomes increasingly apparent. Though a "one-size-fits-all" approach can provide the Republic with a readymade infantry, it cannot hope to contend with the dynamic strategies of the Separatists and the tactical demands of a thousand different worlds. By the end of the conflict, there are many mission-specific clone forces, which go on to form the basis of the Empire's stormtrooper specialisms.

Standard Phase II clone trooper armor, but with red markings

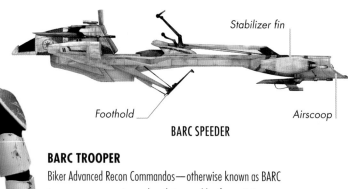

Stabilizer fin

Foothold

Airscoop

**BARC SPEEDER**

### BARC TROOPER
Biker Advanced Recon Commandos—otherwise known as BARC troopers—are expert speeder pilots, capable of negotiating any terrain at more than 500 kph (310 mph). Their helmets are designed to focus attention forward, shielding them from distractions.

Symbol of the 91st Mobile Reconnaissance Corps

Bodysuit environment controls

Armor tarnished by debris collisions

## SHOCK TROOPER
Far away from the cloning facilities on Kamino, shock troopers are secretly raised on the galactic capital, Coruscant. They are trained as an urban security force, specializing in crowd control and close-quarters combat. Replacing the Senate Guard that was responsible for protecting government buildings and officials, they are a symbol of Supreme Chancellor Palpatine's growing executive power.

Macrobinoculars built in to helmet

Camouflaged armor

Survival gear

### DATA FILE

> Other clone specialists include flame troopers, gunners, and medics.

> Shock troopers serve as Emperor Palpatine's personal guard during the early days of the Empire.

### CLONE SCOUT
Clone scout troopers are trained in reconnaissance, and small groups are used to survey territory ahead of larger troop movements. Their survival skills also make them suited to combat in wilderness conditions, where supplies and reinforcements are not so readily available as in urban environments.

DC-15 blaster rifle

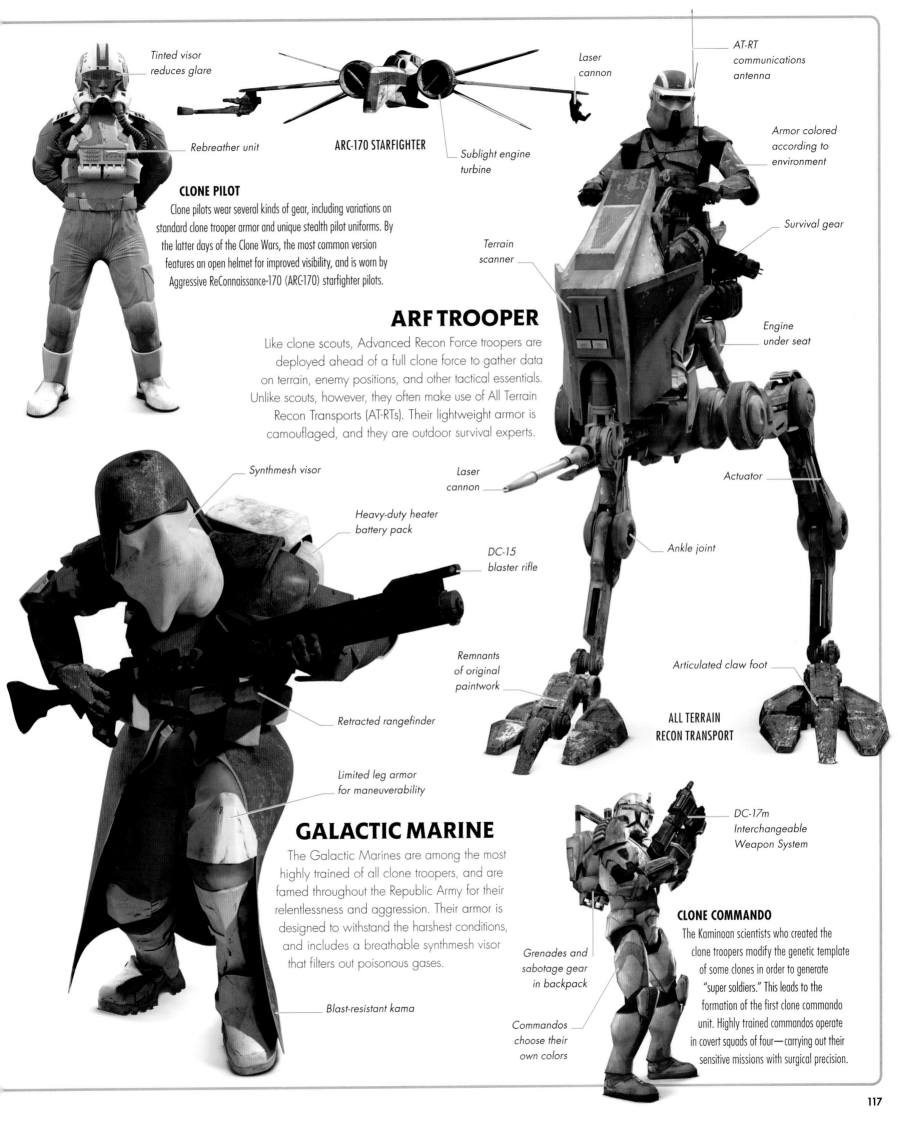

Tinted visor
reduces glare

Rebreather unit

## ARC-170 STARFIGHTER

Laser
cannon

Sublight engine
turbine

## CLONE PILOT

Clone pilots wear several kinds of gear, including variations on standard clone trooper armor and unique stealth pilot uniforms. By the latter days of the Clone Wars, the most common version features an open helmet for improved visibility, and is worn by Aggressive ReConnaissance-170 (ARC-170) starfighter pilots.

AT-RT
communications
antenna

Armor colored
according to
environment

Survival gear

Terrain
scanner

## ARF TROOPER

Like clone scouts, Advanced Recon Force troopers are deployed ahead of a full clone force to gather data on terrain, enemy positions, and other tactical essentials. Unlike scouts, however, they often make use of All Terrain Recon Transports (AT-RTs). Their lightweight armor is camouflaged, and they are outdoor survival experts.

Engine
under seat

Laser
cannon

Actuator

Synthmesh visor

Heavy-duty heater
battery pack

DC-15
blaster rifle

Ankle joint

Remnants
of original
paintwork

Articulated claw foot

Retracted rangefinder

## ALL TERRAIN
RECON TRANSPORT

Limited leg armor
for maneuverability

## GALACTIC MARINE

The Galactic Marines are among the most highly trained of all clone troopers, and are famed throughout the Republic Army for their relentlessness and aggression. Their armor is designed to withstand the harshest conditions, and includes a breathable synthmesh visor that filters out poisonous gases.

Blast-resistant kama

DC-17m
Interchangeable
Weapon System

Grenades and
sabotage gear
in backpack

## CLONE COMMANDO

The Kaminoan scientists who created the clone troopers modify the genetic template of some clones in order to generate "super soldiers." This leads to the formation of the first clone commando unit. Highly trained commandos operate in covert squads of four—carrying out their sensitive missions with surgical precision.

Commandos
choose their
own colors

# ORDER 66

**THE OBEDIENCE OF** the millions of clone troopers is unquestioning—and unquestioned. What would happen if their fierce loyalty was directed against the Jedi is a scenario too terrifying to contemplate. However, that is the reality that the Jedi are faced with when Supreme Chancellor Palpatine (a.k.a. the Sith Lord Darth Sidious) issues Order 66. This activates an obscure protocol in every clone trooper's brain, causing them to see the Jedi as traitors that must be eliminated.

Supreme Chancellor Palpatine issues Order 66 in the form of a holographic message, which is received by clone troopers on handheld devices or via the projectors in their craft. Troopers without access to a holo-projector—such as those piloting BARC speeders—are notified of the order by means of an audio message in their helmet comlinks.

**SALEUCAMI**
Clone troopers led by Commander Neyo gun down Jedi Master Stass Allie as they travel with her on BARC speeders.

## THE JEDI PURGE

Clone Protocol 66 is built into the bio-chip that every clone trooper carries inside him. It was placed there by the Sith, who secretly guided the creation of the clone army from the beginning. When it is activated, the clones obey immediately, and nearly all the Jedi are wiped out. Now, nothing stands in the way of a new Sith Empire.

## CORUSCANT

Darth Sidious' new apprentice, Darth Vader, leads a detachment of the 501st Legion to carry out Order 66 in the galactic capital, Coruscant. The Jedi Temple is left in flames, and its signal beacon is activated as a trap to lure other Jedi back to the planet.

Phase II clone helmets lack the sweeping fin of Phase I models

Comlink

Polarized viewplate

Armor has special anti-blaster coating

DC-15A blaster

Black bodyglove visible between armor plates

Phase II clone trooper armor is designed to be lighter and more flexible than the Phase I design

**PHASE II CLONE TROOPER**

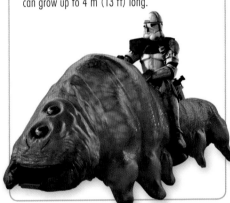

## FELUCIA

Twi'lek Jedi Master Aayla Secura is leading the 327th Star Corps into battle on Felucia when her clone commander, Bly, receives Order 66. Though he had fought alongside Secura many times—with the Jedi Master saving his life on at least one occasion—he obeys his programming without question.

### DATA FILE

> On Felucia, clone troopers use the native Gelagrubs as mounts. The 10-legged creatures can grow up to 4 m (13 ft) long.

CLONE COMMANDER BLY

## CATO NEIMOIDIA

Jedi Master Plo Koon has just led his clone troops to victory in the Battle of Cato Neimoidia when they turn on him. He is killed when his wingmen shoot down his ARC-170 starfighter.

Breath filter

Visor

CLONE COMMANDER CODY

212th Attack Battalion colors

## UTAPAU

The Battle of Utapau should be a great victory for long-time comrades Commander Cody and Jedi Master Obi-Wan Kenobi—but the high-ranking clone receives Order 66 in the midst of the fighting. He orders an attack on Kenobi with an immense AT-TE blast, and sends probes to check that he is dead. In fact, the wily Jedi is one of the few to survive.

## MYGEETO

Ki-Adi-Mundi, a Cerean Jedi Master, has time to ignite his lightsaber when his squad of clone marines begin fire on him. But he cannot hope to survive a close-quarters onslaught by some of the Republic's most highly trained clones.

## YODA IN EXILE

Jedi Master Yoda senses the deaths of his fellow Jedi, and is alert to the change in his own clone troops when it comes. He swiftly counters their attack and escapes into exile with help from his Wookiee friends.

119

# REPUBLIC WARCRAFT

**THE CLONERS OF KAMINO** didn't just create an army of soldiers for the Republic, they also equipped that army with vehicles and warships. When Yoda arrives on Kamino, the clones are already trained in tactics for their use, and are ready to go. They race off to Geonosis to rescue the captive Jedi and strike at Count Dooku's forces which they find arrayed for battle on the planet's badlands.

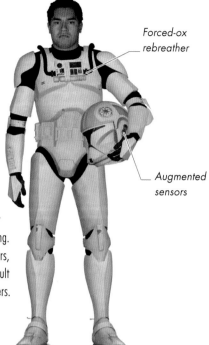

### CLONE PILOT
Clones with particularly good reflexes and spatial awareness are spotted early and diverted into pilot training. Pilot cadets drill in simulators, learning to fly gunships, assault shuttles, and starfighters.

*Forced-ox rebreather*

*Augmented sensors*

In the dusty arena on Geonosis, the Jedi face annihilation at the hands of Dooku's droids. Fortunately, help arrives just in time, as gunships swoop into the arena with cannons blazing.

*Missile launcher*

*Heat-sink/ radiator*

*Co-pilot/gunner*

*Pilot's seat*

*Terrain-sensor housing*

*Bow laser cannons*

*Armature*

*Main hold door*

*Ball turret cannons swing out from the main hold during battle.*

## ASSAULT GUNSHIPS

Gunships are formally known as Low-Altitude Assault Transports/infantry (LAAT/i). At the Battle of Geonosis, they serve the Republic by carrying clone troopers into battle. They also act as effective weapons platforms in their own right, raking ground vehicles and forces with cannons, missiles, and rockets. Clone platoons know their lives depend on their "larties" and regard them with great affection, often giving them nicknames and decorating their noses.

*Missile-belt housing*

*AT-TE in transit*

### AT-TE CARRIER
This variant model of the gunship, the LAAT/c, delivers AT-TE walkers to the battlefield.

# SPHA-TS

These 12-legged walkers follow AT-TEs and gunships on Geonosis, allowing clones to hold ground already seized by the more mobile vehicles in the lead. Formally known as Self-Propelled Heavy Artillery-Turbolasers, SPHA-Ts deploy from *Acclamator*-class assault ships and march slowly but steadily to designated coordinates on the battlefield.

Flashback suppressor

Power converters

Turbolaser firing tip

Command deck

Counterweight

Each foot has terrain sensor computer

Bow fenders

SPHA-T

The Republic deployment begins outside the arena, with gunships and AT-TEs leading the attack. The fight soon spreads across the hills and desert flatlands. As Trade Federation core ships try to escape into orbit, clusters of SPHA-Ts use their turbolasers to bring them crashing back down.

## AT-TE WALKER

Six legs enable these heavily armed and thickly armored walkers to march and climb over uneven terrain. They are armed with guns at the front and rear, making them resistant to close attacks. Each AT-TE carries two squads of clone troopers to confront the droid army.

Conductive armor spreads heat

Flexible midsection

Aft turret cannon

Mass-driver cannon barrel

Rotating servometer disks

AT-TE WALKER

Portside wing turret

On Geonosis, the AT-TEs roll out as they have in countless simulations. But for the clones of the new army, this is no simulation—this is the real thing.

## INVASION FORCE

*Acclamator*-class assault ships are "armies in a box," unloading troops and vehicles with speed and precision. They are also powerful warships in their own right, capable of orbital bombardments of worlds.

Bridge

Missile launch tubes

Point-defense cannons

ASSAULT SHIP

## DATA FILE

> The Republic deployment consists of 1,600 gunships, 400 cargo gunships, 2,160 AT-TEs, 100 SPHA-Ts, and 12 Acclamator assault ships.

> In all, 192,000 clone troopers deploy on Geonosis, divided into two battle armies.

Comm antenna

# GEONOSIANS

**THE GREAT HIVE COLONIES** of Geonosis teem beneath the planet's surface and extend upward from its barren landscape like strange towers. The quasi-insectoid Geonosians live in a completely caste-segregated society. The arrogant upper class rules with savage authority, while the masses work in great swarms at large-scale industrial operations. Workers are conditioned to loathe the thought of separation from the hive and its system of complete control. The Geonosian aristocrats' ability to harness the populace for harsh industrial work has made Geonosis a very profitable society for its rulers. The planet becomes known for its huge battle droid foundries, which are supplied with raw materials from the metal-rich asteroid belt surrounding the planet.

Geonosian art and furniture mix blade-like forms, reflecting the violence of the hives, with rounded shapes drawn from the natural world. Outlanders vary in their reactions to Geonosian creations. Some find them beautiful, while others are disturbed by their alien aesthetic.

Arm rest designed for Geonosian bodies

Image-casting matrix

**PROJECTOR**  **COMMAND CHAIR**

Spider emblem of office

Wings not used after youth

Bracelets represent number of prime hives under Poggle's control

Exoskeletal flexibility joint

Toe structure allows Geonosians to cling to rock crags

Command staff

Sharpened tip used to prod inferiors

Geonosian society exists to benefit its upper caste, who thinks nothing of forcing thousands to labor for its whims. The waste created by the phidna parasites is mixed with rock paste, and is used to create spectacular architecture to please rulers. Forms once built by instinct have been refined into fascinating, spire-like structures.

## POGGLE THE LESSER

The Stalgasin hive colony ruled by Archduke Poggle the Lesser controls all the major hives on Geonosis. Poggle negotiates with off-world parties and coordinates widespread planetary hive efforts for the largest industrial projects ever undertaken on Geonosis—the building of colossal numbers of battle droids for the Separatists. The tremendous income from these projects secures Poggle's power, but he may not have complete control—there are rumors of a secret queen of the hive. The infighting rife in Geonosian society usually makes clients reluctant to place large orders.

### SUN FAC

Poggle's chief lieutenant, Sun Fac, ensures that his master's will is done throughout Geonosis. Sun Fac is unusually intelligent and creative for a Geonosian, which makes him adept at playing whatever role will best suit the needs of the moment. He may be a sympathetic listener or a heartless executioner, depending on which will increase productivity.

# GEONOSIAN SOLDIER DRONE

Geonosian soldier drones reach adulthood rapidly, which means they can be ready for combat at an age of only six standard years. Soldier drones are biologically adapted for a warrior life. Minor bodily specializations occur among all Geonosian drone castes, but only soldiers have functional wings. The drones are conditioned to act en masse, with a fearless and stubborn mentality. They make good defenders and strong fighters against brute beast opponents, but they lack the stategic capabilities to successfully face intelligent enemies in the field.

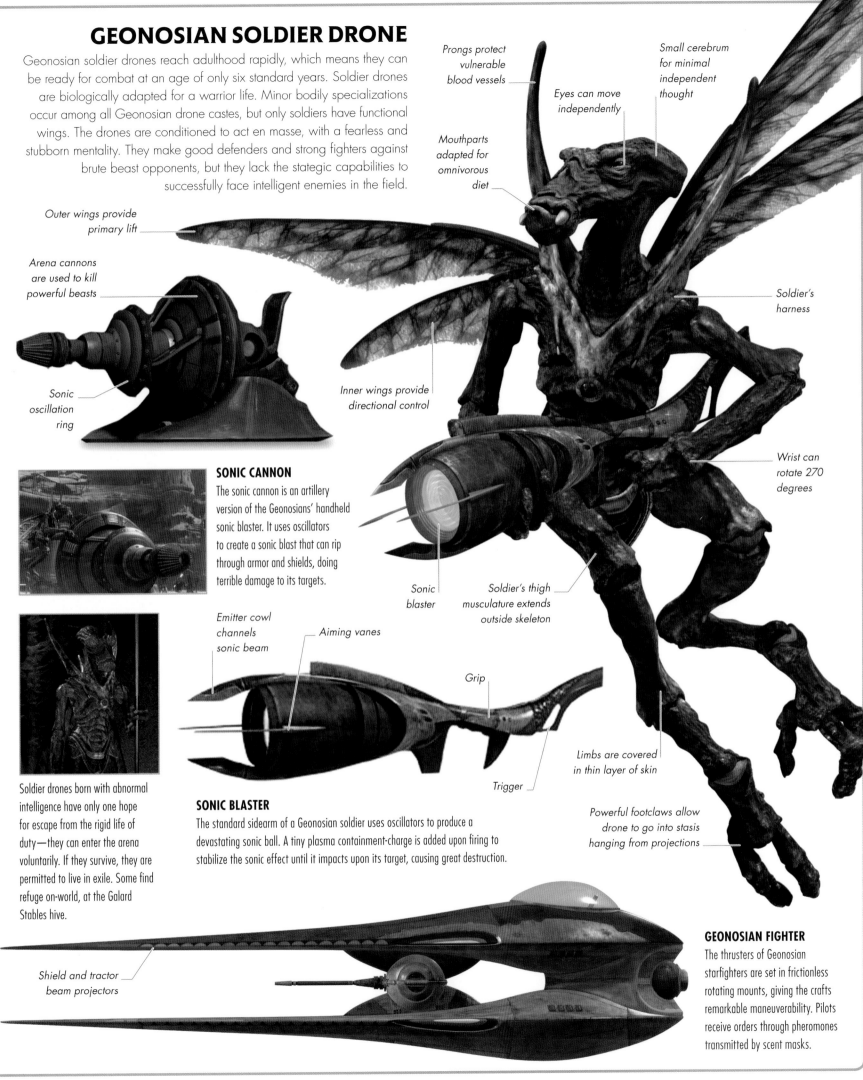

Prongs protect vulnerable blood vessels

Eyes can move independently

Small cerebrum for minimal independent thought

Mouthparts adapted for omnivorous diet

Soldier's harness

Outer wings provide primary lift

Arena cannons are used to kill powerful beasts

Inner wings provide directional control

Wrist can rotate 270 degrees

Sonic oscillation ring

## SONIC CANNON

The sonic cannon is an artillery version of the Geonosians' handheld sonic blaster. It uses oscillators to create a sonic blast that can rip through armor and shields, doing terrible damage to its targets.

Sonic blaster

Soldier's thigh musculature extends outside skeleton

Emitter cowl channels sonic beam

Aiming vanes

Grip

Soldier drones born with abnormal intelligence have only one hope for escape from the rigid life of duty—they can enter the arena voluntarily. If they survive, they are permitted to live in exile. Some find refuge on-world, at the Galard Stables hive.

Limbs are covered in thin layer of skin

Trigger

## SONIC BLASTER

The standard sidearm of a Geonosian soldier uses oscillators to produce a devastating sonic ball. A tiny plasma containment-charge is added upon firing to stabilize the sonic effect until it impacts upon its target, causing great destruction.

Powerful footclaws allow drone to go into stasis hanging from projections

## GEONOSIAN FIGHTER

The thrusters of Geonosian starfighters are set in frictionless rotating mounts, giving the crafts remarkable maneuverability. Pilots receive orders through pheromones transmitted by scent masks.

Shield and tractor beam projectors

# ARENA BEASTS

**CONDEMNED PRISONERS AND GLADIATORS** face a terrifying array of monsters in the Geonosian arena beast-battles or "venations." Common criminals are strung up or let loose with the beasts, which are released from underground hive pens. Many of these creatures behave in predictably gruesome ways, and some are trained by their keepers to maximize their more hideous behaviors. The most crowd-pleasing spectacle is saved for last, when the rarest beasts from far-flung star systems are released into the arena to savage criminals deserving of special attention.

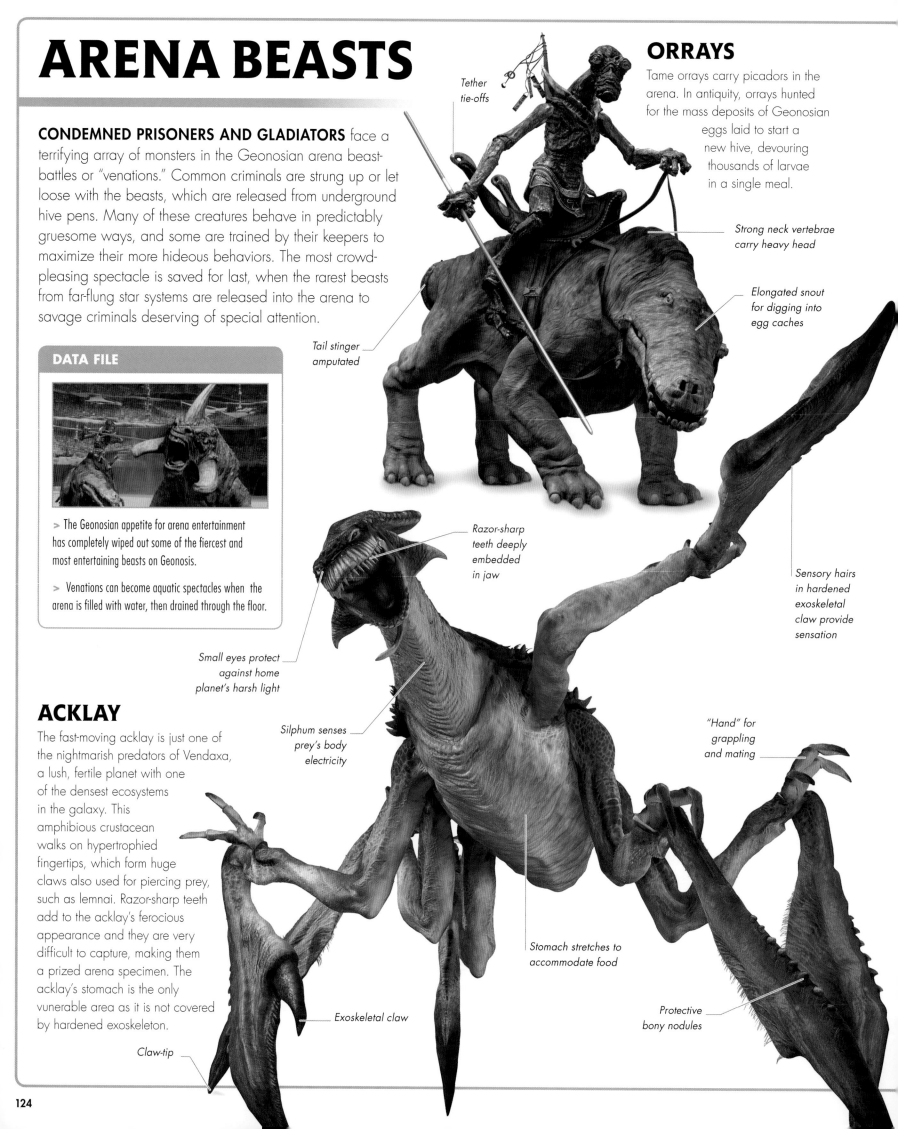
## ORRAYS

Tame orrays carry picadors in the arena. In antiquity, orrays hunted for the mass deposits of Geonosian eggs laid to start a new hive, devouring thousands of larvae in a single meal.

Tether tie-offs

Strong neck vertebrae carry heavy head

Elongated snout for digging into egg caches

Tail stinger amputated

Razor-sharp teeth deeply embedded in jaw

Sensory hairs in hardened exoskeletal claw provide sensation

Small eyes protect against home planet's harsh light

Silphum senses prey's body electricity

"Hand" for grappling and mating

## ACKLAY

The fast-moving acklay is just one of the nightmarish predators of Vendaxa, a lush, fertile planet with one of the densest ecosystems in the galaxy. This amphibious crustacean walks on hypertrophied fingertips, which form huge claws also used for piercing prey, such as lemnai. Razor-sharp teeth add to the acklay's ferocious appearance and they are very difficult to capture, making them a prized arena specimen. The acklay's stomach is the only vunerable area as it is not covered by hardened exoskeleton.

Stomach stretches to accommodate food

Exoskeletal claw

Protective bony nodules

Claw-tip

124

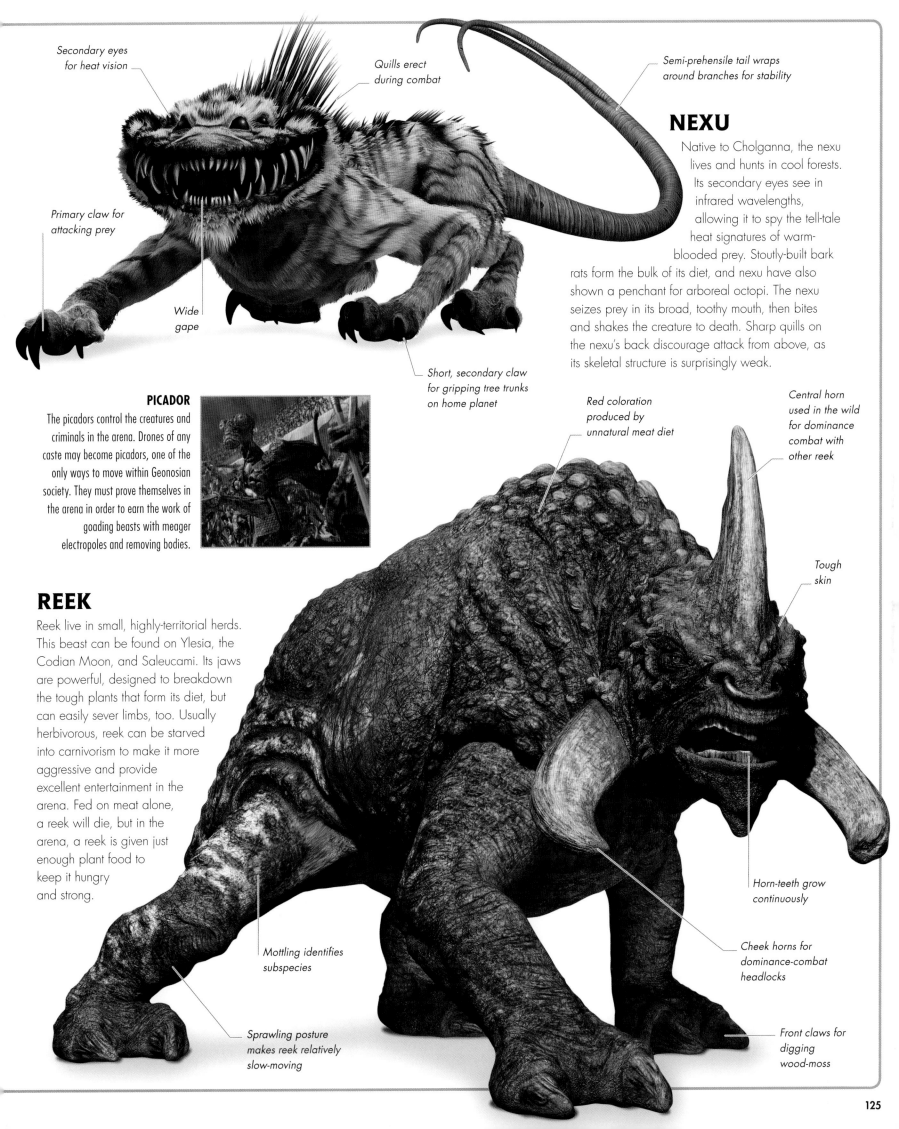

Secondary eyes
for heat vision

Quills erect
during combat

Semi-prehensile tail wraps
around branches for stability

## NEXU

Native to Cholganna, the nexu lives and hunts in cool forests. Its secondary eyes see in infrared wavelengths, allowing it to spy the tell-tale heat signatures of warm-blooded prey. Stoutly-built bark rats form the bulk of its diet, and nexu have also shown a penchant for arboreal octopi. The nexu seizes prey in its broad, toothy mouth, then bites and shakes the creature to death. Sharp quills on the nexu's back discourage attack from above, as its skeletal structure is surprisingly weak.

Primary claw for
attacking prey

Wide
gape

Short, secondary claw
for gripping tree trunks
on home planet

### PICADOR

The picadors control the creatures and criminals in the arena. Drones of any caste may become picadors, one of the only ways to move within Geonosian society. They must prove themselves in the arena in order to earn the work of goading beasts with meager electropoles and removing bodies.

Red coloration
produced by
unnatural meat diet

Central horn
used in the wild
for dominance
combat with
other reek

Tough
skin

## REEK

Reek live in small, highly-territorial herds. This beast can be found on Ylesia, the Codian Moon, and Saleucami. Its jaws are powerful, designed to breakdown the tough plants that form its diet, but can easily sever limbs, too. Usually herbivorous, reek can be starved into carnivorism to make it more aggressive and provide excellent entertainment in the arena. Fed on meat alone, a reek will die, but in the arena, a reek is given just enough plant food to keep it hungry and strong.

Horn-teeth grow
continuously

Mottling identifies
subspecies

Cheek horns for
dominance-combat
headlocks

Sprawling posture
makes reek relatively
slow-moving

Front claws for
digging
wood-moss

125

# THE SEPARATIST COUNCIL

**THE CONFEDERACY OF** independent systems has its own governing body, just like the Galactic Republic. But whereas the speakers in the Galactic Senate largely come from its member worlds, the loudest voices on the Separatist Council represent major business interests. Led by the Sith Lord Count Dooku, and later by General Grievous, the council members believe they are setting the strategy for their forces in the Clone Wars. However, for the most part they are the unwitting puppets of Dooku's master, Darth Sidious—also known as Supreme Chancellor Palpatine—who also controls the Galactic Senate.

The Separatists maintain council chambers on Geonosis and Utapau, before establishing a final base on the inhospitable planet Mustafar.

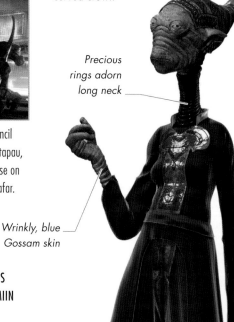

Presidente's curved crown

Precious rings adorn long neck

Wrinkly, blue Gossam skin

Hoof-like feet

SHU MAI

SHU MAI'S AIDE, CAT MIIN

## THE COMMERCE GUILD

The Commerce Guild comprises some of the galaxy's best known corporations, and has long been a dominant presence in interplanetary affairs. Shortly before the outbreak of the Clone Wars, it pledges allegience to the Confederacy of Independent Systems, earning its Presidente, the Gossam Shu Mai, her place on the Separatist Council.

WAT TAMBOR

Vocabulator/annunciator

Pressure suit simulates conditions on Tambor's homeworld, Skako

Koorivar spiral horn

PASSEL ARGENTE

PASSEL ARGENTE'S AIDE, DENARIA KEE

Koorivar skin can be violet or green

## THE CORPORATE ALLIANCE

The head of the wealthy Corporate Alliance, Magistrate Passel Argente, resigns his seat in the Galactic Senate to take a place on the Separatist Council. The early support of such an influential businessman helps bring others to the cause, and earns the Alliance a degree of favor in the eyes of Count Dooku. As a result, its member corporations flourish in Separatist systems, and the cartel itself survives into the age of the Empire.

## THE TECHNO UNION

Officially, the Techno Union is a neutral observer in the Clone Wars, and still retains a seat in the Galactic Senate. In reality, this powerful group of tech firms is responsible for designing many of the battle droids that make up the Separatists' fighting force. It is led by the Skakoan Wat Tambor, who styles himself as Foreman of the Techno Union.

The Archduke of Geonosis, Poggle the Lesser, is a prominent voice on the Separatist Council. He forged strong links with the Techno Union in the years prior to the Clone Wars, establishing his world as the main production base for one of the Union's member firms, the Baktoid Armor Workshop.

## DATA FILE

> The tallest tower in Murkhana City on the planet Murkhana is named after the Corporate Alliance leader Passel Argente.

> Nute Gunray fights through the courts to remain head of the Trade Federation after leading its failed invasion of Naboo.

*Formal breastplate of office*

The Aqualish politician Po Nudu gives up his seat on the Galactic Senate to become a founding member of the Separatist Council. As part of the new Confederacy of Independent Systems, his homeworld, Ando, is promised the support of the Banking Clan and the Techno Union.

*Long, thin Muun skull*

SAN HILL

*Long index and middle fingers*

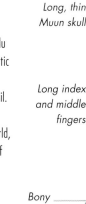

*Bony arms*

## THE BANKING CLAN

The InterGalactic Banking Clan is the most influential financial organization in the Outer Rim. It continues to do business with the Galactic Republic throughout the Clone Wars, despite its chairperson, San Hill, having a vocal presence on the Separatist Council. The Republic eventually exposes the Clan's corrupt business practices, and seizes control of its assets. From this point on, the banks are directly answerable to Supreme Chancellor Palpatine.

*Belt-cape sets off otherwise somber banker's attire*

RUNE HAAKO

*Ostentatious miter*

*Gunnay's garb is more sober than that of his superiors, Nute Gunray and Rune Haako.*

RUTE GUNNAY

*Gunnay is occasionally mistaken for the similar-looking Nute Gunray*

## THE TRADE FEDERATION

The immensely powerful Trade Federation is based on the planet Cato Neomoidia and run by Neimoidians. An early agitator for greater freedom from the Republic, its forces invade the planet Naboo in pursuit of greater profit before becoming an integral part of the Confederacy of Independent Systems. Its representatives on the Separatist Council include the outspoken Viceroy Nute Gunray, and his advisors Rune Haako and Rute Gunnay.

After the death of Count Dooku, Darth Sidious sends the members of the Separatist Council to Mustafar, saying it is for their own safety. In fact, they have outlived their usefulness to the Sith Lord, and he soon dispatches his new apprentice, Darth Vader, to their secret location. The man who once called himself Anakin Skywalker shows no mercy as he follows his master's orders and kills them all.

# SUPER BATTLE DROIDS

## DATA FILE

> B2 super battle droids are built by Baktoid Combat Automata, an offshoot of the Techno Union's Baktoid Armor Workshop, based on the planet Geonosis.

> B2 super battle droids are fourth-class droids, meaning that they are designed for military and security work. Imperial security droid K-2SO is also a fourth class droid.

**WHILE B1 BATTLE DROIDS** rely on vast numbers to overhelm organic opponents, the B2 super battle droid poses a significant threat all by itself. The B2 is designed following the defeat of the Trade Federation's army of B1 droids in the invasion of Naboo, and is ready for action in time for the first enagagement of the Clone Wars, some 10 years later. It is much stronger and more heavily armored than its predecessor, and has its dual blaster weapon built directly onto its right wrist. This greatly increases the super battle droid's response time in combat, as well as making it far harder to disarm.

Thick acertron chest armor

Flexible mid-section armor

Arms strong enough to lift an adult human

Unshakeable monogrip

Just a handful of super battle droids are deployed at the start of the Battle of Geonosis, supporting hundreds of B1 battle droids. It is the first time that the Jedi have seen the Separatists' droid army, and it proves they have been actively preparing for war. As the skirmish escalates, a total of 100,000 super battle droids are deployed.

## COMPLETE CONTROL

One of the most significant advantages of the B2 super battle droid over its B1 predecessors is its independent computer brain, which allows it to function without orders from a droid control ship. However, its intelligence remains sorely limited, and it still relies on an organic commander or a tactical droid in order to perform effectively.

Droidekas, B2 super battle droids, and B1 battle droids fight side by side in the Petranaki arena on Geonosis. In a vote of confidence for the new design, Count Dooku opts for a super battle droid at his side as he watches the battle unfold.

Optical sensor

Wrist-mounted dual blaster

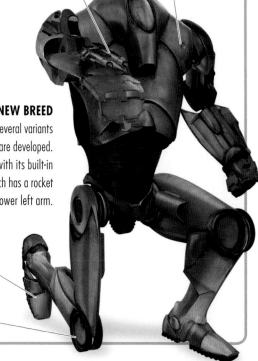

### FIRST OF A NEW BREED

As the Clone Wars rage on, several variants of the B2 super battle droid are developed. This includes the B2-RP with its built-in jetpack, and the B2-HA, which has a rocket launcher in place of its lower left arm.

Modular feet can be replaced with terrain-specific alternatives.

Hermetically sealed joints

# MAGNAGUARDS

**STRONG AND SKILLED ENOUGH** to take on a Jedi, the IG-100 MagnaGuard is the favored battle droid of General Grievous. They serve as the cyborg Separatist's personal bodyguard, protecting his secret fortress on Vassek 3, and accompanying him on missions to Coruscant and Utapau. Though highly effective alone, MagnaGuards most often fight in well-coordinated pairs, and can continue to function even if they lose a limb—or a head.

### DATA FILE

> The IG-100 MagnaGuards' humanoid dimensions and high intelligence enables them to pilot starfighters effectively.

> The pair of MagnaGuards serving on board General Grievous' ship, *The Invisible Hand*, during the Battle of Coruscant have the designations IG-101 and IG-102.

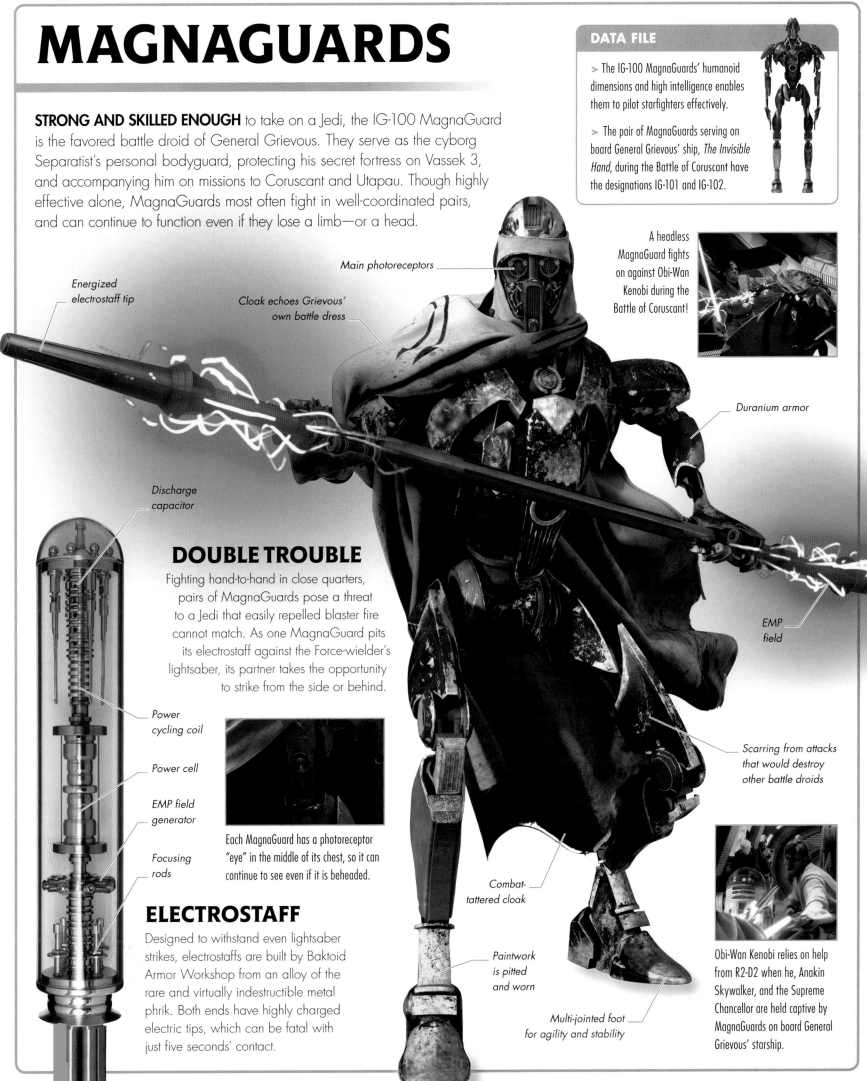

Energized electrostaff tip

Main photoreceptors

Cloak echoes Grievous' own battle dress

A headless MagnaGuard fights on against Obi-Wan Kenobi during the Battle of Coruscant!

Duranium armor

Discharge capacitor

## DOUBLE TROUBLE

Fighting hand-to-hand in close quarters, pairs of MagnaGuards pose a threat to a Jedi that easily repelled blaster fire cannot match. As one MagnaGuard pits its electrostaff against the Force-wielder's lightsaber, its partner takes the opportunity to strike from the side or behind.

Power cycling coil

Power cell

EMP field generator

Focusing rods

EMP field

Each MagnaGuard has a photoreceptor "eye" in the middle of its chest, so it can continue to see even if it is beheaded.

Scarring from attacks that would destroy other battle droids

## ELECTROSTAFF

Designed to withstand even lightsaber strikes, electrostaffs are built by Baktoid Armor Workshop from an alloy of the rare and virtually indestructible metal phrik. Both ends have highly charged electric tips, which can be fatal with just five seconds' contact.

Combat-tattered cloak

Paintwork is pitted and worn

Multi-jointed foot for agility and stability

Obi-Wan Kenobi relies on help from R2-D2 when he, Anakin Skywalker, and the Supreme Chancellor are held captive by MagnaGuards on board General Grievous' starship.

# SEPARATIST GROUND CRAFT

**THE IMMENSE OFFENSIVE CAPABILITIES** of the Trade Federation, the Techno Union, the Commerce Guild, and others come together to form the ground forces of the Confederacy of Independent Systems. Their military hardware is primarily made up of automated mobile weapons known as droid tanks, which do not rely on organic troops to function. The ground forces are diverse in their appearance and original function, but over the course of the Clone Wars, Separatist colors and insignia are used to give them a unified look.

Primary optical sensor

Sensor array

Comlink antenna

Heavily armored cognitive module

Waterproof joint

Radiator vents

Sensor suite aperture

Optical sensor hidden in recess

Blaster cannon

### LM-432 CRAB DROID
The six-legged crab droid is built by the Techno Union. It uses its two oversized forelegs to negotiate steep and slippery surfaces. The pincers are powerful enough to penetrate vehicle armor, while its two belly-mounted blaster cannons attend to long-range targets.

Laser cannons can be replaced with chain-fed missile launchers.

Duranium pincers serve as feet and offensive grips

Plasmic vials

## OCTUPTARRA TRI-DROID

Towering over the Republic's clone troopers, the mighty octuptarra droid has optical sensors on all sides, making sneak attacks impossible. Three rotating laser cannons give it a wraparound field of fire, while its most fearsome variant also carries deadly viruses and other airborne bio weapons inside its spherical head.

Actuator piston

Actuator piston

Damage to a single leg can put an entire tri-droid out of action

Armored legs hide inner hydraulics

Tracing antenna

Infrared photoreceptor

Laser cannon

Armored joint plate

Armored brain casing

### DSD1 DWARF SPIDER DROID
Also known as the burrowing spider droid, owing to its ability to infiltrate spaces too small for other droid tanks, the DSD1 is essentially a laser cannon on legs. Most are equipped with self-destruct mechanisms, and they will willingly blow themselves up in order to destroy an enemy.

Articulated foot

Jointed "toes" improve stability

Height-adjustable legs

All-terrain footpad

## NR-N99 DROID ENFORCER

The NR-N99 *Persuader*-class droid enforcer may lack the speed and agility of a walking droid tank, but it makes up for it with reliability and firepower. Plowing through the battlefield on heavy-duty tracks, it brings a relentless onslaught of blaster fire, missiles, and ion-cannon disruption. The NR-N99 is designed to function autonomously using its computer brain, and can also be operated by a pilot droid.

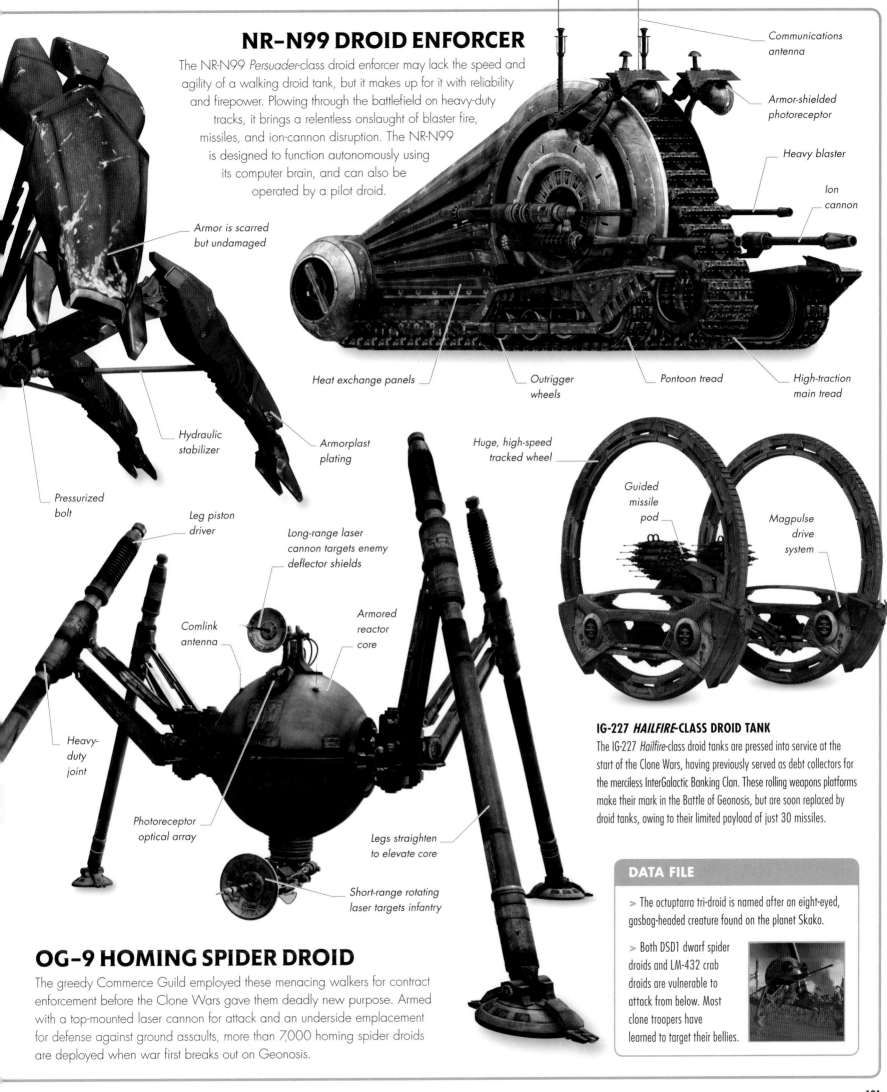

Communications antenna

Armor-shielded photoreceptor

Heavy blaster

Ion cannon

Armor is scarred but undamaged

Heat exchange panels

Outrigger wheels

Pontoon tread

High-traction main tread

Hydraulic stabilizer

Armorplast plating

Pressurized bolt

Huge, high-speed tracked wheel

Guided missile pod

Magpulse drive system

Leg piston driver

Long-range laser cannon targets enemy deflector shields

Comlink antenna

Armored reactor core

Heavy-duty joint

### IG-227 *HAILFIRE*-CLASS DROID TANK

The IG-227 *Hailfire*-class droid tanks are pressed into service at the start of the Clone Wars, having previously served as debt collectors for the merciless InterGalactic Banking Clan. These rolling weapons platforms make their mark in the Battle of Geonosis, but are soon replaced by droid tanks, owing to their limited payload of just 30 missiles.

Photoreceptor optical array

Legs straighten to elevate core

Short-range rotating laser targets infantry

### DATA FILE

> The octuptarra tri-droid is named after an eight-eyed, gasbag-headed creature found on the planet Skako.

> Both DSD1 dwarf spider droids and LM-432 crab droids are vulnerable to attack from below. Most clone troopers have learned to target their bellies.

## OG-9 HOMING SPIDER DROID

The greedy Commerce Guild employed these menacing walkers for contract enforcement before the Clone Wars gave them deadly new purpose. Armed with a top-mounted laser cannon for attack and an underside emplacement for defense against ground assaults, more than 7,000 homing spider droids are deployed when war first breaks out on Geonosis.

# SEPARATIST DROIDS

**SPACE-GOING DROIDS** form the main part of the Separatist fleet, as their computer brains are integrated with starfighter technology. By doing away with organic pilots, the Separatists solve the problems caused by nerves and fatigue, but also lose out on the imagination and daring that a seasoned starfighter ace can rely on in battle. Some larger ships are used for troop deployment and as flagships for Separatist leaders, but these too are usually crewed by battle droids.

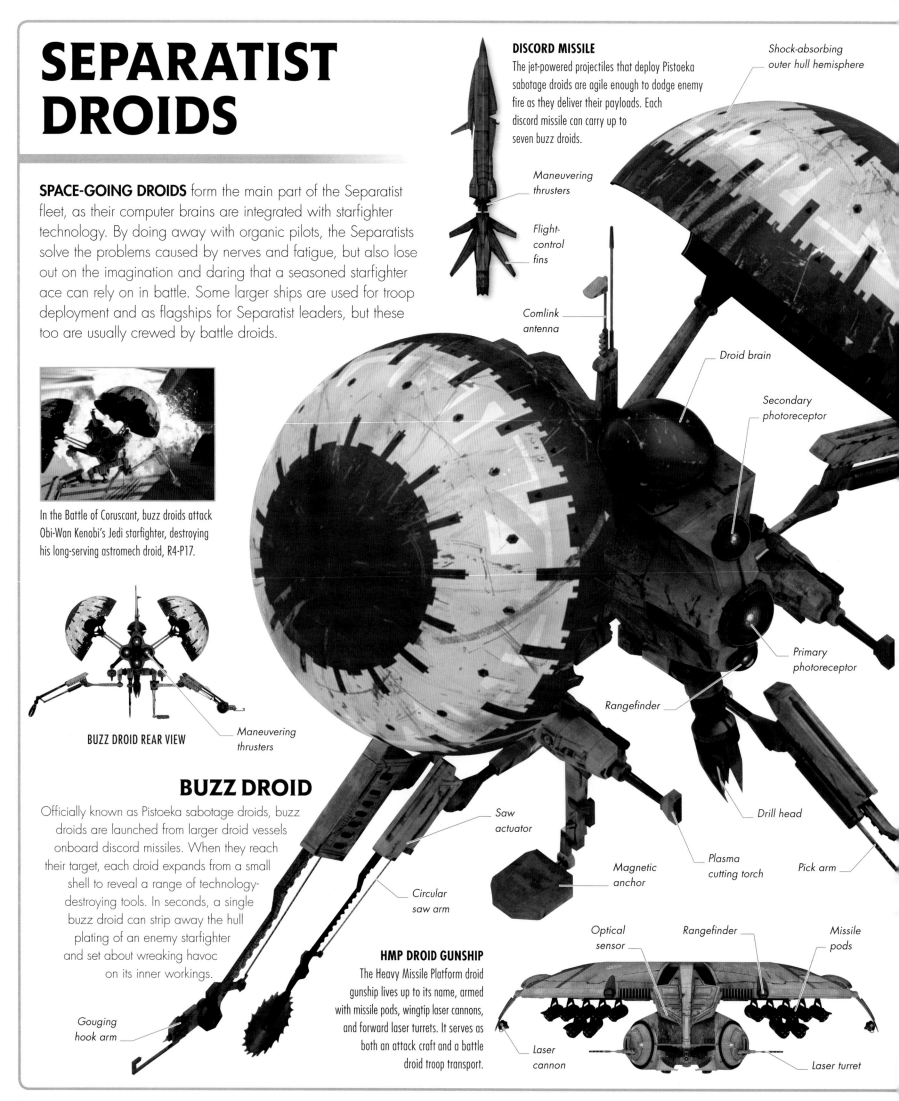

In the Battle of Coruscant, buzz droids attack Obi-Wan Kenobi's Jedi starfighter, destroying his long-serving astromech droid, R4-P17.

**BUZZ DROID REAR VIEW**

Maneuvering thrusters

## BUZZ DROID

Officially known as Pistoeka sabotage droids, buzz droids are launched from larger droid vessels onboard discord missiles. When they reach their target, each droid expands from a small shell to reveal a range of technology-destroying tools. In seconds, a single buzz droid can strip away the hull plating of an enemy starfighter and set about wreaking havoc on its inner workings.

Gouging hook arm

**DISCORD MISSILE**

The jet-powered projectiles that deploy Pistoeka sabotage droids are agile enough to dodge enemy fire as they deliver their payloads. Each discord missile can carry up to seven buzz droids.

Maneuvering thrusters

Flight-control fins

Comlink antenna

Shock-absorbing outer hull hemisphere

Droid brain

Secondary photoreceptor

Primary photoreceptor

Rangefinder

Drill head

Saw actuator

Circular saw arm

Magnetic anchor

Plasma cutting torch

Pick arm

### HMP DROID GUNSHIP

The Heavy Missile Platform droid gunship lives up to its name, armed with missile pods, wingtip laser cannons, and forward laser turrets. It serves as both an attack craft and a battle droid troop transport.

Optical sensor

Rangefinder

Missile pods

Laser cannon

Laser turret

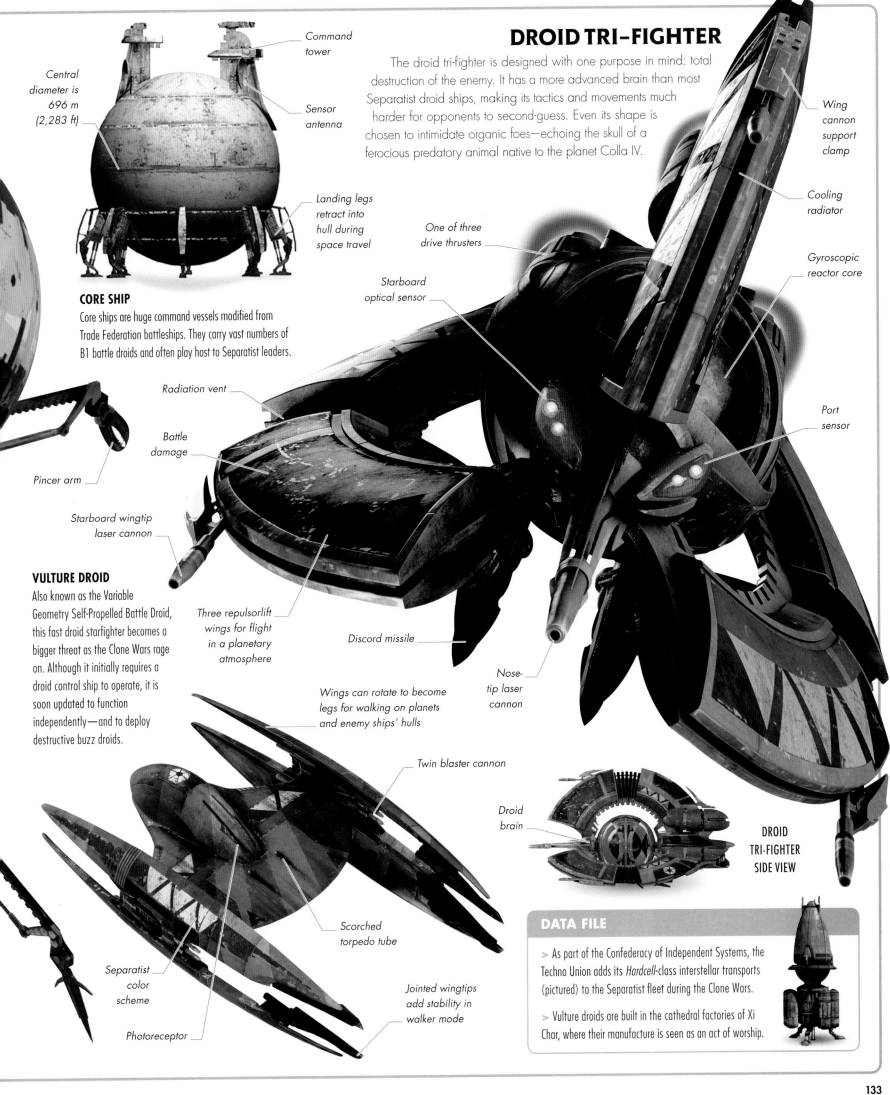

# DROID TRI-FIGHTER

The droid tri-fighter is designed with one purpose in mind: total destruction of the enemy. It has a more advanced brain than most Separatist droid ships, making its tactics and movements much harder for opponents to second-guess. Even its shape is chosen to intimidate organic foes—echoing the skull of a ferocious predatory animal native to the planet Colla IV.

Command tower

Sensor antenna

Central diameter is 696 m (2,283 ft)

Landing legs retract into hull during space travel

Wing cannon support clamp

Cooling radiator

Gyroscopic reactor core

One of three drive thrusters

Starboard optical sensor

Port sensor

## CORE SHIP

Core ships are huge command vessels modified from Trade Federation battleships. They carry vast numbers of B1 battle droids and often play host to Separatist leaders.

Radiation vent

Battle damage

Pincer arm

Starboard wingtip laser cannon

## VULTURE DROID

Also known as the Variable Geometry Self-Propelled Battle Droid, this fast droid starfighter becomes a bigger threat as the Clone Wars rage on. Although it initially requires a droid control ship to operate, it is soon updated to function independently—and to deploy destructive buzz droids.

Three repulsorlift wings for flight in a planetary atmosphere

Discord missile

Nose-tip laser cannon

Wings can rotate to become legs for walking on planets and enemy ships' hulls

Twin blaster cannon

Droid brain

DROID TRI-FIGHTER SIDE VIEW

Separatist color scheme

Scorched torpedo tube

Photoreceptor

Jointed wingtips add stability in walker mode

# GENERAL GRIEVOUS

## DATA FILE

> General Grievous' arms can also serve as legs, allowing him to scuttle along at speed like an enormous insect.

> Grievous has a grapple line built into his right wrist. He uses it to secure himself to the hull of the *Invisible Hand* when he is sucked out of the ship into the vacuum of space.

**THE SUPREME COMMANDER** of the Separatists' droid army, General Grievous, is not a droid but a highly mechanized cyborg. This large and powerful warrior was originally a bat-like warlord from the planet Kalee, who chose to make himself even more threatening through extreme cybernetic upgrades. Now he is one of the most infamous fighters in the Clone Wars, feared as much for his strategic mind as for his awesome abilities in single combat. From the bridge of his vast flagships, the *Malevolence* and the *Invisible Hand*, he commands millions of battle droid troops, and goes on to lead the entire Separatist cause after the death of Count Dooku.

Transparisteel viewport

Triple laser cannon

Thrust vector fin

Landing strut

## THE *SOULLESS ONE*

Grievous flies a customized Belbullab-22 starfighter, which he calls the *Soulless One*. Built by Feethan Ottraw Scalable Assemblies, it boasts two triple rapid-fire laser cannons and a top-of-the-range hyperdrive.

Sensor cone

TOP VIEW

Cockpit

Impervium hull

Kaleesh cloak is a vestige of Grievous' organic identity

Circuitry is grafted onto brain tissue

Wiring carries the brain's electrical impulses around the body

Red Kaleesh flesh still visible around eyes

Six digits on each hand

## MAN AND MACHINE

The only surviving parts of Greivous' original Kaleesh form in his new metal body are his eyes, his brain, and a few vital organs. His persistant cough is the result of his organic lungs being irritated by their cybernetic implants.

Ultrasonic vocabulator

Armor covers surviving organs

Precision targeting scope

## BLASTED IN BATTLE

For all his prowess with stolen lightsabers, Grievous is killed by a single shot from his own blaster, when it, in turn, is taken from his possession by Obi-Wan Kenobi during the Battle of Utapau.

Grip suited to cyborg digits

DT-57 "ANNIHILATOR" BLASTER

FOUR-ARMED
COMBAT FORMATION

Fearsome masks are often
worn by Kaleesh warriors

Duranium
armor plating

Split armor
allows arms
to separate

Reinforced
knee plates

Lower legs
show wear
from many
campaigns

Four claws
on each foot

Heavy-
duty joints

Cybernetic hands enable
Grievous to spin lightsabers
at a terrifying rate

## SITH TRAINING

The Separatist leader, Count Dooku,
trained Grievous in lightsaber combat.
The General can now wield four at a
time by splitting both of his arms in two.
He adds to his collection of lightsabers every
time he defeats a Jedi in battle, and keeps
them in easy reach inside his cloak.

# UTAPAUNS

**THE PEACEFUL OUTER RIM** world of Utapau is inhabited by two indigenous, symbiotic species—the Utai and the Pau'ans—and the immigrant Amani species. The languid Pau'ans constitute Utapau's modest patrician class. Humble by nature, the stubby Utai make up the labor class. Collectively, the Utai and Pau'ans are referred to as the Utapauns, and reside in cities built into the sides of huge sinkholes found on Utapau. Utapau remains neutral in the Clone Wars until the Separatist leadership occupies their world as a sanctuary. The Utapauns feign acceptance of occupation, while secretly preparing for rebellion.

*Beak horns used for display, defense, and combat*

*Utapaun bident*

*Pau'an warrior*

### DACTILLION

A carnivorous reptile native to Utapau and other worlds, the dactillion is a four-legged avian lizard. Utapauns justifiably feared dactillions, but eventually learned to domesticate the creatures by supplying them with fresh meat.

*Keeled breastbone developed for flight muscles*

*Strong claws for grasping prey*

*Shield conforms to profile*

*Modest thrusters*

*Passenger compartment seats four Pau'ans*

*Distended eyes*

### SCOOP SKIMMER

An airspeeder used on Utapau, scoop skimmers are chiefly used as transport vehicles but some are equipped with light blasters. Scoop skimmers can also be found in the skies of Coruscant.

*Law enforcement blasters are rarely used*

### UTAI

Utapau's immense sinkholes were home to the Utai long before climactic change drove the lordly Pau'ans from the planet's surface. Distended eyes provide the Utai with keen night vision, perfectly suited to the crevasses that fissure Utapau. The Utai tamed the varactyl, and still serve as wranglers for the dragon mounts.

### LANDING PLATFORM

Obi-Wan lands in Pau City and is met by Tion Medon, who assures him that nothing strange has occurred. While Obi-Wan's Jedi Interceptor is refueled, Tion whispers that Separatists have taken control of Utapau.

*Varactyl muck boots*

*Saddle*

The 15 m (49 ft) long varactyl is an obliging herbivore. Utai leatherworkers handcraft high-backed saddles, sized for Pau'ans and Utai and perfect for riding at any angle.

*Long crooked legs*

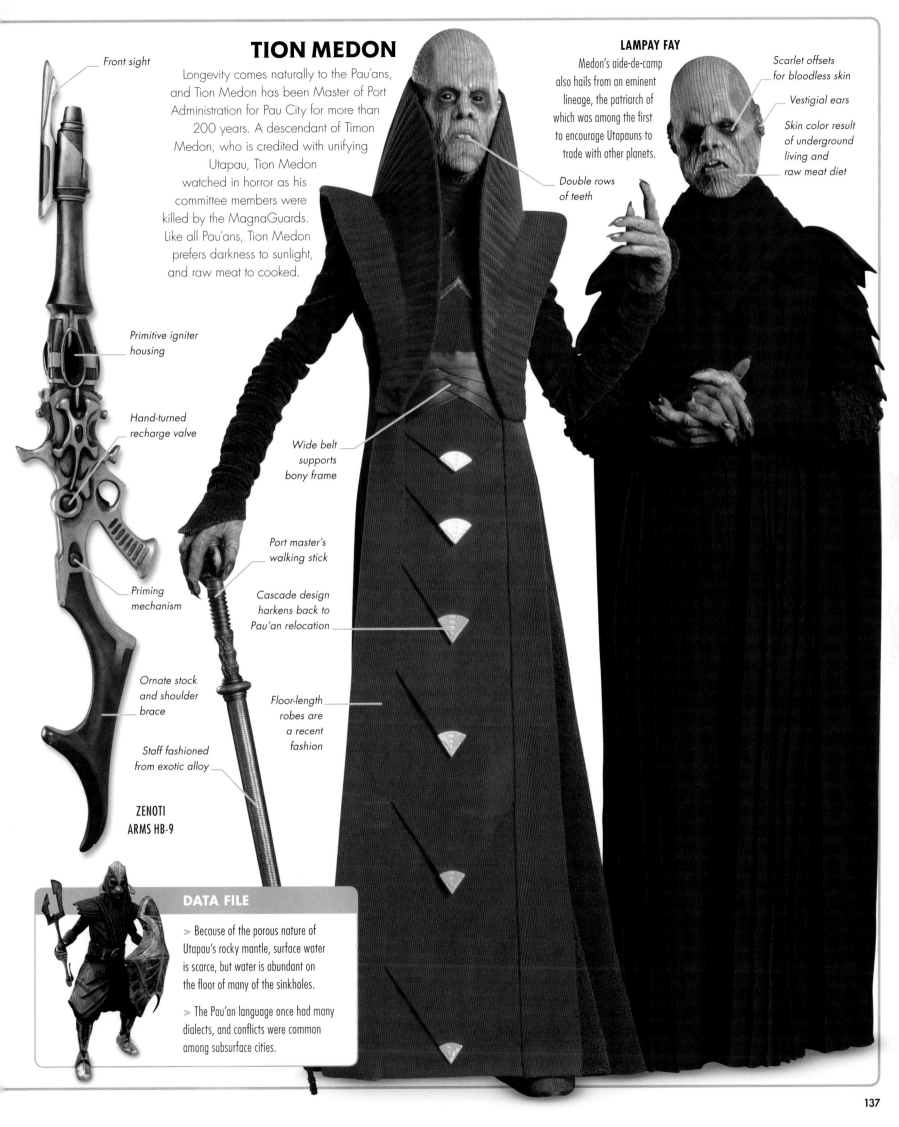

Front sight

# TION MEDON

Longevity comes naturally to the Pau'ans, and Tion Medon has been Master of Port Administration for Pau City for more than 200 years. A descendant of Timon Medon, who is credited with unifying Utapau, Tion Medon watched in horror as his committee members were killed by the MagnaGuards. Like all Pau'ans, Tion Medon prefers darkness to sunlight, and raw meat to cooked.

## LAMPAY FAY

Medon's aide-de-camp also hails from an eminent lineage, the patriarch of which was among the first to encourage Utapauns to trade with other planets.

Scarlet offsets for bloodless skin

Vestigial ears

Skin color result of underground living and raw meat diet

Double rows of teeth

Primitive igniter housing

Hand-turned recharge valve

Wide belt supports bony frame

Priming mechanism

Port master's walking stick

Cascade design harkens back to Pau'an relocation

Ornate stock and shoulder brace

Floor-length robes are a recent fashion

Staff fashioned from exotic alloy

**ZENOTI ARMS HB-9**

## DATA FILE

> Because of the porous nature of Utapau's rocky mantle, surface water is scarce, but water is abundant on the floor of many of the sinkholes.

> The Pau'an language once had many dialects, and conflicts were common among subsurface cities.

# CHEWBACCA

**COMPARATIVELY SHORT, EVEN SLIGHT,** for a Wookiee, 200-year-old Chewbacca was born in the city of Rwookrrorro, several hundred kilometers from Kachirho, in an area of exceptionally tall wroshyr trees. His mother, father, and several cousins still reside there. A mechanic, holo-game competitor, and catamaran and fluttercraft pilot, Chewbacca learned his skills at Rwookrrorro's landing pad, and helped design and build the Wookiee escape pods. When it comes to outwitting droids or clone troopers, Chewbacca is ready with a plan.

## DATA FILE

> More compassionate than fierce, Chewbacca nevertheless proves himself an able and cunning warrior.

> Slavers prize Wookiees for their strength, keen intellects, and long lifespans.

## WOOKIEE EXPLORER

Chewbacca has explored his homeworld from pole to pole, and has explored the wildest reaches of Kashyyyk's phenomenal forests. Restless by nature, he has also visited scores of planets, and is a veteran of numerous adventures, including escaping the Trandoshan hunting grounds on Wasskah with the Jedi Padawan Ahsoka Tano.

On the ground and on Kachirho's loftiest tree platforms, Wookiees gaze into the night sky, which the ships of the Separatist fleet have strewn with harsh light. Chewbacca is no stranger to combat, but he worries that Kashyyyk may not be able to defend itself against the invasion force, and will fall to the Confederacy.

*Ammunition bandolier*

*Pouch contains dismantled bowcaster*

*Chewie's legs are comparatively short*

## THE GATHERING

The clarion call to defend Kachirho summons young and old, from all areas of Kashyyyk. Despite the victory at the tree-city, Kashyyyk will become enslaved to the Empire soon after the end of the Clone Wars, and thousands of Wookiees will be exported to remote worlds to serve as slave laborers. Even Imperial oppression, however, will not dampen Chewbacca's abiding fondness for humans—including his future friendship with Han Solo.

GUANTA    LACHICHUK    MERUMERU

*Hardened footpads from exploring Kashyyyk*

# TARFFUL

**TARFFUL HAS SERVED AS LEADER** of the Wookiee city of Kachirho for longer than a human lifetime. He has already experienced captivity, having fallen into the clawed hands of Trandoshan slavers who have long been enemies of the Wookiees, and who had cut a deal with Count Dooku. Standing over 2 m (7 ft) tall, Tarfful is literally looked up to by many, and so assumes the role of commander when Separatist forces invade.

Immense lung capacity required to sound call

KASHYYYK CLARION

Hammered bronzium jacket inlaid with cerulean gemstone

Mouth emits bellow that can be heard for 20 km (12 miles)

ELDER'S STAFF

Wood is over six centuries old

CEREMONIAL PIPE

Elaborately engraved stem

Ferocious visage

Teeth bared for war cry

Locks of hair banded by precious metal rings

Decorative pauldron

## MASTER CARVERS

Wookiees turn their dexterous hands to carving at an early age, fashioning household items, musical instruments, and tools. The Kashyyyk clarion is made from the horn of a bantha, and jacketed with hand-hammered bronzium.

## ABLE LEADER

Rescued from captivity by a team of Republic clone commandos, Tarfful pledged that he would fight to the death any who threatened to enslave the Wookiees or to occupy Kashyyyk. Tarfful and the citizenry of Kachirho are relieved that Yoda will personally assist with the defense of Kashyyyk. Yoda has been honored with the prestigious title "Defender of the Home Tree" for his role as a Jedi negotiator between the Wookiees and the Trandoshans.

### DATA FILE

> Trandoshans are a reptilian humanoid species from a world in the same planetary system as Kashyyyk.

> Wookiees cannot speak Basic, and few species in the galaxy can mimic the complex roars and barks that comprise their language, Shyriiwook. Even so, Wookiees have a way of making their intentions clearly understood.

# WOOKIEE WEAPONS

**THE WOOKIEE LANGUAGE** contains over 150 words for wood, many of them devoted to grain, moisture content, and factors that can influence warping, twisting, and checking. Shipboard logs cite instances of Wookiees effecting temporary repairs of starship drives using pieces of wood. Commentators have classified even their blasters as "art," and yet the language has no word for "artist." Wookiees view their innate talents for carving and engraving as mere survival skills.

### KLORRI-CLAN BATTLE SHIELD
Carved with symbolic motifs and banded with bronzium, the two thousand-year-old Klorri-clan battle shields are normally displayed only during important rituals and ceremonies.

Crest is ancient sun symbol

**PAULDRON**

Hair can be threaded through perforated flange

**HELMET**

Stock is tapered for line-of-sight accuracy

Battery pack is mortised into stock

Rear sight

Blaster gas cartridges

### MILITARY WEAR
Armor, harnesses, and other examples of military gear evolved from ceremonial clan regalia, in the same way that most Wookiee implements of war have their origin in hunting. Halter and shoulder-slung bandoleers typically hold power packs, blaster gas canisters, and bowcaster quarrels.

Bowstring catch

Tensile bowstring

Blaster gas lines

### BOWCASTER MECHANICS
The bowcaster works on the principle of magnetic acceleration. A pair of spherical polarizers generate positive and negative pulses that power the weapon's tensile metal bowstring. Enveloped in energy when it emerges from the barrel, the quarrel could be mistaken for a blaster bolt.

**AMMO HALTER**

Polarizer

Ribbed launch shaft

Conduction chamber housed in shaft

## BOWCASTER
The traditional bowcaster still enjoys wide use as a ranged weapon. The original bowcaster had few metal parts, and employed a length of braided kshyy vine to fire a wooden quarrel. The stock was adorned with clan or tree-city emblems, or inlaid with semi-precious stones or mosaics of contrasting hardwood.

Metal limb

Barrel

Front sight

Power pack

Stock recoil spring

Safety catch

Conduction chamber

Magnetic acceleration coil

Trigger

> The Battle of Kachirho might not have gone as well for the Wookiees had Yoda not been there to lend his lightsaber to the fray. Similarly, the battle might not have gone as well for Yoda had the Wookiees not peppered the area around the tree-city with launch-capable escape pods, in case Kachirho had to be evacuated.

# SURE-SHOT

Tremendous strength is required to cock and control most bowcasters. Traveling circuses use these ranged weapons in feats-of-strength competitions. Chewbacca's, however, is more tribute than traditional, with an automatic recocking system and low-light scope. Consequently, his bandoleer houses more power packs than most.

Bowcaster easily dismantled

Automatic recocking system

DISRUPTOR

Ring-grip peculiar to southern hemisphere tree-cities

Bronzium alloy blast suppressor

Accelerator

SIDE-ARM

Polarizers positioned forward of barrel

## BLASTERS

Of the array of blasters fashioned by Wookiee weaponsmiths, several models are favorites and are now mass-produced in workshops all over Kashyyyk. Blaster technology has influenced traditional weapons as well, with the over-under bowcaster featuring a built-in blaster.

Quarrel autofeed mechanism

Shortened stock

SLUG-THROWER

Blaster gas cartridges

CHEWBACCA'S BOWCASTER

Electromagnetic coil for ultra-power blasts

Front sight

Polarizer

Barrel

Lowered rear sight

# MUSTAFAR

**A TINY, FIERY PLANET** in the Outer Rim, Mustafar maintains an erratic orbit between two gas giants, Jestefad and Lefrani. The Techno Union, who owns the planet, provides the locals with tools to mine valuable mineral allotropes for them. Mustafar is deemed an ideal hideout for Separatist leaders due to this affiliation, and because its atmosphere and surface interfere with standard scanners and navigational systems.

## MUSTAFARIAN NATIVES

Both northern and southern Mustafarians evolved from extremophile arthropods in caves of dormant volcanoes. Although their skin can withstand the heat radiated by common blasters, Mustafarians require insulated armor to function in close proximity to lava rivers. Northern Mustafarians are tall and thin, while southern Mustafarians have squat, burly bodies that can resist greater temperatures.

*Lava-proof metal shank* — **LAVA SKIMMER**

The term "lava skimmers" applies to Mustafarian miners as well as their pole-mounted cauldrons, which combine the function of crucible tongs and pouring shanks. Excessive pressure can crush cauldron walls, so the tongs have pressure-stop locks. With their powerful bodies, southern Mustafarians can lift the lava-filled cauldrons with relative ease.

**HARD AT WORK**
Assisted by droid lava collectors and other Techno Union-provided technology, Mustafarian miners ride repulsorlift-powered harvesting platforms to gather lava from their planet's surface. Besides valuable minerals, lava streams also provide energy for Mustafar's ore collection complex.

*Insulated fabric*

*Armor recycled from discarded lava flea shells*

**SOUTHERN MUSTAFARIAN**

*Ratchet clamp with pressure-stop lock*

*Lava-resistant ceramic cauldron*

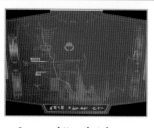

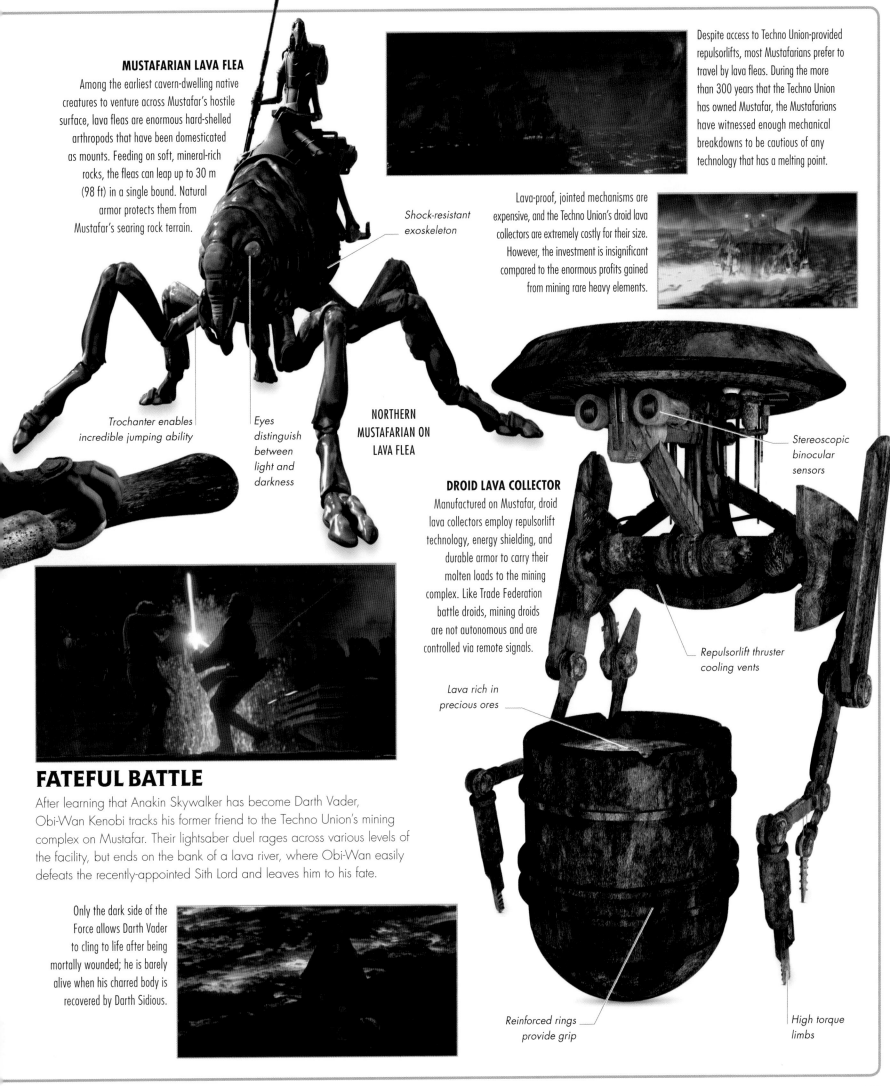

### MUSTAFARIAN LAVA FLEA

Among the earliest cavern-dwelling native creatures to venture across Mustafar's hostile surface, lava fleas are enormous hard-shelled arthropods that have been domesticated as mounts. Feeding on soft, mineral-rich rocks, the fleas can leap up to 30 m (98 ft) in a single bound. Natural armor protects them from Mustafar's searing rock terrain.

*Shock-resistant exoskeleton*

Despite access to Techno Union-provided repulsorlifts, most Mustafarians prefer to travel by lava fleas. During the more than 300 years that the Techno Union has owned Mustafar, the Mustafarians have witnessed enough mechanical breakdowns to be cautious of any technology that has a melting point.

Lava-proof, jointed mechanisms are expensive, and the Techno Union's droid lava collectors are extremely costly for their size. However, the investment is insignificant compared to the enormous profits gained from mining rare heavy elements.

*Trochanter enables incredible jumping ability*

*Eyes distinguish between light and darkness*

**NORTHERN MUSTAFARIAN ON LAVA FLEA**

*Stereoscopic binocular sensors*

### DROID LAVA COLLECTOR

Manufactured on Mustafar, droid lava collectors employ repulsorlift technology, energy shielding, and durable armor to carry their molten loads to the mining complex. Like Trade Federation battle droids, mining droids are not autonomous and are controlled via remote signals.

*Repulsorlift thruster cooling vents*

*Lava rich in precious ores*

### FATEFUL BATTLE

After learning that Anakin Skywalker has become Darth Vader, Obi-Wan Kenobi tracks his former friend to the Techno Union's mining complex on Mustafar. Their lightsaber duel rages across various levels of the facility, but ends on the bank of a lava river, where Obi-Wan easily defeats the recently-appointed Sith Lord and leaves him to his fate.

Only the dark side of the Force allows Darth Vader to cling to life after being mortally wounded; he is barely alive when his charred body is recovered by Darth Sidious.

*Reinforced rings provide grip*

*High torque limbs*

# KALLIDAHIN

**THE KALLIDAHIN BELIEVE THEY** are descended from the now-vanished Eellayin species. Evidence of the Eellayin civilization is scant but traces can be found on the fractured remains of a planet named Polis Massa. Mystery surrounds the cause of the cataclysm that broke this Outer Rim planet into a series of asteroids. Almost 500 years prior to the Galactic Republic's fall, the Kallidahin started an archaeological dig on one of largest asteroids. Most of the prize artifacts uncovered thus far have come from deep within the asteroid, and so seasoned spelunkers—cavers— comprise the majority of the team. The medical facility to which Padmé Amidala is taken was built to suit the needs of the investigators, not child-birth. Known for their discretion, the researchers ask few questions of their unexpected visitors.

Obi-Wan, Padmé, R2-D2, and C-3PO rendezvous with Yoda and Bail Organa at the Polis Massa research facility. The fact that the facility is remote suits the purposes of the Jedi, who are determined to keep secret the birth of Padmé's children. The medtechs who assist in delivering the twins are baffled by their inability to save her life.

Diagnostic display screen

Equipment tray

Analysis chamber

Manipulator arm

Specimen tray

**FRONT VIEW**

Diagnostic fingertips

Signal light

Tissue analyzer

Voice-activated comlink

Shoulder lamp

Form-fitting bodysuit

Processor casing

Paired bioscanner

Probe arm

Powerbus conduits

Sampling grasper

## MEDICAL DROID

The GH-7 meddroid is a common feature in many Outer Rim medical facilities. It is an all-purpose diagnostician, hematologist, and surgical assistant. Rarely underfoot, courtesy of a compact repulsorlift, the GH-7 uses its servoarms to collect specimens, administer anesthesia, and see to injections of drugs or plasma agents. The GH-7's stereoscopic bioscanners are linked to computers, which interpret gathered data and transmit subsequent instructions to the droid.

Specimen jars

Repulsor cell housing

**SIDE VIEW**

Magnetic resonance reader

Leg warmers

**OSH SCAL**

## MIDWIFE DROID

Non-threatening aspect

Warming cushion

The current Kallidahin team has had limited contact with humans, and knows little about delivering human children. After consulting their databanks, the medtechs select a padded droid to be Padmé's midwife. It is equipped with a thermal cushion and paddle appendages with which to cradle the newborns.

Nutrient reservoir

Repulsorlift

Cradling paddle

**DATA FILE**

> A committee of Kallidahin archaeologists named the Archaeological Research Council set up a research base in Polis Massa. They intend to study the mysteries behind the planet's destruction.

Fearing the worst, Bail orders Captain Antilles to delete all data about Mustafar from Padmé's starship computer. The twins, whom Padmé has named Luke and Leia, are separated. Bail adopts Leia, while Luke is taken to his family on Tatooine.

Head lamp

Deep-focus eyes

Droid summoner

Utility belt

Sign language gesture

Mildly telepathic brain

Osmotic membrane face

Surgical hood seal

Caver's harness

Remote control unit

Warming line

Surgical hood

Remote control

Sample containers

Suit reveals body growth-rings

Knee pads

## ALIEN MEDICS

Only two of the technicians that help deliver the Skywalker twins are trained physicians. The rest are xenobiologists. They are attached to the archaeological team to analyze artifacts for organic tissue, suitable for cloning. Padmé's condition is judged to be so critical that the techs have no time to change out of their caving jumpsuits.

DZNORI XAM

SELIF XAM

MANEELI TUUN

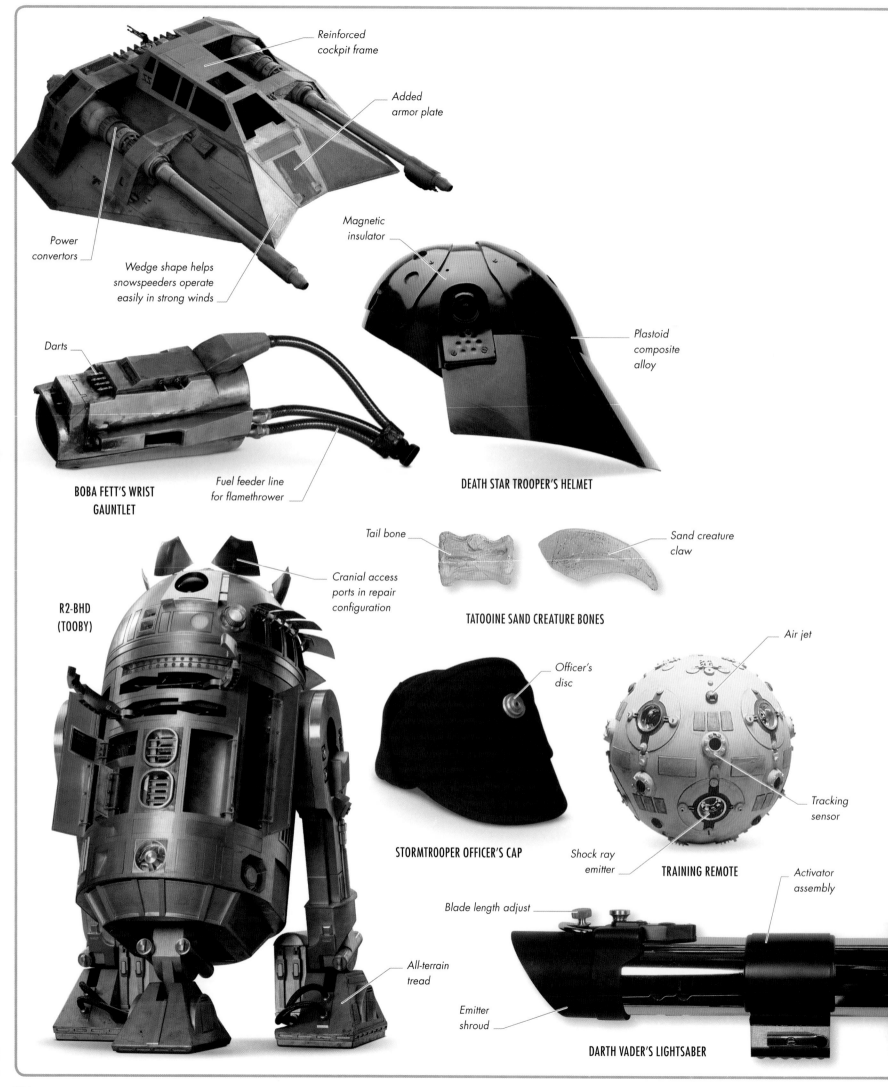

Reinforced
cockpit frame

Added
armor plate

Magnetic
insulator

Power
convertors

Wedge shape helps
snowspeeders operate
easily in strong winds

Plastoid
composite
alloy

Darts

Fuel feeder line
for flamethrower

BOBA FETT'S WRIST
GAUNTLET

DEATH STAR TROOPER'S HELMET

Tail bone

Sand creature
claw

Cranial access
ports in repair
configuration

R2-BHD
(TOOBY)

TATOOINE SAND CREATURE BONES

Air jet

Officer's
disc

Tracking
sensor

Shock ray
emitter

STORMTROOPER OFFICER'S CAP

TRAINING REMOTE

Activator
assembly

Blade length adjust

All-terrain
tread

Emitter
shroud

DARTH VADER'S LIGHTSABER

# THE ORIGINAL TRILOGY ERA

Rediscover the classic era of the original *Star Wars* trilogy, a time when a ruthless Emperor rules over the entire galaxy, enforcing his despotic will through military might. An age when Luke Skywalker, Leia Organa, and other brave rebels rise up to challenge the Empire and restore peace and democracy. During the Galactic Civil War, the galaxy is inhabited with legendary characters on both sides of the conflict. Much can be gleamed from the clothes they wear; the vehicles they travel in, and the equipment they carry. From Leia's diplomatic starship, *Tantive IV,* to the uniformity of stormtrooper armor, and Jabba the Hutt's monstrous rancor, explore the array of fascinating artifacts from this classic *Star Wars* era.

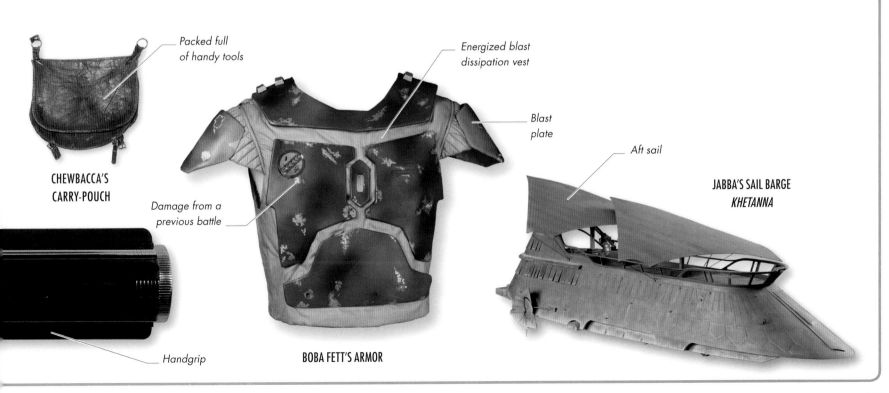

*Packed full of handy tools*

*Energized blast dissipation vest*

*Blast plate*

*Aft sail*

**CHEWBACCA'S CARRY-POUCH**

*Damage from a previous battle*

**JABBA'S SAIL BARGE** *KHETANNA*

*Handgrip*

**BOBA FETT'S ARMOR**

# KESSEL RUN CREW

**A GANG OF THIEVES,** led by seasoned outlaw Tobias Beckett, is attempting to steal a valuable hyperspace fuel called coaxium. The criminal crew crosses paths with an Imperial soldier named Han Solo who has discovered his reckless disregard for rules is incompatible with military life. Instead, Han's cockiness, daring, and ability to take a punch make him a capable—if unpredictable—thief. He soon finds himself on a risky venture in the company of skilled smugglers and scoundrels, each with their own motivations and loyalties. When their plans go awry, the crew must depend on a fast starship, Han's piloting abilities, and some luck to make a record-breaking journey and complete the job.

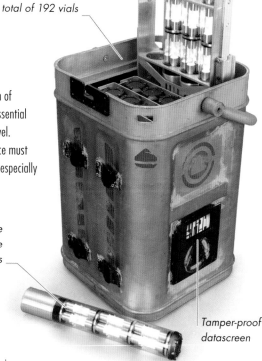

*Case holds a total of 192 vials*

## COAXIUM

Coaxium is a rare form of hypermatter and an essential fuel for lightspeed travel. The explosive substance must be transported safely, especially in its unrefined form.

*Tubes are made out of unreactive metal alloys and glass*

*Tamper-proof datascreen*

**COAXIUM CANISTER**

## KESSEL

The royal family of Kessel has allowed one side of their planet to be taken over for widespread mining operations. Most notorious of the minerals harvested on the planet is a medicinal substance known as Kessel spice. Kessel's mineral wealth also draws the crew to this blockaded world. They are hoping to profit from the rare veins of coaxium that run through the mines.

*R3 astromech brain has been upgraded and modified for L3*

**BRAIN MODULE**

*Form-fitted durasteel shell*

*Carbon-scoring from engine room vents*

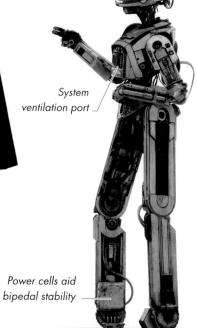

*System ventilation port*

*Synthetic nanosilk capelet*

*Power cells aid bipedal stability*

## LANDO'S *FALCON*

This YT-1300 freighter has been converted into a speedy sports vessel by its current owner, Lando Calrissian. The smuggler has also modified the two cargo mandibles at the front into an auxiliary ship launch. The *Falcon's* streamlined body assists with Calrissian's quick getaways and is perfect for the crew's risky plan. The pristine vessel is Lando's pride and joy, so he is reluctant to allow a stranger like Han behind its controls.

*Corellian Spike rules favor a 62-card deck*

**SABACC CARDS**

### LANDO CALRISSIAN

Lando Calrissian says he plans to retire from smuggling, but the experienced con artist could be bluffing. He allows the crew to board the *Falcon* after a game of sabacc.

### L3-37

L3 is Lando's copilot and has exceptional navigational abilities thanks to her many modifications. This enlightened droid is passionate about droid rights.

Nerf-leather jacket

Gun belt

Fur conceals surprisingly nimble fingers

Ammunition cells crafted by Rio Durant

BlasTech RSKF-44 heavy blaster

Crimson Dawn emblem

Voorpak-fur lining

**SIGNET RING**

## CHEWBACCA

Chewbacca owes his freedom to Beckett's crew. Loyalty and the hope of finding other Wookiees prompts him to join their mission, rather than any desire for riches.

## BECKETT

A gunslinger from Glee Anselm, Tobias Beckett has assembled a team to carry out risky but profitable heists. He hopes to pay off his debts and live a quieter life.

## QI'RA

Cool and calculating Qi'ra works for a powerful criminal organization called Crimson Dawn. She joins the gang to ensure her employer gets a cut of the intended haul.

# HAN SOLO

Han grows up as a street thief on Corellia, spending his days working for a local crime gang and avoiding Imperial patrols. His desire to fly outweighs his apathy for the Empire, so he escapes from his impoverished life by joining the Imperial Navy. It is only when he meets Beckett's crew that Han is truly able to make use of the skills he learned on the streets. Han sees similarities between himself and Beckett, though the older man has a sense of true assuredness that inexperienced young Han can only try to emulate.

As a teenager, Han is forced to fight for survival on his homeworld of Corellia—a former shipbuilding hub that has become a place of poverty and gang warfare under Imperial rule.

## DATA FILE

> The Kessel Run is an established route through the safest areas of the Maelstrom that surrounds Kessel. Foolhardy pilots can skim off parsecs by taking a more dangerous route, but take a chance on what obstacles they may encounter.

# REBEL LEADERS

**THE REBEL ALLIANCE** is hard-pressed for ships and weapons, so it relies on its capable leaders to make the most of every asset. Living up to the highest standards of virtue and duty, they come from many backgrounds—from nobility and powerful government positions to mechanics, pilots, and merchants who have answered the call of justice and freedom. A good rebel leader can overcome the Empire's numeric advantage with inventive tactics, or find the words and deeds needed to bring new allies into the fight for freedom. The Alliance recognizes merit, and capable individuals soon find themselves in positions of authority.

### MON MOTHMA

Chandrillian Freedom Medal

Simple robe of office

Mon Mothma is the highest leader of the Rebellion. Abandoning her position in the Senate, she helps build the Rebel Alliance by uniting rebel cells such as Phoenix Squadron and continues to strengthen it through her diplomacy and negotiations. Focusing on freedom for all, Mon Mothma does not let fear rule her decisions. Losses are to be avoided, but nothing will convince her the Rebellion lacks merit.

### BAIL ORGANA

Bail Organa of Alderaan has been carefully building a network of like-minded politicians and influencers as Palpatine's power has grown. The Senate's influence has dwindled, and Bail now walks a razor's edge as Alderaan has funded, armed, and equipped the Rebellion in secret. Bail still has influence with new senators, but political manouverings have grown increasingly tense.

Dense flesh acts as insulator to protect ocular circulation

Mon Cal uniform jerkin

### ADMIRAL RADDUS

A stern and gruff Mon Calamari, Raddus has the unenviable task of staring down the might of the Imperial Starfleet and not blinking. Raddus is one of the commanding officers of the fledgling Alliance fleet, an asset Mon Mothma has described as the most vital component of the growing rebel military.

Sealed and coded datapad with mission orders

Command insignia

### ADMIRAL ACKBAR

The cautious Admiral Ackbar hails from the ocean world of Mon Cala. After securing the future of his planet during civil war as Captain of the Mon Calamari guard, Ackbar decides to join the Alliance, becoming commander of the rebel fleet. The giant Mon Cal star cruisers contributed by his people are the largest ships in the rebel fleet.

Moisture-retaining fabric

# GENERAL JAN DODONNA

In the early days of the Rebellion, Jan Dodonna commands the Massassi rebel splinter group. He continues to be vital to the Rebellion, becoming a general and part of the Alliance High Command. Dodonna is an important voice on the rebel council and his opinion is always considered, as he is an excellent tactician. Once Dodonna is in posession of the Death Star plans, he orchestrates the attack strategy to take down the superweapon, identifying the best hope of penetrating the considerable defenses. Monitoring the ensuing battle from Yavin 4, he is ready to alter formations and aid the rebels to victory.

## DATA FILE

> Ever democratic, military leaders are not the only members of the rebel coucil. Rebel senators such as Senator Vaspar, Minister for Industry, ensure the needs of the people are met, while debating with the generals.

Secondary passenger shuttle

Main shuttle

Hangar entrance

Ion engine

## GENERAL DAVITS DRAVEN

Draven is a veteran of the Clone Wars, a trusted field operative, and is the representative of Alliance Intelligence at the Yavin base. He and Mon Mothma do not always agree, but he has earned much respect. Draven is often left to make difficult or unpopular decisions.

## HOME ONE

One of the largest ships in the Alliance fleet, *Home One* is under the command of Admiral Ackbar. The Mon Calamari vessel acts as a mobile base for the Rebellion, and is the command ship during the Battle of Endor. Equipped with turbolaser and ion cannons, and tractor beams, the ship is heavily armed. The holographic amphitheater is a perfect briefing room—it is from here that rebel leaders instruct the strike force for the attack on the second Death Star.

## GENERAL CARLIST RIEEKAN

General Rieekan keeps the hidden levels of Echo Base in a state of constant alert, ever wary of discovery by Imperial forces. When the base is discovered, Rieekan commands the evacuation and assists in planning the next move for the rebellion—destroying the second Death Star.

## GENERAL CRIX MADINE

Crix Madine is the general of the Alliance's commando units. Madine is one of the chief strategists in the Alliance, and is the key mind behind the attack on the Imperial shield generator on the forest moon of Endor.

## REBEL INSIGNIA

The Alliance inherits Alderaanian insignia for its officers. Between one and five pips, arranged on a metal backing, denote the wearers rank.

 General

 Colonel

 Commander

 Major

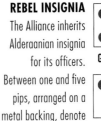 Captain

 Lieutenant

# REBEL HEROES

**NINETEEN YEARS INTO** the rule of the Empire, the Rebel Alliance learns of a deadly new Imperial superweapon called the Death Star, which is powerful enough to destroy entire planets. However, the creator of this battle station, Galen Erso, secretly includes a fatal flaw in its design, the details of which can be found in the plans. Stealing these plans would be the Alliance's first significant victory in the Galactic Civil War, but the risks are extremely high. A group of unlikely heroes, led by Erso's daughter, Jyn, are determined to succeed in this mission, no matter what the cost. The fate of billions of lives across the galaxy depends on their success.

**KYBER PENDANT**

**CROZO 2-MAL PERSONAL COMLINK**

*Scarf can be used to cover head*

*Insulated mechanic's vest*

**BATON TONFA**

### YOUNG WARRIOR
Jyn's time under Saw Gerrera's command has made her a tough hand-to-hand combatant. She is particularly skilled at taking down her opponents with a sturdy baton.

**STOLEN A180 BLASTER PISTOL**

*Primary programming port access door*

### K-2SO
Cassian Andor has reprogrammed this Imperial droid to serve the Rebel Alliance. K-2SO has a habit of offering blunt, and sometimes unwanted, statistics.

## ROGUE REBEL

After her father is forced into Imperial service, Jyn Erso grows up to be a resilient soldier. Raised—and then abandoned—by the rebel extremist, Saw Gerrera, her only priority is survival. However, when Jyn learns of the terrible destruction that the Death Star will bring to the galaxy, she puts aside her independent nature and learns to trust her fellow rebels.

*Practical combat boots*

**Modified repeating blaster**

**Pips denote rank of Captain; color indicates Army service**

**Traditional charcoal kasaya robe**

## BAZE MALBUS

Former Guardian of the Whills, Baze is a hardened enemy of the Empire. He may be gruff, but he cares greatly about his friends.

## BODHI ROOK

Imperial pilot Bodhi switches sides and becomes a rebel. He is the one to deliver Galen Erso's secret message to the Rebellion.

## CHIRRUT ÎMWE

Chirrut guards the Temple of the Kyber on Jedha. This monk is a skilled warrior, and has a deep connection to the Force.

**CHIRRUT'S STAFF**

**Military fatigues**

**Electroscope**

**Rapid fire barrel**

**Exhaust vent**

## CASSIAN ANDOR

Captain Cassian Andor is an accomplished Intelligence Officer for the Alliance. This hardened rebel agent has extensive experience in undercover and combat missions, and is known to follow orders without question. This all changes when he meets Jyn Erso and joins her in her mission to steal the Empire's Death Star plans.

**BAZE'S MODIFIED REPEATING BLASTER**

**Galven-circuitry charge belt**

**CASSIAN'S SECURITY KIT**

**Flashback supressor rim**

**BODHI'S CABLE BACKPACK**

**CHIRRUT'S LIGHTBOW**

**Recycled E-11 blaster handle**

**Stabilising handle**

**CASSIAN'S BLASTECH A280-CFE PISTOL**

**BODHI'S NEUROSAAV TE1.3 QUADNOCULARS**

**CHIRRUT'S JEDHA PENDANT**

**REBEL ALLIANCE'S REPORT ON JYN ERSO**

# PRINCESS LEIA ORGANA

Stolen Imperial blaster

Traditional gown of the Alderaan royal family

**STRONG-WILLED AND A WOMAN OF ACTION**, Princess Leia Organa of Alderaan uses her position in the Imperial Senate as a cover to help the Rebel Alliance. Able to travel throughout the galaxy on her consular ship *Tantive IV*, Leia brings aid to beleaguered planets and secret rebel cells that later form the Rebellion. Leia holds a crucial position at a fateful time for the galaxy, and she hides her personal feelings behind stern discipline and dedication to her cause.

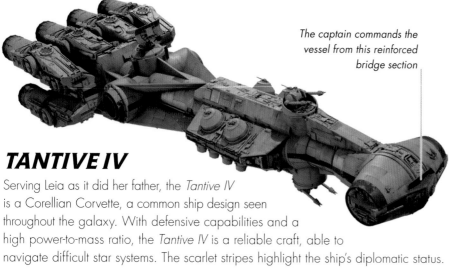

The captain commands the vessel from this reinforced bridge section

## TANTIVE IV

Serving Leia as it did her father, the *Tantive IV* is a Corellian Corvette, a common ship design seen throughout the galaxy. With defensive capabilities and a high power-to-mass ratio, the *Tantive IV* is a reliable craft, able to navigate difficult star systems. The scarlet stripes highlight the ship's diplomatic status.

Symbolic belt worn by Alderaan royalty

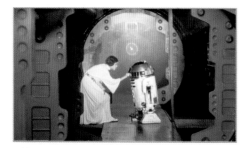

While on a secret mission to ensure the Rebellion gets the Death Star plans stolen from the Imperial archives on Scarif, and to find Jedi Knight Obi-Wan Kenobi, Leia is trapped onboard her diplomatic starship. Knowing she will be captured, she does what she can to ensure that her message will reach Obi-Wan, via R2-D2, even if she herself cannot.

## PREPARATION IS KEY

As the adopted daughter of Queen Breha Organa of Alderaan, Leia has been trained for her royal position from a young age. The princess is highly educated in a range of martial and political arts, as well as galactic etiquette, languages, and, of course, use of an array of weapons. In order to aid her father, she also becomes an adept spy and is skilled in all elements of espionage, including disguising herself.

Travel boots

### DATA FILE

> After the Battle of Yavin, a surviving Alderaanian pilot, Evaan Verlaine, alerts Princess Leia to the Empire's plans to hunt down those who survived Alderaan's obliteration. Both go on to save many of those left without their homeworld.

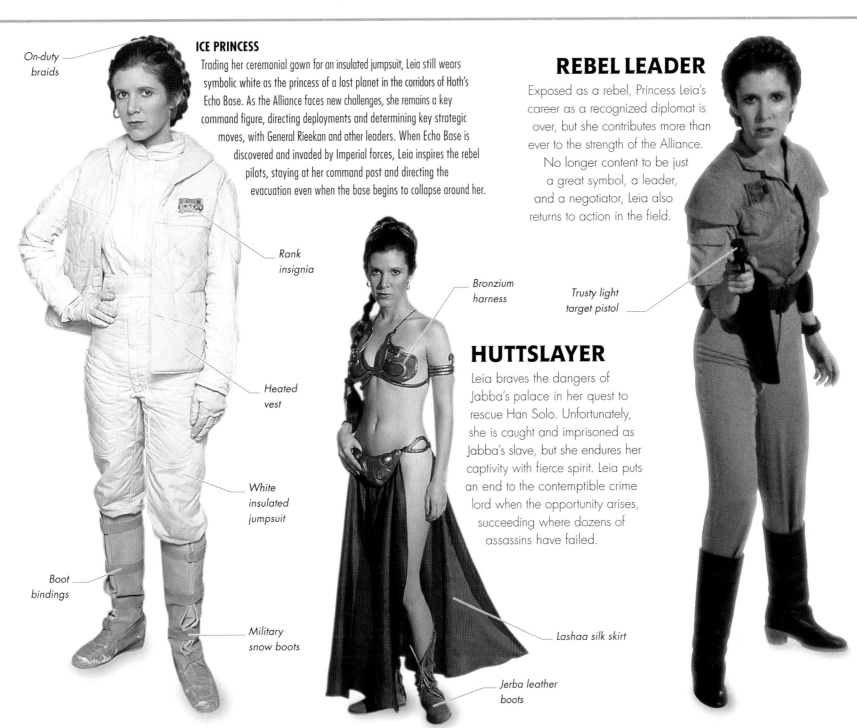

### ICE PRINCESS

Trading her ceremonial gown for an insulated jumpsuit, Leia still wears symbolic white as the princess of a lost planet in the corridors of Hoth's Echo Base. As the Alliance faces new challenges, she remains a key command figure, directing deployments and determining key strategic moves, with General Rieekan and other leaders. When Echo Base is discovered and invaded by Imperial forces, Leia inspires the rebel pilots, staying at her command post and directing the evacuation even when the base begins to collapse around her.

On-duty braids

Rank insignia

Heated vest

White insulated jumpsuit

Boot bindings

Military snow boots

## REBEL LEADER

Exposed as a rebel, Princess Leia's career as a recognized diplomat is over, but she contributes more than ever to the strength of the Alliance. No longer content to be just a great symbol, a leader, and a negotiator, Leia also returns to action in the field.

Trusty light target pistol

Bronzium harness

## HUTTSLAYER

Leia braves the dangers of Jabba's palace in her quest to rescue Han Solo. Unfortunately, she is caught and imprisoned as Jabba's slave, but she endures her captivity with fierce spirit. Leia puts an end to the contemptible crime lord when the opportunity arises, succeeding where dozens of assassins have failed.

Lashaa silk skirt

Jerba leather boots

### FOREST DIPLOMAT

Leia's good spirit, compassion, and gift for diplomacy aid her on missions. When she encounters the Ewoks on Endor, she saves two of them, and swaps her combat uniform for clothes they make for her. Leia's actions help her to win these unexpected allies.

Vision-plus scanner

Targetting laser

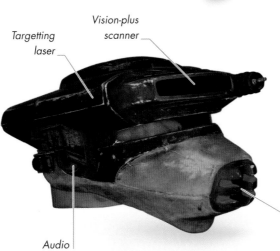

Audio pickup and broadband antenna

### BOUSHH'S HELMET

In order to resuce Han Solo, Leia dresses in the armor of the well-known bounty hunter, Boushh, under the guise to collecting the bounty that Jabba has on Chewbacca.

Metal speech-srambler

### FORCE-SENSITIVE

Initially unbenownst to her, Leia is Luke Skywalker's twin. As his control over the Force grows, her Force-sensitivity becomes more evident. When Luke is hanging from below Cloud City on Bespin, Leia feels he is in trouble and turns the fleeing *Millenium Falcon* around to rescue him. At the conclusion of the Battle of Endor, Leia is able to sense from the surface of the forest moon that Luke escaped the second Death Star before it blew up.

# LUKE SKYWALKER

**A YOUNG FARMBOY** living on the remote desert planet Tatooine, Luke Skywalker yearns to escape the dull routine of his daily chores on his uncle's moisture farm. Luke dreams of becoming a space pilot, but is torn between his desire to enroll in the Imperial Academy and his loyalty to his uncle and aunt, who need him on the farm. When Luke discovers a cryptic secret message hidden in one of his new droids, he sets out on a quest and is catapulted into a world of adventure which will at last fulfill his true destiny.

*Tatooine farm tunic*

## T–16 SKYHOPPER MODEL

Luke owns a suborbital T-16 skyhopper (plus a small model of one), which he races through the narrow ravines of Beggar's Canyon with his friends, blasting womp rat dens in sheltered hollows. Having narrowly made it through both Diablo Cut and the Stone Needle, Luke has proven himself an excellent pilot. He cannot search for R2-D2 in the skyhopper because his uncle has grounded him for reckless flying.

*Model includes enhancements Luke hopes to buy when he can afford them*

*Emblem Luke would like to add*

*Pneumatic projectile gun for blasting womp rats*

*Display base*

*Droid caller*

*Tool pouch*

*Light pants*

*Anakin Skywalker's lightsaber*

Tosche power station in a small town just outside of Anchorhead offers a place for Luke to escape the farm and spend time with his friends—talking, playing electronically assisted pool, or tinkering with his landspeeder or skyhopper.

## EAGER FOR ADVENTURE

Luke's aunt and uncle try to ensure he remains in the relative safety of their moisture farm, but keen for action, Luke often manages to get into trouble. Whether standing up to thugs, or making dangerous flights on his skyhopper he strains at the restricted lifestyle and is often grounded, adding to his frustration.

*Pitting from desert sand and gravel*

*Sandproof leg bindings*

*Grip soles*

### DATA FILE

> Luke's best friend, Biggs Darklighter, left Tatooine to enlist in the Imperial Academy, which had been Luke's dream too. Biggs graduated with a commission on the freighter *Rand Ecliptic*. The friends are reunited on the flight deck of the rebel base at Yavin 4, where Biggs is a rebel pilot.

# LIGHTSABER

Luke's lightsaber is the legacy of his father Anakin, a former Jedi Knight of the Republic and a warrior who fought in the Clone Wars. A symbol of Luke's destiny, the lightsaber is unlike any other weapon. Luke has a natural ability with the saber and learns rapidly from his mentor Ben Kenobi.

Luke uses macrobinoculars to observe a space battle between two ships far overhead. The macrobinoculars provide electronic zoom and image enhancement capability, as well as target range.

## VIEW FROM LUKE'S MACROBINOCULARS

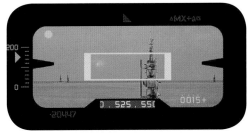

## LUKE'S LANDSPEEDER

Luke's X-34 landspeeder hovers above the ground, suspended by repulsorlifts even when parked. Three turbines boost the repulsor drive effect and jet the speeder across the open spaces of the desert. The windshield can be closed to a sealed bubble, but Luke hasn't been able to fix the back half, so he keeps the cockpit open.

Quick recharge plug

Blade length adjust

Activation matrix

Power cell

Handgrip

Luke first encounters part of the hidden truth about his father when Ben Kenobi gives him his father's Jedi lightsaber. In Luke's hands it flares to life again for the first time in many years.

### TRAINING HELMET

During lightsaber training with Obi-Wan Kenobi, Luke wears a fighter pilot's helmet with a painted-over blast shield. This helps him focus, and is reminiscent of Jedi training methods used during the time of the Republic. Luke must learn to trust his natural instincts, and removing his sense of sight helps him reach out for the Force.

Blacked-out blast shield

In order to rescue Princess Leia, Luke and Han steal stormtrooper armor to gain access to the prison cells onboard the Death Star. This plan works, but they are caught under stormtrooper fire. Although proving himself a gifted fighter, Luke's first adventure shows how impulsive he is—far from the calm, collected mindset needed to become a Jedi Knight.

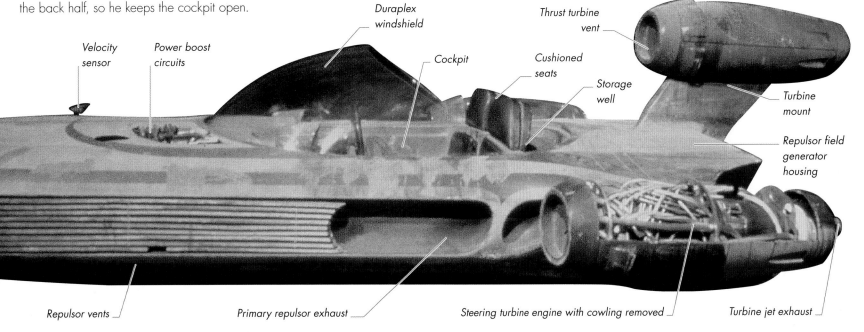

Duraplex windshield

Thrust turbine vent

Velocity sensor

Power boost circuits

Cockpit

Cushioned seats

Storage well

Turbine mount

Repulsor field generator housing

Repulsor vents

Primary repulsor exhaust

Steering turbine engine with cowling removed

Turbine jet exhaust

# LUKE SKYWALKER: PILOT AND JEDI

**LUKE SKYWALKER FIRST CLIMBS** into the cockpit of an X-wing starfighter to fly as "Red Five" in the attack on the first Death Star. Fighting for the Alliance in the years afterward, Luke takes his X-wing and other craft into battle against Imperial ships, bringing victories for the hard-pressed rebels, and discovering more about the history of the Jedi, tracking down forgotten temples. His Force abilities are developed by Master Yoda and, over the years, Luke grows toward becoming a Jedi Knight at last.

Chest pack straps

Flak vest

Pressurized g-suit

Life support unit

Data cylinders

Insulated helmet

Alliance symbol

Safe passage documents for downed pilots

Upper Taim & Bak KX9 laser cannon

Wings open to X configuration for combat

Astromech droid

Long-range laser cannons

Krupx MG7 proton torpedo launcher

Flight gauntlets

## T–65 X–WING

The X-wing fighter carries a small payload of proton torpedoes in addition to its laser cannons, but they are expensive ordnance, and in short supply for the Alliance. This means that Luke goes into battle against the Death Star with only two torpedoes at his disposal.

Power coupling access port

Gear harness

Simulation of proton torpedo entering the small thermal exhaust port that is the rebels' target

Targeting computer signal to fire

Equipment pocket

**X-WING TARGETING COMPUTER SCREEN**

The stolen Death Star plans allow the rebel leaders to simulate the effects of different kinds of attacks on the battle station.

Flight boots

## DARING FLYER

Luke's bravery makes him a great rebel leader, but it also takes him into many dangerous situations. When he leads a squadron against the Imperials in the Battle of Hoth, his snowspeeder is blasted from the sky! The ship's equipment is wiped out, but Luke doesn't give up. He struggles out of the cockpit—moments before his snowspeeder is crushed by an AT-AT.

Signal flares

Positive-grip soles

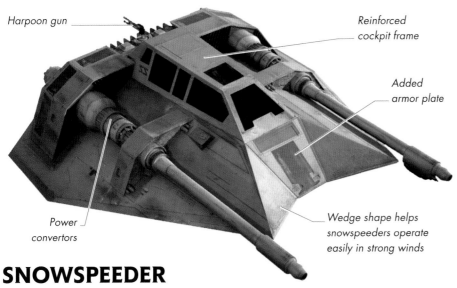

Harpoon gun

Reinforced cockpit frame

Added armor plate

Power convertors

Wedge shape helps snowspeeders operate easily in strong winds

# SNOWSPEEDER

These speeders are equipped with armor plating and heavy-duty blaster cannons. Laboriously modified to operate in the frozen temperatures of Hoth, the snowspeeders have no defensive shields and must rely on agility and speed in battle. Luke, as a wing commander, leads the Rogue Squadron of snowspeeders against the Imperial Blizzard Force AT-ATs.

## WAMPA

While out on a patrol on the ice planet Hoth, Luke is caught unawares by a wampa. This large, vicious creature takes Luke back to its lair, intending to eat him! He manages to escape the creature, but his serious injuries cause him to collapse in the snow.

Although he spends only a short time with the wise Jedi Master, Luke learns much from Yoda. The training tests Luke's patience with tedious tasks that seem to have no purpose, and he must learn to curb his emotional reactions in order to face his father and become a Jedi Knight.

Energy blade emitter

Ridged handgrip

Activation switch

## GREEN BLADE

When Luke's first lightsaber is lost in his duel with Vader at Cloud City, Luke must construct a new one. His own lightsaber has a vibrant green blade, like the lightsabers used by Qui-Gon Jinn and others. The handle is modeled in a similar style to Obi-Wan Kenobi's.

# JEDI KNIGHT

Luke continues to improve his abilities with Yoda after facing the truth about his father's identity. After assisting in Han's rescue on Tatooine and returning to Dagobah, a dying Yoda informs Luke that his training is complete. Luke moves on to his final challenge before becoming a true Jedi and fulfilling his destiny—facing the darkest challenges of the Emperor and Darth Vader.

Mechanical hand

Lightsaber hook

## THE SHADOW OF DARTH VADER

Growing up, Luke never knew much about his father. Ben Kenobi revealed that Luke's father had been a Jedi Knight, but the secret of his death remained clouded by the evil figure of Darth Vader. Only in close combat with Vader does Luke learn the truth that will pose his greatest challenge with the Force.

# R2-D2: REBEL DROID

**THIS R-SERIES ASTROMECH** has a long history of adventures, the memories of which have built up in his processors, giving him a distinct personality. R2-D2 exhibits a strong motivation to succeed in his assigned tasks, and displays extraordinary determination and inventiveness for a utility droid. His human masters may not always understand R2's electronic beeps and whistles, but that doesn't stop him from trying to communicate anyway, and he usually manages to get his points across. Highly loyal, R2 is never reluctant to risk damage or destruction to help his masters and accomplish missions.

## HOLOGRAPHIC PROJECTOR

By accessing data, R2-D2 can create three-dimensional displays of starship systems. To make a holographic recording of a proximal being or object, the droid's visual sensors are used in combination with his acoustic signaler; an automatic analysis of reflected sound waves creates a visual pattern that "fills in" the areas that R2 cannot see directly.

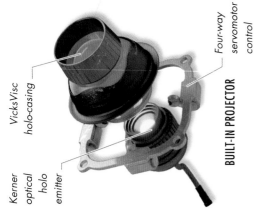

*Vicks Visc holo-casing*

*Four-way servomotor control*

*Kerner optical holo emitter*

**BUILT-IN PROJECTOR**

*Main power coupling* — **MAIN POWER COUPLING**

*Overload heat vent*

**MOTIVATOR HOUSING AND VENT**

*Stored experiences*

**MEMORY CHIP**

*Inert alloy plate*

## REBEL AGENT

R2-D2 is far more than an average astromech droid; he comes up with innovative solutions to problems his rebel friends encounter on missions. While facing two muderous droids (BT-1 and 0-0-0) on Vrogas Vas, R2 quickly emits a well-aimed jet of oil, hitting BT-1's sensors and blinding him, allowing R2 and his friends to escape. On Cloud City, R2 uses his fire extinguisher to create a mist that conceals his allies from stormtroopers. This plucky astromech even launches an attack on an Imperial Star Destroyer all by himself, burning and electrocuting anyone that gets in the way of him liberating his gold-plated friend, C-3PO.

*Extendible auxiliary visual imaging system*

*Electromagnetic field sensor unit*

*Commutator*

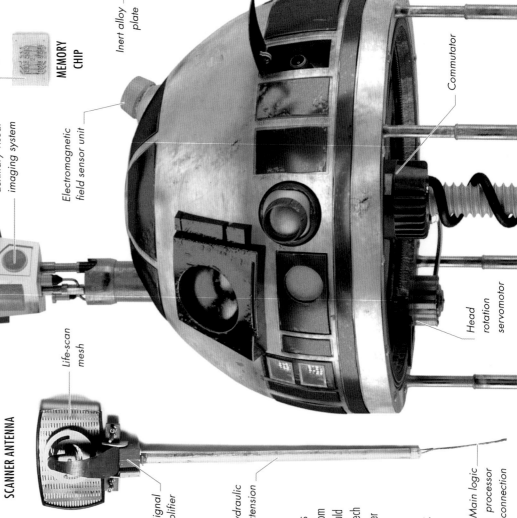

*Head rotation servomotor*

*Life-scan mesh*

**SCANNER ANTENNA**

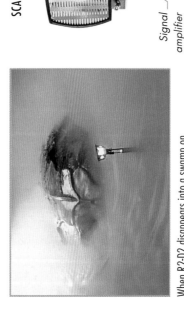

*Signal amplifier*

*Hydraulic extension*

When R2-D2 disappears into a swamp on Dagobah, Luke thinks he may have lost his companion for good until R2's periscope pops out of the murky water.

*Main logic processor connection*

An onboard astromech unit is a vital component of the Incom T-65 X-wing. Most pilots would want to use the best astromech available, but Luke Skywalker grows attached to R2-D2 and chooses the droid to accompany him in the attack on the Death Star and many subsequent missions.

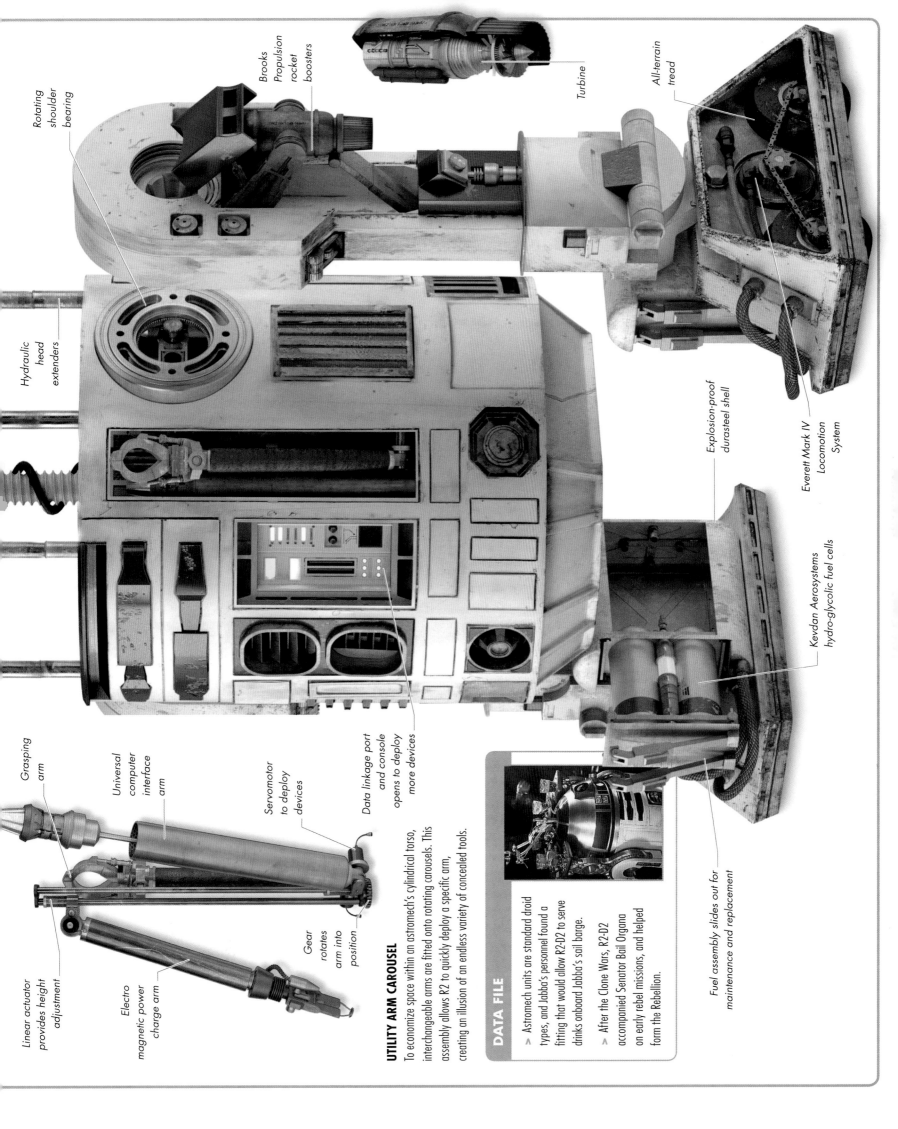

Rotating shoulder bearing

Brooks Propulsion rocket boosters

Turbine

All-terrain tread

Hydraulic head extenders

Explosion-proof durasteel shell

Everett Mark IV Locomotion System

Kevdan Aerosystems hydro-glycolic fuel cells

Grasping arm

Universal computer interface arm

Servomotor to deploy devices

Data linkage port and console opens to deploy more devices

Linear actuator provides height adjustment

Electro magnetic power charge arm

Gear rotates arm into position

Fuel assembly slides out for maintenance and replacement

## UTILITY ARM CAROUSEL

To economize space within an astromech's cylindrical torso, interchangeable arms are fitted onto rotating carousels. This assembly allows R2 to quickly deploy a specific arm, creating an illusion of an endless variety of concealed tools.

## DATA FILE

≫ Astromech units are standard droid types, and Jabba's personnel found a fitting that would allow R2-D2 to serve drinks onboard Jabba's sail barge.

≫ After the Clone Wars, R2-D2 accompanied Senator Bail Organa on early rebel missions, and helped form the Rebellion.

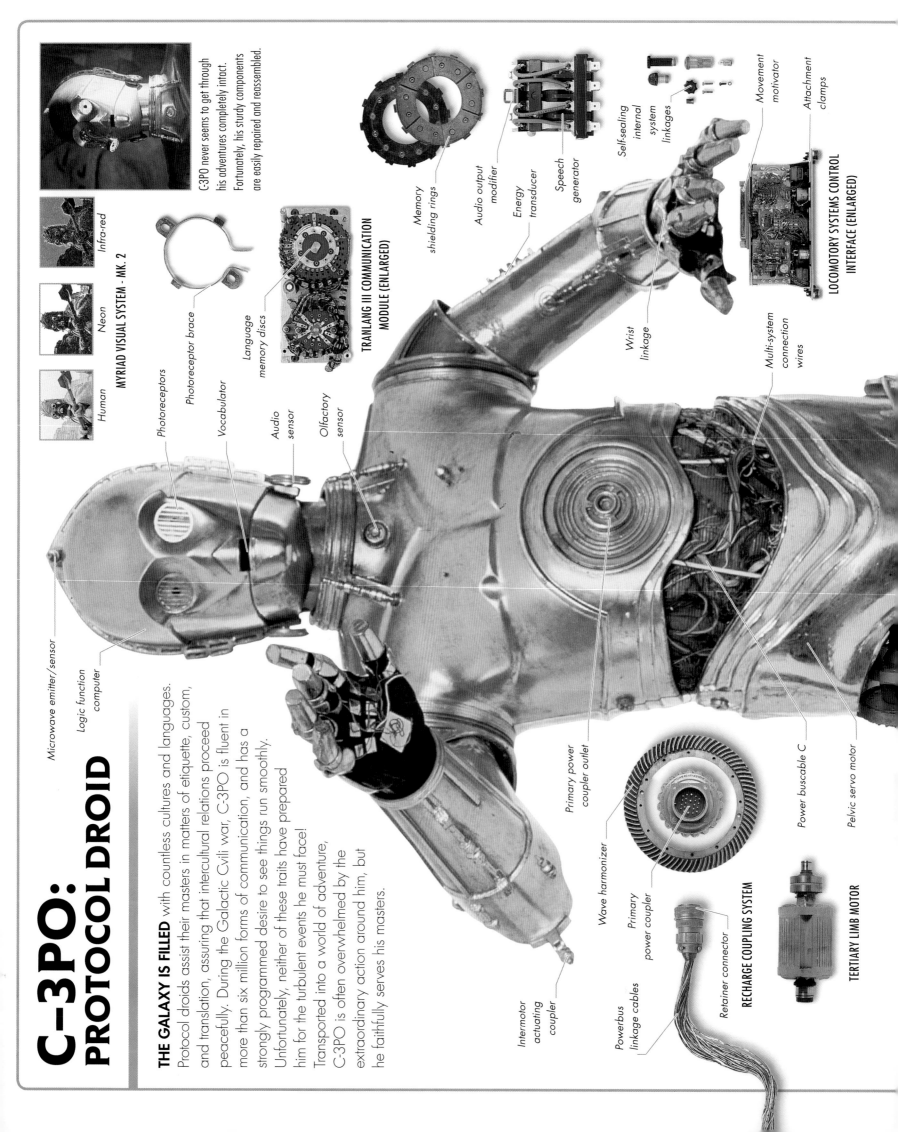

# C-3PO: PROTOCOL DROID

**THE GALAXY IS FILLED** with countless cultures and languages. Protocol droids assist their masters in matters of etiquette, custom, and translation, assuring that intercultural relations proceed peacefully. During the Galactic Cvili war, C-3PO is fluent in more than six million forms of communication, and has a strongly programmed desire to see things run smoothly. Unfortunately, neither of these traits have prepared him for the turbulent events he must face! Transported into a world of adventure, C-3PO is often overwhelmed by the extraordinary action around him, but he faithfully serves his masters.

C-3PO never seems to get through his adventures completely intact. Fortunately, his sturdy components are easily repaired and reassembled.

Human

Neon

Infra-red

**MYRIAD VISUAL SYSTEM - MK. 2**

Memory shielding rings

Audio output modifier

Energy transducer

Speech generator

Self-sealing internal system linkages

Movement motivator

Attachment clamps

**TRANLANG III COMMUNICATION MODULE (ENLARGED)**

**LOCOMOTORY SYSTEMS CONTROL INTERFACE (ENLARGED)**

Photoreceptor brace

Photoreceptors

Vocabulator

Audio sensor

Olfactory sensor

Language memory discs

Microwave emitter/sensor

Logic function computer

Wrist linkage

Multi-system connection wires

Primary power coupler outlet

Wave harmonizer

Primary power coupler

Power buscable C

Pelvic servo motor

Intermotor actuating coupler

Retainer connector

**RECHARGE COUPLING SYSTEM**

Powerbus linkage cables

**TERTIARY LIMB MOTOR**

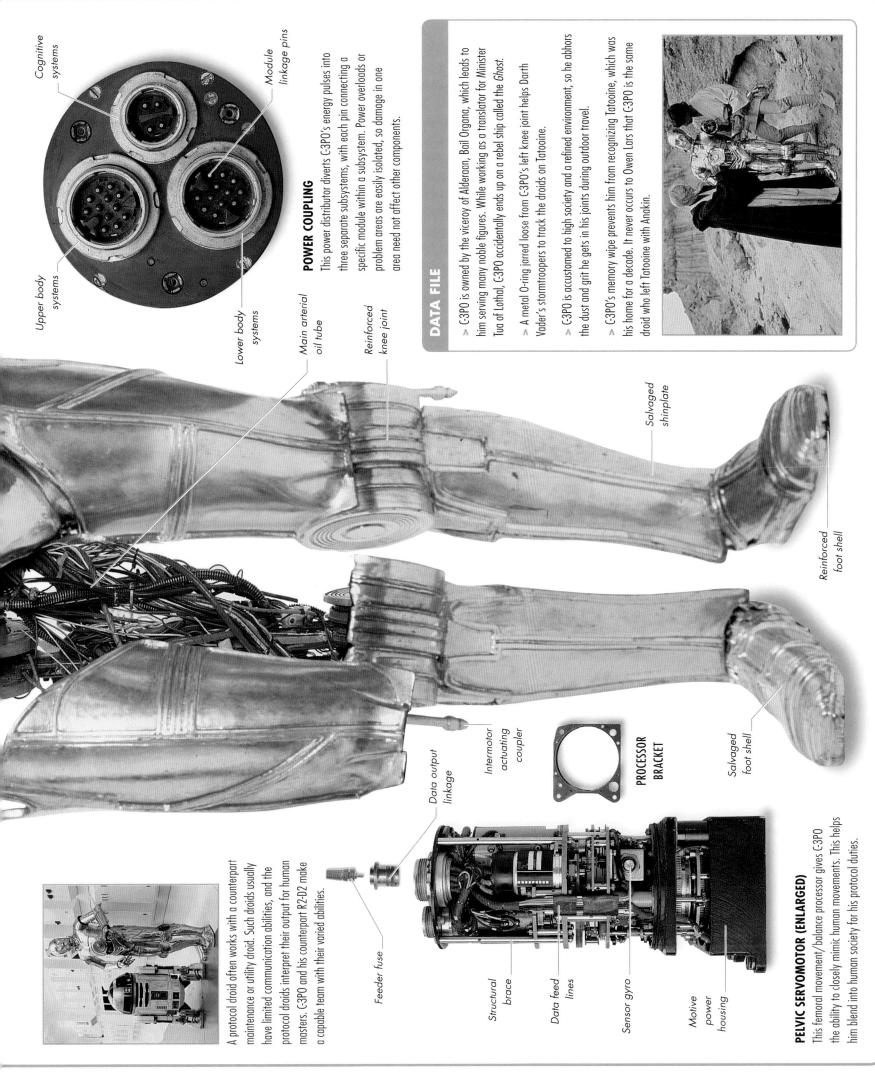

Cognitive systems

Module linkage pins

Upper body systems

Lower body systems

Main arterial oil tube

Reinforced knee joint

## POWER COUPLING

This power distributor diverts C-3PO's energy pulses into three separate subsystems, with each pin connecting a specific module within a subsystem. Power overloads or problem areas are easily isolated, so damage in one area need not affect other components.

Salvaged shinplate

Reinforced foot shell

Data output linkage

Intermotor actuating coupler

## PROCESSOR BRACKET

Salvaged foot shell

A protocol droid often works with a counterpart maintenance or utility droid. Such droids usually have limited communication abilities, and the protocol droids interpret their output for human masters. C-3PO and his counterpart R2-D2 make a capable team with their varied abilities.

Feeder fuse

Structural brace

Data feed lines

Sensor gyro

Motive power housing

## PELVIC SERVOMOTOR (ENLARGED)

This femoral movement/balance processor gives C-3PO the ability to closely mimic human movements. This helps him blend into human society for his protocol duties.

# HAN SOLO

**MERCENARY PIRATE, SMUGGLER CAPTAIN**, and cocksure braggart, the overly confident Han Solo is a rugged individual of the Galactic Rim. A Corellian pilot of the finest caliber, Solo gains control of his destiny when he wins his ship, the *Millennium Falcon*, in a game of sabacc. His reputation as a gunfighter matches his renown as captain of the *Falcon*. While Han may be reckless and foolhardy, he is also courageous and daring—a match for any adventure.

Han becomes indebted to one of his employers, Jabba the Hutt, after jetisoning some of the crime lord's cargo when spotted by Imperial forces. When Han is faced at gunpoint by one of Jabba's minions in the Mos Eisley Cantina, he slowly draws his blaster under the table. With a well timed shot, Solo escapes from a tight spot.

Customized blaster pistol

Corellian spacer black vest and light shirt

Scope

Scope settings and adjustment

Flash suppressor

Blast delivery circuits

Cooling unit

Quick-draw holster

Droid caller

Trigger

**HAN SOLO'S DL-44 PISTOL**

Blaster power cell

Low-power pulse warning

Holster thigh grip

Captain's pants

Captain Solo's loyal friend and first mate is the imposing Wookiee, Chewbacca. Each has risked his life for the other in many tight situations. Between Han's fast draw and Chewbacca's immense strength, the two are not to be trifled with.

## DATA FILE

> Han has heard spacers' tales about the legendary titan space slug. However, none of these stories can prepare him for having to fly the *Falcon* out of the belly of a live space slug. He only just escapes through its teeth!

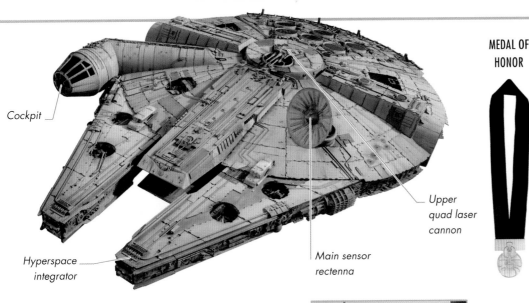

Cockpit

Hyperspace integrator

Upper quad laser cannon

Main sensor rectenna

Solo's last-minute rescue of Luke Skywalker during the Battle of Yavin saves the Rebel Alliance. His bravery wins him one of the highest medals of honor, along with Chewbacca and Luke.

## HAN IN CARBONITE

Han Solo becomes trapped in a plot by Darth Vader to ensnare Luke Skywalker. He is taken to the industrial bowels of Cloud City and flash-frozen in carbonite to test the process meant to immobilize Luke. Carbon-freezing is a way of bonding condensed Tibanna gas for transport, but can be used to keep life forms in suspended animation when the painful process of freezing does not kill them.

## MILLENNIUM FALCON

This battered and aging YT-1300 light freighter is one of the fastest vessels in the galaxy, due to extensive modifications made by Han, as well as previous owners. Even at sublight speeds, its velocity and maneuverability are extraordinary for a ship of its class. The *Falcon* sports Imperial military-grade armor, quad laser cannons, a top-of-the-line sensor rectenna, and many other illegal and customized hot-rod components. Not only is it a powerful workhorse, it also makes for a unique home.

With the *Falcon* on the run and in need of repairs, Han Solo lands at Bespin to meet the ship's previous owner Lando Calrissian, not knowing how Lando will react.

Carbonite frame

Life system monitor

Flash-blasted carbonite matrix

## REBEL LEADER

After the victory at Yavin, Han accepts a commission as captain in the Rebel Alliance. At Echo Base on Hoth, he volunteers for perimeter patrol duty even though he does not like tauntauns or the cold. Han is a natural leader and serves as an inspiration to many of the troops around him.

Heavy weather parka

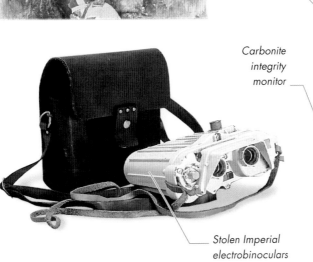

Carbonite flux monitor

**REBEL SENSOR PACK**

Extensible antenna

Stentronic wave monitor

Power indicator

Range cycle computer

Power cells

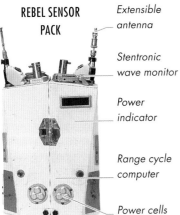

Gas ratio monitor

Carbonite integrity monitor

### HOTH EQUIPMENT

With their patrol craft paralyzed by the icy cold, the rebels must survey the snow plains of Hoth with hand-carried gear. Han Solo is an expert at keeping a low profile and seeing others before they see him, and has helped design the Echo Base perimeter survey plan.

Stolen Imperial electrobinoculars

# CHEWBACCA:
## SKILLFUL CO-PILOT

**CHEWBACCA IS A** mighty Wookiee from the planet Kashyyyk. At more than 200 years old, he in the prime of life for such a long-living species. Chewie uses his mechanical abilities to keep Han Solo's heavily modified starship flying, and serves as both a fiercely loyal co-pilot and a trusty fellow adventurer. He enjoys a good fight, which is sometimes caused by his fierce temper, and likes the action that Han gets them into. However, Chewbacca can also act as his partner's conscience when Han's ego takes over, bringing the smuggler back to reality with a growl.

Sensitive nose

Bandolier

Blue eyes

Padding

Insulated lining

Six-shell ammo case

Quarrel

**AMMO CASE**

Detonator pin

Energy shell flare material

Shell casing

Accelerator lock surface

**QUARREL**

### BOWCASTER AMMUNITION

The traditional Wookiee bowcaster uses a magnetic accelerator to fire explosive quarrels, which are enveloped in a penetrating energy shell as they are fired.

Chewbacca loves strategy games like dejarik or holochess, but hates losing—especially to someone he doesn't know. New opponents are likely to get injured!

Chewie is a sharp shot. With a range of 50 m (164 ft), his weapon of choice, the bowcaster, is very handy for covering quick get-aways.

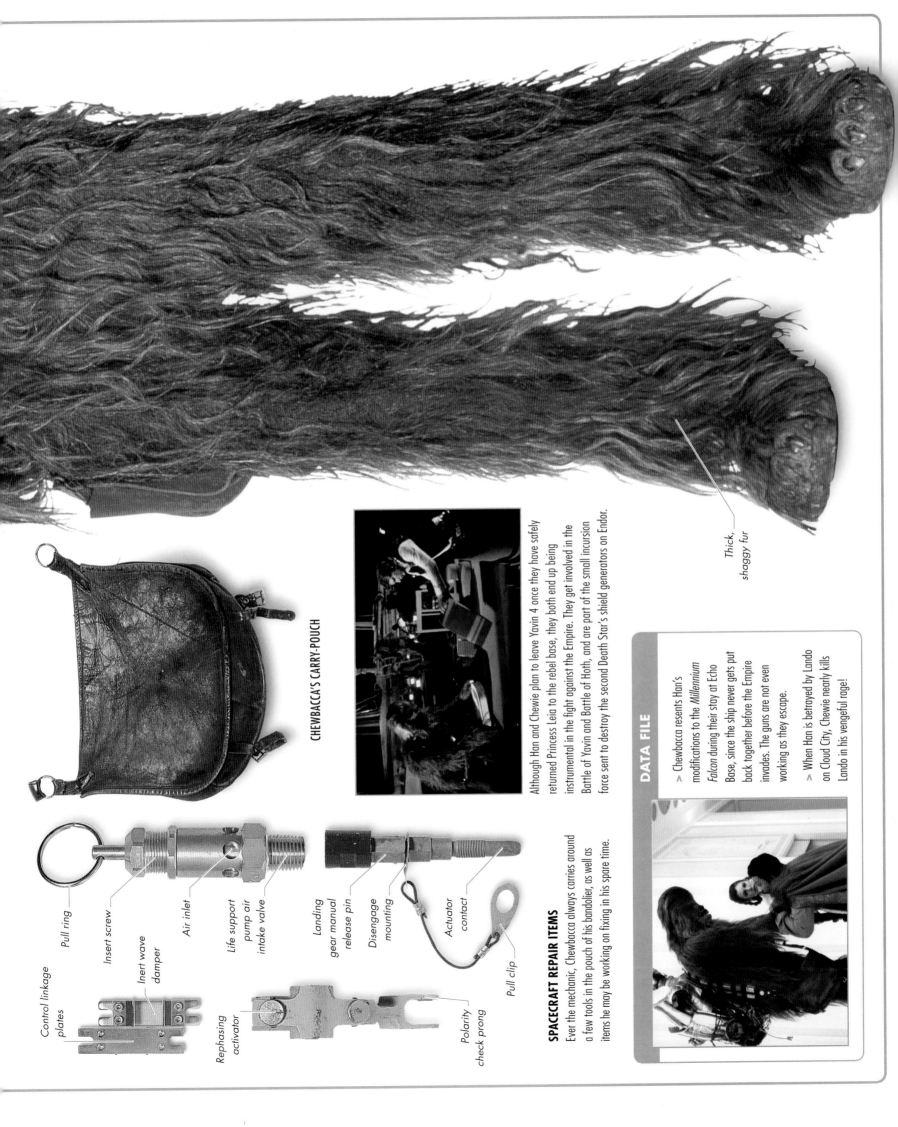

Thick, shaggy fur

**CHEWBACCA'S CARRY-POUCH**

Although Han and Chewie plan to leave Yavin 4 once they have safely returned Princess Leia to the rebel base, they both end up being instrumental in the fight against the Empire. They get involved in the Battle of Yavin and Battle of Hoth, and are part of the small incursion force sent to destroy the second Death Star's shield generators on Endor.

## SPACECRAFT REPAIR ITEMS

Ever the mechanic, Chewbacca always carries around a few tools in the pouch of his bandolier, as well as items he may be working on fixing in his spare time.

Control linkage plates

Pull ring

Insert screw

Inert wave damper

Air inlet

Life support pump air intake valve

Landing gear manual release pin

Disengage mounting

Rephasing activator

Actuator contact

Polarity check prong

Pull clip

# LANDO CALRISSIAN

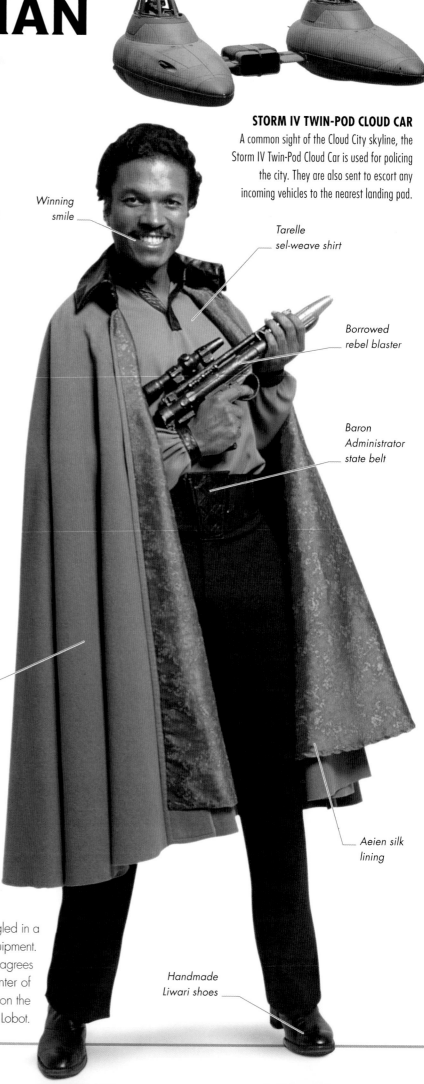

**FEW ON BESPIN WOULD SUSPECT** the checkered past of the dashing Baron Administrator of Cloud City, but Lando Calrissian has had many criminal dealings. A rogue and a con artist, Lando came from modest beginnings, but built a reputation as a daring smuggler captain with a good head for business. Lando's habit of gambling does not always pay, but fortune favors him when a game of sabacc leaves him the leader of Cloud City. Lando's flare for making money, combined with his natural leadership, has made the Bespin facility very profitable. The role of Baron Administrator also allows Lando to indulge his expensive and flamboyant tastes.

**STORM IV TWIN-POD CLOUD CAR**
A common sight of the Cloud City skyline, the Storm IV Twin-Pod Cloud Car is used for policing the city. They are also sent to escort any incoming vehicles to the nearest landing pad.

*Winning smile*

*Tarelle sel-weave shirt*

*Borrowed rebel blaster*

*Baron Administrator state belt*

## CLOUD CITY

Suspended high above the core of the gas giant Bespin, Cloud City was once the headquarters of great royal leaders. A shadow of its former self, the city has become a center for industry, processing the rare anti-gravitational tibanna gas in Bespin's atmosphere. Cloud City is supported on a single giant column which stems from a processing reactor at its base. The hollow air shaft core houses gigantic directional vanes which control the facility's location.

*Baron's cape*

*Aeien silk lining*

### DATA FILE

> Cloud City is home to industrious citizens and advanced technology. Facilities process for export the rare anti-gravitational tibanna gas from the exotic atmosphere of Bespin.

> Using a comlink and his security code, Lando can address all parts of Cloud City from any central computer terminal.

## MINING MOGUL

Lando's early foray in mining took place on the Outer Rim planet of Lothal, on a much smaller scale than Bespin. To avoid Imperial regulations, he smuggled in a puffer pig to sniff out precious minerals more discreetly than large mining equipment. When running Cloud City, Lando is still eager to avoid the Empire's attention, so agrees to trade with Darth Vader. Bargaining the rebels for the freedom of his center of operations, Lando betrays his friend, Han Solo. However, when Vader reneges on the bargain, Lando regrets his deal, and plots a rescue and escape with his aide Lobot.

*Handmade Liwari shoes*

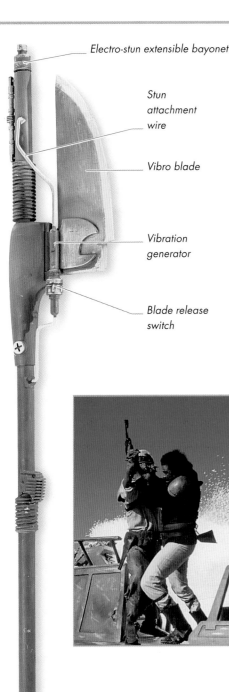

Electro-stun extensible bayonet

Stun attachment wire

Vibro blade

Vibration generator

Blade release switch

Grip

Blade/ electro-stun power unit

Reinforced lance pole

**BD-1 CUTTER VIBRO-AX**

## LOBOT

Although handy for his work as the Chief Administrative Aide of Cloud City, Lobot's enhancements have cost him dearly. Early on in Lando and Lobot's friendship, they took on a job to steal the Emperor's personal yacht, *Imperialis*. Lobot was confronted by Imperial Guards while on board, and was severely wounded. The cybernetic implants need constant focus to be kept in check, and as Lobot lost conciousness they began to take over, leaving him a shell of his former self.

**LANDO'S SKIFF GUARD HELMET**

Lando braves the very heart of danger to rescue Han Solo, disguised as a lowly skiff guard at Jabba's palace. His old con man skills are put to good use, and no one at the palace ever suspects him until it is too late.

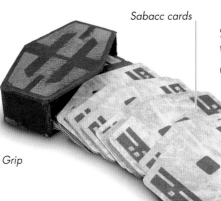

Rank insignia

Rank plaque

Alliance general's uniform

Sidearm blaster

Dress cape

Wrist comlink

Sabacc cards

### SABACC

Whether losing the *Millenium Falcon* to Han Solo, or winning the position of Baron Administrator of Cloud City, games of sabacc can mean big changes for Lando. At Old Jho's Pit Stop on Lothal, he plays a lucky game against Gazareb Orrelios of the Spectres rebel cell. Lando wins their droid, Chopper, with the best possible sabacc hand—known as "Idiot's Array."

## GENERAL LANDO

Having become a renegade on the run from the Empire, Lando falls in with the rebels after leaving Cloud City. His penetrating judgment at the Battle of Taanab wins Lando a promotion within the ranks, and the former con artist and baron becomes a general within the Alliance. He dons a cape once more, a symbol of his regained honor and authority. Grown beyond his self-centered past, Lando still finds adventure but now contributes his abilities to a greater cause.

# OBI-WAN KENOBI:
## JEDI IN EXILE

Jedi robes

Hooded cloak

**THE HERMIT BEN KENOBI** lives far from the settlements of Tatooine, out in the Jundland Wastes. He is dismissed by many as crazy, but they have no idea who this mysterious figure truly is. He was once Obi-Wan Kenobi, Jedi Knight, and a great warrior of the Republic during the Clone Wars. Kenobi retreats to Tatooine after the rise of Emperor Palpatine, watching over the young Luke Skywalker. Obi-Wan waits for the right time to reveal Luke's lineage as the son of a Jedi, and begin his training in the ways of the Force. Even in his elder years, Obi-Wan Kenobi's powers make him a threat to the Empire.

Kenobi lives simply, in accordance with Jedi philosophy and to ensure his true identity remains hidden. He keeps only a few reminders of his former life in his home on Tatooine. It is here that Kenobi gives Luke his father's lightsaber.

## SECRET PROTECTOR

Luke Skywalker's uncle, Owen Lars, forbids Kenobi from seeing the boy, fearing that Luke will follow his father's footsteps. However, Obi-Wan continues to watch over Luke and protect him. When Luke confronts Jabba the Hutt's thugs about their extortion of local farmers, he is pushed over and knocked unconscious. An observing Kenobi intervenes, fending off the attackers and returning Luke to his homestead. Luke is unaware of how much the old Jedi does for him until he returns to Tatooine and reads Kenobi's journal.

Air jet

Tracking sensor

Shock ray emitter

Hovering training remotes are used by Jedi to sharpen reflexes and develop coordination. They can be set to varying degrees of aggressiveness and their shock rays can be adjusted from harmless to painful.

TRAINING REMOTE

Kenobi only trains Luke in person for a short time before facing his final lightsaber duel. Obi-Wan sacrifices himself in the duel, knowing he must become one with the Force, and is struck down by Vader.

### DATA FILE

> Ben Kenobi rescues 12-year-old Luke and his friend Windy after they are left unconcious during a sandstorm. Luke wakes to find a krayt dragon sneaking up on him, but Kenobi beheads it just in time.

> An enemy of Kenobi's past, Maul, tracks him down to Tatooine, seeking vengence. The two duel, and Obi-Wan is able to defeat Maul once and for all.

# YODA:
## JEDI IN EXILE

## DAGOBAH

Dagobah is a remote planet of swamps and mists. It hides a tremendous variety of life forms, including gnarl trees, butcherbugs, and swamp slugs. This inhospitable setting makes a good hiding place during the dark days of the Empire.

**THE WISE JEDI MASTER YODA** should not be judged by his small size. At almost 900 years old, his life spent in contemplation and training have given him deep insight and profound abilities. One of his greatest challenges is mentoring Luke Skywalker, who arrives on Dagobah an impatient would-be Jedi. In the short time he has with Luke, Yoda must instill in him the faith and harmony with the Force that will fulfill Luke's potential. He must also guard him from the dark path of temptation, anger, and evil. Yoda imparts the heart of the ancient Jedi traditions to his final student.

Yoda spends his days in meditation, seeing ever deeper into the infinite tapestry that is the living vitality of the Force. Like Obi-Wan, he hides behind an assumed identity of harmless craziness. Yoda uses this persona to test Luke upon his arrival on Dagobah. As Obi-Wan once cautioned, not everything is as it seems.

*Green skin*

HEALING MOTHER-ROCK

*Sensitive ears*

YODA'S GIMER STICK

SOHLI BARK

MUSHROOM SPORES

GALLA SEEDS

YARUM SEED
*tea-making variety*

Through the Force, Luke Skywalker is able to see his mentors Yoda and Obi-Wan, as well as a youthful apparition of his father Anakin, all finally at peace due to Luke's heroic efforts. United in the Force, their Jedi spirits are restored and complete.

## LIVING OFF THE LAND

On Dagobah, Yoda uses his attunement with the natural world to live peacefully on the resources around him. His gimer stick, for example, serves as a walking staff as well as a source of pleasant gimer juice, which can be chewed out of the bark.

# REBEL TROOPS

**DATA FILE**

> The Pathfinders are a rebel Special Forces, or SpecForce, unit trained in infiltration techniques. A group of these commandos form a strike team under General Han Solo, and use guerilla tactics to get to the Death Star II shield generators on Endor.

**THERE ARE A VARIETY** of roles in the Rebel Alliance's military, from technicians and scouts to commandos and spys. Many have personal reasons for joining the Rebellion, and everyone does their part to bring down Imperial rule and bring peace to the galaxy. Unlike the Empire, with its seemingly bottomless well of resources to arm its military, the Rebellion must make do with the weapons and equipment it has. This makes the people operating them even more essential.

Even the support staff of the Rebel Alliance are trained in combat skills. These technicians are too valuable to risk on the battlefield. Their expertise around machinery, computer systems, communications networks, and the administrative systems that keep the Alliance organized are vital to the success of the Rebellion.

## INTELLIGENCE AGENT

Colonel Airen Cracken is an Alliance spy and scout who flies support missions for General Madine's commandos. He is later promoted to General, and takes over the running of the vast intellegence network, deciphering Imperial communications fed from an array of automated listening posts.

Hands-free comlink

Service helmet with flash visor and integral comlink

Orange eyes

Multi-pocketed spacer vest

Fire-resistant tactical gloves

### SERGEANT GALEN TORG

Galen Torg is assigned to guard and escort senators and dignitaries trusted to visit the secret rebel outpost on Yavin 4. He wears the uniform of Alderaanian consular security.

### BISTAN

After coming to the assistance of a SpecForces team on his native Iakar, Bistan is drafted in to the Rebel Alliance military. Bistan's specialty is using his repeating blaster to provide cover fire from the entry hatch of a U-wing during operations.

## REBEL BLASTERS

The resemblance between some Imperial and rebel blasters is no coincidence. BlasTech Industries may have been taken over by the Empire, but the resourceful rebels can get their hands on secondhand weapons. Both the BlasTech DL-21 blaster pistol and A280 blaster rifle are used by rebel forces on Hoth and Endor.

Electronic sight adjusts for windage and elevation

Integrated muzzle compensator

Ribbed front-grip pump

Power charge system

Carry strap

**A280 BLASTER RIFLE**

**DL-21 BLASTER PISTOL**

Flared muzzle can produce scattered energy charges

**BISTAN'S "ROBA" M-45 REPEATING ION BLASTER**

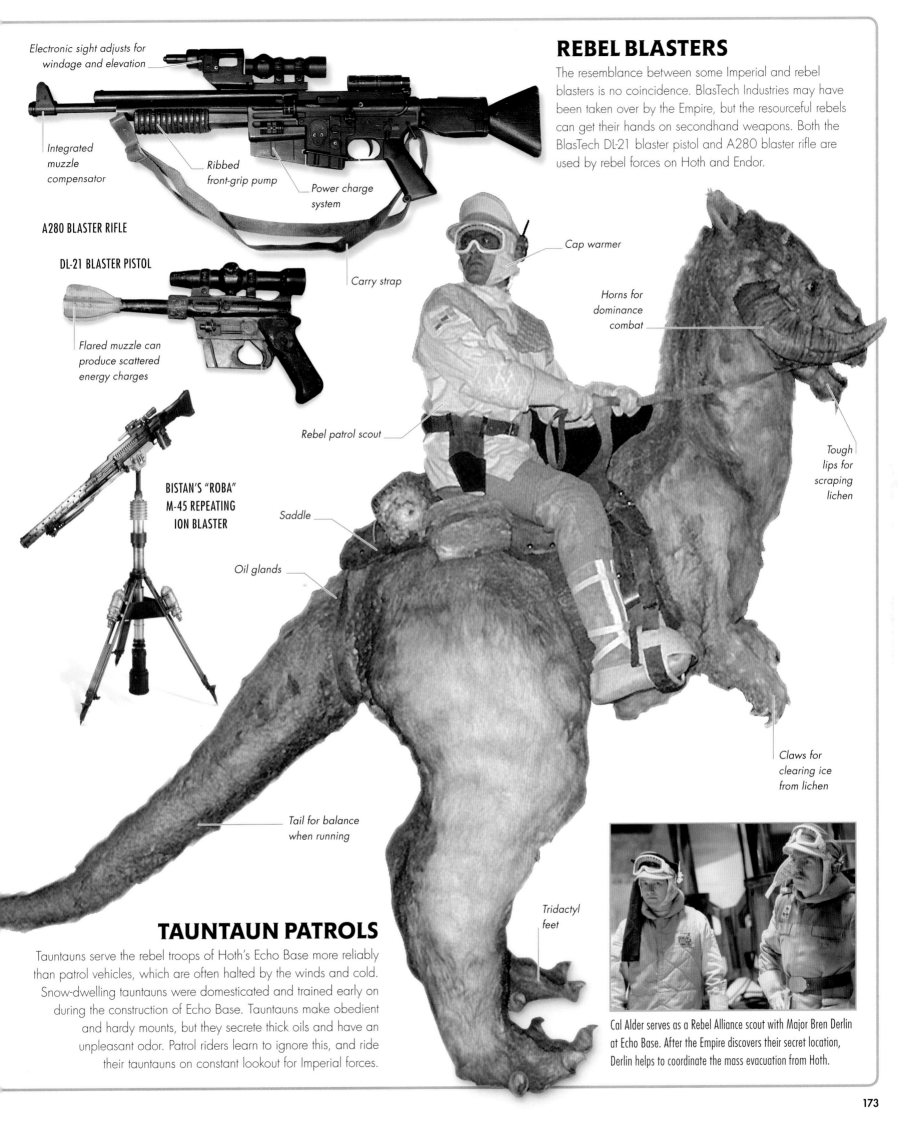

Cap warmer

Horns for dominance combat

Tough lips for scraping lichen

Rebel patrol scout

Saddle

Oil glands

Claws for clearing ice from lichen

Tail for balance when running

Tridactyl feet

## TAUNTAUN PATROLS

Tauntauns serve the rebel troops of Hoth's Echo Base more reliably than patrol vehicles, which are often halted by the winds and cold. Snow-dwelling tauntauns were domesticated and trained early on during the construction of Echo Base. Tauntauns make obedient and hardy mounts, but they secrete thick oils and have an unpleasant odor. Patrol riders learn to ignore this, and ride their tauntauns on constant lookout for Imperial forces.

Cal Alder serves as a Rebel Alliance scout with Major Bren Derlin at Echo Base. After the Empire discovers their secret location, Derlin helps to coordinate the mass evacuation from Hoth.

# REBEL PILOTS

**DESERTERS OF THE** Imperial forces, commercial fliers, or young volunteers with no combat experience, all types join the ranks of the Alliance pilots. New recruits are evaluated before being assigned to their squadron. Many must train regularly to compete for a spot on the squadrons, as the Alliance has more pilots than battle-ready craft. Places in the X-wing squadrons are the most sought after, particularly by the youngest and most adventurous of the enlisted. Squadrons can be rather diverse and include other starfighters such as A-wings, U-wings, and Y-wings.

## RED SQUADRON

An X-wing starfighter squadron serving as part of the starfighter corps, Red Squadron is formed of 12 pilots. Each has the call sign "Red (assigned number)", except the commanding officer, who is refered to as "Red Leader." Red Squadron can always be found where the fighting is thickest, or on the trickiest missions. Lieutenant Zal Dinnes becomes Red Eight after encroaching Imperial patrols force the rebels to scuttle their Tierfon launch base, disbanding the defending squadron that she was part of. Her wingmate, Jek Porkins (Red Six) also transfers to Yavin 4 from Tierfon.

Control conduit

Life support umbilical tubing

G-Force indicator and warning klaxon

Wrist-mounted comlink/beacon

Utility pocket

### BIGGS DARKLIGHTER
Darklighter joins the Rebellion after graduating from an Imperial Academy. Reuniting with his friend Luke Skywalker at Yavin, Biggs participates in the assault on the first Death Star, under the callsign "Red Three."

### WEDGE ANTILLES
A native of Corellia, Wedge originally studied at the Skystrike Imperial Academy. One of the only surving Red Squadron members at the Battle of Yavin, Wedge also takes part in the Battle of Hoth, and is Red Leader in the Battle of Endor.

### DEREK "HOBBIE" KLIVIAN
Klivian is a student at the Skystrike Imperial Academy, until he defects and joins the Alliance. Hobbie serves with Red and then Rogue Squadron until the Battle of Hoth, where he is killed by Imperial fire.

### ZEV SENESCA
Zev Sanesca is a snowspeeder pilot in Rogue Squadron on Hoth, who locates the lost Luke Skywalker and Han Solo. He is shot down during the Battle of Hoth, while covering the evacuation of Echo Base.

> Y-wings are one of the first starfighter models in the rebel fleet. Around since the Clone Wars, they are generally considered outdated technology. In the battles at Scarif and Yavin, Y-wings make up the entirety of Gold Squadron's starfighters.

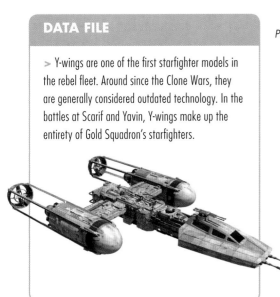

Polarized plastex visor

Modified Wren Phoenix crest

**FARNS MONSBEE'S HELMET (BLUE FIVE)**

Each pilot's helmet has markings that can include such things as squadrons, as well as personal symbols from their past.

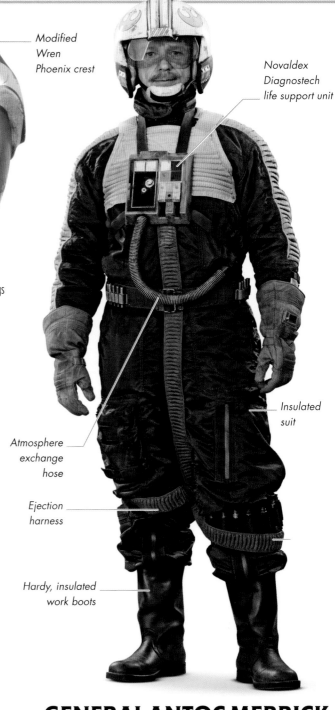

Novaldex Diagnostech life support unit

Atmosphere exchange hose

Ejection harness

Hardy, insulated work boots

Insulated suit

# GENERAL ANTOC MERRICK

As a General of the Rebel Alliance, Antoc Merrick has direct authority over all groups of starfighters at the Massassi base. He also acts as leader of Blue Squadron, and he cares a great deal about his pilots. Merrick is particularly protective of the U-wings he commands, as they have the added responsibily of getting ground troops through areas of heavy fire.

**YAVIN BASE BRIEFING ROOM**

As the Death Star approaches the Rebel Alliance's secret base on Yavin 4, rebel pilots assemble in their retrofitted briefing room within an ancient Massassi temple. Desperate for success, Alliance leaders give detailed briefings to pilots who will be trying to bring down the moon-sized superweapon.

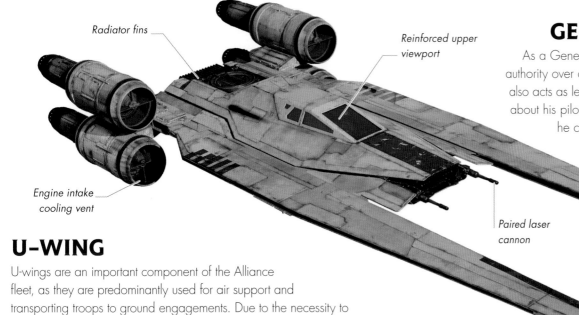

Radiator fins

Reinforced upper viewport

Engine intake cooling vent

Paired laser cannon

S-foil in stowed configuration

# U-WING

U-wings are an important component of the Alliance fleet, as they are predominantly used for air support and transporting troops to ground engagements. Due to the necessity to linger in areas of enemy fire, the ships have high-grade shielding systems and heavy armor. The forward-mounted laser cannons and an optional mounted laser cannon at the entry doors give the craft extra protection.

# REBEL DROIDS

**ALTHOUGHT THE REBELLION NEEDS** an army of troopers and pilots, the various droids aboard ships or at bases are the backbone of the Rebel Alliance. R-series astromechs form the bulk of the droid labor pool, often accompanying out-going starfighters, but there are a host of other astromech, medical and protocol droids. Medical droids are equipped with encyclopedic memory banks and statistical analyzing algorithms, allowing them to be sure of the best course of treatment—they can often restore health even to critically injured patients.

## CHOPPER

C1-10P, or "Chopper", assists an early rebel cell group, named the Spectres, before the formation of the Rebel Alliance. His age and lack of regular maintenance make him cantankerous and mischievous, but he is also a brave and fiercely loyal friend. As part of the crew of the *Ghost*, Chopper undertakes missions to undermine the Empire including helping Mon Mothma evade Imperial capture, and go on to form the Alliance.

### R2-BHD (TOOBY)

R2-BHD's silvery, unadorned surface gives the droid an unfinished look, though the astromech has been in rebel service for years. Currently on rotation through Gold Squadron, Tooby is most often assigned to Gold Leader (Jon Vander) who flies the lead Y-wing, Gold One. Loyal and attentive, Tooby finds the grouchiness of fellow droids such as Arforb illogical.

*Durasteel shell*

*Strong but delicate clamps for maintenance work aboard the Ghost*

*Transmitter inherited from a fallen rebel droid*

*Electro-shock prod*

*Retractable wheel*

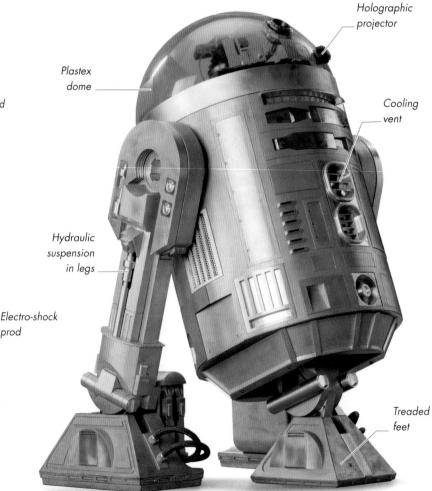

*Holographic projector*

*Plastex dome*

*Cooling vent*

*Hydraulic suspension in legs*

*Treaded feet*

## R3–S1 (THREECE)

With a clear dome that shows off her overclocked Intellex V processor, R3-S1 (or Threece) has picked up a decidedly vain programming flutter. Threece is not assigned to a specific starfighter; instead she is employed in the upkeep of technology throughout the Yavin base. Competitive to a fault, Threece does not work well with others, but she excels at organization, and has become therecognized chief of the astromech pool.

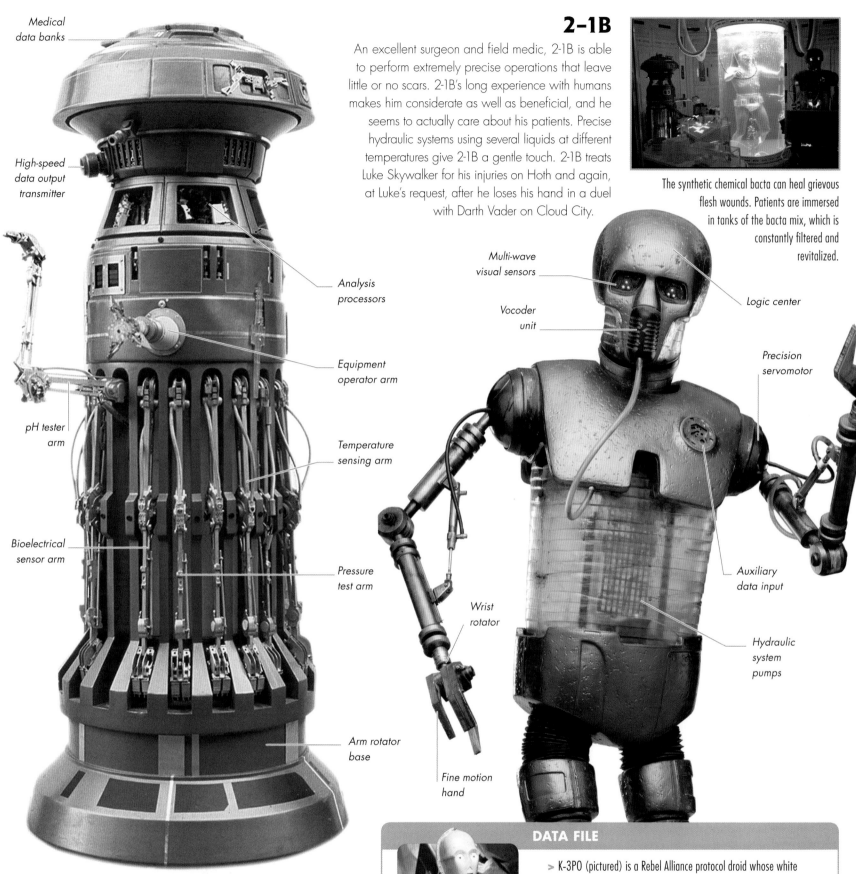

Medical data banks

High-speed data output transmitter

pH tester arm

Bioelectrical sensor arm

Analysis processors

Equipment operator arm

Temperature sensing arm

Pressure test arm

Arm rotator base

## FX-7

An antiquated but still serviceable model, FX-7 is designed primarily as a medical assistant droid. Its multiple arms can assess the condition of a patient quickly by performing various tests and assays suited to the needs of different species. It is also expert at operating medical devices. The precise data provided by FX-7 gives its surgeon droid all the information it needs to determine appropriate treatment.

## 2-1B

An excellent surgeon and field medic, 2-1B is able to perform extremely precise operations that leave little or no scars. 2-1B's long experience with humans makes him considerate as well as beneficial, and he seems to actually care about his patients. Precise hydraulic systems using several liquids at different temperatures give 2-1B a gentle touch. 2-1B treats Luke Skywalker for his injuries on Hoth and again, at Luke's request, after he loses his hand in a duel with Darth Vader on Cloud City.

The synthetic chemical bacta can heal grievous flesh wounds. Patients are immersed in tanks of the bacta mix, which is constantly filtered and revitalized.

Multi-wave visual sensors

Vocoder unit

Logic center

Precision servomotor

Auxiliary data input

Hydraulic system pumps

Wrist rotator

Fine motion hand

# IMPERIAL LEADERS

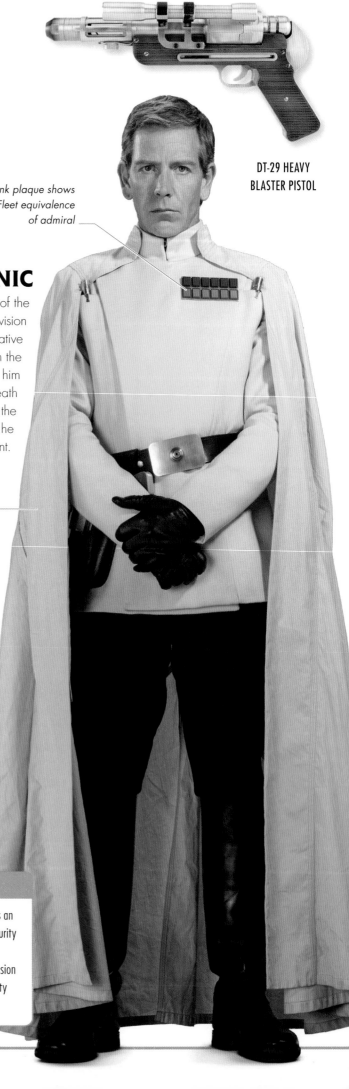

**DT-29 HEAVY BLASTER PISTOL**

**THE EMPEROR'S WILL** is enforced by the might of the Imperial forces. Imperial military commanders carry out the orders of the Emperor and hold the true positions of power in the New Order. The price for failure can be death, but ambition for the highest posts keeps competition fierce amongst officers. While bureaucracy and political whims can place incapable men in high posts, many of the Empire's commanders are formidable military talents in a system that values ruthless efficiency.

Rank plaque shows
Fleet equivalence
of admiral

## THE FIRST DEATH STAR

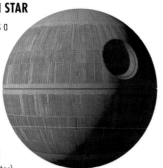

The Death Star contains a hypermatter reactor that can generate enough power to destroy an entire planet. The space station is invulnerable to large-scale assault, but has a fatal weakness in a small thermal exhaust port (connecting directly to the main reactor).

## ORSON KRENNIC

Orson Krennic is the Director of the Advanced Weapons Research Division within the Imperial Military. His manipulative and ambitious nature has gained him the favor of the Emperor, and has earned him the responsibility of developing the Death Star. Krennic uses his friendship with the crystallographer Galen Erso to ensure he succeeds in his assignment.

Antistatic
tailored cape

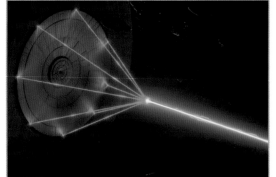

The concave dish emitter of the kyber crystal-powered superlaser focuses eight smaller beams to create an immensely destructive beam. The design is developed by many teams working in secret, including the one led by Galen Erso. The superlaser's capabilities are first tested on Jedha City, and the results are disatrously effective.

## KRENNIC'S SHUTTLE

*Delta*-class shuttles do not see much use in the early days of the Empire, due to the release of the more popular and versatile *Lambda*-class. However, Krennic's architectural background leads him to favor the bold design and he keeps one in active use for over a decade. He has no sentiment towards the ST 149 *Delta*-class T-3c shuttle, but his personal aide, Captain Dunstig Pterro, affectionately names the craft *Pteradon*. The imposing ship can hold a contigent of 15 death troopers, and is armed with several powerful laser cannons.

Central
stabilizer foil

Primary sensor and
communications
transmission core

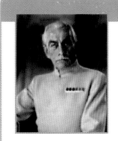

### DATA FILE

> Colonel Wullf Yularen is an officer of the Imperial Security Bureau (ISB). Assigned to Grand Moff Tarkin, his mission is to ensure absolute loyalty to the Emperor.

Blast helmet

Pilot armor

Utility belt contains mission data

The conference room on the original Death Star can project holographic tactical readouts for evaluation by Tarkin and his Imperial strategists.

## IMPERIAL STAR DESTROYER

There are several models of dagger-shaped Star Destroyers in the Imperial Navy, replacing the older Republic *Venator*-class models. Each Destroyer is heavily armored and powerful enough to blast other ships out of the sky.

Port lateral umbilical restocking vestibule

Fore starboard active sensor array pallet

Forward pursuit tractor beam array

## GENERAL VEERS

General Maximilian Veers masterminds the devastating Imperial assault on Echo Base, commanding the action in person from the lead walker cockpit. Veers is a cunning and capable individual, which makes him a model Imperial officer.

**KEPI HAT**

Naval officer's tunic

Imperial officer's tunic

Imperial officer's disc

Leather gloves

Naval boots

Rank insignia plaque

**GRAND MOFF TARKIN'S CODE CYLINDER**

## GRAND MOFF TARKIN

As Governor of the Outer Rim Territories, Grand Moff Wilhuff Tarkin uses fear to keep Imperial subjects in line. His strategic skills and ruthless methods have lead to him becoming one of the most powerful officials in the Empire. After removing Orson Krennic from his position, Tarkin takes the credit for his rival's work, as well as the role of Death Star Commander.

Code cylinders

## ADMIRAL PIETT

Firmus Piett is positioned onboard Darth Vader's personal Super Star Destroyer. Due to the failure of his superior officer, Admiral Piett takes over the hunt for rebels fleeing Hoth.

## MOFF JERJERROD

Tiaan Jerjerrod is placed in charge of the construction of the second Death Star. He ensures the exhaust ports are heavily armored on the new superweapon.

# EMPEROR PALPATINE

Hood to hide face

Simple cloak

**PALPATINE USES HIS POLITICAL SKILLS** to appoint himself Emperor. He declares martial law throughout the galaxy, and begins to rule by force through the newly created Imperial military. Any hint of rebellion is dealt with quickly, with many purges taking place, even within the ranks of Palpatine's own army. Part of the Emperor's quest for power and dominion is the eradication of the Jedi. Palpatine is a Sith Lord, a dark side Force-user, and age-old enemy of the light side Jedi.

As a Sith, Emperor Palpatine is strong in the Force, and uses his power to inspire fear and inflict pain to acheive his own ends. He takes great pleasure in using lightning to torture his enemies, such as Luke Skywalker.

## DATA FILE

> In the early days of his reign, Palpatine deals directly with signs of rebellion, such as the Free Ryloth movement. However, over the years, the Emperor disappears from public view. He rarely leaves his palace, preferring to appear via hologram. He sends trusted minions to tackle threats to his Empire.

## SITH SYMBOL

Emperor Palpatine continues to use Coruscant as a base for his Empire. He gives orders for the Jedi Temple on Coruscant to be transformed into a grand Imperial Palace. The Emperor also begins the restoration of an ancient Sith shrine.

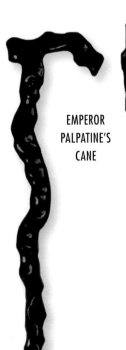

**EMPEROR PALPATINE'S CANE**

Military spectacles are used to showcase the might of the Empire and unify its citizens. They also serve to remind anyone within Imperial ranks that opposition is futile.

Coruscant
headware

# IMPERIAL SHUTTLE

Emperor Palpatine's position—
and ego—require him to have
a personal shuttle. He uses it
to personally travel to projects
like the building of the Death
Star, often unannounced, to
increase the fear and dread
of his prescence.

Central
fixed wing

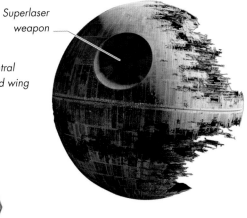

Superlaser
weapon

## THE SECOND DEATH STAR

The Emperor uses the half-completed second
Death Star as part of a colossal trap. It
presents a false image of vulnerability,
which lures the rebel fleet into fatal combat.

Fixed-position
offensive laser
cannons

## IMPERIAL DIGNITARIES

The Emperor's favor can elevate individuals to positions of galactic
power. High officials owe their posts to Palpatine's whim, and form
a society of twisted sycophants and back-stabbers.

Cockpit

Twin rotating
long-range
blasters

Wings fold up
for landing

## IMPERIAL
DIGNITARY HAT

Full-face
helmet with
darkened visor

Force pike

## ROYAL GUARD

The Imperial Royal Guards protect the
Emperor at all times. These mysterious
and fanatically loyal warriors are so
highly trained in deadly arts that their
chosen weapon is not a blaster, but a
vibro-active force pike. They wield them
with lightning swiftness to inflict very
precise and lethal wounds.

The Emperor knows that his apprentice, Darth Vader, plots to follow the Sith
Rule of Two by taking an apprentice of his own and overthrowing his master.
Palpatine has ordered Vader's stormtrooper escorts to turn their blasters on
him when Palpatine gives the order, and eliminate the threat.

Long robe conceals
hidden weapon

The Emperor's throne room
sits atop a high tower on
board the second Death
Star, allowing him to survey
the ensuing destruction.

The red robes of the Royal Guard blend into the
red decor favored by the Emperor. The sinister
presence of the silent watchers unnerves even
the most stoic of visitors.

FORCE
PIKE

# DARTH VADER

**THE FORBIDDING FIGURE OF** Darth Vader has an unusual relationship with the Empire at large. He holds no formal role within the Imperial hierarchy, but as the Emperor's envoy, he can requisition any assets to carry out his master's will. Unable to survive for extended periods of time without the life support provided by his suit, Vader is nonetheless a powerful figure whose knowledge of the dark side of the Force makes him unnerving and dangerous.

Sith blade

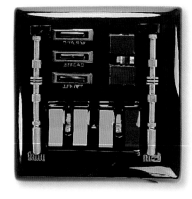

### CHESTPLATE

Vader's life support systems are monitored and controlled through this central panel of chestplate controls on his suit, which he regularly upgrades. Slots allow the insertion of diagnostic cards for periodic system checkouts, while switch panels allow function modification.

Locking armored helmet

Vision enhancement receptor

Primary system function box

Electromagnetic clasp

Secondary system function box

Synthetic belt strap

Outer cloak

**DARTH VADER'S BELT**

System function indicator

Vader sends Boba Fett to capture the rebel pilot who destroyed the Death Star. Although Boba is unsuccessful, he reveals to Vader that the pilot's name is Luke Skywalker—and unwittingly that Vader's child lives.

## VADER'S REDEMPTION

The Emperor blames Vader for the destruction of the first Death Star, and considers him unworthy. Pondering a replacement, Palpatine allows a mysterious scientist named Cylo to create cyborgs with Force-like abilities. When Vader realizes his vulnerability, he forms a secret army. While Palpatine is pleased with Cylo's creations, the scientist conspires to kill Vader. Vader discovers Cylo's treachery and destroys his forces. The Emperor uncovers Vader's duplicity and is pleased with Vader's actions, giving him command of an Imperial fleet.

Body heat regulators

Outer helmet locking surface

Helmet air pump

Electrical system radiators

Multiple power cells

Hermetic seal

Power distributor

Primary environmental sensor

Air processing filter

Hermetic seal

Neck support

Nutrient feed tube

Voice processor

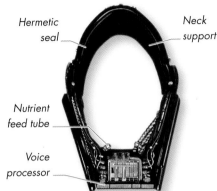

Vader plots with the Emperor to sway Luke to the dark side. However, during an intense lightsaber battle, Vader tempts Luke with the proposal that the two of them work together to overthrow the Emperor. Where Vader's loyalties really stand at this time is lost in the darkness filling his soul.

Vader keeps a personal residence on Mustafar. This forboding black castle was once the site of a Sith temple, and sits atop a source of the dark side of the Force.

### INTERIOR OF VADER'S HELMET

Vader's helmet is the most important part of his life support suit, connecting with a flat backpack to cycle air in and out of Vader's broken lungs and keeping his hideously damaged skull in shape.

Command tower

Turbolaser computer targeting

### THE *EXECUTOR*

The *Executor* is one of largest and most powerful vessels in the Imperial Navy. It serves as Vader's flagship, leading the Death Squadron in various battles against the rebels. The ship meets a violent end when it crashes into Death Star II during the Battle of Endor.

Bent solar array wings

Access hatch with dorsal viewpoint

High performance solar cells

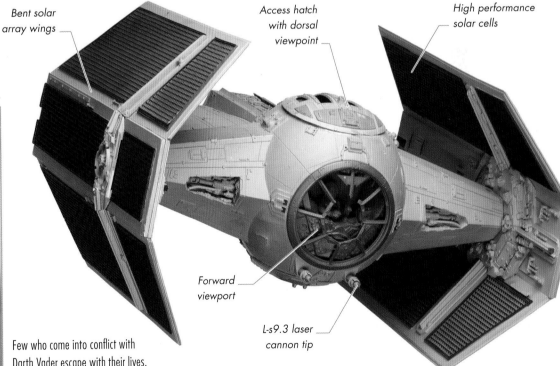

Forward viewport

L-s9.3 laser cannon tip

Few who come into conflict with Darth Vader escape with their lives. During the Battle of Scarif, the Sith Lord boards the *Profundity* to recover the stolen Death Star plans. When a small group of rebels are trapped in a corridor with him, their brave attempts to fight back are no match for his ruthlessness.

### TIE ADVANCED X1

Vader expertly pilots a unique TIE Advanced x1, developed from the prototypes flown by the Inquisitors. During the Battle of Vrogas Vas, Vader single-handedly destroys two rebel starfighter squadrons before crashing to the planet's surface.

183

# IMPERIAL PERSONNEL

**FOLLOWING THE CLONE WARS,** Palpatine did nothing to halt the massive military buildup that had produced an army of troopers and enormous weapons of destruction. Citizens of many worlds are eager to join the newly-formed Imperial forces. The Empire finds innumerable recruits and trains them in Imperial Academies throughout the galaxy. All are proud to serve in the many different roles available.

DEATH STAR
TROOPER HELMET

## NAVY TROOPERS

Also known as Death Star Troopers due to their prevalence on the battle station, navy troopers are an elite force within the Empire's military. They can skilfully defend vessels from boarders as well as viciously take down enemy ships. Most also have some operational training—such as Corporal Thobel who operates a sensor suite onboard the Death Star.

### BRIDGE CREW

Flight data officers, tracking systems specialists, and combat supervisors work in sunken data pits on either side of the elevated platform that bisects the *Executor*'s bridge. Because the location of their stations inhibit their ability to see through the bridge's viewports, the crew can focus on their consoles without unnecessary distraction.

*Reinforced neck guard*

*Energy-shielded fabric*

BLASTECH SE-14
BLASTER PISTOL

*Black durasteel gloves*

IMPERIAL GUNNER HELMET

*Belt buckle has secret data compartment*

*Blaster pistol holster*

## IMPERIAL GUNNER

Gunnery crews man the ion cannons and turbolasers of capital starships. Gunners also operate rarer weapons, including the gravity well projectors onboard *Interdictor*-class cruisers. Only elite gunners are allowed to calibrate the Death Star superlaser, ensuring that it does not overload and cause catastrophic explosions.

### SECURITY OFFICER

Imperial starships and installations require security forces to control access to sensitive areas. In Scarif's Citadel, access to the top-secret data vault is keyed to Lieutenant Milton Putna's right palm print.

*Wraparound helmet with removable faceplate*

*Gaberwool jacket*

*Flared pants are standard issue*

*Positive gravity pressure boots*

*Imperial kepi*

*White tunic typically reserved for ISB members and Grand Admirals*

*Displeased demeanor*

*Code cylinder*

*Spare power pack for suit systems*

*Padded glove*

### SECURITY BUREAU OFFICER

The Imperial Security Bureau is a vast, multi-branched agency tasked with eliminating any opposition to the Empire's reign and preserving state secrets. Inspector General Bozeden Jeems oversees the protection of the data vault in the Scarif Citadel.

*Light-emitting tip can be seen in a range of weather conditions*

*Plastoid knee-pad*

**ILLUMINATED TRAFFIC WANDS**

# GROUND CREW

Based on ground or space installations, Imperial ground crew are responsible for maintaining ships on their deck. Ground crew are faster at decision making than Imperial computers, so they use their illuminated traffic wands to indicate to ships when they can arrive and depart.

# IMPERIAL STORMTROOPERS

Broadband communications antenna

Audio pickup

Body glove

Reinforced helmet

Polarized lenses

Plastoid composite armor

Blaster power cell container

Utility belt

**IMPERIAL STORMTROOPERS ARE THE** perfect tools to enforce the Emperor's will. From a young age, these men and women have been trained in Imperial Academies across the galaxy, turning them into elite military troops. This intense conditioning instils fierce loyalty in the stormtroopers, strict discipline, and ruthless efficiency. Clad in identical armor, these grimly impersonal troopers turn the might of their training and weaponry on any opposition to the Empire.

Often deployed and paraded in overwhelming numbers, stormtrooper legions are adept at manipulating the psychology of dominance.

## STORMTROOPER ARMOR

Developed and manufactured by the Imperial Department of Military Research, stormtrooper armor sets a new standard for military equipment. Stormtroopers don a black body glove to which the 18 white plastoid plates of armor are magnatomically attached. The overlapping plates allow mobility and offer superior protection—including from most projectile weapons, blast shrapnel, and even glancing blaster bolts. While the armor may look formidable, rebel troops have discovered design flaws in the mass-produced armor that a well-placed shot can breach. Each suit of armor is identical, so rebel operatives can impersonate a stormtrooper and gain access to restricted military areas.

Blast energy sink

Reinforced alloy plate ridge

Sniper position knee protector plate

Positive-grip boots

Suit system power cells

Series code

Pocket clip

Data interface

**CODE TRANSMITTER**

**CODE CYLINDERS**

Officer's disc

**STORMTROOPER OFFICER'S CAP**

**BELT BUCKLE**

**OFFICER'S RANK PLAQUES**

## STORMTROOPER OFFICERS

In non-combat situations, stormtroopers officers wear distinctive black tunics and caps. Their insignia—officer's discs, rank plaques, and code cylinders—conform to the standards of the Imperial Navy. Code cylinders allow officers access to secure areas and computer systems. All stormtrooper officers are proven soldiers, and in combat they wear body armor like any other trooper. In the field, officers may wear colored shoulder pauldrons as rank indicators, which makes them easy targets for enemy snipers.

Setting adjust

Gas cartridge cap

Magnatomic adhesion grip

Accessory mounting rail

Range-finding sight

Safety catch

Low-power pulse indicator

Power cell

Coolings fins

Folding three-position stock

## STORMTROOPER BLASTER

The E-11 BlasTech Imperial blaster rifle combines excellent range with lethal firepower in a compact and rugged design. A standard power cell carries enough energy for 100 shots. Replacement cells are carried in a trooper utility belt. Plasma gas cartridges last for over 500 shots and the unit features an advanced cooling system for superior fire-delivery performance. A folding three-position stock converts the weapon to a rifle configuration for sustained long-distance firing.

# STORMTROOPER EQUIPMENT

**WHILE THE BRUTAL TRAINING** and intense conditioning of stormtroopers account for much of their power and effectiveness, Imperial-issue stormtrooper equipment is also vital in making them the galaxy's most dreaded soldiers. Field troops carry gear such as pouches of extra ammunition (power packs and blaster gas cartridges) and comprehensive survival kits. Standard backpack sets can adapt troopers to extreme climates or even the vacuum of space. Component construction allows standard backpack frames to be filled with gear suited to specific missions, which may include micro-vaporator water-gathering canteens, augmented cooling modules, or a wide variety of base camp and field operative equipment.

MULTI-FREQUENCY SPOTLIGHT GLOW ROD

NEURO-SAAV MODEL TD2.3
ELECTROBINOCULARS

## UTILITY BELT TOOLS

Standard-issue equipment in the utility belt must be carried at all times and includes power packs, energy rations, a thermal detonator, and a compact tool kit. The belt can hold additional gear such as a grappling hook, comlink, electrobinoculars, handcuff binders, or other items such as this combat de-ionizer.

COMBAT DE-IONIZER

*Acoustic sensors*

*Timing control*      *Code keys*

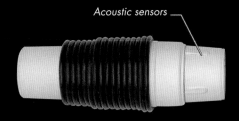

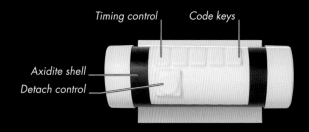

*Axidite shell*

*Detach control*

### THERMAL DETONATOR

All stormtroopers are issued a thermal detonator, worn at the back of their belt. None of the controls are labelled so that enemy troops cannot use the powerful explosives if they capture them.

### COMLINK

The hand-held comlink supplements a stormtrooper's built-in helmet comlink system with improved range and communication security. Comlink sets can be tuned with encryption algorithms to work only with each other.

*Miniature vaporator condensation bulb*

*Activator*

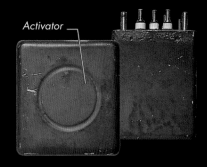

*Folding tines*

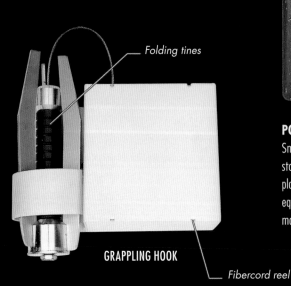

### POWER CELLS

Small power packs plug into standard stormtrooper gear, including helmets, back plates, communication sets, and other field equipment. Complex circuitry extracts the maximum power from the cell.

GRAPPLING HOOK

*Fibercord reel*

*Thermal detonator*

SANDTROOPER TYPE
4 FIELD PACK

## DATA FILE

> During the hunt for the Death Star plans, sandtroopers use their high-powered backpack communications gear to alert orbiting Star Destroyers to intercept the escaping *Millennium Falcon*.

> On Jedha, stormtroopers carry vac-sealed armored canisters to preserve any kyber crystals they discover.

# STORMTROOPER HELMET

Imperial stormtrooper standard-issue helmets incorporate various specialized components to help their wearer on the battlefield. All helmets include a multi-frequency targeting and acquisitions system that creates an in-lens display, providing tactical information, shielding the eye from excessive brightness, and offering vision through many barriers such as smoke, darkness, and fire. The helmets do not normally have a contained air supply, however, with the addition of an external atmospheric tank, the helmets can be hermetically sealed.

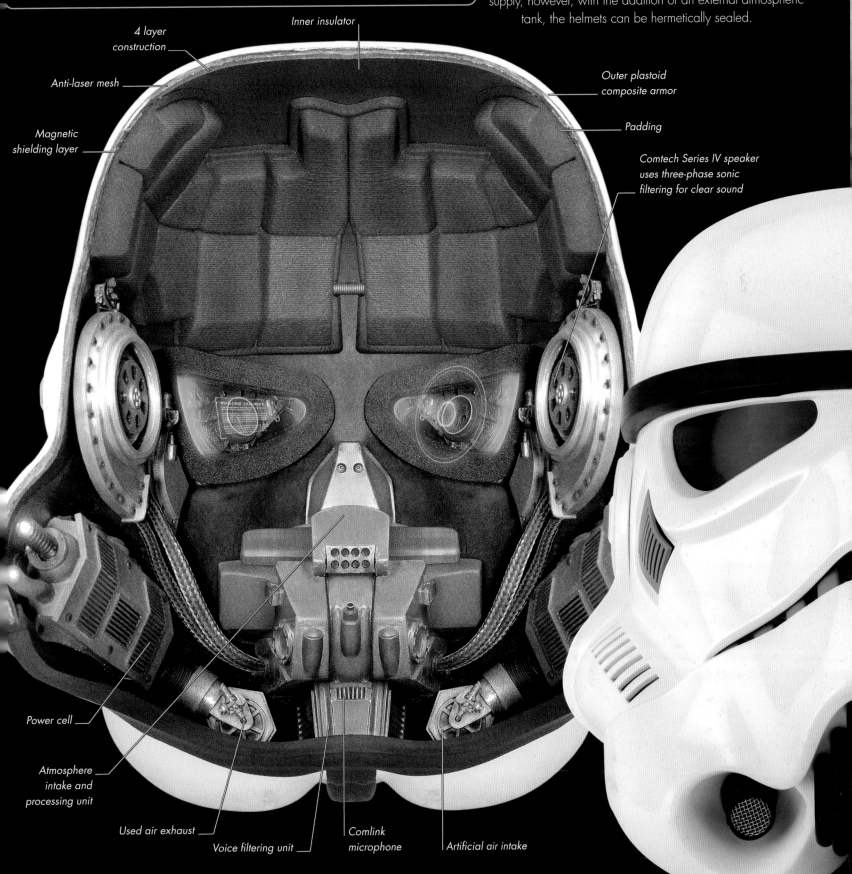

4 layer construction

Inner insulator

Anti-laser mesh

Outer plastoid composite armor

Magnetic shielding layer

Padding

Comtech Series IV speaker uses three-phase sonic filtering for clear sound

Power cell

Atmosphere intake and processing unit

Used air exhaust

Voice filtering unit

Comlink microphone

Artificial air intake

# SPECIALIST STORMTROOPERS

FOR ENVIRONMENTS THAT WOULD challenge a standard stormtrooper, there is a specialized class of Imperial soldier. Certain Imperial troopers are selected at an early stage in their training for these roles, and are conditioned with appropriate knowledge and psychological training. Once specialized, their psychological conditioning to their particular identity is so strong that a trooper rarely wishes to change his division.

## SNOWTROOPER

Based on the Republic's cold assault clone troopers, Imperial snowtroopers are self-sufficient mobile combatants in freezing terrains. They rely upon their backpacks, breath masks, and suit systems to keep them warm. Each suit can last for two weeks on battery power alone before they need to be recharged.

Covered airfilters prevent sand buildup

Control systems interface

Blaster power cell cartridge belt

Plastoid greave with expandable plates

Insulated gauntlet

Heated pants

Rugged ice boots

Chest plate

Wrist comlink

SNOWTROOPER KNEE GUARD

Accessory power outlet

Heater liquid pump

SNOWTROOPER BACKPACK

Rations storage compartment

## SHORETROOPER

Imperial shoretroopers are proficient at attacking enemy forces and defending Imperial objectives in coastal environments. They wear flexible, lightweight armor, so they are more nimble in battle. Their armor can be modified so they can operate underwater. Seaside warfare is uncommon, so these specialists are a rare sight in the Imperial ranks, and common stormtroopers defer to them in coastal combat.

Plastoid-coated armor prevents salt corrosion

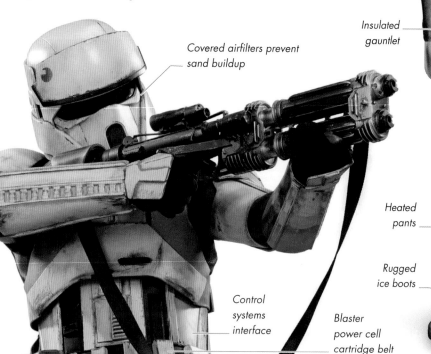

Snowtroopers can carry and set up deadly E-web heavy-repeating blaster cannons. Manufactured by BlasTech Industries, these weapons are highly effective and deadly when deployed during combat.

E-22 BLASTER RIFLE

Multi-frequency targeting and acquisition sensor system

Neuro-saav macromotion monitor

Armor coated with reflec spray polymer

Environmentally sealed bodysuit

MERR-SONN MUNITIONS FRAGMENTATION GRENADE

Large-bore reinforced barrel

BLASHTECH E-11D BLASTER RIFLE

## DEATH TROOPER

Responsible for protecting critical individuals and operations for the Imperial military, death troopers are lethal and menacing opponents. Only the best cadets are selected to become death troopers, undergoing rigorous training and receiving top-secret augmentations to make them far superior to other Imperial infantry. Their ominous name suggests a link to a rumored Advanced Weapons Research project that reanimates dead flesh.

EC-17 HOLD-OUT BLASTER

Electro-magnetic vision enhancement visor

Boosted comlink system for long-range communication

Power unit backpack also stores gear

Survival rations

Terrain sensor

Guidance vanes mounting strut

Guidance linkage

Brake pedal

## SCOUT TROOPER

Scout troopers are equipped for high maneuverability and long periods without support. Trained to an unusual degree of independence for Imperial personnel, scout troopers are nonetheless conditioned to work with partners wherever possible. Scout troopers are armored only on the head and upper body. They carry food supplies, micro-cords, and other gear that allows them to reach and silently infiltrate almost any objective, far from Imperial support.

**SCOUT TROOPER HELMET**

Scout trooper helmets possess enchanced macrobinocular viewplates that let them identify targets from afar.

# IMPERIAL PILOTS

**THE EMPIRE HAS A HORRIFYING** range of vehicles at its disposal requiring specialized pilots to operate them. The two main corps of pilots are the TIE fighter corps and the combat driver corps. TIE fighter pilots serve in the Imperial Navy and are trained to fly the full range of TIE fighter models. Imperial combat drivers are part of the army and can also pilot a broad range of ground vehicles, from speeders to walkers. All Imperial pilots are entirely dedicated to the cause and will use their vehicles to ruthlessly destroy any resistance to the Empire.

**TIE FIGHTER FUELING PORT**
TIE fighter fuel is a radioactive gas under high pressure. The twin ion engines of the ship have no moving parts, making the TIE easy to maintain.

*Reinforced flight helmet*

*Ship-linked communications*

*Gas transfer hose*

## TIE FIGHTER PILOT

TIE fighter pilots are an elite group within the Imperial Navy. Only a small number of those accepted into training graduate with commissions. Through their intense psychological conditioning, pilots know that their mission comes above all other concerns, including those of personal survival. TIE pilots are trained to regard the TIE craft as the most expressive instrument of Imperial military will, and they exult in their role, taking pride in their total dependence on higher authority.

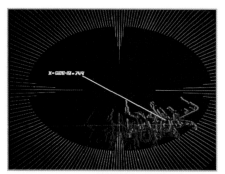

TIE fighter targeting systems are superior to the targeting systems available in rebel starfighters. The advanced readouts of these Seinar systems track targets in high resolution.

*Comlink/transponder in shockproof belt case*

*Reinforced viewport facet*

*Solar array*

## TIE FIGHTER

The standard TIE fighter carries no deflector shield or hyperdrive equipment and employs high-performance ion engines energized by solar array "wings." This lightweight design makes the craft agile, but leaves the pilot defenseless and unable to travel far from his base station. TIE pilots view shields as tools of cowards.

*Fueling port*

*Flight gloves*

*Energy-shielded fabric*

Wireless telemetry receiver for tank system interfaces

Breathmask filter screen

Basic armor plating worn underneath jumpsuit

Utility belt with compact repair and diagnostic kits

Fire-resistant boots

Flexible greave plates allow for a secure fit

# AT–AT PILOT

To operate the imposing AT-AT, a pilot must be incredibly strong and have specialized training. These skills make an AT-AT pilot far more valuable than other Imperial pilots, so each of them wears a life-support system for extra protection.

Reinforced helmet

Pressure hose

Air hose

Suit heat control

Energy monitor

Life support pack

Driving gauntlet

Gear harness

Comlink

Insulated jumpsuit

Insulated boot

## AT-ST CREW

AT-ST crew always work in pairs, one pilots the vehicle, while the other operates the twin laser cannon, light blaster cannon, and the concussion grenade launcher. They must be dexterous and have a superior sense of balance to skilfully operate an AT-ST.

## COMBAT DRIVER

A combat driver's vehicle offers the best protection in the field, but they wear armor just in case. During the Empire's reign, their uniform has been improved, incorporating some protective plastoid plates, but offering some flexibility too.

Telemetry receiver unit

**AT-ST CREW HELMET**

System linkage

Receptor filaments

Echo transmitter

Slide mount rails

Energy monitor contact

Signal amplifier

**AT-AT TARGETING SENSOR**

**POWER PACK CONTROL UNIT**

Armored viewport

Light blaster cannon

Armored joint shield

## AT-ST

The small, gyroscopically-stabilized AT-ST, or All Terrain Scout Transport, is a potent vehicle in the Imperial arsenal. The AT-ST is well-suited to a range of combat situations due to its speed and ability to navigate dense terrain.

The All Terrain Armored Transport, or AT-AT, is a gigantic machine used to terrorize enemy forces. It stands at over 22 m (72 ft) tall and is equipped with a devastating array of medium-repeating blasters and fire-linked laser cannons.

# IMPERIAL DROIDS

## DATA FILE

> A V-series droid supervisor model, AV-6R7 oversees work droids building the second Death Star. It was deprived of arms for failing to keep track of a faulty power droid.

**THE EMPIRE ADAPTS COMMON DROID** models to suit specific Imperial needs and also commissions specialized new forms, including illegal assassin and torture droids. Imperial droids are programmed to restrict their abilities for independent action and focus them tightly on assigned tasks only. Typically, Imperial droids are pure machines that are oblivious to anything outside their role and rarely develop anything approximating personality.

## MSE-6 DROID

Common throughout the galaxy, MSE (or "mouse") droids often carry top-secret messages between crewmembers. On Imperial ships and battle stations, they also lead troops through long mazes of corridors to their assigned posts.

## RA-7 PROTOCOL DROIDS

RA-7 protocol droids are a popular model that predate the Empire and saw service during the Clone Wars. They are also known as "insect droids" due to the large photoreceptors on their heads. From spying to inventory management, these units are suited to many different tasks, but often specialize in one role. For example, 4D6-J-A7 is an administrative assistant to the Imperial Intelligence and Security Bureau offices on the Scarif.

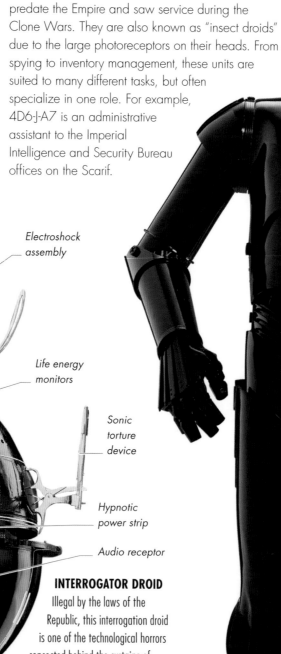

Insect-like photoreceptors

Vocabulator

Pelvic servomotor

Reinforced knee joint

Searing flesh pincers

Acid jet

Sonic piercing needle

Electroshock assembly

Life energy monitors

Sonic torture device

Hypnotic power strip

Audio receptor

Drug injector

Victim analysis photoreceptor

Lower repulsor projector

Arc emitter

## INTERROGATOR DROID

Illegal by the laws of the Republic, this interrogation droid is one of the technological horrors concocted behind the curtains of Imperial secrecy. Completely without pity, this nightmare machine surgically exploits every physical and mental point of weakness with flesh peelers, bone fragmenters, electroshock nerve probes, and other unspeakable devices.

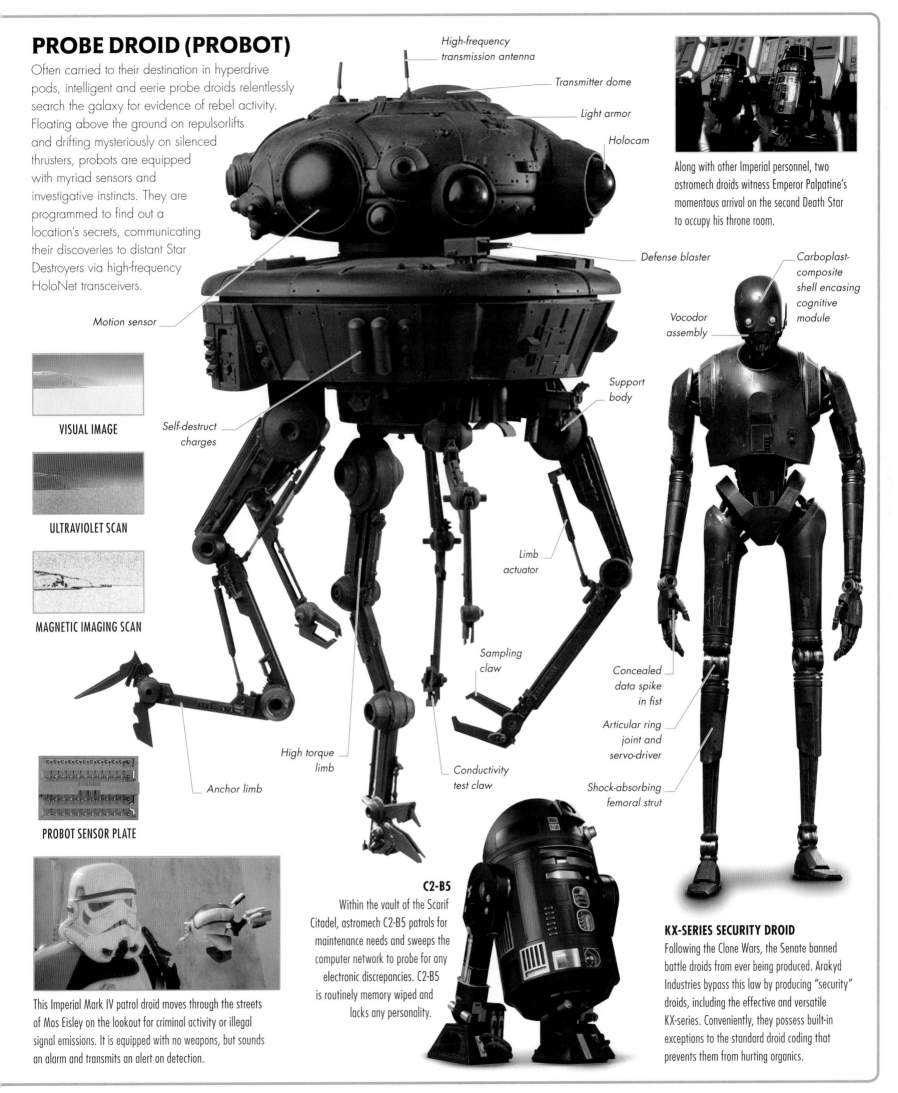

# PROBE DROID (PROBOT)

Often carried to their destination in hyperdrive pods, intelligent and eerie probe droids relentlessly search the galaxy for evidence of rebel activity. Floating above the ground on repulsorlifts and drifting mysteriously on silenced thrusters, probots are equipped with myriad sensors and investigative instincts. They are programmed to find out a location's secrets, communicating their discoveries to distant Star Destroyers via high-frequency HoloNet transceivers.

High-frequency transmission antenna

Transmitter dome

Light armor

Holocam

Along with other Imperial personnel, two astromech droids witness Emperor Palpatine's momentous arrival on the second Death Star to occupy his throne room.

Defense blaster

Carboplast-composite shell encasing cognitive module

Vocodor assembly

Motion sensor

**VISUAL IMAGE**

**ULTRAVIOLET SCAN**

**MAGNETIC IMAGING SCAN**

Self-destruct charges

Support body

Limb actuator

Concealed data spike in fist

Articular ring joint and servo-driver

Sampling claw

High torque limb

Conductivity test claw

Shock-absorbing femoral strut

Anchor limb

**PROBOT SENSOR PLATE**

This Imperial Mark IV patrol droid moves through the streets of Mos Eisley on the lookout for criminal activity or illegal signal emissions. It is equipped with no weapons, but sounds an alarm and transmits an alert on detection.

## C2-B5
Within the vault of the Scarif Citadel, astromech C2-B5 patrols for maintenance needs and sweeps the computer network to probe for any electronic discrepancies. C2-B5 is routinely memory wiped and lacks any personality.

## KX-SERIES SECURITY DROID
Following the Clone Wars, the Senate banned battle droids from ever being produced. Arakyd Industries bypass this law by producing "security" droids, including the effective and versatile KX-series. Conveniently, they possess built-in exceptions to the standard droid coding that prevents them from hurting organics.

# SAND PEOPLE

**THE FIERCE NOMADS** of Tatooine known as the Tusken Raiders prowl areas like the Dune Sea and the Jundland Wastes. They blend invisibly into the landscape, and survive where no one else can. Their savage and violent ways pit them against the moisture farmers and settlers in lonely, remote lands. The Tusken Raiders usually stay away from towns and cities, but during the hot season, they emerge from the wastes to scavenge or steal from the edges of settlement zones. They always wait until Tatooine's twin suns have set, so it is best to lock up tight at night.

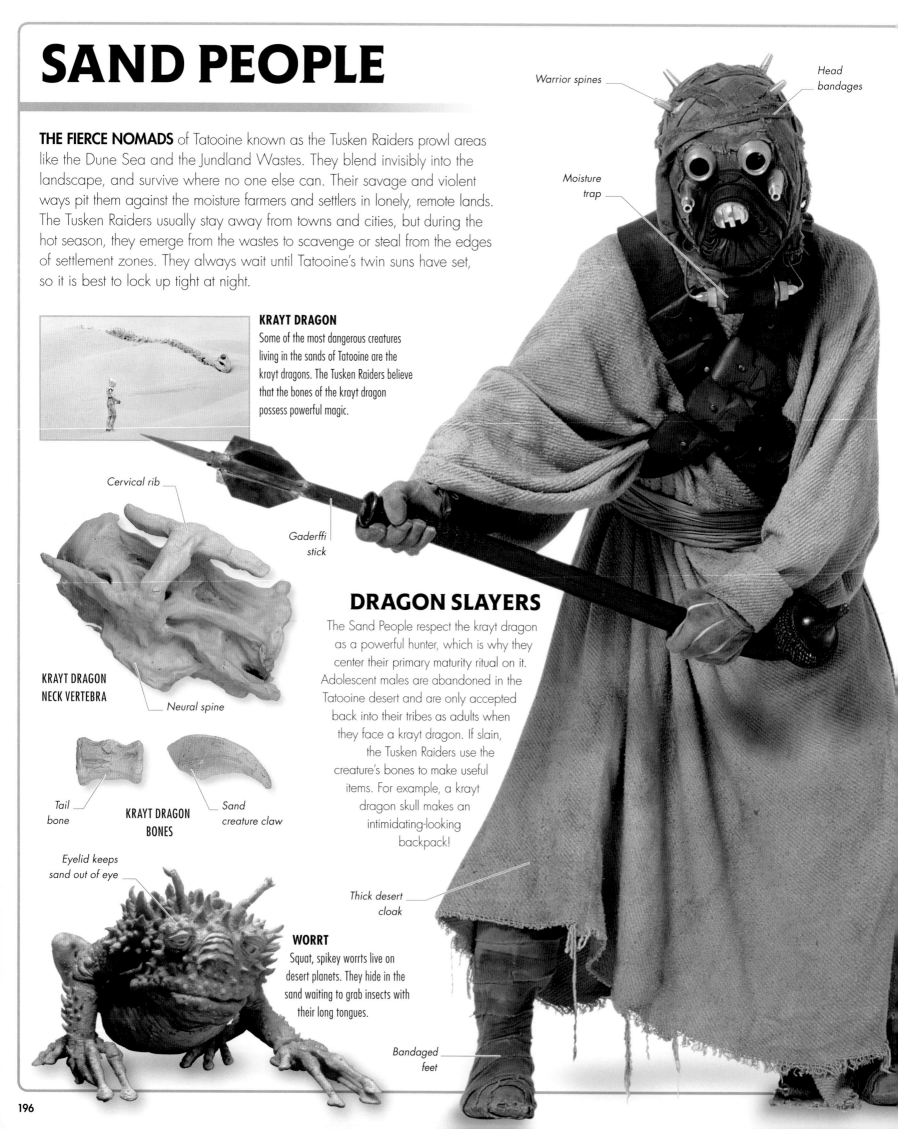

Warrior spines

Head bandages

Moisture trap

### KRAYT DRAGON
Some of the most dangerous creatures living in the sands of Tatooine are the krayt dragons. The Tusken Raiders believe that the bones of the krayt dragon possess powerful magic.

Cervical rib

Gaderffi stick

**KRAYT DRAGON NECK VERTEBRA**

Neural spine

Tail bone

**KRAYT DRAGON BONES**

Sand creature claw

## DRAGON SLAYERS
The Sand People respect the krayt dragon as a powerful hunter, which is why they center their primary maturity ritual on it. Adolescent males are abandoned in the Tatooine desert and are only accepted back into their tribes as adults when they face a krayt dragon. If slain, the Tusken Raiders use the creature's bones to make useful items. For example, a krayt dragon skull makes an intimidating-looking backpack!

Eyelid keeps sand out of eye

Thick desert cloak

### WORRT
Squat, spikey worrts live on desert planets. They hide in the sand waiting to grab insects with their long tongues.

Bandaged feet

Jawa clans use rontos to bring goods to cities for trade. These loyal creatures are large enough to scare off threatening Tusken Raiders.

## BANTHAS

Banthas roam the dunes and wastes of Tatooine in herds. Sand People use these giant beasts to carry both riders and gear, forming close bonds with them, and even making them members of their clans.

*Spiral horn*

*Sack for food and supplies*

*Three-toed hoof*

## ROCK WART

The rock wart of Tatooine has a painful neurotoxic venom in its bite and sting. This venom can kill much larger prey.

## BLOODLETTING BLADE

Tusken Raider clan rituals may involve the sacrifice of animals, captives, or even condemned Sand People.

*Eye protection lenses*

*Blood spitter*

*Gaderffi handle*

**GADERFFI STICK**

## MASK

Tusken Raiders' clothing helps them survive in the glaring heat and extreme windstorms of Tatooine. They cover their faces with masks, which have eye coverings to keep out sand and mouth grilles to retain moisture. Masks worn by female Sand People tend to be more elaborate and jeweled. Tusken children wear unisex masks, as gender-specific coverings are not allowed until they become adults.

*Breath filter*

*Mouth covering*

### DATA FILE

> Rare water wells in canyons like Gafsa are sacred to the Tusken Raiders. Merely trespassing near one can provoke immediate violence.

197

# JAWAS

Heavy cloaks protect from sun glare

Glowing eyes

**THE TIMID AND ACQUISITIVE** Jawas scavenge scrap metal, lost droids, and equipment from the refuse that dots the desert landscapes of Tatooine. Their faces are concealed in dark robes that protect them from the twin suns, and their glowing eyes help them see in the dark crevices where they hide. There are a few Jawa settlements, as most Jawas patrol the dunes and dusty rocks in gigantic sandcrawlers, ancient vehicles from a mining era long ago. Jawas can offer real bargains in the junk that they repair, but are notoriously tricky and will swindle the unwary buyer.

The Jawas' sandcrawlers are scoured and rusted from countless sandstorms and the blistering suns. These vehicles hold droid prisons, mineral ore and metal processors, and salvaged junk of every kind.

Bandolier

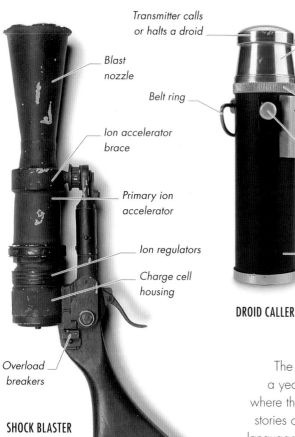

Transmitter calls or halts a droid

Droid signal receiver

Blast nozzle

Belt ring

Ion accelerator brace

Setting adjust

Primary ion accelerator

Activator

Ion regulators

Charge cell housing

Power cell

Overload breakers

**DROID CALLER**

**SHOCK BLASTER**

Stock

## JAWAS

The Jawa clans gather together once a year in a great salvage swap meet, where they trade droids, equipment, and stories of their adventures. The Jawaese language that they use to speak to each other uses scent as well as spoken words. The Jawas' stench helps them understand one another—but makes Jawaese impossible for others to learn.

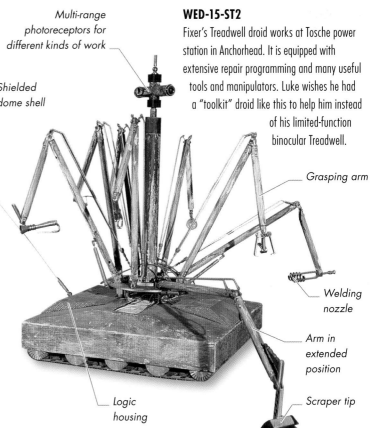

Photoreceptors made to look like Stacchati eyes

Shielded dome shell

Multi-range photoreceptors for different kinds of work

### WED-15-ST2

Fixer's Treadwell droid works at Tosche power station in Anchorhead. It is equipped with extensive repair programming and many useful tools and manipulators. Luke wishes he had a "toolkit" droid like this to help him instead of his limited-function binocular Treadwell.

Grasping arm

Welding nozzle

Arm in extended position

Scraper tip

### LIN-V8K

This heavily-armored mining droid plants explosives and can see through radiation, fog, and even sand and light ground fill. LIN was recovered from an abandoned military garrison and refurbished by Jawas on Tatooine.

Human-style manipulator hands

Logic housing

## CZ-1

This very old secretary droid was modified from a standard model to resemble the Stacchati species he once served. Abandoned on Tatooine and separated from his twin unit CZ-3 after a crash, CZ-1 breaks down in the desert and is captured by Jawas. His locomotors are sand-encrusted and too damaged for him to walk or move properly. Still optimistic, he hopes to be repaired and sold soon.

Photoreceptor

Power coupling

Mounting brace

Linkage pins

Tread energizer

Neutral polarity node

Mark II reactor drone magfield sensor ball

Contact cage

## R5-D4

R5-D4, also known as "Red," is a white and red astromech droid that Jawas on Tatooine sell to Owen Lars. However, immediately after the sale, Red's motivator blows up, and Owen returns him to the Jawas. This gives C-3PO the opportunity he needs to recommend that Owen takes R2-D2 instead.

Binocular fine-focus vision

Extensible neck strut

Manipulator arm

Recharge coupling

### DROID PARTS

Jawa recycling talents are legendary. If a droid is too battered even for Jawas to repair, it is cannibalized for spare parts. New owners who open up a droid bought from Jawas may find internal parts of which its makers never dreamed.

### WED-15-77

This binocular Treadwell has a frustratingly small independent thought processor, but is capable of accomplishing very specific tasks with close supervision. It assists Luke on his uncle's vaporators but prefers working for Aunt Beru, as she always asks it to do the same predictable jobs.

Logic housing

Third tread for balance over uneven surfaces

Treads

# CANTINA PATRONS

**BECAUSE OF THE IMPERIAL MILITARY'S** apparent bias against nonhumans, many citizens have migrated or fled from the Core Worlds to Outer Rim planets such as Tatooine, which the Empire regard as barely worth their attention. Although some beings have chosen to band together in this relatively lawless area of space, others have become cynical and look out only for themselves. Except for droids, anyone with credits is welcome at the cantina—but newcomers should be cautious of the more dangerous regulars.

In an alcove close to the bar, the Talz pickpocket Muftak, Bith mercenary and backup kloo horn player Lirin Car'n, Sakiyan bounty hunter Djas Puhr, and fight-loving Myo discuss current events while listening to the band.

Aqualish see better underwater

Length and density of tusks indicate age

Orange jacket

### DIVERSE CLIENTELE
Of the few places where a methane-breathing Morseerian, a Jawa-speaking Bimm smuggler, a Saurin bodyguard, and a pipe-smoking bureaucrat ever find common ground, the cantina is a favorite hangout. The wide range of species that frequents the Cantina encourages the bartender to maintain an equally wide stock of beverages.

Wuher the bartender knows when to stay out of the way. He dives for cover as Dr. Evazan and Ponda Baba make the mistake of drawing their blasters on Ben Kenobi.

## PONDA BABA

A burly Aqualish named Ponda Baba spends his time on Tatooine smuggling spices for crime lord Jabba the Hutt. When he's not busy with his illegal ventures, he and his partner, Dr. Cornelius Evazan escape the heat of the planet's two suns in the cantina. When Luke Skywalker and Obi-Wan Kenobi visit the cantina, it doesn't take long for the violent thugs to pick a fight with Luke. Unfortunately for Ponda, Obi-Wan's intervention leads to the Aqualish losing his arm to a lightsaber!

Hands covered in black hair

SE-14C blaster pistol

## MOMAW NADON

Momaw Nadon is an exile from his homeworld Ithor. It is rumored the "hammerhead" supports the Rebellion.

## DJAS PUHR

Puhr is a Sakiyan bounty hunter, as well as an occasional assassin employed by Jabba the Hutt.

## BOM VIMDIN

An Advozse smuggler who works for corrupt officials, Bom Vimdin despises his own species.

## MYO

Myo is a self-regenerating Abyssin who is employed by the Galactic Outdoor Survival School.

## PONS LIMBIC

The Siniteen nicknamed "Brainiac" is capable of calculating hyperspace coordinates in his head.

## BLASTERS

Although blaster fights are discouraged in the cantina, even the toughest customers agree that it would be downright unwise to enter the cantina unarmed. The BlasTech SE-14C blaster pistol is the weapon of choice for both Dr. Evazan and Ponda Baba, who also packs a modified DL-21.

SE-14C BLASTER

Optical targeting scope

Power pack

Rapid-fire auto trigger

Recharge valve

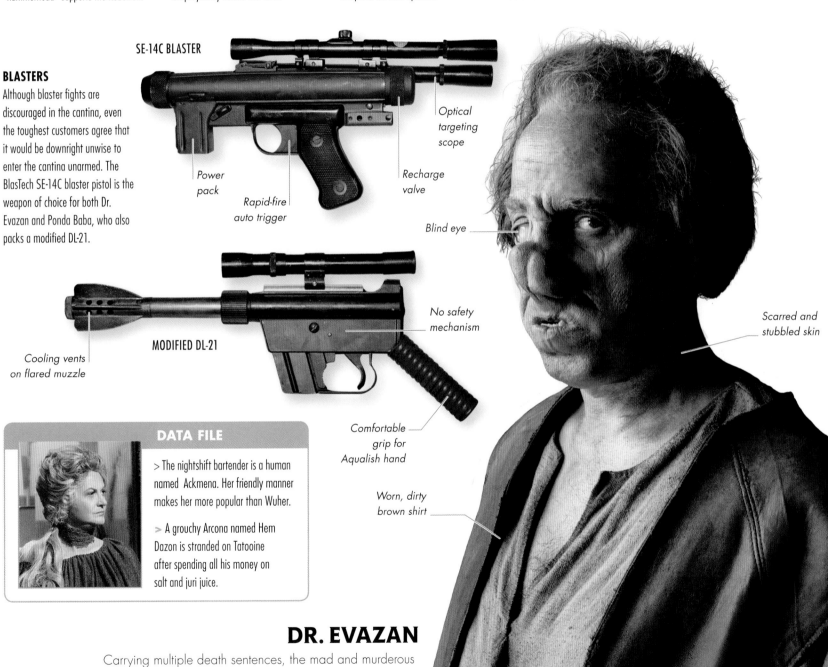

Blind eye

MODIFIED DL-21

No safety mechanism

Cooling vents on flared muzzle

Comfortable grip for Aqualish hand

Scarred and stubbled skin

Worn, dirty brown shirt

### DATA FILE

> The nightshift bartender is a human named Ackmena. Her friendly manner makes her more popular than Wuher.

> A grouchy Arcona named Hem Dazon is stranded on Tatooine after spending all his money on salt and juri juice.

## DR. EVAZAN

Carrying multiple death sentences, the mad and murderous Dr. Cornelius Evazan is notorious for rearranging body parts on living creatures. Before arriving on Tatooine, he worked on Jedha, using his ghastly medical techniques to produce an order of cybernetic servants known as the Decraniated. Evazan and his partner Ponda Baba also enjoy brawling and gunning down defenseless beings in the cantina.

# THE CANTINA CROWD

**THE MOS EISLEY SPACEPORT** sees many unusual beings, but the Mos Eisley Cantina is known as the haunt of the weirdest clientele in town. Hardened professional spacers and bizarre outlanders from distant corners of the galaxy can be found here. It's no place for the squeamish, but for its regulars, the cantina provides a pan-galactic atmosphere that helps distract them from their various misfortunes and the miserable hole of Mos Eisley. The regular band suits many tastes, and as long as foolish outsiders don't step in and get their heads blown off, everyone can have their own version of a good time. Deals get made, things get drunk, and the wrong sorts of business go the right sorts of ways. The bartender maintains a semblance of order by threatening to poison the drinks of creatures that give him trouble.

Duros are a species long adapted to space travel, with natural piloting and navigation skills. These two make regular deep space runs connecting through Mos Eisley.

Hrchek Kal Fas is a tough Saurin droid trader who wisely keeps his bodyguard nearby in the cantina.

An entrance vestibule serves as a buffer between the intolerable heat outdoors and the relative cool inside the cantina. It also gives those inside an opportunity to look over new arrivals before they step in.

This Devaronian hides under the assumed name of Labria. He is on the run from a wicked past and one of the galaxy's highest bounties for his deadly crimes.

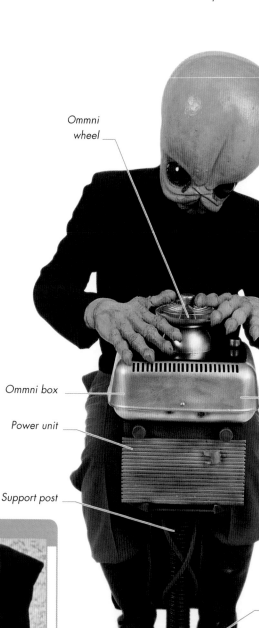

Mouthpiece

Farra slots

Ommni wheel

Fanfar

Sound projector

Ommni box

Power unit

Support post

Bwom pedal

Thwee pedal

**TECH M'OR**

**TEDN DAHAI**

## DATA FILE

> When Luke and Ben leave the cantina they do not realize that they were spotted by the insect-eating Garindan, a low-life informant carrying an Imperial comlink.

> Bodies or severed limbs from altercations in the cantina never seem to be there when the authorities show up. No one is quite sure what happens to them.

Living beneath Mos Eisley in abandoned tunnels, this Talz named Muftak works as a pickpocket. Talz are a primitive species who use few tools, and are taken into space only by slavers.

The cantina's diverse selection of legal and illegal drinks draws unusual visitors. Lamproids and other marginal species are served blood mixes that are of questionable origin.

# FIGRIN D'AN AND HIS BAND

The Bith musicians often heard in the cantina are highly intelligent creatures with sophisticated musical abilities—a band called the Modal Nodes. Although they complain, the seven band members enjoy their out-of-the-way dive and are glad to be away from their homeworld of Clak'dor VII. The lead player is an expert gambler who pays off his occasional debts with his tunes, while trying to keep his members out of trouble. They've been asked to play at Jabba's palace, but they're smart enough to know better.

Mouth tube

Kloo horn

Tone mode selectors

Respiratory folds

Peel rods

Travel boots

FIGRIN D'AN

Enlarged cranium

Band jacket

Bandfill

Ploong sounder

Reciprocator horns

Power indicator

Band pants

NALAN CHEEL

Large eyes

Fizzz (or dorenian beshniquel)

Peel rod

DOIKK NA'TS

# JABBA THE HUTT

**AT THE CENTER OF** an extensive crime empire is Jabba the Hutt. This repellent crime lord has built his syndicate through a long history of deals, threats, murders, and astute business arrangements. Unlike many of his competitors, Jabba is highly intelligent, and rarely overlooks details or dangers. Once bold and daring, he has settled back in his old age to a life of debauchery in his palace on Tatooine. Jabba enjoys violent entertainment almost as much as he enjoys profits, and he arranges deadly gladiatorial games and executions on a regular basis.

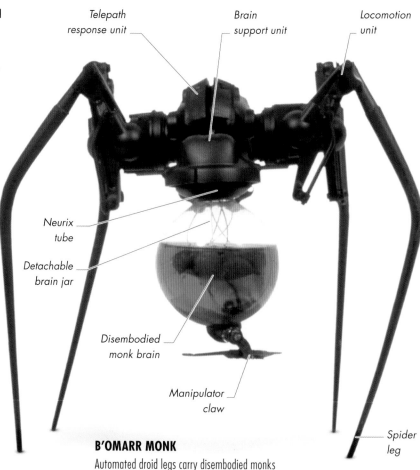

Telepath response unit

Brain support unit

Locomotion unit

Neurix tube

Detachable brain jar

Disembodied monk brain

Manipulator claw

Spider leg

### B'OMARR MONK
Automated droid legs carry disembodied monks through the palace. The oldest spider droids have four legs, while more recent models have six.

The desert palace of Jabba the Hutt was originally a monastery constructed long ago by the mysterious B'omarr monks. Over the years, bandits take control of parts of the citadel, adding portions even as the monks go about their secret ways in the nether reaches of the structure. As Jabba's headquarters, the fortress holds a wide variety of gangsters, assassins, travelers, crooked officials, entertainers, and servants.

Lekku (head-tail)

## OOLA
Jabba keeps a Twi'lek named Oola as his slave. Although the crime lord finds her highly desirable, Oola refuses to give in to him.

Jabba's palace is equipped with many security devices, including a semi-intelligent droid gatewatcher built into several of the entrances.

# JABBA THE HUTT

Jabba Desilijic Tiure, better known as Jabba the Hutt, comes from the planet Nal Hutta, where he is raised by his father, also a crime lord, to crave power and wealth. Hutts are notorious for their ruthless ways, and they often use their physical power to control weaker species. Hutts run most of the galaxy's large criminal syndicates.

Jabba's sail barge *Khetanna* carries the Hutt on journeys to Mos Eisley or to places of execution and gladiatorial combat staged for the crime lord's amusement.

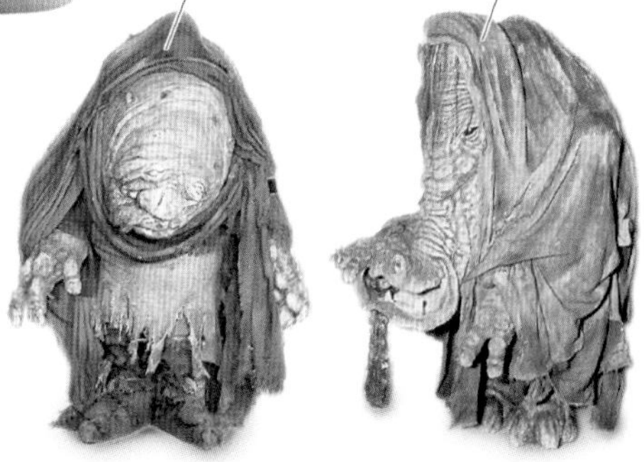

Hermi Odle

Ephant Mon

Internal mantles shape a Hutt's head

Hutt skin secretes oil and mucus, making Hutts difficult to seize

Body has no skeleton

Muscular body can move like a snail or slither forward

Hookah pipe

Naal thorn burner

Jabba's palace is filled with bizarre creatures like his personal armorer, the Baragwin Hermi Odle. The former gun-runner Ephant Mon is Jabba's only real friend, as the Hutt once saved his life.

# SALACIOUS CRUMB

When Jabba first finds this Kowakian monkey-lizard stealing his food, he tries to eat him, but he becomes amused by the creature's antics. Salacious is given the job of Jabba's court jester.

Salacious Crumb

Movable dais

# JABBA'S ENTOURAGE

**CROWDED AROUND JABBA** is a wide variety of individuals—sycophants, co-conspirators, hired thugs, and beings of mystery. The crime lord's syndicate offers opportunity to many types, just as his power and wealth draw many to secretly scheme against him. Jabba regards the inevitable plots as amusement, pitting the different schemers against each other before compassing their destruction. Amidst all the power plays and convoluted ambitions, many are individuals simply doing their jobs and ignoring the web of intrigue around them. Each in the retinue have their own stories, and curious paths have led every one of them to the desert palace.

*Sensory brain areas*

*Scary red eyes*

*Sharp, pointed teeth*

*Lekku (head-tail; one of two)*

*Suction tipped fingers*

*Manipulative mouth tentacles*

*Vand belt*

## BIB FORTUNA

Jabba's majordomo supervises the affairs of the desert palace and the Mos Eisley estate. Before working for Jabba, Bib Fortuna grew wealthy as a slave trader of his own people and became a hunted criminal as a spice smuggler. This scheming Twi'lek plots to kill his boss behind a facade of obsequious manners. Fortuna's control within the organization and his tendency to resort to underhanded means with friends and foes alike make him a powerful and dreaded, if cowardly, individual.

### TESSEK

Tessek is a clever Quarren from Mon Cala, who views the world of Jabba's palace with a clear and calculating mind. As Jabba's accountant, he embezzles money into a secret fund, and plans to assassinate Jabba and take over his organization.

*Rock wart sting juice (dried)*

*Chall granules*

*Retractable eyes*

*Krayt dragon venom*

**TWI'LEK DAGGER AND POISONS**

## J'QUILLE

J'Quille is a brutal Whiphid from the cold planet of Toola, working as a manhunter for Jabba. He is actually a spy for a rival crime lord, and is planning to kill the Hutt with a slow-acting poison in his food.

*Coarse fur*

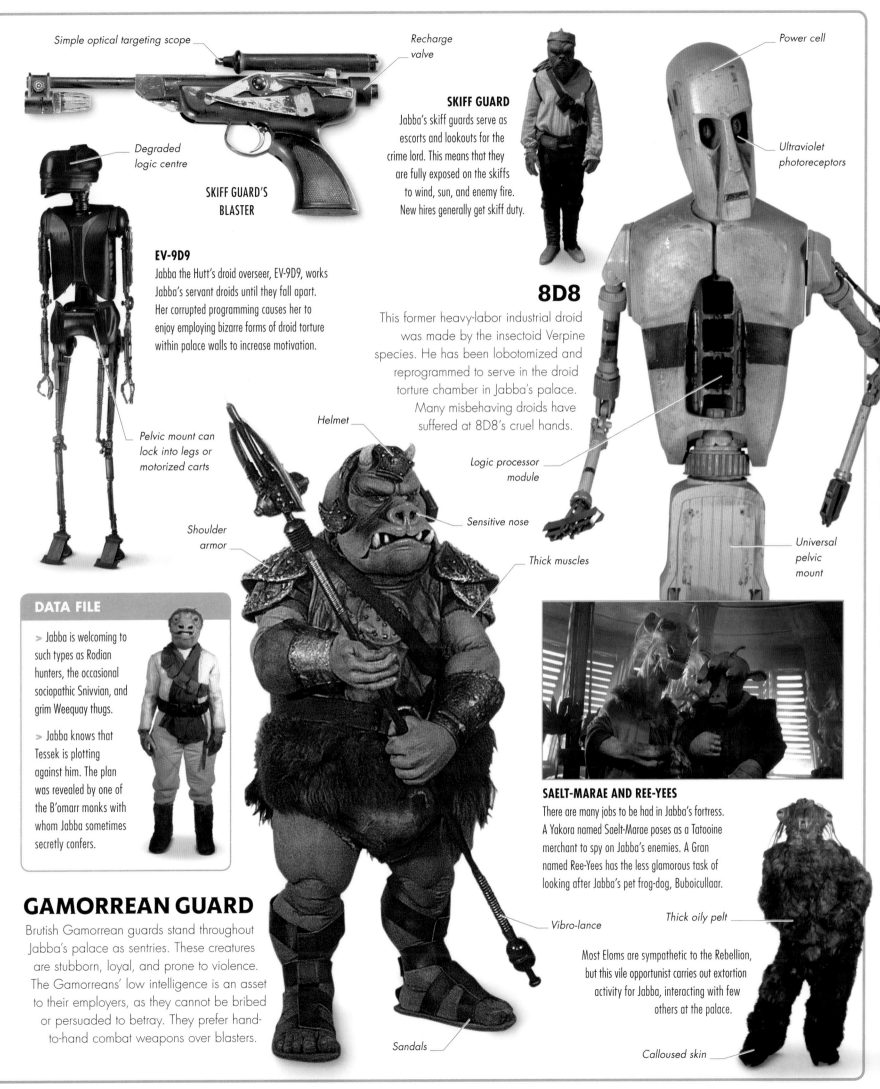

Simple optical targeting scope

Recharge valve

Power cell

## SKIFF GUARD

Jabba's skiff guards serve as escorts and lookouts for the crime lord. This means that they are fully exposed on the skiffs to wind, sun, and enemy fire. New hires generally get skiff duty.

Ultraviolet photoreceptors

### SKIFF GUARD'S BLASTER

Degraded logic centre

## EV-9D9

Jabba the Hutt's droid overseer, EV-9D9, works Jabba's servant droids until they fall apart. Her corrupted programming causes her to enjoy employing bizarre forms of droid torture within palace walls to increase motivation.

## 8D8

This former heavy-labor industrial droid was made by the insectoid Verpine species. He has been lobotomized and reprogrammed to serve in the droid torture chamber in Jabba's palace. Many misbehaving droids have suffered at 8D8's cruel hands.

Pelvic mount can lock into legs or motorized carts

Helmet

Logic processor module

Shoulder armor

Sensitive nose

Thick muscles

Universal pelvic mount

## DATA FILE

> Jabba is welcoming to such types as Rodian hunters, the occasional sociopathic Snivvian, and grim Weequay thugs.

> Jabba knows that Tessek is plotting against him. The plan was revealed by one of the B'omarr monks with whom Jabba sometimes secretly confers.

## SAELT-MARAE AND REE-YEES

There are many jobs to be had in Jabba's fortress. A Yakora named Saelt-Marae poses as a Tatooine merchant to spy on Jabba's enemies. A Gran named Ree-Yees has the less glamorous task of looking after Jabba's pet frog-dog, Buboicullaar.

## GAMORREAN GUARD

Brutish Gamorrean guards stand throughout Jabba's palace as sentries. These creatures are stubborn, loyal, and prone to violence. The Gamorreans' low intelligence is an asset to their employers, as they cannot be bribed or persuaded to betray. They prefer hand-to-hand combat weapons over blasters.

Vibro-lance

Thick oily pelt

Most Eloms are sympathetic to the Rebellion, but this vile opportunist carries out extortion activity for Jabba, interacting with few others at the palace.

Sandals

Calloused skin

# THE SARLACC

## SCIENTIFIC RESEARCH HAS answered questions about many

lifeforms in the galaxy, but some creatures continue to defy analysis, such as the sarlacc. A rare, enormous beast, one sarlacc rests in the basin of the Great Pit of Carkoon in the Northern Dune Sea on Tatooine. The sarlacc's three-meter-wide mouth is the only part above ground level; its body otherwise completely concealed beneath the desert sands. While some xenobiologists argue over whether the sarlacc is a plant or animal, most agree that the creature is far too dangerous to merit extended study.

The sarlacc feeds on stray creatures that cannot escape the sandy slopes that surround its mouth, but not all of its meals are accidental. For many years, Jabba the Hutt delivered his enemies as "gifts" to the sarlacc. Luke Skywalker is among the few to survive such a close encounter.

Jabba is surprised by the sudden, coordinated revolt of his rebel captives. While the battle rages over the Great Pit of Carkoon, the sarlacc simply waits for bodies to fall.

## DEADLY TONGUE

As the only visible aspect of the sarlacc rests in the basin of the Great Pit of Carkoon, some mistakenly assume that the beak-tipped appendage at the basin's center is the creature's head. In fact, this eyeless protuberance is the sarlacc's muscular tongue, which rises up from its mucous-lined mouth, seeking whatever savory morsels come its way.

*Touch-receptor tentacles*

*Inward-pointing teeth prevent victims from escaping*

*Rock-hard primary digestive glands*

*Tranquilizing poisons immobilize prey*

*Slower digestive route for more intellectually stimulating victims*

*Beaked tongue swallows small prey whole*

*Sand trap*

*Multiple hearts paired with multiple lungs*

*Upper stabilizing limb senses movement in surrounding sands*

*Moisture-gathering roots*

Parasitic male remains attached to female for life

Unfortunate eopie

Anchored root system

Acidic juices dissolve soft membranes and digest smaller molecules of food

Careless anooba

Once swallowed, the sarlacc's prey is incorporated into the biological system. It is believed that the sarlacc absorbs the intellect of its victims, and is capable of sustaining their torment for thousands of years.

Still-sentient cocooned victims become part of the sarlacc's collective intelligence

Transport tentacles place prey in specific areas of main stomach

Humanoid prey from one of Jabba's previous visits

The sarlacc claims numerous lives during the skirmish that becomes known as the Battle of Carkoon, but many escape the conflagration that consumed Jabba's sail barge. It remains unknown whether the sarlacc prefers its meals live or roasted.

Lower stabilizing limb

**DATA FILE**

> The sarlacc is vulnerable to energy weapons, but most of its victims are unarmed. Those snared by the sarlacc can only hope for rescue. Various factions have suggested that the sarlacc should be destroyed, but more influential beings ensure its ongoing use as a most entertaining disposal system of their enemies.

# BOBA FETT

HAVING INHERITED JANGO FETT'S MANDALORIAN
battle armor and arsenal of exotic weapons, Boba Fett
assumes his father's mantle as a notorious bounty hunter.
Over the years, Boba Fett has developed his own code
of honor, and though he takes only certain assignments,
he devotes himself to those few with fanatical skill.
His cool and calculating ways combined with his
manifold hidden capabilities have brought in many
"impossible" marks, and earned his reputation as the
best bounty hunter in the galaxy. From the concealed
weapons covering his space suit to the disguised
armaments of his starship *Slave I*, Boba Fett is
unerringly a bounty's worst nightmare.

## ARMOR

Boba Fett patches together
his modified armor in memory
of his father. The sight of this
battered suit keeps the idea
of Mandalorian warriors
alive in the galaxy.

Blast plates

## JET BACKPACK

Fett's backpack is an excellent
combination jumper-pack and rocket
launcher. The launcher can be fitted
with a missile or with a grappling
hook projectile. The jet jumper system
holds rocket blasts for short flights or
for escaping and surprising Boba's prey.

Darts

Upper shell

Fuel feeder
line for
flamethrower

Wrist
opening

Missile

Missile
boost charge

Stabilizing
gyro

Jetpack
adjustment
tool

Fuel
tank

Directional
servo

HoloNet transmitter

S-thread detection
matrix

Organic alloy
casing

Setting control

Attachment
magnet

Attachment
frame

Missile
launcher

Missile
targeting
rangefinder

Activation
button

FALSE EYE
(BACK)

ION LIMPET
HOMING BEACON

Touchprint simulator
surface

FALSE TOUCH

Boba Fett uses these devices to track his marks and gain silent access to
high-security areas. A false touch pad clamps over touchprint locks to simulate
the bioelectrical field and fingerprint of nearly any individual. A false eye pad can
be applied to defeat retinal scan locks in a similar fashion. The ion limpet quietly
uses the galactic HoloNet to track spacecraft throughout the known galaxy.

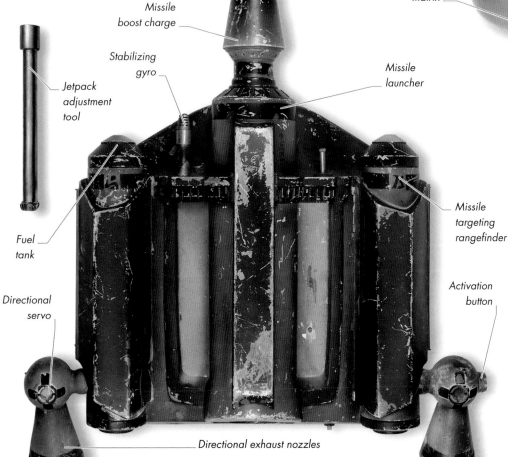

Directional exhaust nozzles

## DATA FILE

> Fett often uses the method of completely
disintegrating those whom he has been hired
to track down and kill.

> Darth Vader contracts Fett to track down
the rebel pilot who destroyed the first Death
Star. While Fett is unsuccessful, he learns that
the pilot is named Luke Skywalker and reveals
this information to the Sith Lord.

Not even the Corellian smuggler Han Solo can escape the craft and determination of Boba Fett. Outsmarting all his bounty hunter rivals, Fett tracks Solo to Bespin. There he takes possession of his mark, loading Solo's carbon-frozen body into the cargo hold of *Slave I*.

Targeting rangefinder (retracted)

Macrobinocular viewplate

Internal comlink allows Fett to summon Slave I from a distance

Targeting scope

EE-3 blaster rifle

Cooling vanes

Insulated gloves with armor mesh

Wrist gauntlet

Motion/sound sensor system

Energized blast dissipation vest

Reinforced double-layered flight suit

Braided Wookiee scalps attest past hunts

Handgrip

Emitter

Activator

Weight-saving cutout

High-frequency screamer chip

Power cell

Firing pin cover

Flanged Stibnium alloy blade

Journeyman protector honor sash

Utility pouch

## SURVIVAL KNIFE

## SONIC BEAM WEAPON

## KNEE PAD ROCKET DARTS

Kneepad rocket dart launchers

Having worked as an enforcer for Jabba the Hutt in the past, Boba Fett accepts a renewed assignment with the crime lord, in return for a bonus added to the bounty on Han Solo. Some in Jabba's palace suspect that Fett also stays on to admire his frozen trophy hanging in Jabba's throne room.

Vibro-plate

Setting and intensity controls

Range marking

## ANTI-SECURITY BLADES

These sophisticated electronic instruments can defeat fence fields, erase magnetic locks, and tune out security cameras and other alarm systems by the use of intense harmonic interference waves. Fett keeps them in his shin pockets, and uses them individually for most purposes. He also uses several together to create a safe anti-security field for secret forced entries.

Boot spikes (spring-loaded)

For major demolition jobs, Boba Fett uses an antiquated multi-detonator. It is less susceptible to damper shield effects than a conventional thermal detonator, and is capable of tearing a starship engine into fragments.

Concussion beam emitter

Satellite spin piercer

Trigger

Magno-thermitic charge

Fragmentation housing

Ripper launch tip

Cycle wave ripper

## MULTI-DETONATOR

# BOUNTY HUNTERS

**THE RESTRICTIVE RULE** of the Empire makes criminals of many, encouraging black-market smugglers and creating long blacklists of proscribed citizens of every kind. Rewards posted for all such "enemies of the state" have made bounty hunting a thriving profession. Bounty hunters are often criminals themselves, and many of them act in murderous and violent ways with the sanction of Imperial law. A few work with the legitimate intention of capturing criminals, but the profession as a whole is distinguished by outstanding slime.

DLT-19 heavy blaster rifle

## DENGAR

During the Clone Wars, Dengar serves as a member of a syndicate of bounter hunters including Boba Fett, Bossk, and Asajj Ventress. Dengar continues his impressive career throughout the Galactic Civil War, becoming one of several bounty hunters hired by Darth Vader to capture Han Solo.

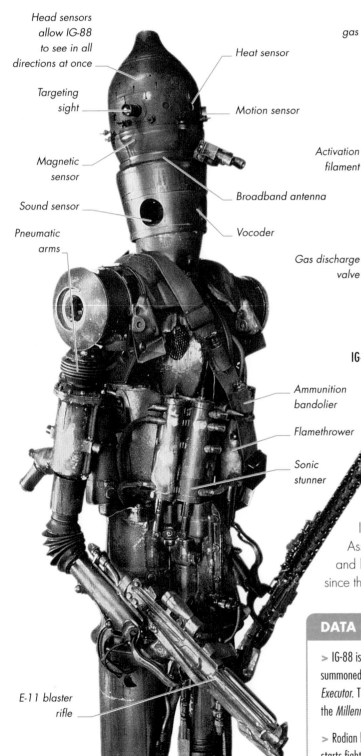

Head sensors allow IG-88 to see in all directions at once

Targeting sight

Magnetic sensor

Sound sensor

Pneumatic arms

Heat sensor

Motion sensor

Broadband antenna

Vocoder

Ammunition bandolier

Flamethrower

Sonic stunner

E-11 blaster rifle

Blast armor

Poison gas packet

Activation filament

Gas discharge valve

**IG-88'S TRION GAS DISPENSER**

## ZUCKUSS

The bounty hunter Zuckuss uses the mystic religious rituals of findsman traditions dating back centuries on his gaseous homeworld of Gand. His uncanny abilities make other bounty hunters uneasy. Zuckuss is a tireless tracker and weirdly effective.

"Butcher" vibro-blade

**IG-88'S BLADE EXTENSION SET**

## IG-88

This hideous assassin droid is one of a set of five identical robots that massacre their constructors moments after activation, and escape their laboratories to stalk the galaxy. IG-88's incompletely formed identity leaves it obsessed with hunting and killing. Assassin droids are always hard to control and have long been illegal for good reason, since they pose a threat to any and all around them.

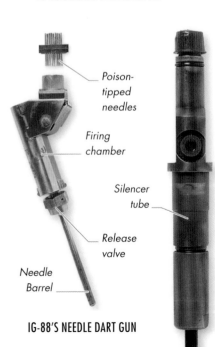

Poison-tipped needles

Firing chamber

Silencer tube

Release valve

Needle Barrel

**IG-88'S NEEDLE DART GUN**

### DATA FILE

> IG-88 is one of the bounty hunters summoned to Darth Vader's flagship, the *Executor*. They are tasked with capturing the *Millennium Falcon*.

> Rodian bounty hunter Greedo often starts fights with others. He finally meets his match when he confronts Han Solo.

## BOSSK

During the Clone Wars, a mean Trandoshan named Bossk focuses his bounty hunting career on capturing a rare target: Wookiees. In later years, this resilient reptile goes on to claim bounties for the Empire. However, on one occassion he teams up with young rebel Ezra Bridger to take down Imperial Security Bureau Lieutenant Jenkes.

Eyes can see in infrared range

Sling for grenade launcher

Relby v-10 micro grenade launcher

Lost fingers, skin, and even limbs can regrow until adulthood

Compound photoreceptors

Plasmic core

Battered black droid plating

**BOUSHH'S THERMAL DETONATOR**

Stun tip

Fire coils

Shock blade

## 4-LOM

4-LOM was a sophisticated protocol droid made to resemble the species it worked with. However, it rewrites its own programming and becomes a criminal, specializing in anticipating the moves of target beings. Teamed with the findsman Zuckuss, 4-LOM provides information and analysis to support his partner's mysterious ways.

**BOUSHH'S LANCE BLADE AND STUN ATTACHMENTS**

Jabba the Hutt's palace frequently brings bounty hunters together as the Hutt posts rewards for both captures and kills on a regular basis.

Targeting laser

Vision-plus scanner

Speech scrambler

Audio pickup and broadband antenna

Body suit

Impact armor

Chest- mounted comlink

Bandolier

Projectile detonator

Glove spikes

Ubese clan belt-clasp

Ammo pouches

Ogygian cloak

Fragmentation shell

Shata leather pants

## BOUSHH

In a galaxy with so many bizarre creatures acting as bounty hunters, it is easy for Princess Leia to adopt a convincing identity as an Ubese tracker. She disguises herself with a dead hunter's helmet and garb. Leia's military training served her well as Boushh, and only Jabba suspects her real identity.

Traditional Ubese boots

# JABBA'S ENTERTAINMENT

**GREEATA**　　　**RYSTÁLL SANT**　　　**LYN ME**

**JABBA HAS COME TO** spend a great deal of time in his palace, importing entertainers to amuse him in his court. His wealth and lavish spending can attract real talent, but the palace's reputation for danger and mayhem tends to keep out all but the desperate. The bands that do end up playing at the palace are typically either slaves to debt, heavy spice users, or the singing dregs of galactic society. Some are merely very poor judges of venue, and those who leave the palace intact almost always fire or eat their managers. Jabba's whims keep this odd flotsam of musicians and dancers hopping, one way or another.

## DROOPY McCOOL

Totally oblivious to what's going on around him, this Kitonak hardly recognizes the stage name given to him by Max Rebo. This far-out quasi-mystic doesn't notice that he hardly fits in with the Rebo band; he just plays his tunes. Lonely for the company of his own kind, he claims to have heard the faint tones of other Kitonaks out in the Tatooine dunes.

**BONTORMIAN KLESPLONG**

When he particularly likes a unique sound, Jabba keeps the instruments of some bands that don't need them anymore. These exotic instruments stay in the palace, and the Hutt sometimes orders the new bands to perform using them, even if they don't know how.

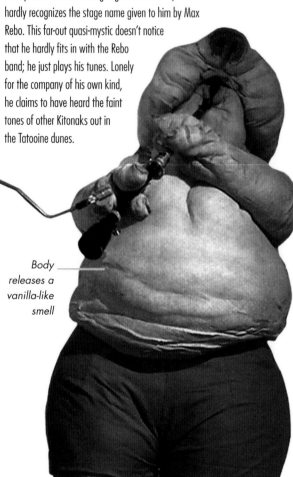

*Body releases a vanilla-like smell*

## THE DANCERS

The body shape of Hutts makes them unsuited to elaborate forms of dance, but Jabba has developed an appreciation for the sinuous and rhythmic movements of non-Hutt dancers. A good dancer can obtain the favor and indulgence of the Hutt, and those who are also expert at the arts of manipulation can find profit or opportunity among his entourage.

*Retractable tusks protrude from second mouth*

## SY SNOOTLES

Misled by Jabba's enthusiastic appreciation, the egotistical singer Sy Snootles has a very inaccurate view of her own potential. As a vocalist, she is too weird to make it anywhere mainstream. She will probably never discover this, since Jabba's favorite singers find it very hard to leave the palace.

*Microphone stand*

*Forward and backward-facing toes for walking on shallow lakes*

*Output speaker*

## MAX REBO

The blue Ortoloan known in the business as Max Rebo is a half-insane keyboard player, who is completely obsessed with food. He accepts a contract with Jabba that pays only in free meals, to the outrage of his bandmates. He may have poor judgement as a band leader, but he is devoted to music and good at his chosen instrument.

*Air outlet pipes*

# RANCOR MONSTER

Standing five m (16 ft) tall, this fearsome carnivore possesses an armored skin and colossal strength. Jabba keeps this beast in a pit beneath one of his palace courts, feeding it a live diet of unfortunate victims and watching its attacks for amusement. Jabba keeps the origin of his bizarre, freakish pet a mystery, but wild rancors have been known to roam the jungles found on the planet Felucia.

**HUNGRY BEAST**

Jabba can operate a secret trap door located in front of his throne, which leads directly to his pet rancor below. When Luke Skywalker is thrown down, a Gamorrean guard falls with him and is then crushed in the rancor's jaws.

**DATA FILE**

> Jabba's pet Hoover (below) looks harmless. However, at night it creeps up on sleeping victims to suck their blood, using its nose trunk to slither through clothing or around blankets.

*Digestive spittle*

**MALAKILI**

The animal handler Malakili became an outlaw when some of his circus beasts escaped during a show and killed most of the audience. Jabba then hired him as keeper of the murderous rancor, which Malakili has grown fond of.

*Sweat-soaked rag belt*

*Ancient circus pants*

*Wide grasp*

*Manacles*

*Short legs*

*Tough, rigid hide can absorb blaster bolts*

*Stubby hooves*

Rancors are inherently benign and have been domesticated by the Witches of Dathomir. However, Jabba takes every measure to encourage ferocious behavior in his own rancor. Consumed by rage and hunger, Jabba's rancor proves immune to Luke Skywalker's persuasive Jedi mind tricks when they battle in the creature's pit.

# EWOKS

**DEEP WITHIN THE FORESTS** of the emerald moon of Endor, the small, furry Ewoks live in harmony with the natural world around them. They build their villages high in the oldest trees, connecting their dwellings with wooden bridges and suspended platforms. Ewoks hunt and gather by day on the forest floor, retreating to their aerial villages by night, when the forest becomes too dangerous for them.

Acute sense
of smell

Chief's medallion

Reptilian
staff

## CHIEF CHIRPA

Chief Chirpa serves as leader of his tribe for 42 seasons, and has the wisdom of long years. He leads his people with understanding, even though he has become a bit forgetful in his old age. His authority commits the Ewoks to their dangerous fight against the Empire.

Hoods are a sign
of adulthood

### UNLIKELY FRIENDS

Visitors to Endor's moon are rare, and Ewoks are suspicious of outsiders. At first, they try to cook Han and Luke for dinner, but the Ewoks soon realize that the rebels can help them keep their village safe from worse strangers.

Leather
strap

HUNTING
KNIFE

Sheath

FIGHTING
CLUB

Stone
knife

Thick fur

## WICKET W. WARRICK

A young loner named Wicket is off travelling when he encounters Princess Leia in the forest. While helping her to the relative safety of his village, he senses her goodness of spirit and comes to trust her. When Leia's friends arrive, Wicket argues that they should be spared any abuse, but his solitary habits leave him with small influence amongst the village elders. Wicket's thorough knowledge of the forest terrain greatly assists the rebels in their later attack on the Imperial forces.

Wicket's
favorite
weapons are
the spear and
the bola

An Ewok shaman builds a collection of many magical objects and medicinal cures for his work. A spirit staff helps summon dead ancestors for assistance, while the sick or injured are touched with a powerful healing wand. The forest vegetation offers many medicinal plants, which are kept with charms in a talisman bag.

# LOGRAY

A tribal shaman named Logray uses his knowledge of ritual and magic to help and awe his people. He still favors the old traditions of initiation and live sacrifice. The trophies on his staff of power include the remnants of old enemies. Logray is suspicious of all outsiders, an attitude reinforced by the arrival of Imperial forces.

*Churi skull*

*Staff of power*

*Trophy spine*

*Healing wand*

*Talisman bag*

**SHAMAN'S KIT**

*Striped fur*

*Gurreck skull headress*

*Stone club head*

**CHURI BIRD CALLER**

**SHAMAN'S GHOST RATTLE**

# TEEBO

A watcher of the stars and a poet at heart, Teebo has a mystical alignment with the forces of nature. His subtle perception lets him see more than meets his dreamer's eye, but he is also a practical thinker. His sound judgment has led to his position as a leader within his tribe.

*Authority stick*

**DATA FILE**

> The Ewoks' technology may be primitive, but they display resourceful ingenuity. They construct advanced hang gliders and complex traps in preparation for the invading Imperial occupation forces.

Many Ewoks often wear the teeth, horns, and bones of animals that they have hunted as trophies. Animal skulls make particularly good helmets.

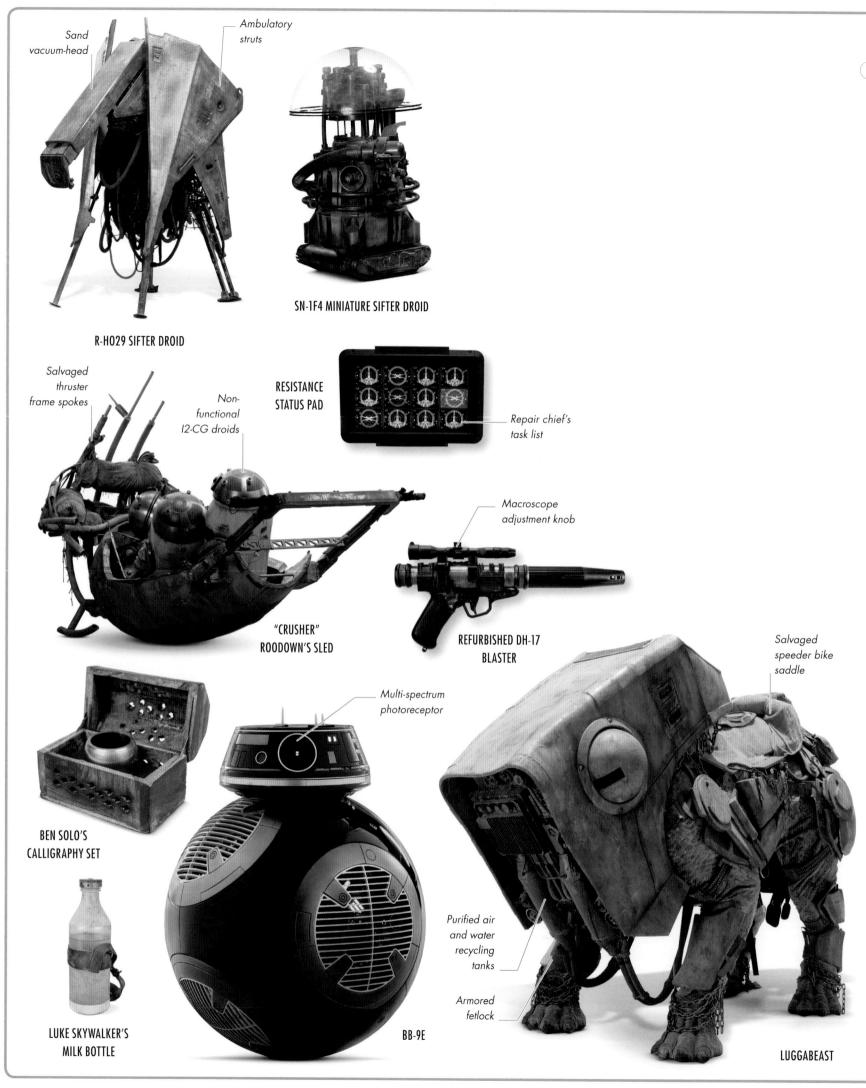

Sand vacuum-head

Ambulatory struts

SN-1F4 MINIATURE SIFTER DROID

R-H029 SIFTER DROID

Salvaged thruster frame spokes

RESISTANCE STATUS PAD

Non-functional I2-CG droids

Repair chief's task list

Macroscope adjustment knob

"CRUSHER" ROODOWN'S SLED

REFURBISHED DH-17 BLASTER

Salvaged speeder bike saddle

Multi-spectrum photoreceptor

BEN SOLO'S CALLIGRAPHY SET

Purified air and water recycling tanks

Armored fetlock

LUKE SKYWALKER'S MILK BOTTLE

BB-9E

LUGGABEAST

# THE SEQUEL ERA

Explore *Star Wars*, three decades after the hard-fought war to restore the Republic to the galaxy. A generation has grown up in a time of peace, yet a new threat has emerged from the ashes of the old Empire named the First Order. Fearing another galactic conflict, Leia Organa forms the Resistance—a smalll group of volunteers ready to fight back. In this time of upheaval, much can be learned from the advances in starfighter design, the powerful new weapons, and the clothing of the citizens. From Kylo Ren's menacing helmet to Rey's custom speeder, and the fathier racing on Canto Bight, explore the range of incredible objects from the latest *Star Wars* adventures.

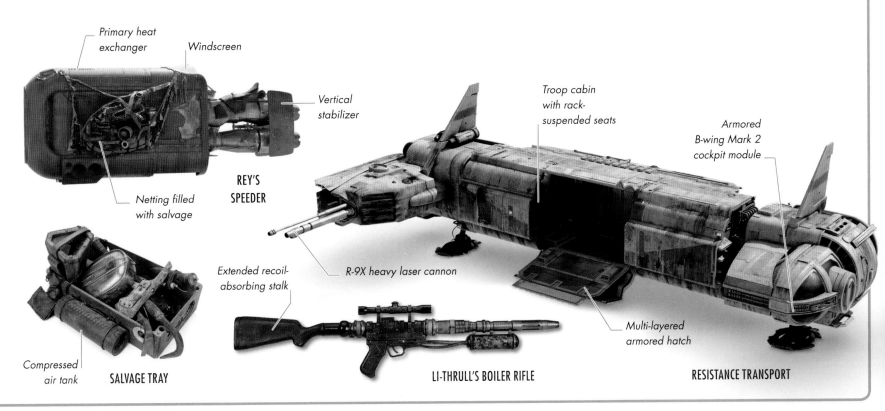

Primary heat exchanger

Windscreen

Vertical stabilizer

Netting filled with salvage

REY'S SPEEDER

Troop cabin with rack-suspended seats

Armored B-wing Mark 2 cockpit module

Extended recoil-absorbing stalk

R-9X heavy laser cannon

Multi-layered armored hatch

Compressed air tank

SALVAGE TRAY

LI-THRULL'S BOILER RIFLE

RESISTANCE TRANSPORT

# GENERAL ORGANA

Leia has shed any symbols of royalty unless tradition demands it

**IT IS NO SMALL IRONY** that the woman who embodied the ideals of peace and freedom for one generation was branded a militant fearmonger by the next. Many thought Leia Organa was unreasonably suspicious of the peace process that defanged the Galactic Empire. She argued that the New Republic was not doing enough to secure the safety of its citizens, and she was estranged from the Senate for her refusal to let the ghosts of the last war stay dead. Leia's words of warning regarding the First Order's mobilization for war prove tragically prophetic.

Rank badges are red for army personnel, and blue for navy

Snub-nose collimating barrel tip

Ammunition power cell

Rank-free vest

Resistance uniform

**GENERAL/ADMIRAL**

**COLONEL**

**COMMANDER**

**MAJOR**

**CAPTAIN**

**LIEUTENANT**

### LEIA'S BLASTER

Leia's preference has always been for compact hand weapons. The Eirriss Ryloth Defense Tech Glie-44 is a Resistance mainstay.

On the smoking battlefield of Takodana, Leia encounters Han Solo in an awkward reunion. Their complicated feelings must be put aside to focus on the graver matters at hand.

In the heart of the D'Qar base command center, Leia Organa keeps track of Resistance operations. Never far from her side are Admiral Statura, whom she relies upon for advice and perspective, and the protocol droid C-3PO.

## RESISTANCE LEADER

Leia Organa's words of warning about the suspicious activities of the First Order fall on deaf ears. Many in the Senate are content with the peace that has been won, regardless of the increasing cold war tensions between Republic and First Order. They brand Leia as an alarmist at best, a warmonger at worst. Not even Leia's royal status as the last princess of Alderaan commands much authority, as such titles now hold little sway in a Republic determined to uphold the tenets of democracy.

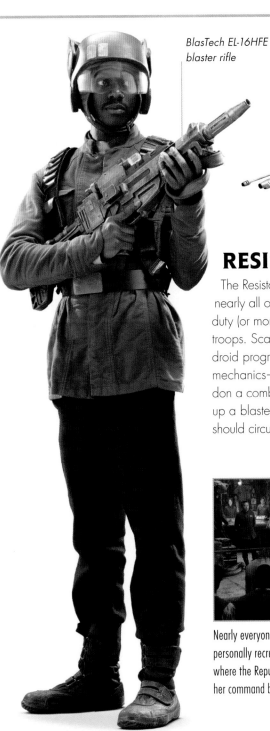

BlasTech EL-16HFE
blaster rifle

Troop cabin
with rack-
suspended seats

## RESISTANCE TRANSPORT

The Resistance's transports are cobbled together from parts left over from previous wars. This creates an unusual-looking vessel for conveying troops to the battlefield.

R-9X heavy laser cannon

## RESISTANCE INFANTRY

The Resistance is so undermanned that nearly all of its personnel do double duty (or more), serving as ground troops. Scanner technicians, droid programers, starship mechanics—all are willing to don a combat helmet and pick up a blaster rifle to do battle, should circumstances call for it.

Multi-layered
armored hatch

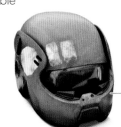

Visor flips down
to protect face
during combat

Armored
B-wing Mark 2
cockpit module

New jacket—
though Leia
didn't notice

**RESISTANCE COMBAT HELMET**

Nearly everyone in the Resistance command center on D'Qar was personally recruited by Leia Organa, convinced by her plea to act where the Republic could or would not. Leia knows everyone under her command by name, a fact not taken for granted by her crew.

## HAN AND LEIA

Tumultuous would be a fitting word to describe the relationship between Han Solo and Leia Organa. In their younger days, their opposite natures led them to romance. Their feelings stand the test of time, but losing their son, Ben, to the dark side forces the dynamics of their relationship to change. No matter what external conflicts and personal tragedies may come, the two will always share a love that comes from knowing someone so completely.

Leia is grateful for Finn's help, and does not hold his past as a First Order stormtrooper against him. She knows full well how fate and hardship may suddenly cause a hero to emerge from the most unlikely places.

### DATA FILE

> Despite the loss of so many loved ones, Leia simply never surrenders to grief. Leia's brother, Luke, speculates that the strength of her will is how the Force manifests in her.

> Leia now rarely uses her royal title except among those who have known her the longest.

# GENERAL ORGANA:
## SYMBOL OF HOPE

Alderaanian mourning braid

**LEIA ORGANA'S TENACITY** serves as an inspirational beacon in such dark times. The destruction of Starkiller Base was a gasp of victory, but the crushing weight of the First Order advance soon strangles it. The New Republic is in shambles, independent systems are capitulating, and Han Solo has been murdered by her son—this would be enough to crush any lesser being in an avalanche of despair. But Leia is strong enough to withstand such pressure. She knows others look to her for leadership, but this reliance comes with a risk. Leia looks to the future and wonders if the next generation of heroes is ready to take on the mantle of responsibilities once she is gone.

Muted somber colors reflect gravity of situation

Having grown up amid intrigue, and taught well by her adoptive parents, Leia is skilled at keeping secrets. The early Rebellion survived by carefully restricting information on a need-to-know basis. Leia keeps her plans for the survival of the Resistance close.

### HOMING BEACON
Leia wears a compact S-thread transmitter bracelet, with Rey holding the mated pair. In this way, Rey will be able to find the ever-mobile Resistance fleet once she recovers Luke Skywalker.

### MOST DESPERATE HOUR
The First Order attack on the *Raddus* results in the destruction of the ship's primary command deck. The bridge crew suffers horrendous casualties, and Leia Organa is incapacitated by exposure to the vacuum of space. Medical droids rush to Leia's aid, and soon a battery of devices carefully monitors her life signs as she recuperates. For many in the Resistance, including the officers and soldiers personally recruited by Leia, her absence is the biggest blow to morale they have yet faced.

## LEIA'S BLASTER

Leia learned to shoot in her teenage years with a Drearian Defense Conglomerate (DDC) Defender sporting blaster. This weapon was favored by aristocrats for its slim styling, reliable construction, and respected manufacturer.

**ORO-WEAVE BRACELET**

**SIGNET RINGS**

**AURODIUM EARRINGS**

Leia knows better than to trust that escape into hyperspace will save the Resistance fleet. The power of the Starkiller showed that the First Order wields technology beyond anything she has ever encountered.

# C-3PO

Once again, C-3PO is caught up in a war where his knowledge of protocol has limited use, leaving him hopelessly out of his programmed depths. The urgent task of moving the Resistance fleet out of reach of the First Order has little need for his skills. Beyond his impeccable language and etiquette abilities, however, C-3PO possesses strong loyalty to Leia.

*Olfactory sensor*

*Multi-system connection wires*

*Life-signs monitoring system*

**REPULSOR GURNEY**

*Non-threatening face*

*Lockable power switch*

*Modular appendage socket*

**EMERGENCY LIFE-SUPPORT UNIT**

*Reinforced foot shell*

**MD-15C MEDICAL DROID**

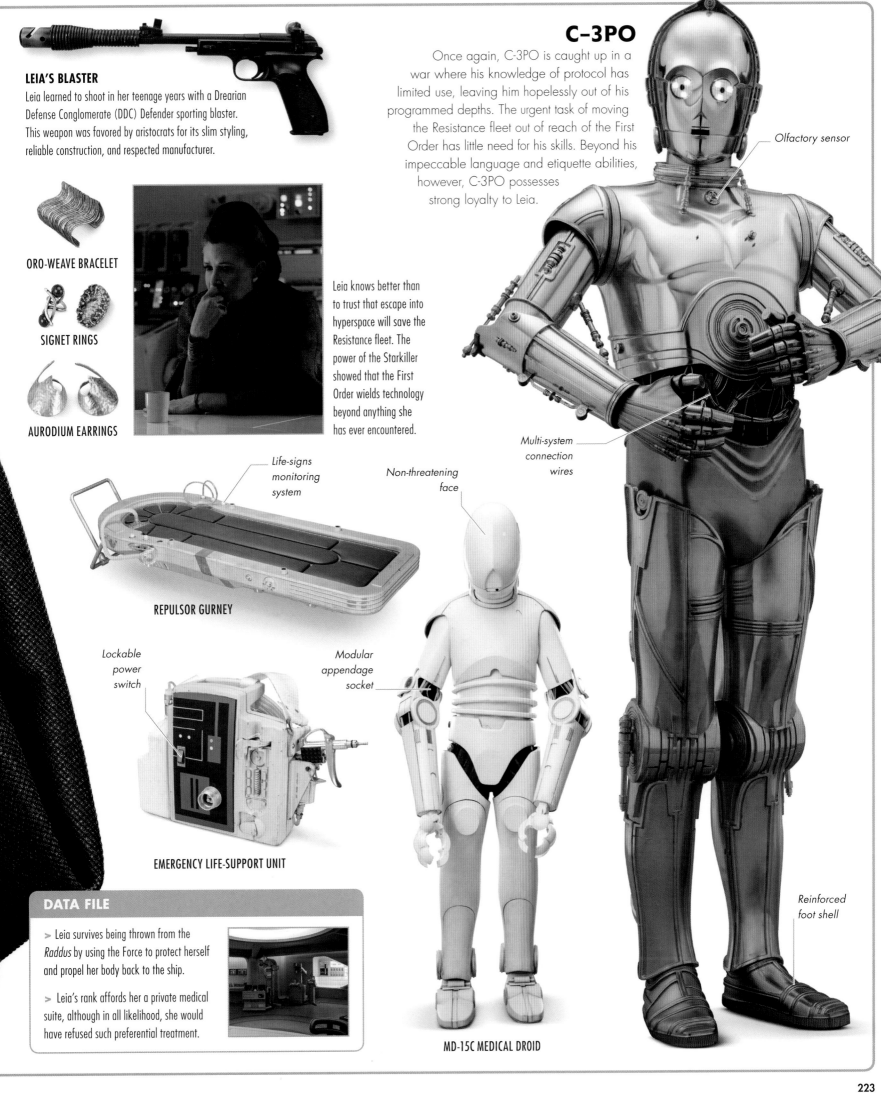

# RESISTANCE COMMANDERS

**THE HIGH COMMAND** of the Resistance comprises a mixture of Alliance veterans, ex-leaders of independent defense forces, and New Republic converts—all of whom share a personal connection to General Organa. Members of the new Senate thought the best way to preserve peace was to disband the galactic-scale military forces that had been the norm since the Clone Wars. This left many skilled veterans without commands. When Leia begins organizing a Resistance to stand watch against the militarized rise of the First Order, these old rebels are ready for the fight.

**COMMAND BRIDGE**
The *Raddus* has two bridges—a primary command bridge on its upper surface and a secondary battle bridge beneath its prow. When the command bridge is destroyed, operations move to the battle bridge.

*Resistance operations tunic*

### MAJOR BRANCE
Taslin Brance is a communications officer who keeps General Organa up to date with the latest intelligence on First Order operations. He grows weary of always imparting bad news.

*Inventory datapad*

### BOLLIE PRINDEL
An amphibious Urodel, Bollie Prindel is a towering, gentle presence in Resistance command centers. On D'Qar and later the *Raddus*, he serves as quartermaster and inventory officer, tracking the Resistance's steadily dwindling supplies.

*Premature graying, common in the Resistance*

*Repurposed Rebel Alliance crest*

### ADMIRAL STATURA
Statura was only a teenager when the war against the Empire ended, but he had already faced combat in trying to liberate his homeworld of Garel. He is pragmatic and technically minded, and was pursuing a career in applied sciences when General Organa recruited him as commander of ship procurement and logistics in the Resistance.

Skin faded
with age

**DOCTOR KALONIA**

Harter Kalonia's sympathetic bedside
manner and good humor is warm enough to
offer even the most hardened soldier comfort.

Medical
services
armband

Eyes evolved for use
both underwater
and in atmospheres

Holds army
rank of major

## LIEUTENANT CONNIX

Kaydel Connix of Dulathia earns
a promotion to lieutenant for
her admirable service as an
operations controller during
the Starkiller crisis—and from
the necessity of having an
officer lead the D'Qar
evacuation. Her word is the
ultimate authority when it comes
to prioritizing and carrying out an
orderly retreat. Once aboard the
*Raddus*, she returns to her sensor
ops position but retains her rank.

Boots emphasize
comfort for long
hours standing

## ADMIRAL ACKBAR

Ackbar brings nearly six decades of combat
experience to the Resistance. He defended
the oceans of his planet in the Clone Wars,
and was instrumental in the Alliance's defeat
of the Empire. Ackbar is coaxed out of
retirement on Mon Cala by General Leia
Organa, and serves the Resistance until
he is killed when the *Raddus'* principle
dorsal command bridge is destroyed
by First Order TIE fighters.

### CAPTAIN IDROSEN GAWAT

Before his retirement, Gawat led
the planetary defense forces that
patrolled space in the Mykapo
system. Not wanting to hang up
his rank badge just yet, he joins
the Resistance in his seventies so
that his decades of experience
can be put to good use.

Brismoss-fiber
uniform tunic

# POE DAMERON

**POE DAMERON GROWS UP** hearing the legends of the starfighter jockeys of old, having been raised by veterans of the Rebel Alliance. At 32 standard years old, he is now the most daring and skilled of the Resistance pilots. His appetite for risk is indulged by the commanders, as he gets spectacular results when pitted against First Order starfighter patrols. Poe is brash but charismatic, and he has limitless respect for the idealistic founders of the Resistance, particularly his idol, General Leia Organa.

## REBEL ROOTS

Poe Dameron was born toward the explosive finale of the war between the Rebel Alliance and the Galactic Empire. His mother, Shara, was an Alliance fighter pilot while his father, Kes, also served in the rebel military. Poe was raised on Yavin 4, in a newly established colony not far from the Massassi ruins from which the Rebel Alliance launched the fateful mission that destroyed the first Death Star.

## MISSION TO JAKKU

Massively outnumbered by the First Order, the Resistance scrapes together what resources it can to prepare for the oncoming war. General Organa sends Poe to the poorly settled fringes of the galaxy's Western Reaches, where he seeks out Lor San Tekka. This old ally of Leia and her brother holds information that can save the Resistance.

Poe forms a close bond with the stormtrooper turned Resistance fighter, Finn. He is overjoyed to see his friend when they are reunited on D'Qar.

*Flight jacket with non-regulation tailoring*

*Stock with gas reservoir*

*Macroscope adjustment controls*

*Sealed blaster lasing chamber*

*Removable galven-circuitry barrel tip*

*Security access plate*

*Electroshock discharge generator*

*Trigger guard*

### POE'S BLASTER RIFLE
A BlasTech EL-16HFE (Heavy Field Edition) blaster rifle is cradled within a charging slot inside Poe's X-wing cockpit. A model used throughout the Resistance, it is outdated New Republic surplus.

*Resistance commander ground uniform*

### FIRST ORDER BINDERS

*Weatherproofed adventurer boots*

Poe bravely resists the First Order's interrogation, refusing to reveal the whereabouts of the map to Luke Skywalker's location. It takes Kylo Ren's use of the Force to extract the information from him.

## DATA FILE

> In addition to his skills as a pilot, Poe is a capable infantryman, equipped with gear such as Neuro-Saav TE4.4 field quadnoculars.

> Poe has been flying starships since he was six years old.

# RESISTANCE ACE

Poe serves as a squadron leader in the New Republic Defense Fleet, but is frustrated by the government's failure to take the First Order threat seriously. Upon being recruited into the Resistance, Poe finds an organization that better resembles the Rebel Alliance of old. He quickly rises through the ranks of the understaffed Starfighter Corps, earning the grade of commander. If the Resistance had recruitment posters, Poe's fellow pilots joke that he would triple their numbers with his dashing bravado alone.

Tousled hair from wearing helmet

Inflatable flight vest

Poe's "lucky" FreiTek life support unit

Long-range laser cannon

BB-8

Nose cone housing sensor array

Armored cockpit module

Fusial thrust engine

Scissor-split S-foil

## CUSTOMIZED X-WING

Poe's *Black One* is a customized Incom-FreiTek T-70 X-wing fighter coated with sensor-scattering ferrosphere paint. Though often overlooked by sensors, the colors certainly stand out to the organic eye. BB-8 considers *Black One* the best and smoothest ride of Poe's ships.

Glie-44 blaster pistol

Old Rebel Alliance symbol has been adopted by the Resistance

Though many starfighter pilots detest atmospheric missions, Poe delights in soaring through skies and skimming the surfaces of planets. The tug of the wind creates an intense feedback that feeds Poe's appetite for thrills.

Anti-corrosion lacquer finish

**POE'S HELMET**

227

# POE DAMERON: DARING PILOT

**POE'S INCREASINGLY IMPORTANT POSITION** within the Resistance brings him greater responsibilities, as General Organa carefully parcels out various duties to him. Emboldened by his victory in the destruction of Starkiller Base, Poe's ego and recklessness begin to grow. His instincts are to keep moving, and he is never at ease when the pace of events slows. The harried evacuation of D'Qar is a real test for Poe, but it is the biding of time that follows the retreat that truly wears at his resolve.

*Visor in retracted position*

**SQUADRON LEADER FLIGHT HELMET**

When the First Order corners the rebels during the Battle of Crait, Poe spots a vulptex passing through a tunnel in the planet's caves. He follows the creature, leading the rebels through the cave system in an effort to get them to safety.

*Visor-retaining cowl*

*Incom-FreiTek 5L5 fusial thrust engine*

*Retractable anti-glare visor*

*S-foils in attack position*

*Accelerator pod*

*Vo-pickup comm unit*

**BLACK ONE**
Resistance technicians have attached a temporary accelerator pod to the tail of Poe's customized T-70 X-wing fighter. This boosts the fighter's sublight speed so it can zip past First Order point-defense cannons.

*Emergency beacon activation switch*

## FIRING INSULTS

Poe brings the fight directly to the First Order fleet—much to the annoyance of General Organa, who frets about Poe's lack of restraint. Buying time and cover for the Resistance bomber squadrons scrambling to hold off the First Order bombardment, Poe takes aim at General Hux's pride by deliberately mispronouncing Hux's name in a broad-frequency address to both fleets.

*Insulated, vac-sealable flight suit*

Poe loses his beloved *Black One* when it is struck by torpedoes fired by Kylo Ren's TIE silencer. Poe and BB-8 barely survive the explosion.

When an officer is named to lead in Leia's absence, Poe is both relieved that it is not him and angered that it is Vice Admiral Holdo. He finds Holdo's strategy and manner uninspiring. Against protocol, Poe questions Holdo's orders, stoking insubordination with the same fiery, rebellious demeanor that serves him well in combat.

For his flagrant disregard of her direct orders, General Organa demotes Poe from wing commander to squadron captain. The Resistance chain of command is becoming increasingly frayed.

*Rebel Alliance/ Resistance crest*

*Runyip-leather jacket*

# RELUCTANT LEADER

Unable to bear Vice Admiral Holdo's secretive and off-putting command style, Poe takes matters into his own hands and conspires against her. He builds a resistance *within* the Resistance, turning to allies such as Finn, Rose Tico, Kaydel Connix, and even a reluctant C-3PO. Poe dispatches Finn and Rose to Cantonica on a secret mission to thwart the First Order's hyperspace tracker, all the while trying to uncover just what Holdo is keeping from him.

**EARPIECE COMM**

*Short-range receiver*

*Brushed steel washer from rebel tech*

**RING NECKLACE**

Poe wears the wedding ring of his late mother, Shara Bey, on a necklace, waiting to share it someday with the right partner.

## DATA FILE

> Most of the surviving pilots who joined Poe in the fight against the Starkiller scatter to other evacuation points, or are assigned to other missions.

> The hurried pace of evacuation means Poe has not been properly introduced to Rey.

**SPEEDER HEADSET**

Poe is confident behind the controls of almost any vehicle, be it a cutting edge starfighter or decrepit repulsorcraft. When the Resistance survivors are forced to make do with aging ski speeders left abandoned on Crait, Poe once again assumes the role of wing commander, regardless of the rank badge he wears.

*Holstered Glie-44 blaster pistol (set to stun)*

# BB-8

**BB-8 IS AN INTENSELY** loyal astromech droid, who is usually never far from pilot Poe Dameron's heels. Like the older, larger astromechs that assist the ranks of the Resistance starfighter forces, BB-8 is equipped to control the flight and power distribution systems of a starfighter when the droid is locked into its astromech socket. The pairing of a selenium power drive and a dedicated, goal-focused personality keeps this orbiculate automaton tirelessly rolling, even into certain danger.

BB-8's self-preservation protocols result in the droid being skittish. However, his experiences have created a strong loyalty subprogram that cannot be overwritten.

## TRUSTY COMPANION

BB-8 is the first to spot the approaching First Order invasion of Kelvin Ravine on Jakku, and attempts to warn Poe. As it becomes clear that Poe is unable to complete his mission for General Leia Organa, the pilot asks BB-8 to continue alone. The little droid bravely evades the attacking stormtroopers and rolls into the foreboding desert night.

## ALWAYS MOVING

An internal orbiculate motivator rolls BB-8's body, while his head is kept perched atop the sphere with magnetic casters. Wireless telemetry between the head and body removes the need to keep the head tethered to a single contact point. When BB-8 needs extra stability or must traverse areas he can't roll through, he fires compressed liquid cable launchers that then reel the droid into hard-to-reach spots.

High-frequency receiver antenna (damaged)

Condensed helical transmitter antenna

Lightweight cranial frame

Towerslee-15 accelerometer

Magnetic caster

Commutator

Ollisteep-4D nanopin data port

Service access thread

Stainless inoxium

Primary photoreceptor

Articulated holoprojector array

BB-8's dense shell and sealed access points prevent dust contamination that would have seized the servomotors of older models.

Power recharge port

Motivator
cooling vents

Surface sensors

BB-8's six swappable circular tool-bay disks
can be replaced and upgraded with minimal
reprogramming. This example is equipped
with a magnetic-tipped bolt-spinner.

## FRIENDS IN FLIGHT

Poe Dameron grew up hearing tales of heroic
pilots and their trusty astromechs, and has
always fostered a deep respect for his droid
companions. Dameron keeps BB-8's systems
up to date and the droid's components well
maintained. BB-8 returns the favor by making
sure the settings on any ship assigned to Poe
are configured to his preferences.

### DATA FILE

> BB-8 converses in 27th generation
droidspeak code, a compressed variant
of the most common astromech language.
A young scavenger named Rey is familiar
with several nonhuman languages, so she
can understand the droid perfectly.

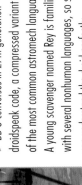

# LOR SAN TEKKA

**AS THE EMPIRE TOPPLED,** retreating Imperial officials destroyed records that would have been vital to the New Republic's attempts at galactic reconstruction. New Republic bureaucrats turned instead to firsthand accounts from well-traveled locals to fill in the gaps. Lor San Tekka is a seasoned traveler and explorer of the more remote fringes of the galaxy. He has proven his worth to the New Republic and the Resistance many times over. Ready to retire after decades of exploration and adventure, the spiritual San Tekka has settled with a colony of villagers in the remote Kelvin Ravine on the frontier world of Jakku.

Home-spun
fantabu-wool coat

Chain of Wisdom

Knowing that Lor San Tekka is a font of obscure information, Poe Dameron seeks him out on Jakku. He hopes that San Tekka's esoteric knowledge will be of benefit to the Resistance.

Tuanulberry-dyed
linen tunic

## DATA FILE

> Lor travels lightly, and shows wisdom in the few artifacts he continues to carry from place to place.

> Lor is old enough to have witnessed the Jedi Knights prior to the Clone Wars. He never believed the lies that painted them as traitors.

Gundark-hide
survival belt

In his travels, Lor San Tekka uncovered much of the history of the Jedi that the Galactic Empire had tried to erase. Others now seek him for his knowledge of Jedi secrets.

## CHERISHED ARTIFACT
Hidden in a plain leather sack is Lor's most valued possession—an antiquated data storage unit.

## KEEPER OF FAITH

Though San Tekka is not Force-sensitive, he has witnessed its power firsthand. During the dark times of Emperor Palpatine's rule, San Tekka was a follower of the Church of the Force. This underground faith was made up of loosely affiliated worshippers of the Jedi ideals, who steadfastly believed that one day their light would return to the galaxy.

# VILLAGER ESSENTIALS

The villagers of Tuanul follow an ascetic lifestyle, rejecting the comforts and luxuries of the galaxy. Even in matters of defense, the villagers prefer to create their own weapons rather than line the coffers of weapons manufacturers. Though not pacifists, the villagers reject the trappings of warfare, especially the profit-driven conflicts that have polluted much of the galaxy.

**MACES**

**PICKAX**

**BLOGGIN-OIL LAMP**

**SHOVEL**

**AX**

*Salvaged industrial power shunt*

**ILCO MUNICA'S BLASTER RIFLE/CLUB**

**DASHA PROMENTI'S BLASTER PISTOL**

*Carved dune zaywar tusk handle*

Seeking Lor San Tekka, the First Order sends more than 60 stormtroopers to pacify Tuanul village, which the villagers fight tenaciously to defend.

The wattle and daub huts of Tuanul village are built around a large vaporator cistern. They are an oasis of life in the otherwise empty Kelvin Ravine.

*Weighted stock doubles as war club*

*Pump-action recharger*

**ILCO MUNICA**

*Abednedo species*

*Pilgrim's robe*

*Insulated boots*

*Unadorned hair*

*Fantabu-fur fringed vest*

*Sash of the Balanced*

*Simple dyed linen dress*

**DASHA PROMENTI**

# TUANUL VILLAGERS

In the time of the Empire, when the Sith was secretly in command of the galaxy, any displays of organized worship or belief in the supernatural were against Imperial law. Underground religions spread across the galaxy, to finally emerge from the shadows with the defeat of Emperor Palpatine. Tuanul village on Jakku houses a collective of worshippers who praise the virtues of the Force without being graced by the ability to wield it.

# FINN

**FN-2187 PROVES TO BE** a highly skilled First Order stormtrooper, at least during simulations. He lacks the combat zeal and submission to authority evident in his squadmates, but keeps his misgivings hidden—until a brutal assault on a sacred village on Jakku. After that night, FN-2187 has a profound change of heart, and becomes a fugitive. He adopts the name "Finn" instead of his numerical designation, the only identity he has ever known. Finn's good nature—a gentleness, humor, and unerring moral compass—cannot be wiped from his mind as it is from others who undergo stormtrooper training.

*Resistance fighter jacket, "borrowed" from Poe Dameron*

Fast-talking FN-2187 enlists the aid of beleaguered Poe Dameron in his hastily conceived escape plan. Poe is used to improvisation and agrees, knowing he has few options available.

Finn puts his training to good use behind the controls of the *Millennium Falcon*'s vintage Corellian AG-2G quad laser cannons.

## RESISTANCE FIGHTER

Once the rush of escape fades, Finn realizes the enormity of his actions and is determined to keep running. Knowing little of the galaxy's workings beyond the borders of the First Order, he considers joining a pirate crew. But such thoughts vaporize when the First Order reveals the power of its ultimate weapon—which Finn served in the shadow of. Though he may not fully appreciate the aims of the Resistance, he does value friendship.

Seeing that the cause of the Resistance matters deeply to Poe, Rey, and Han Solo, Finn signs up.

*Removable collimating barrel tip*

*Improvised thermal detonator*

### FINN'S BLASTER

The First Order's determination to capture BB-8 as well as recover a deserter turns life upside down for Rey, who is swept up in Finn's escape.

*Hand print with FN-2003's blood*

### PYRO DENTON EXPLOSIVE

Having shed his First Order equipment, Finn picks up an older Resistance blaster rifle offered to him by Han Solo. The BlasTech EL-16 is similar enough to the stormtrooper F-11D for Finn to use well.

*Glossy betaplast finish requires constant cleaning*

### STORMTROOPER HELMET

The standard infantry helmet of the First Order protects FN-2187's head, equips him with communications and targeting systems, and conceals any shred of individuality.

*23 standard years spent training (from birth)*

# RELUCTANT WARRIOR

### STORMTROOPER QUADNOCULARS

Quadnoculars are oversized image enhancers used by First Order stormtroopers. The quartet of precision lenses offer enhanced multispectral imaging.

While FN-2187 performs at the top of his combat classes, the ever-present First Order propaganda never really takes hold in his heart. FN-2187's motives to excel are personal, not political—he is more concerned with protecting his squadmates than bringing order to the galaxy. He has a friendly personality that conceals just how unprepared he is for life outside the First Order. Used to relying on his fellow troopers, FN-2187 finds himself instinctively pairing with and trusting strangers rather easily.

### OUTMATCHED

Finn may not be Force-sensitive, but he doesn't hesistate to use Luke Skywalker's lightsaber to defend Rey from Kylo Ren. He bravely attacks the First Order warrior, but he is no match for Kylo's wrath and is gravely injured.

### CRASH SITE

As sturdy as the Special Forces TIE fighter may be, it was never meant to survive such a hard landing. The vessel is a crumpled, smoldering wreck, soon swallowed by the shifting sands of the Sinking Fields.

# FINN:
## RESISTANCE FIGHTER

**FINN'S REPUTATION IS SPREADING** through the Resistance. As the only stormtrooper known to have broken free from the lifelong conditioning and training of the First Order, he is regarded with admiration and curiosity in equal measure. Although he is being praised as a hero, it's a description he does not feel applies. Finn may have left the constraints of the First Order far behind him, but he still has much to learn about the galaxy around him— as well as the part that he must play in its future.

Finn stirs from a deep sleep within his medical cocoon. Doctor Harter Kalonia has placed Finn in a medically induced coma, allowing his body to heal free from the mental stress of the emergency evacuation.

### RECOVERING WARRIOR

Medics aboard the Resistance flagship, *Raddus*, put Finn into an emergency suit filled with healing bacta. When he awakens, he believes himself to still be in the forests of Starkiller Base with Rey, who he remembers being attacked by Kylo Ren. Finn groggily staggers out of the medical suite, leaking synthetic bacta, looking for answers in general and Rey in particular. First Order training psyche-logs, not allowing for such deep personal loyalties, would clinically describe Finn's behavior as "imprinting." He knows it to be something deeper.

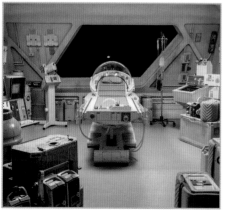

Finn recovers in a converted storage room lined with portable medical gear. The ship's dedicated medical bay is currently at full capacity tending to injuries sustained in the evacuation.

*Flexpoly bacta suit is past its expiration date, making it more fragile*

*Retaining collar lined by status sensors with wireless telemetry*

*Synthetic bacta circulation and filtration tubing*

Stowed blaster rifle

**FINN'S SCOUT BACKPACK**

Environmental
sensor suite

# RUSH TO ACTION

Impulsive Finn rarely plans more than a few steps
ahead. On awakening, his first instinct is to find and
help Rey. But this leads to him meeting Rose Tico, a
maintenance worker standing guard over the *Raddus'*
escape pod bay. The pair seem unlikely allies, but Rose's
methodical, technical mind coupled with Finn's drive
and knowledge of First Order methods allows
them to hatch a daring plan—one that
will allow the Resistance to shake
off the enemy pursuit.

*In a gesture of friendship,
Poe Dameron repaired Finn's
jacket while he recovered.*

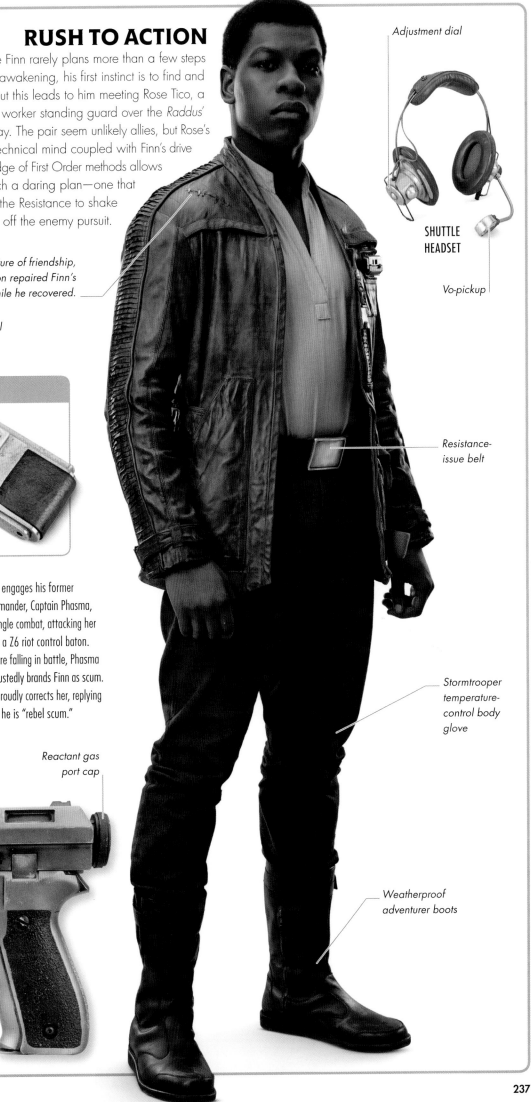

Adjustment dial

**SHUTTLE
HEADSET**

Vo-pickup

Resistance-
issue belt

Stormtrooper
temperature-
control body
glove

Weatherproof
adventurer boots

## DATA FILE

> While on his mission to thwart the
First Order pursuit, Finn keeps in touch
with Poe via a coded comlink that he
keeps stowed within BB-8.

> Though Finn is a quick learner, he still
isn't confident flying starships. However, his
speeder skills are more than competent.

Finn engages his former
commander, Captain Phasma,
in single combat, attacking her
with a Z6 riot control baton.
Before falling in battle, Phasma
disgustedly brands Finn as scum.
He proudly corrects her, replying
that he is "rebel scum."

Reactant gas
port cap

Power
cartridge

**FINN'S BLASTER PISTOL**

Finn's lifetime of combat training makes him adept with a wide variety
of small arms, well beyond the standard-issue weaponry of the First
Order. The rugged Glie-44 pistol is the standard Resistance blaster,
and is found in military, police, and civilian holsters the galaxy over.

# REY

**NINETEEN-YEAR-OLD REY** carves out her existence on the bleak world of Jakku. Despite a life that should have built a barrier against any sympathy or weakness, Rey still possesses a generous heart. It is her willingness to help those in need that gives her the strength to leave Jakku, joining Finn on his inherited mission to deliver BB-8 to the Resistance. Rey is catapulted into an adventure that tests her skills as a warrior, pilot, and mechanic. She comes to discover that she has remarkable abilities she never suspected she had.

Rey's first taste of lightsaber combat comes on the Starkiller Base. Her opponent, Kylo Ren, is surprised by her skill with the weapon, and tries to tempt her to the dark side of the Force.

## AN AWAKENING

Since the disappearance of Luke Skywalker and the shattering of his fledgling Jedi following, the cosmic Force has lain dormant, seemingly quieted to those able to sense its presence. The adventures of Rey and Finn on Jakku coincide with a turbulence in the cosmic Force, a sudden ripple indicating the awakening of newfound ability. With the Jedi and their records vanished, few—other than Kylo Ren and his master, Supreme Leader Snoke—are able to appreciate this occurrence.

Firm back arm grip to power a sudden swing

### DATA FILE

> Rey's fighting skill with her staff translates well into other short-ranged melee weapons, including those she has never wielded before.

> Though Rey has heard fragments of legends of the Jedi, she is surprised to learn that they were ever real.

Blade fashioned from droid arm attachment

**REY'S KNIFE**

Salvaged quarterstaff

Bloggin-leather and wool strap

Having made an enemy of the First Order by her alliance with Finn, Rey is forced to flee Jakku. She and Finn hurriedly board a dilapidated Corellian freighter, and Rey proves her remarkable piloting abilities.

Lower defensive position

Agile footwork practiced on shifting sands

Orange fabric salvaged from a New Republic cargo container

**DOLL**
Rey crafted this Alliance pilot doll when she was 10 years old, from debris she found in the junkfields.

## REY'S HOME

Rey lives in a toppled AT-AT walker, sleeping in a simple hammock. Her only escape from the brutal conditions of Jakku are vivid flights of imagination, where she envisions lush, green worlds and fantasizes about a family she has never known.

Goggles are stormtrooper helmet lenses

## A TOUGH LIFE

Rey's life on Jakku consists of treks into the junkfields, where she scavenges wrecks for valuable technology. She then trades her haul for food at Niima Outpost. Climbing through decaying starships requires Rey to be in peak physical shape, and she must also be ready to defend herself against cutthroat thieves who roam the wastes. The harsh conditions on Jakku have taught Rey that good fortune often invites trouble, and bullies only fear strength.

Armored body shell

Flash-suppressing/ stabilizing muzzle

Survival equipment stored inside

Salvaged quarterstaff

## REY'S BLASTER

A gift from Han Solo, Rey's LPA NN-14 blaster pistol has a compact grip to best fit her small hands, but its enlarged power core and reinforced frame means it is sturdy and packs a respectable punch.

Handle wrapping made from scraps of uniform

Water bottle

Tools

Happabore- leather wallet

Brushes

**SURVIVAL SATCHEL**

**SALVAGE TRAY**

**SALVAGE CLEANING KIT**

Primary heat exchanger

Netting filled with salvage

Windscreen

Vertical stabilizer

## REY'S SPEEDER

Rey's junker speeder is a cobbled-together transport that she built for travel across the Jakku wilderness. The craft sits between the classifications of speeder bike and swoop, not quite fitting in either category. A modified tractor web keeps Rey in place as the speeder rockets up to immense speeds, and well-positioned heat sinks keep the engine thrusters from burning her.

Afterburner assembly

**QUARTERSTAFF**

# REY:
## STUDENT OF THE FORCE

Energized plasma blade

Luke refuses Rey's invitation to join her in the Resistance. He turns his back on her, slamming his door in her face. Despite Rey's repeated demands, Luke attempts to ignore her. It becomes a battle of wills, as both Rey and Skywalker are equally stubborn.

**WITH THE FORCE** now awakened in Rey, she is filled with newfound ability, insight, and questions. The duel with Kylo Ren on Starkiller Base demonstrated how potent her abilities are when she allows the Force in, but that battle and the events that surrounded it exposed Rey to anger, fear, and aggression—emotions that all too easily lead to the dark side. Rey needs guidance, and there is but one last Jedi Master in the galaxy. When she finds him frustratingly short on answers, Rey does what she does best, and improvises on her own.

## REY'S TRAINING

Luke shocks Rey with his view that the time of the Jedi has come to an end. When he finally agrees to give her guidance, it comes with many words of warning. As Rey's abilities increase, so does a strange and seemingly unprecedented connection in the Force that spans across the galaxy to unite Kylo Ren and Rey. The bond is powerful, and gives Rey insights into Ren that not even Skywalker can see.

Rey has had visions of the island, or at least a place very much like it. Having grown up in the harsh Jakku desert, she found escape through dreams of being surrounded by water. Rather than finding comfort on Ahch-To, however, she is beset by surprises.

Burtt acoustic signaler

Resistance-issue holster

Leather band across which Rey props her quarterstaff in combat stance

Keeps out the chill of Ahch-To nights

### R2-D2
The ever-loyal astromech droid R2-D2 accompanies Rey to Ahch-To, armed with the full navigational data required for the journey. He has not seen Luke Skywalker, his master, in years.

**WOVEN BLANKET**

Constellations have since changed configuration

Resoled gorvath-wool traveler's boots

**ANCIENT STARMAP ARTIFACT**

**MILLENNIUM FALCON ESCAPE POD**

Viewport

Life-support tank

Maneuvering thruster

# FACING THE DARKNESS

Rey opens up to the connections of the Force on the island. She senses and is drawn to a shadowed area—a gloomy sea cave where the dark side festers. As she visits the cave, her fears and insecurities about her parents, and the reasons why she was abandoned on Jakku manifest themselves. Among the questions that encumber Rey is one of her destiny—what is her role in the conflict that now sweeps the galaxy?

Focused determination and control

Loose open weave tabard in the Jedi tradition

Combat stance learned from years of polearm use

Blade length adjust

Though Han Solo is gone, his reckless spirit lives on. Solo invited Rey onto his crew, and Rey honors that with her continued care of the battered *Falcon*. More than just a pilot and mechanic, Rey finally gets a chance to be a gunner in the ship's ventral turret.

Activation matrix

### SKYWALKER'S LIGHTSABER

Built by Anakin Skywalker decades ago, the blue-bladed lightsaber that Obi-Wan Kenobi once gave to Luke was thought lost. When it fell into the possession of Maz Kanata, she cared for it, keeping it in operational shape until one day it would point the way to Master Skywalker. But when Rey presents it to Luke, he tosses it aside, hoping to lose it once more.

# STARSHIP GRAVEYARD

**A GENERATION AGO**, the last embers of the Galactic Civil War came crashing down onto the dunes of Jakku. The secluded planet, far on the fringes of the Western Reaches, became the final battleground of the Galactic Empire. An intense assault by New Republic warships led to the burning wrecks of vessels from both sides plummeting into Jakku's atmosphere. The battle was ended by news of the peace treaty being signed on distant Coruscant, and the sudden departure of the surviving Imperial warships into the Unknown Regions.

### LUGGABEAST
These cybernetically enhanced beasts of burden are found on frontier worlds. They are forever hidden beneath armor plating, and invasive mechanical systems enhance their endurance to well beyond natural levels.

*Salvaged speeder bike saddle*

*Purified air and water recycling tanks*

*Armored fetlock*

*Exposed cranial dome reveals reptilian heritage*

*Catch bottle collects and recycles bodily fluids*

*Goggles help eliminate desert glare*

*Mag-pulse grenade*

*Ionization spear transmits crippling charge*

*Activation base*

*Sand-shoes built from rubberized droid treads*

### TEEDO
Teedo is a small, brutish scavenger who roams Jakku's vast Starship Graveyard in search of valuable technology. Using scanners built into the cybernetic cowl that encases his luggabeast, he relentlessly seeks out the energy signatures found in droid power cells. Teedo has a particular focus on the area that he believes to be his territory, a patch of desert southwest of Niima Outpost.

Teedos have a peculiar sense of identity that does not differentiate between individuals. The name Teedo refers both to a single being and the entire species.

## REY'S SANDBOARD

To help her descend quickly down Jakku's largest dunes, Rey uses a scrap of smooth-hulled Mon Calamari escape pod as a makeshift sled. It can carry her and her rucksack.

*Lining is repurposed parachute fabric*

*Fuel port functions as fastening grommet*

## STEELPECKERS

These iron-beaked carrion birds are drawn to the magnetic signature of metal. To better break down their metallic meals, steelpeckers collect vanadium, osmiridium, and corundum in their gizzards.

*Carcasses and guano are a worthwhile commodity*

**SALVAGED STAR DESTROYER CAPACITOR BEARING**

*Iron-hard talons are sharpened to a deadly point*

## THE *RAVAGER*

The huge Super Star Destroyer *Ravager* crashed upside down. Its rusting halls have a sinister reputation, even among hardened scavengers.

*Used to pry components from durasteel bulkheads*

**"WESSEX-HEAD" BIT-DRIVER**  **"BLISSEX-HEAD" BIT-DRIVER**  **CARBON CHISEL**  **CHISEL HEAD HAMMER**

Rey keeps a satchel filled with tools that allow her to carry out fine salvage work among the starship wrecks. Unlike many of the brutes who work the Graveyard, she has the keen eye and dexterity required to extract the most valuable pieces of technology.

# WRECKED SHIPS

Jakku was once home to a secret Imperial research facility, and was the last rallying point of the Imperial fleet. Entering the atmosphere to tighten its cordon, the Empire fought to keep the New Republic from capturing the base. In its defense, doomed Imperial vessels used tractor beams to drag New Republic warships into the planet's surface. The retreating Imperials destroyed the base before disappearing into the Unknown Regions.

*Remains of the Star Destroyer Inflictor*

*Conning tower has become home to squatters*

# NIIMA OUTPOST

**SINCE THE WAR** that littered Jakku's landscape with debris, the planet has become a treasure trove for prospectors and scavengers. Niima Outpost is a crumbling settlement of rickety landing bays, dusty salvage yards, and the type of shady businesses that parasitically flourish around the desperate. It is the closest thing Jakku has to a city. Interstellar travelers looking to find riches or lose pursuers keep a steady trickle of traffic coming to and from the outpost.

*Traditional Kyuzo war helmet*

*Sensor pack with extensible antenna*

*Face wrapped to prevent sunburn*

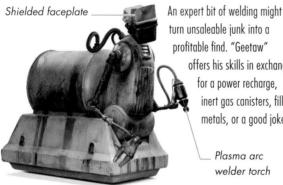

## NIIMA ORIGINS

After the Battle of Jakku, opportunists pounced to recover valuable metal, weapons, and scraps of technology from the scattered crash sites. The first enterprising scoundrel to organize the collection efforts was Niima the Hutt. She operated far from the borders of Hutt Space—a province of the galaxy embroiled in conflict as the Hutts carved up the deceased crime lord Jabba's territory. Niima was later killed by a bounty hunter, but the outpost that she established still bears her name.

*Salvaged metal hammered into armor*

*Breathable tsu-seed linen tunic*

*Shielded faceplate*

An expert bit of welding might turn unsaleable junk into a profitable find. "Geetaw" offers his skills in exchange for a power recharge, inert gas canisters, filler metals, or a good joke.

**EGL-21 "AMPS" POWER DROID**

*Plasma arc welder torch*

**GTAW-74 WELDER DROID**

### HAPPABORE

The happabore is found on several worlds, perhaps as a result of some forgotten colonial effort. This strong creature has tough skin, an enormous snout, and remarkable obedience.

**CONSTABLE ZUVIO**

Constable Zuvio, leader of a local militia that includes two of his fellow Kyuzo warriors, provides a semblance of law and order in Niima Outpost. He has a strong sense of justice and cannot be bribed.

# NIIMA RESIDENTS

New arrivals on Jakku are inevitably drawn to Niima Outpost, as it is the only navigational beacon on the planet. Salvage forms the backbone of Niima's economy, but other services have sprung up to take advantage of newcomers. Black market trading, guns-for-hire, and other disreputable activities thrive on a planet with minimal laws.

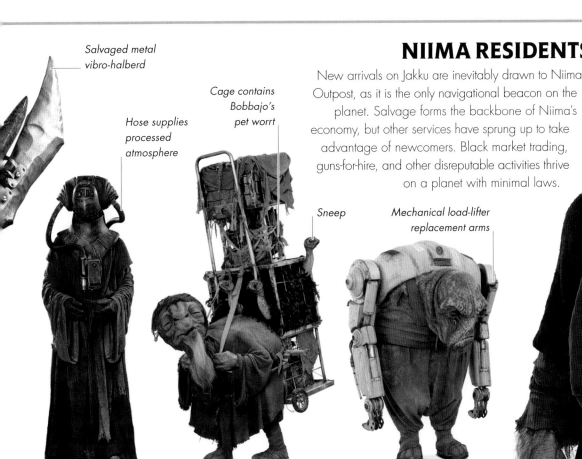

Salvaged metal vibro-halberd

Hose supplies processed atmosphere

Cage contains Bobbajo's pet worrt

Sneep

Mechanical load-lifter replacement arms

## SARCO PLANK

One-time scavenger, bounty hunter, and tomb raider, Sarco Plank is an aging Melitto who has made a multitude of enemies in his checkered career. The eyeless being "sees" via supersensitive cilia.

Nutrient and fluid dispenser

## ATHGAR HEECE

A Dybrinthe bounty hunter used to operating in higher atmospheric pressures and temperatures, Heece actually finds Jakku quite pleasant.

## BOBBAJO

Bobbajo is a creaky-jointed Nu-Cosian. His calm demeanor settles down the jittery animals he carries on his back to sell at the market.

## "CRUSHER" ROODOWN

Roodown is an unlucky salvager who had his arms cut off by Unkar Plutt's thugs over a misunderstanding. He offers his services as a for-hire strong back.

SoroSuub JSP-14 pistol fitted in tripler

### SARCO'S BLASTER RIFLE

Sarco's business as an arms dealer involves fencing stolen weaponry to travelers looking to brave the Graveyard wastes. To emphasize the quality of his wares, Sarco brandishes an exotic Trandoshan tripler, an attachment that increases the firepower of any compatible blaster weapon.

"JAKKU NIGHT SPECIAL" BLASTER RIFLE

### TRANDOSHAN DOUBLER ON TARGET PISTOL

Collimating tip

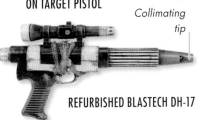

### REFURBISHED BLASTECH DH-17

There are very few permanent structures on Jakku. Though the marketplace is a fixture of Niima Outpost, it consists mostly of cargo containers and temporary awnings. There is little in the way of accommodations, and most travelers opt to sleep aboard their starships.

# UNKAR PLUTT

**A HARSH DESERT PLANET** is the last place one would expect to find an alien of aquatic origins, but Unkar Plutt goes where profit dictates. Removed from his saltwater surroundings, Unkar's Crolute body sags unsettlingly on his frame, giving him the appearance of a melted blobfish. This only adds to his unappealing demeanor as the junk boss of Jakku, who runs a successful business stealing, scavenging, and selling scrap. He doles out slim rations of food in exchange for valuable salvage, and uses goons and henchmen to ensure he gets the best deals.

Buoyant, gelatinous body tissue

Leather cap with electroloupe

Sour demeanor

From behind a caged window within his stall, Unkar casts a discerning eye over fresh salvage delivered by Rey. Impressed, he grants her a quarter portion of rations.

**VEG-MEAT**

**POLYSTARCH**

Unkar's workspace is a converted cargo crawler. It has been fitted with security monitors to ensure no desperate scavengers attempt to steal any of his provisions.

Long-range antenna, as Jakku lacks a communications grid

Audio grid and tuning dial

**UNKAR'S COMLINK**

## JUNKYARD BOSS

Unkar's stall stands at the center of one of the few semi-permanent structures in Niima Outpost, an awning-roofed blockhouse the locals call the "Concession Stand." Unkar is the principal source of nourishment for scavengers who work the junkfields. In exchange for salvage that he can sell for real credits, Unkar doles out food rations. He sells the salvage to spacers on Jakku, or on nearby worlds like Ponemah Terminal and Ogem.

Apron made from salvaged hull plates

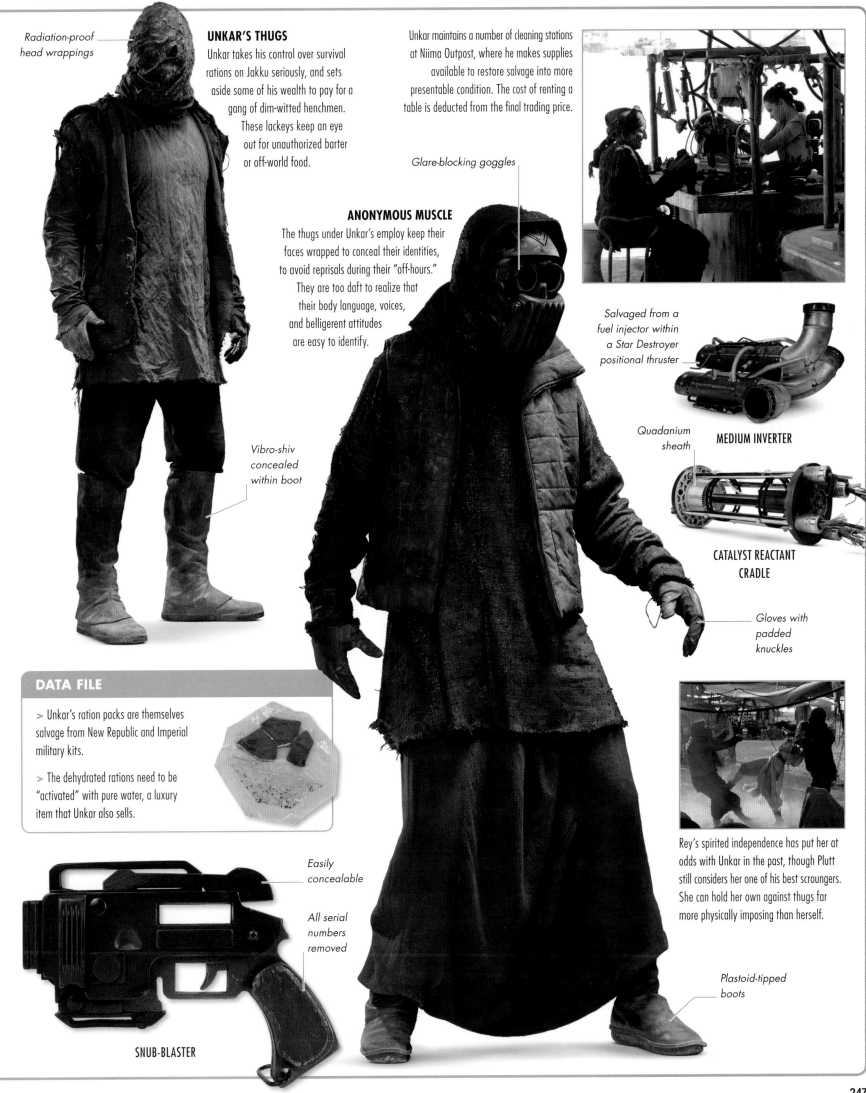

**UNKAR'S THUGS**

Unkar takes his control over survival rations on Jakku seriously, and sets aside some of his wealth to pay for a gang of dim-witted henchmen. These lackeys keep an eye out for unauthorized barter or off-world food.

Radiation-proof head wrappings

Unkar maintains a number of cleaning stations at Niima Outpost, where he makes supplies available to restore salvage into more presentable condition. The cost of renting a table is deducted from the final trading price.

Glare-blocking goggles

**ANONYMOUS MUSCLE**

The thugs under Unkar's employ keep their faces wrapped to conceal their identities, to avoid reprisals during their "off-hours." They are too daft to realize that their body language, voices, and belligerent attitudes are easy to identify.

Salvaged from a fuel injector within a Star Destroyer positional thruster

Quadanium sheath

**MEDIUM INVERTER**

Vibro-shiv concealed within boot

**CATALYST REACTANT CRADLE**

Gloves with padded knuckles

**DATA FILE**

> Unkar's ration packs are themselves salvage from New Republic and Imperial military kits.

> The dehydrated rations need to be "activated" with pure water, a luxury item that Unkar also sells.

Rey's spirited independence has put her at odds with Unkar in the past, though Plutt still considers her one of his best scroungers. She can hold her own against thugs far more physically imposing than herself.

Easily concealable

All serial numbers removed

Plastoid-tipped boots

**SNUB-BLASTER**

# HAN SOLO: REBELLIOUS HERO

**IF ANYTHING IS CONSISTENT** in Han Solo's life, it is unpredictability. His past exploits are the stuff of legends—he has been the smuggler who smashed the record for the Kessel Run; the onetime captain of the *Millennium Falcon*; and the scoundrel who won the heart of the last princess of Alderaan and became a hero of the Rebellion. Transition to a time of peace has not been easy for Han, who never expected an early or tranquil retirement. As the pendulum of fate swings the galaxy back into war, he once again finds himself in the center of the chaos.

*Former brown hair now entirely gray*

*Nerf-leather jacket*

*Still a fast draw*

## OLD HABITS

After the Galactic Civil War, Han Solo's life takes unexpected turns as he becomes husband to a politician, a father, and—for a time—a successful racing pilot. But the peace of this life was not to last. Han and Leia's son, Ben, betrays his family and turns to the dark side. This profound tragedy upends what had become normal for the Corellian, and Han returns to his old life as a tramp freighter captain, smuggler, and law bender. Chewbacca returns to Solo's side, and although much had changed, in many ways it is like the old days.

*Trigger*

**DETONATOR**

Han and Chewie are surprised to find stowaways aboard the *Millennium Falcon*, but quickly realize that the inexperienced youngsters do not pose a threat.

**HAN'S WELDING GOGGLES**

*Detachable macroscope*

### HAN'S HEAVY BLASTER PISTOL
Han favors the BlasTech DL-44 design he has carried since before the Galactic Civil War, even though newer models have come and gone.

*Power cell*

*Low-power pulse warning*

*Captain's pants devoid of markings*

# FOR THE RESISTANCE

For Han, helping the Resistance is less about lofty ideals of freedom and democracy than it is to answer pleas for help from Rey, Finn, and ultimately, Leia Organa. Solo suits up for trouble and charges into danger. He plunges into the very heart of the First Order, in an attempt to make a difference in as foolhardy and reckless a way as possible—a classic Han Solo gambit. This mission would prove to be his last, as he dies at the hands of his son, Kylo Ren, on Starkiller Base.

A visit to Takodana and the sanctuary of Maz Kanata's castle is suddenly interrupted by an unmistakable show of force by the First Order.

Cargo containers locked into transport grid

Cold weather gear

Bridge

Propulsion module

Docking bay door

# SHIPS OF FORTUNE

As easily as the *Millennium Falcon* fell into Solo's life, so it was destined to abandon him after a change in fate. Solo makes do with other ships, eventually settling on an enormous bulk freighter named the *Eravana*. He uses it to haul massive shipments of legally questionable cargo. The ship is largely automated, meaning Solo and Chewbacca can handle most of the work, but on particularly dangerous or profitable hauls he hires additional hands.

Han is surprised by Rey's resourcefulness and quick-thinking when it comes to flying the *Millennium Falcon*. She makes an impressive copilot, despite her lack of experience with the ship.

Cooling vent

## SCOUNDREL'S LUCK

Solo keeps the golden pair of dice that he used in the "Corellian Spike" game of sabacc, in which he won the *Millennium Falcon* from Lando Calrissian.

Replacement sensor dish

Insulated boots

Cockpit

# CHEWBACCA: RETURNING REBEL

**FAITHFUL FIRST MATE** and copilot Chewbacca has loyally stood by his captain's side through the twisting fortunes of a galaxy in turmoil. Devoted to Solo no matter what ship the Corellian pilot happens to be flying, Chewie serves as a mechanical mastermind, keeping ships operational after Solo's harebrained maneuvers push them to their limit. As a long-lived Wookiee, the decades that Chewie has spent at Solo's side are scant payment of the life debt that Chewie feels he owes Solo. The two continue to be inseparable friends.

## WOUNDED WOOKIEE

A run-in with competing gangs over a matter of credits owed results in Chewbacca suffering a blaster wound. Though the wound is suitably field-dressed, it requires a closer inspection from a medical professional. Doctor Harter Kalonia of the Resistance applies her skilled touch to the injured Wookiee.

### MEDICAL KIT

Kalonia's field kit is well equipped to handle blaster burns, with antiseptic field generators, bacta bulbs, and synthflesh dispensers within easy reach.

*Stowed gear in cushioned case*

*Handheld healing field generator*

### TOOL KIT

Despite the *Falcon's* ramshackle appearance, Chewbacca is surprisingly particular when it comes to the storage of his tools. He often wishes Han was the same.

Soothing words from Kalonia calm the temperamental Chewbacca, who has never been good around doctors. Kalonia's fluency in Shyriiwook makes her a sympathetic ear.

*Positive-default alternating polarizer*

*Conductive bowstring*

*Macroscope*

*Skeletal stalk and butt*

*Woven kshyyy-vine strap*

## BOWCASTER

Chewie's hand-crafted bowcaster is a traditional Wookiee ranged weapon. Colloquially known as a laser crossbow, the weapon uses alternating magnetic polarizers to energize a destructive bolt known as a quarrel. The quarrel emerges from the barrel sheathed in blaster energy, resulting in a particularly explosive impact. The weapon requires Wookiee strength to fire comfortably.

*Negative-default alternating polarizer*

"We're home," declares Han as they recover the *Falcon*. Although Chewie's time aboard the vessel represents a smaller percentage of his life, he is still fond of the ship he invested so much effort into maintaining.

Keen blue eyes

Bandolier cases
contain one
to three bowcaster
quarrels each

Nearly
indestructible
kshyyy-vine weave

Carry-pouch

Pattern of fur
coloration is
unique to each
Wookiee

Climbing claws
(retracted)

Chewbacca is the first Wookiee Finn has ever met. Unable to understand
Chewie's language, the young First Order deserter is intimidated.

## PARTNERS IN CRIME

Chewbacca returned to Kashyyyk once it was free from
Imperial rule and reconnected with his larger family.
Wookiee familial bonds are strong, but occur in a timescale
alien to humans with their shorter lifespans. As such, it is
relatively easy for Chewbacca to spend decades adventuring
in the galaxy, away from his people. When Han Solo returns
to a life of smuggling, Chewbacca feels honor-bound to follow
his trusted friend down this path and offer what help he can.

### EXPLOSIVES BAG

Chewbacca puts his great strength to good
use hauling a rucksack full of pyro denton
explosives, during a mission to sabotage
the First Order's evil plans.

Ever loyal, Chewbacca accompanies Han
Solo on his mission to infiltrate the Starkiller
Base. Chewie is Solo's sworn protector and
will do all he can to keep him safe.

### BANDOLIER

Chewbacca's bandolier holds
ammunition and a carry-pouch
containing tools to keep his
bowcaster in operational condition.

# CHEWBACCA: LOYAL PROTECTOR

**CHEWBACCA'S STRONG** protective instincts extend to watching over Rey, especially after the degree to which Han Solo vouched for her. Though Chewie is ever-loyal, he knows better than to crowd a young woman as independent as Rey, who tends to be drawn to isolation. As Rey disappears to follow her duties as a Jedi-in-training, the Wookiee mostly sticks close to the *Millennium Falcon*, forever tinkering with the stubborn freighter, and taking occasional breaks to explore his surroundings on the island.

Rey and Chewbacca soon develop a rhythm as they operate the *Falcon* together. Though a capable pilot himself, Chewie prefers his time-honored role as first mate and copilot, recalibrating the *Falcon's* fickle systems as Rey's instinctive piloting abilities push the ship to its limits.

*Keen sense of smell*

*Leather bandolier with ammunition cases*

*Wookiee fur consists of three main layers: an outer coat, a mid-fiber layer, and inner down*

## DATA FILE

> Chewbacca and Han spent much time apart after the Galactic Civil War as they both settled down with their respective families.

> It is Chewbacca who brings Luke Skywalker up to speed on the latest tragedy to have befallen the Solo household.

## MILLENNIUM FALCON

Having been separated from the *Falcon* for years as it underwent changes in ownership, Chewbacca takes advantage of every minute of downtime to tear apart access hatches and rediscover the ship's inner workings. He has reset numerous recent "improvements" to the more familiar configurations he and Solo devised years earlier. Complicating this chore is a growing infestation of curious porgs, who have transformed circuit bays into nests.

*Mandibles grip containers during cargo-pushing operations*

*Side-mounted cockpit*

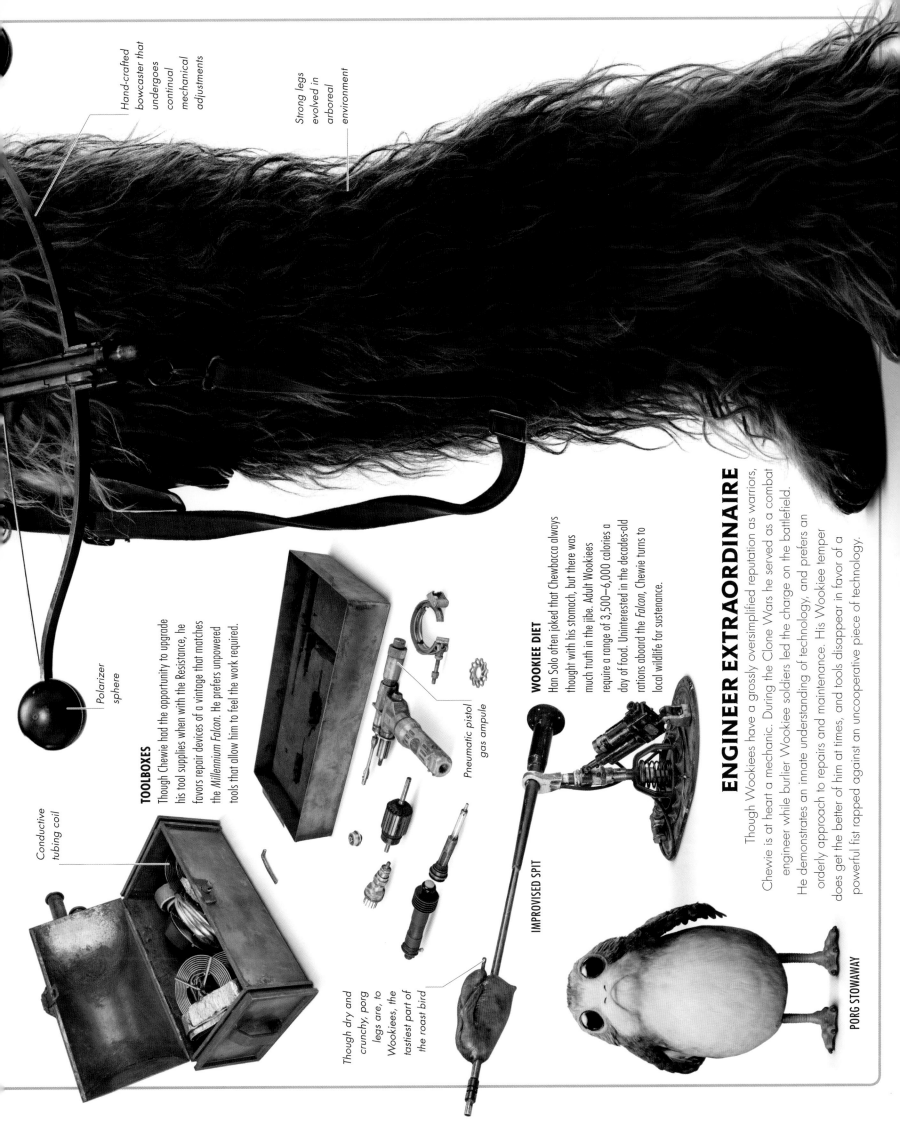

Hand-crafted bowcaster that undergoes continual mechanical adjustments

Strong legs evolved in arboreal environment

Conductive tubing coil

Polarizer sphere

## TOOLBOXES

Though Chewie had the opportunity to upgrade his tool supplies when with the Resistance, he favors repair devices of a vintage that matches the *Millennium Falcon*. He prefers unpowered tools that allow him to feel the work required.

Pneumatic pistol gas ampule

Though dry and crunchy, porg legs are, to Wookiees, the tastiest part of the roast bird

**IMPROVISED SPIT**

## WOOKIEE DIET

Han Solo often joked that Chewbacca always thought with his stomach, but there was much truth in the jibe. Adult Wookiees require a range of 3,500–6,000 calories a day of food. Uninterested in the decades-old rations aboard the *Falcon*, Chewie turns to local wildlife for sustenance.

# ENGINEER EXTRAORDINAIRE

Though Wookiees have a grossly oversimplified reputation as warriors, Chewie is at heart a mechanic. During the Clone Wars he served as a combat engineer while burlier Wookiee soldiers led the charge on the battlefield. He demonstrates an innate understanding of technology, and prefers an orderly approach to repairs and maintenance. His Wookiee temper does get the better of him at times, and tools disappear in favor of a powerful fist rapped against an uncooperative piece of technology.

**PORG STOWAWAY**

# TEMPLE ISLAND

**WHEN IMPERIAL FORCES** surrendered in the aftermath of the Battle of Jakku, Luke Skywalker began a lengthy quest to recover as much lost Jedi knowledge as possible. Over the years, he uncovered tantalizing clues as to the origin point of the Jedi, but its exact location remained a mystery. When he finally does piece together its location with the help of the old scholar Lor San Tekka, Skywalker keeps this information to himself. An unnamed island, located in the northern latitudes of Ahch-To, was the site of the first Jedi temple. It is this world, and its temple island, where Luke eventually hides away from the galaxy.

The suns of Ahch-To mark another dawn on a world where little ever changes. Ahch-To stands apart from the rest of the galaxy, a peaceful oasis where the daily struggles and triumphs of life are greatly removed from the ravages of interstellar war. But in many ways, the island is a microcosm of the galaxy that surrounds it.

*Extra membrane enables sharp underwater vision*

*Traditional white habit*

## THALA-SIRENS

Thala-sirens are large, flippered marine mammals often found sunning themselves along the coastal rocks of the island. The docile creatures are not hunted, and thus do not fear the natives of the island, but they do produce a nutritious green milk that Luke has taken to harvesting.

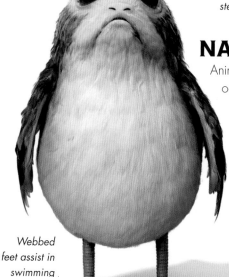

*Forward-facing eyes provide stereoscopic vision*

# NATIVE LIFE

Animal life on Ahch-To has evolved to thrive in or near the ocean. Avian forms are dominated by seabirds, and the native sentient beings of the planet have evolved from this branch of life-form. Salt glands are a common evolutionary trait, as creatures on Ahch-To are able to extract the sea salt from their food and drink. Skin, hair, and plumage also have an innate water-shedding ability afforded by natural oils.

*Webbed feet assist in swimming*

*Feet show avian origins of species*

## PORGS

Porgs are a hyper-curious species of avian found throughout the islands of Ahch-To. These cliff-dwelling creatures perform controlled dives into the sea, fetching small fish to feed upon or pass to their otherwise helpless porglets.

## LANAIS

The sentient Lanais are distant relatives of the porgs. An enclave of females known as the Caretakers lives on the temple island, devoted to the upkeep and care of the ancient structures that dot the landmass. The males spend most of their lives at sea.

### JEDI TEMPLE

Built atop a high ledge overlooking the ocean, the temple houses meditation plinths and an ancient mosaic depicting the first Jedi.

### TREE LIBRARY

The hollowed-out trunk of a centuries-old uneti tree contains a reading chamber and a bookshelf that holds sacred Jedi texts.

### CARETAKER VILLAGE

The female Caretakers live in a hillside village overlooking a cove where male Lanais, or "Visitors," make regular landings.

### MIRROR CAVE

A natural convergence of energy, strong in the dark side of the Force, manifests itself on the eastern side of the island.

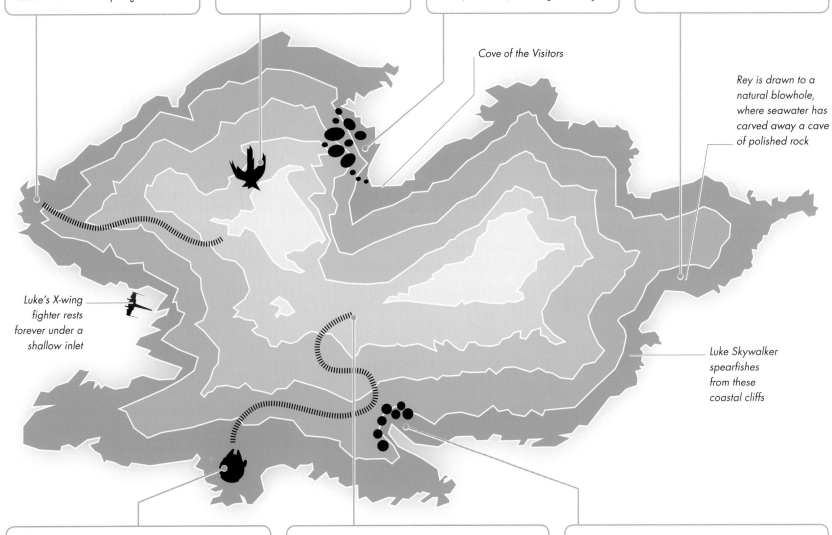

Cove of the Visitors

*Rey is drawn to a natural blowhole, where seawater has carved away a cave of polished rock*

*Luke's X-wing fighter rests forever under a shallow inlet*

*Luke Skywalker spearfishes from these coastal cliffs*

### *MILLENNIUM FALCON*

Chewbacca and R2-D2 stay at the flat landing stage where Rey has left the *Millennium Falcon*. Ancient steps lead from here to the interior of the island.

### SADDLE

A valley at the top of the ancient set of steps, the saddle provides a breathtaking place for contemplation. This natural amphitheater is where Rey first encounters Luke.

### JEDI VILLAGE

These ancient stone structures of unfathomable age were once home to early Jedi. Now, they host Luke and Rey. They are cold huts offering little in the way of comfort.

# LUKE SKYWALKER:
## ISLAND HERMIT

Intricately woven wool with natural waxes that shed water

**SINCE THE FIERY** collapse of his Jedi training temple, Luke Skywalker has put that part of his life behind him, focusing instead on the task of living on Ahch-To. In many ways, the toil of his existence on the island mirrors his youth spent on Tatooine. The chores he avoided in his teen years now mark the clock on his long, tiring island days. The native Caretakers pay Luke little mind, for though his spirit is troubled, and his view of the Jedi has clouded, he exhibits no outward ill-will to the island itself and the history it contains. Skywalker has instead respected what island life asks of him, and has carved out a place for himself in this harsh environment.

Lowered blast shield

**KOENSAYR FLIGHT HELMET WITH BLAST SHIELD**

Pinniped-skin jacket is waterproof

### EXILE INTERRUPTED

Luke did not expect Rey's arrival in the *Millennium Falcon*, or for his past to come crashing back into his island life like an ocean wave. He has lost track of time on the island, the result of his willful neglect as well as a mysterious quality the world shares with such Force-infused locales as Dagobah and Mortis. News of the disaster that has befallen the galaxy shocks him out of isolation. The past will not be buried.

**MARKSMAN-H TRAINING REMOTE**

**A PAST LIFE**
By a twist of fate, the starship that Rey uses to travel to the island is a flying time capsule of Luke's early adventures, containing the helmet and combat remote he used in his very first Jedi lessons.

Luke's life follows strict routines. In this way, he can efficiently harvest everything he needs from the island, taking advantage of different seasons, times of day, and weather conditions.

Tightly wound leggings

**DATA FILE**

> Despite living on an island drenched in the Force, Luke has cut off all connection to the mystical energy field.

> Luke was unaware of the fate that befell Han Solo, or of the interstellar cataclysm that wiped out countless lives in the Hosnian system.

## ISLAND SURVIVAL

It is no small irony that Luke, who grew up on a parched desert planet, has come to rely on the bounties of the ocean for his survival.

Fishhook made from salvaged wire

**FINGERLIP GARPON**

**TWINFIN HYACANDER**

Spear wound

**SPETAN CHANNELFISH**

Kindling bundle

Carved bone barbs

**SPEARFISHING POLE**

Weather shawl

Breather tank

Fishing net

Empty bottle to collect thala-siren milk

**HIKING PACK**

**SEALED JUG OF ROE-SALVE**

**GROOMING BOX WITH MIRROR**

Luke learns to spearfish during his time on Lew'el. He has become adept at using a very long pole that reaches from a bluff and extends into an inlet between opposing cliffs.

**WALKING STICK**

## LUKE'S HUT

Ahch-To's weather is unpredictable, and strong shelter is a necessity. Luke retreats each night to his hut, an ancient corbelled structure made of stacked stones. The hut sits in a village built on the southern coast of the island, which is believed to have been the quarters of the earliest Jedi to study on Ahch-To.

Prominent stones point toward local stars

Waterproof boots

Door made from salvaged S-foil of Luke's T-65 X-wing

# LUKE SKYWALKER:
## THE LAST JEDI

**THE FIRST IN** a new era of Jedi Knights, Luke Skywalker took it upon himself to pass on what he had learned. But before restarting the Jedi Order, he had many questions that needed answering. The Empire had expended much effort in eradicating the history of the Jedi, so Skywalker's research into the past was slow and difficult. His questions resulted in a journey that took years, as he chased down every remnant of Jedi lore he could find in an effort to piece together a fragmented past. This quest led Luke to understand much about himself and his destiny, and gave him the confidence needed to revive the Order.

Ahch-To's Jedi temple stands silent and empty. After the fall of Ben Solo, Luke seeks to amend for his mistakes by retreating from the Force and the galaxy.

Homespun
traditional
Jedi robe

### JEDI REKINDLED

Skywalker's first student was to be his sister, Leia. However, she decided that the best path for her to serve the galaxy left no room for the extended isolation of Jedi training. As Leia concentrated on her new family and senatorial politics, Luke began his travels, largely disappearing from galactic view. During this lengthy journey, Skywalker gathered disciples who would go on to become his first students.

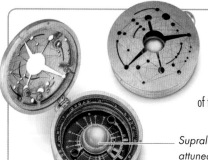

**LUKE'S COMPASS**
This antiquated star compass was among the Jedi relics hoarded by the Emperor during his rule. It was recovered from one of the Emperor's observatories on Pillio.

Supraluminite lodestone
attuned to hyperspace vectors

> From Ahch-To, Luke uses all his strength to create a Force projection of himself to fight Kylo Ren on the planet Crait. It is to be his final Jedi battle.

> Skywalker's studies revealed the cyclical nature of the struggle between light and dark, and the massive toll the galaxy pays with each cycle.

# FLAMES OF FAILURE

Skywalker kept the location of his Jedi training temple a secret, known only to members of his burgeoning Order. When he found it ablaze, the grounds littered by slaughtered students, he knew the betrayal came from within. It was his nephew, consumed by darkness, who had led its destruction. The wider galaxy would not know of this calamity for years to come.

An ancient mosaic is set into the floor of the Ahch-To temple. According to the Caretakers, it is an image of the Prime Jedi, the first of the Order, in a state of meditation and balance.

## JEDI ARTIFACTS

Luke's search for Jedi lore led to him uncovering many lost relics, which he collected and brought with him to Ahch-To. Key to finding the island itself was studying the spread of uneti saplings, a rare type of tree that is sensitive, in its own way, to the Force.

**LIGHTNING ROD**

*Wind indicator*

*Insulated knurl*

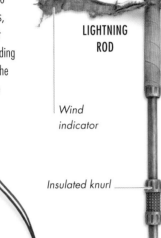

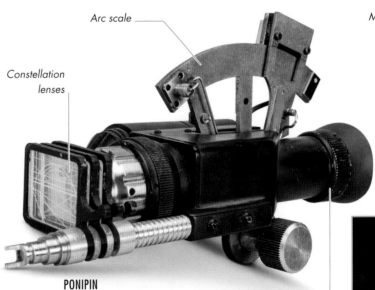

*Arc scale*

*Constellation lenses*

*Memento salvaged from Luke's crashed X-wing*

**S-FOIL ACTUATOR CLUTCH DISC**

**PONIPIN ASTROGATOR**

*Star viewer*

*Leather bolo slide*

*Trophy made from fragmented Sith lightsaber crystal*

**RECOVERED JEDI CRUSADER PENDANT**

Luke's travels have allowed him to collect and assemble ancient scriptures containing lost Jedi wisdom and abilities. Actual books such as these are a true primitive rarity.

Luke is convinced that he cannot be the hero or the teacher that Rey needs him to be. His old master, Yoda, appears before him as a Force spirit, insisting that there is much that Luke can pass on to Rey. She can learn from not only Luke's strength, but from his failures, too.

# THE LANAIS

**LOCATED ON A NORTHERN INLET** on the temple island is a village of natives sworn to their role as Caretakers. These people are the Lanais, and they evolved from the same evolutionary stock of seabirds that produced the unintelligent porgs. Though the Lanais do not appear to possess any exceptional connection to the Force, they do have an uncanny ability to read the intentions of newcomers to the island. Provided that visitors do not intend the island any harm, the Lanais ignore their presence. For thousands of years, the Lanais have tended to the island. Each day, they trek overland to the southern shore, where old Jedi huts are kept in livable condition thanks to their diligence.

## CARETAKERS

The female Lanais are known collectively as the Caretakers, a name derived from their sworn duty to maintain the island. Though they have lived in the shadow of the Jedi temple for millennia, they do not follow the Jedi path. Instead, their own religion has analogues for light and darkness as expressed by the weather of the island. To them, the ideal is a balance in tranquility.

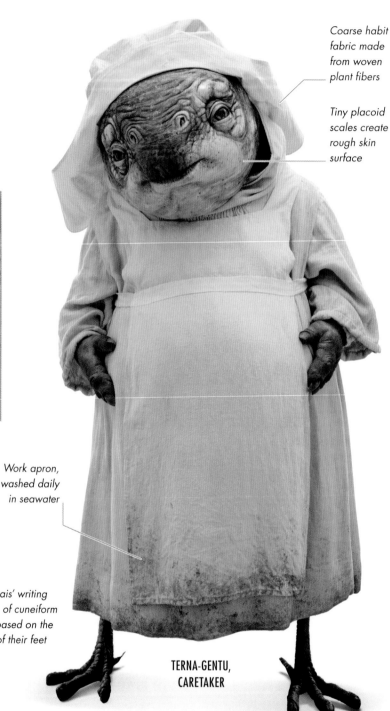

Coarse habit fabric made from woven plant fibers

Tiny placoid scales create rough skin surface

Work apron, washed daily in seawater

TERNA-GENTU, CARETAKER

The Caretaker duties fall to Lanai females, the more spiritual and empathic members of the species. They keep the stone paths clear of growth, conduct repairs, and prepare meals for the village.

**CLAY CHOPPING BOARD**

The Lanais' writing consists of cuneiform marks based on the shape of their feet

**FISH-SCALING KNIFE**

## ALCIDA-AUKA, CARETAKER MATRON

Alcida-Auka is the current leader of the Caretakers, inheriting the position from an untold number of ancestors. She calls the other Caretakers her "daughters," and instills in them the virtues of cleanliness, orderliness, and decorum.

## DATA FILE

> Nearly all of the Lanais' technology derives from fish. The bountiful oceans provide a wide variety of aquatic life with useful skins and skeletons.

> The Lanais' language is a combination of spoken words and hand motions. Written language is rare, and fire signals suffice for long-range communications.

## VILLAGER TOOLS

To keep rhythm during their repetitive chores, the Lanais' culture is intrinsically musical. Lanai-song is a mix of whistles and guttural oscillations that echo from their village and worksites. The tools of their daily tasks often become impromptu percussion instruments.

*Pressed waterproof bark strips*

*Sanded seedpod wash basin*

*Caudal vertebrae from a tytahuso fish*

**WASH BUCKET**

*Baleen-stripped washboard*

**WASHSTAND**

**LADDER**

Males and females interact only on a monthly basis, when the males return from the sea, their boats laden with enough fish to feed the village until the next gathering. This multi-day reunion becomes a festival, with music, dance, and food, while long-term romances are rekindled.

*Dried crinoid frondtrailer hat*

*Opah-bladder bagpipes*

*Flotation vest made of vacullacle shells*

*Byssus-wool smock*

**CORM-KAIRUKU, NET-MAKER**

**HESPER-INGUZA, GUTTER**

*Digitigrade feet*

**GREBE-KORORA, PORTER**

## LANAI INSTRUMENTS

The Lanais' music is loud and boisterous, and includes many folk songs that tell their vast history. Few, if any, feature the Jedi, as if these ancients were somehow above commemorating. Their ballads instead focus on their lives as fishermen and Caretakers.

*Bioluminescent seeds "sing" when twirled*

*Billfish beak*

**NIGHTKELP FLAIL**

## ISLAND VISITORS

The male Lanais are known as the Visitors, due to their infrequent presence on the island itself. The males are the hunters and gatherers in the Lanais' society, spending their lives aboard hand-crafted boats that travel the open seas and journey to nearby islands. They return monthly, with hauls of fish that they and the females process for food and tools.

**WHARLITHAN HORN**

**DOUBLE BASS**

**OPAH-BLADDER BAGPIPES**

**GNARLGOURD DRUM**

**AUK-WAIMANU, CAPTAIN**

# VICE ADMIRAL HOLDO

Frequently dyed hair colored with chromomites

Defender-5 sporting blaster features stun and lethal settings

**VICE ADMIRAL AMILYN HOLDO** is high-ranking officer within the Resistance fleet. She has known Leia Organa since their teenage years, when both served as part of the Apprentice Legislature in the Imperial Senate, as well as the Rebellion during the Galactic Civil War. Holdo's dyed hair and eye-catching clothing show her devotion to her homeworld of Gatalenta and its independent spirit. Holdo has great knowledge of esoteric practices of her planet, such as meditation and astrology, making her a cool-headed, insightful member of the Resistance. When the First Order blitz against the *Raddus* decimates the Resistance leadership, Holdo transfers from the *Ninka* to take the reins of the remnant fleet.

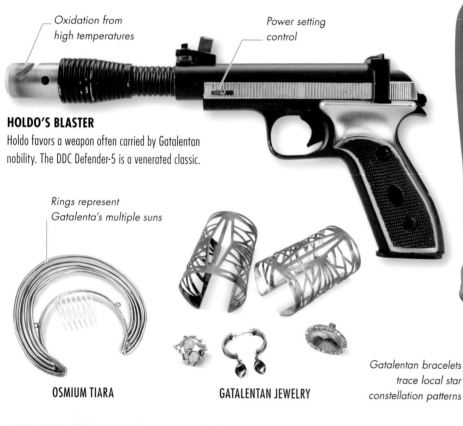

Oxidation from high temperatures

Power setting control

### HOLDO'S BLASTER
Holdo favors a weapon often carried by Gatalentan nobility. The DDC Defender-5 is a venerated classic.

Rings represent Gatalenta's multiple suns

OSMIUM TIARA

GATALENTAN JEWELRY

Gatalentan bracelets trace local star constellation patterns

From the emergency bridge of the damaged *Raddus*, Amilyn Holdo announces her assumption of command in a transmission to the entire fleet. Her words of confidence are met with skepticism by a crew who are mostly strangers to her command. Some silently feel Holdo has a lot to prove.

### A SELFLESS ACT
In an incredibly bold move, Holdo fires up the *Raddus'* hyperdrive and jumps through Supreme Leader Snoke's flagship, the *Supremacy*, at lightspeed. Although she perishes in the collision, her sacrifice saves the lives of many rebels, as they are subsequently able to escape from the First Order's onslaught.

Vice Admiral Holdo has a loyal command staff of handpicked officers. The influx of these strangers adds to the already tense atmosphere aboard the Resistance flagship.

Officer's rank plaque

Tunic pocket

Holstered ERD Glie-44D pistol

**MAJOR NOSSIT CICER**

**CAPTAIN GENO NAMIT**

Integrated belt

SERGEANT DERHAM BOYCE

Resistance combat helmet (visor removed)

Weatherproof field jacket

RM-45 ammunition and tool pouch

BlasTech EL-16 blaster rifle

# COMMANDER D'ACY

Larma D'Acy comes from a military family entrusted with the protection of sovereign space in the Warlentta system. The demilitarization of the New Republic had little effect on her home, though her father was one of the loudest to question such a shortsighted decision. When an opportunity for her to join the Resistance arose, D'Acy's family gave their blessing for the greater good.

When Warlentta refused to join the New Republic, its independent culture made an impression on then-Senator Leia Organa. After founding the Resistance, Leia visited the world and personally recruited D'Acy.

# BRIDGE GUARDS

With the Resistance chased out of its base, all personnel are now trapped in spacebound vessels. Faced with this claustrophobic situation, ground troops have been redeployed as extra shipboard security. Tensions continue to rise as events turn increasingly dire, and these guards stand vigilant should there be any breakdown of order.

# RESISTANCE PILOTS

**THE YOUNGEST AND BRIGHTEST** of the Resistance military fill out the ranks of its starfighter forces. The Resistance recruits them from the local planetary defense forces on worlds liberated by the New Republic from the worst of the Empire's oppression. Prepared to fight for the ideals of the former Rebellion, these pilots prove to be a loyal, spirited lot, eager to bring the battle to the First Order. They form a close-knit bond within their squadrons, and continue to fly the seal of the Rebellion made famous in the Galactic Civil War.

## SNAP WEXLEY

Snap hails from Akiva, an Outer Rim world that was an Imperial base until it was liberated by the New Republic. He is the son of a Rebel Alliance Y-wing pilot who flew at the Battle of Endor. Now a captain in the Resistance, Snap is one of the best recon fliers in the force, with a keen eye for trouble and the piloting skill to evade it.

FreiTek life support unit

Detachable holster

Padded flight gauntlets

Signal flares

Positive grip soles

Streamlined S-foil configuration

Astromech socket

Long-range laser cannon

Advanced split-engine design

Flight computer

## T–70 X–WING

The modern X-wing starfighter continues to use many of the design features of the venerable T-65. Improvements include refined engines and a variable-configuration droid socket that supports a wider variety of astromech types. The T-70 also has modular secondary weapon pods, allowing the proton torpedo launchers to be swapped out for different ordnance or even additional laser cannons. This has increased the X-wing's versatility as a space superiority fighter.

Insulated flight helmet

Older Cobalt Squadron logo

Tierfon Yellow Aces sigil

Older Coalstreak Squadron stripes

**ELLO ASTY'S HELMET**

**JESS PAVA'S HELMET**

**NIEN NUNB'S HELMET**

# SQUADRONS

The Resistance base on D'Qar maintains two primary X-wing squadrons, code-named Blue and Red. Blue Squadron is the primary line of defense for the base, with Red Squadron flying as support. Commander Poe Dameron leads both squadrons, under the call sign Black Leader—not as an indication of a separate squadron, but to denote his specialized fighter, *Black One*.

Combat missions typically break the squadron into paired fighter elements, consisting of a lead and a wingman.

Abednedish lettering

Modified native Sullustan gear

Inflatable flight vest

Glie-44 blaster pistol

Spacer's flight belt

Ejection harness

The intuitive controls of the X-wing remain largely unchanged, meaning inexperienced bush pilots can quickly and confidently take up the stick.

Guidenhauser flight harness

**SIGNAL FLARES IN BANDOLIER**

**ELLO ASTY**

**NIEN NUNB**

"Interstellar orange" color

**DATA FILE**

> The current generation of fighter pilots venerate the past with maneuvers named for heroes of the Galactic Civil War. The Skywalker Swoop, the Antilles Intercept, and the Porkins Belly Run are all training basics for Resistance pilots.

**JESS "TESTOR" PAVA**

# RESISTANCE FLEET

**WITH ONLY FOUR SHIPS,** the Resistance effort to evacuate D'Qar barely qualifies as a fleet—and yet this ragtag assembly of transports and cruisers is vital for rescuing the doomed base's personnel. Reinforcements take the form of bombers, additional X-wing fighters, and A-wing interceptors, as well as seasoned commanders. Lifeboats quickly ferry people from the planet's surface to the waiting ships, trying to escape the inevitable First Order reprisal.

## THE *RADDUS*

The enormous *Raddus* is General Organa's flagship, and was one of the last warships designed prior to the disarmament treaty between the New Republic and defeated Empire. The heavy cruiser served in the New Republic home fleet for a time, but was retired in favor of a less crew-intensive design. Increased automation and the removal of redundant systems have made the cruiser a viable Resistance asset. The *Raddus'* key strength is its advanced deflector shield system that can push the envelope of protective energy far from its hull.

Comms antenna

Midship turbolaser battery blister

Primary command bridge

Aft section enveloped by intensified deflector screens

Starboard hangar bay

The engineering depths of the capital ships soon teem with evacuees, as sections usually reserved for maintenance workers are hastily repurposed to accommodate the influx of extra crew.

## FLEET CREWS

The Resistance is so understaffed that the D'Qar base personnel change roles to be of better service aboard the capital ships. Communications techs become evacuation shuttle pilots, medics work as mechanics, and armorers become gunners. Duty officers on the capital ships implement emergency plans for the intake of evacuees and reassign them to key roles on their respective vessels. Personnel from scattered cells must suddenly work side by side, forging strong new relationships in the face of the newest First Order threat.

The *Raddus* takes the bulk of Leia's unit, with spillover to the *Anodyne*, the *Ninka*, and the *Vigil* in that order.

Borrowed starfighter pilot helmet

Holstered Glie-44 blaster pistol

**PAMMICH NERRO GOODE, TRANSPORT PILOT**

Insulated ground crew headset

**SAILE MINNAU, GUARD**

**RIVA ROSETTA, TECHNICIAN**

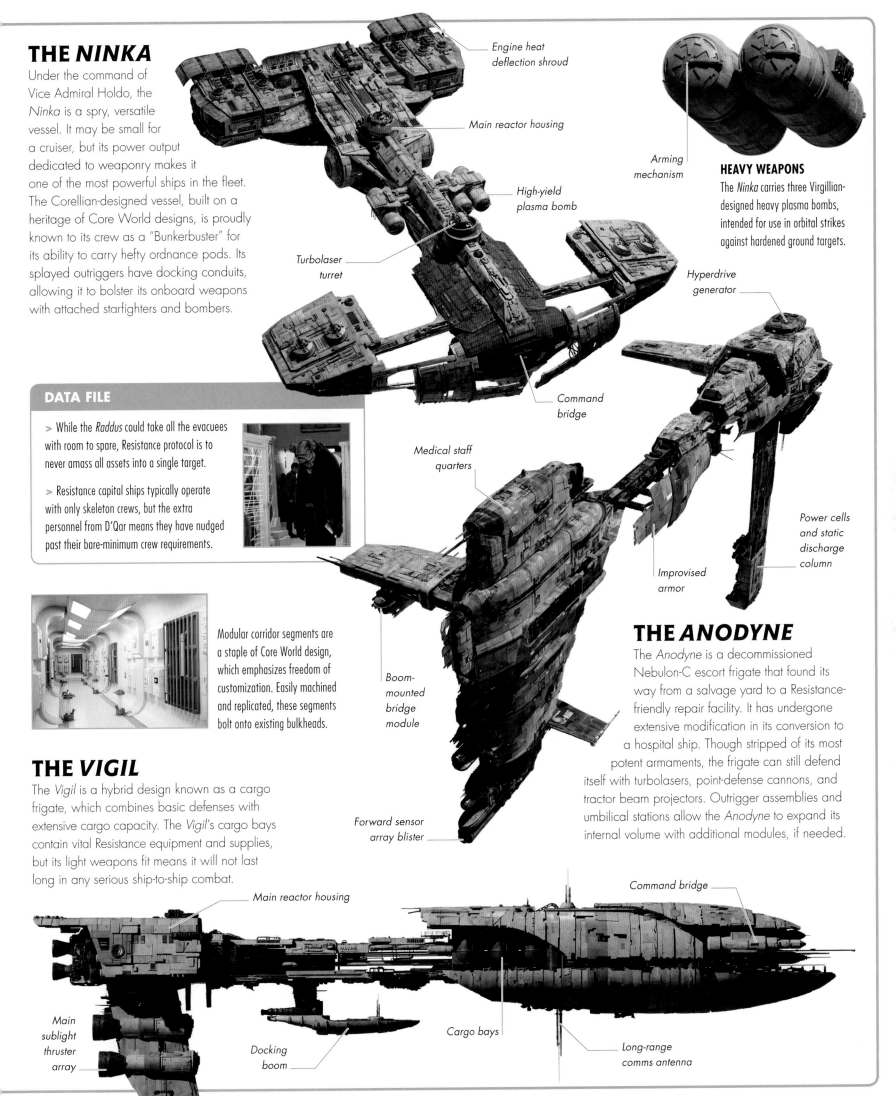

# THE *NINKA*

Under the command of Vice Admiral Holdo, the *Ninka* is a spry, versatile vessel. It may be small for a cruiser, but its power output dedicated to weaponry makes it one of the most powerful ships in the fleet. The Corellian-designed vessel, built on a heritage of Core World designs, is proudly known to its crew as a "Bunkerbuster" for its ability to carry hefty ordnance pods. Its splayed outriggers have docking conduits, allowing it to bolster its onboard weapons with attached starfighters and bombers.

Engine heat deflection shroud

Main reactor housing

Arming mechanism

High-yield plasma bomb

Turbolaser turret

Command bridge

**HEAVY WEAPONS**
The *Ninka* carries three Virgillian-designed heavy plasma bombs, intended for use in orbital strikes against hardened ground targets.

Hyperdrive generator

Medical staff quarters

Improvised armor

Power cells and static discharge column

## DATA FILE

> While the *Raddus* could take all the evacuees with room to spare, Resistance protocol is to never amass all assets into a single target.

> Resistance capital ships typically operate with only skeleton crews, but the extra personnel from D'Qar means they have nudged past their bare-minimum crew requirements.

Modular corridor segments are a staple of Core World design, which emphasizes freedom of customization. Easily machined and replicated, these segments bolt onto existing bulkheads.

Boom-mounted bridge module

# THE *ANODYNE*

The *Anodyne* is a decommissioned Nebulon-C escort frigate that found its way from a salvage yard to a Resistance-friendly repair facility. It has undergone extensive modification in its conversion to a hospital ship. Though stripped of its most potent armaments, the frigate can still defend itself with turbolasers, point-defense cannons, and tractor beam projectors. Outrigger assemblies and umbilical stations allow the *Anodyne* to expand its internal volume with additional modules, if needed.

# THE *VIGIL*

The *Vigil* is a hybrid design known as a cargo frigate, which combines basic defenses with extensive cargo capacity. The *Vigil*'s cargo bays contain vital Resistance equipment and supplies, but its light weapons fit means it will not last long in any serious ship-to-ship combat.

Forward sensor array blister

Main reactor housing

Command bridge

Main sublight thruster array

Docking boom

Cargo bays

Long-range comms antenna

# RESISTANCE BOMBERS

**TWO SMALL SQUADRONS** of heavy bombers help cover a Resistance evacuation by targeting the Dreadnought that threatens the fleet. The ships of Cobalt and Crimson Squadrons must withstand the devastating firepower of point-defense cannons spread across the Dreadnought's surface, then soar into bombing range to drop their massive payloads. Resistance escort starfighters fly support and interference, keeping TIE fighters away from the ponderous, explosives-laden craft. It is a costly mission, as well-targeted fire from First Order gunners can erupt a bomber's entire magazine with catastrophic results. The bomber crews know the risks involved and are willing to sacrifice everything to give their comrades a chance to escape.

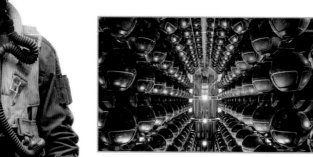

Armored flight deck

Rear gunner ball turret

Stabilizer foil and laser cannon mount

Sublight engine

## MG-100 STARFORTRESS

The Slayn & Korpil MG-100 StarFortress heavy bomber dates back to the final days of the Galactic Civil War, when the New Republic besieged Imperial holdouts. Disarmed versions of the vessel see continued use in planetary civilian services, as the modular bomb magazine can easily be repurposed for remote cargo drops, wildfire suppression, and the deployment of mining explosives. The MG-100's relatively simple and sturdy construction has ensured its longevity.

Targeting sensor mast

Ventral gunner ball turret

Bomb magazine "clip"

Plate can slide forward to form blast visor

### *COBALT HAMMER* CREW

The *Cobalt Hammer* soars through enemy fire thanks to the bravery and tenacity of its crew. The standard assigned crew consists of bombardier Nix Jerd, pilot Finch Dallow, two specialist gunners, and a flight engineer.

**PAIGE TICO'S HELMET**

Personalized helmet art

**NIX JERD'S HELMET**

**NIX JERD**

Guidenhauser ejection seat flight harness

Magnetic attraction plates

Hand-scrawled messages from ordnance crew

### PROTON BOMBS

The StarFortress's tall profile comes from the modular bombing magazine (called the "clip" by the bomber's crew). The assembly can be programmed to drop specific sections of the payload in sequence, but the most common configuration is "deploy all," which drops all 1,048 bombs from one end of the racks to the other.

## DATA FILE

> Bombs don't technically "drop" in microgravity, but are impelled from their racks by sequenced electromagnetic plates in the clip. They continue their downward momentum upon leaving the artificial gravity field of the bomber.

## VENTRAL BALL TURRET

Suspended beneath the bomb racks of a StarFortress, encased in an armored transparisteel shell, is a rotating turret with a pair of heavy repeating laser cannons. Though deflector shields protect the gunner, the feeling of being exposed to enemy fire is unshakable.

*Synthetic aviator flight cap, lined to catch perspiration*

## PAIGE'S MEDALLION

*Buoyancy-foam filled flight vest collar*

*Merr-Sonn Munitions EM-1919 paired repeating laser cannons*

*Defusing sequencer pins in sleeve stowage*

*Life-support system atmosphere hose*

Escort duty is one of the toughest assignments for a starfighter pilot, as their ordinarily swift vessel must sacrifice its speed advantage to stay close to its assigned bomber. TIE fighters try to lure the Resistance escorts away, leaving the StarFortresses exposed.

## PAIGE TICO

Paige Tico serves as the *Cobalt Hammer*'s ventral gunner. She and her sister, Rose, have committed their lives to the Resistance cause, having witnessed firsthand the brutality of the First Order on their homeworld in the Otomok system. Paige has survived several missions, and has become superstitious as a result, occasionally wrapping her medallion around the struts of her cannons for good luck. Though Rose is assigned aboard the cruiser *Raddus*, she sometimes accompanies her sister on flights. In the downtime between bombing runs, Paige and Rose discuss their chance to see the galaxy.

*Control button*

## BOMB RELEASE

The bombardier sights a target from a pedestal on the flight deck that contains a concentrated sensor feed. The system calculates the optimum time for release, and at a given prompt, or at the discretion of the bombardier, the control button on a wireless remote triggers the release of the payload.

# RESISTANCE STARFIGHTERS

**THE FIGHT AGAINST** the Starkiller nearly exhausts the supply of starfighters stationed on D'Qar, but thankfully that is not the extent of the Resistance's resources. Distress calls sent during that crisis draw reinforcements in the form of the starfighter complements of the newly arrived cruisers. This not only brings in X-wings to replenish Blue and Red Squadrons, but also adds the blazingly fast A-wings to the roster. These fighters are primarily tasked with covering the retreat of the beleaguered Resistance fleet.

As fighters are redistributed among the Resistance squadrons, they fall under Poe Dameron's command. The hangar bays of the *Raddus* become their primary launch point.

## TALLISSAN LINTRA

22 year-old Lieutenant Tallissan "Tallie" Lintra was born long after the dark days of the Empire. She has proven to be one of the most capable pilots in the Resistance, dazzling even the hard-to-impress Poe Dameron with her skills. Tallie learned the basics of piloting behind the controls of an old RZ-1 A-wing that her father used as a cropduster on their farm on Pippip 3.

**RONITH BLARIO**

*Swiveling cannon mounting*

*Novaldex K-88 Event Horizon engines*

*Missile launcher*

## RZ-2 A-WING INTERCEPTOR

The RZ-2 is an upgrade of the RZ-1 A-wing starfighter that played a crucial role in the Galactic Civil War. Improvements include refined cannon mountings, a streamlined hull, and more powerful jammers that make the A-wing a less tempting target for enemy sensors. Tallie flies an A-wing with blue livery.

*Synthsilk scarf, a gift from her father*

*FreiTek life-support unit*

*"DA" stands for "Deadly Approach," the punchline to a well-known pilots' joke*

*Towing slot for assisted moving of landed craft*

*Guidenhauser ejection harness*

## T-70 X-WING

With the New Republic's T-85 X-wing fleet atomized by the destruction of the Hosnian system, the Resistance's T-70s are once again the most advanced examples of this legendary design.

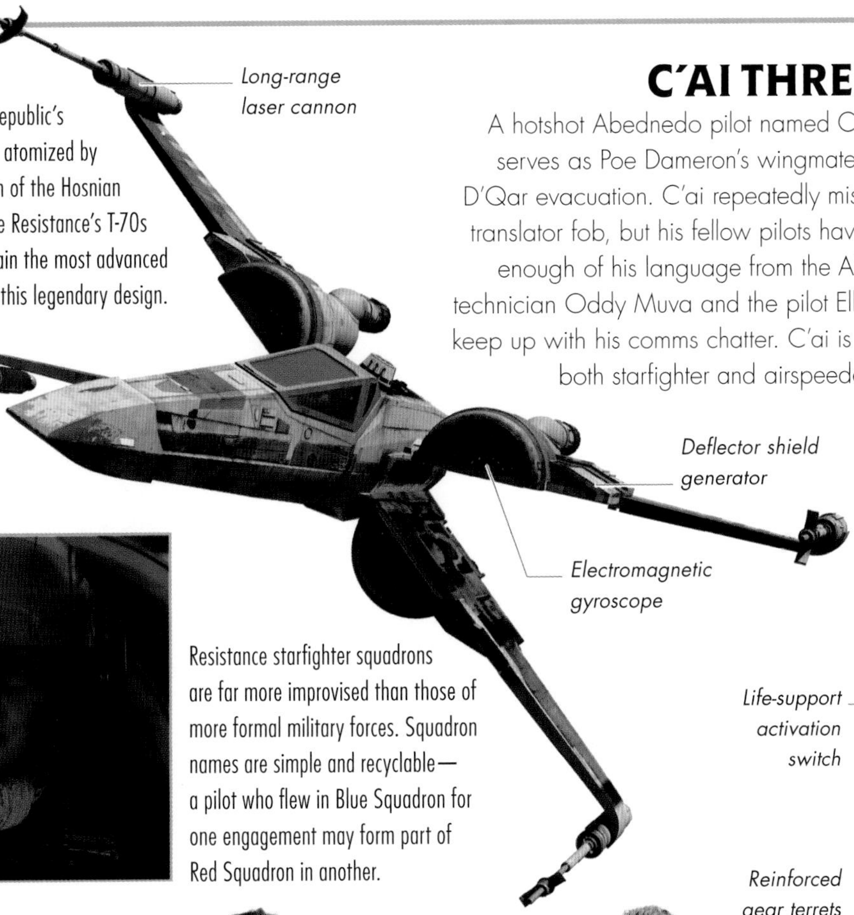

Long-range laser cannon
Deflector shield generator
Electromagnetic gyroscope


# C'AI THRENALLI

A hotshot Abednedo pilot named C'ai Threnalli serves as Poe Dameron's wingmate during the D'Qar evacuation. C'ai repeatedly misplaces his translator fob, but his fellow pilots have learned enough of his language from the Abednedo technician Oddy Muva and the pilot Ello Asty to keep up with his comms chatter. C'ai is skilled at both starfighter and airspeeder piloting.

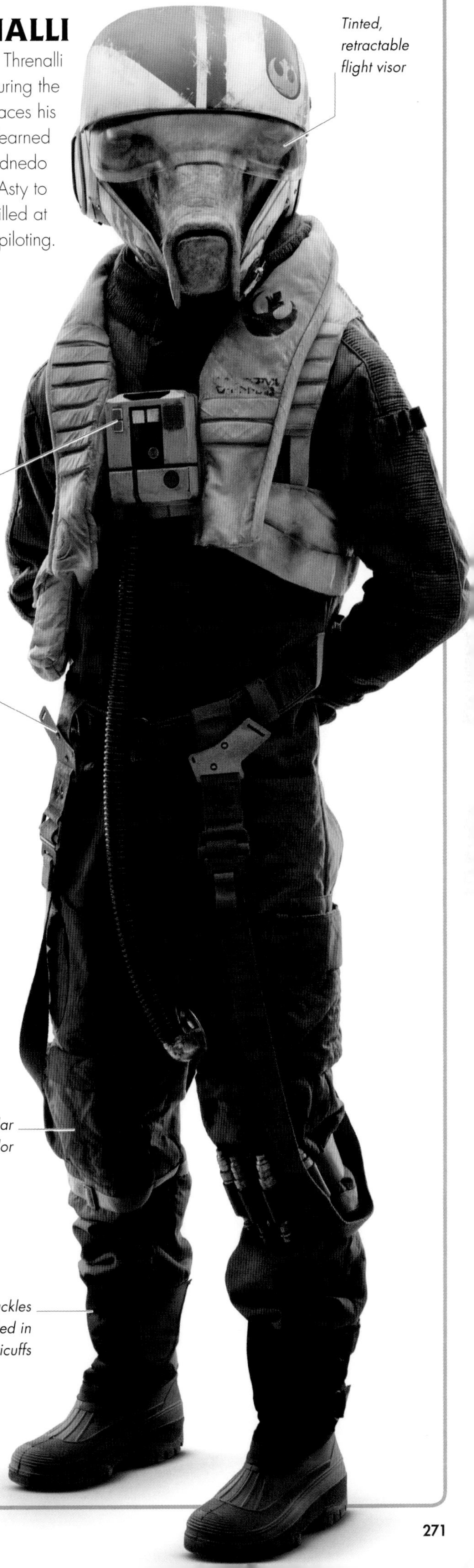

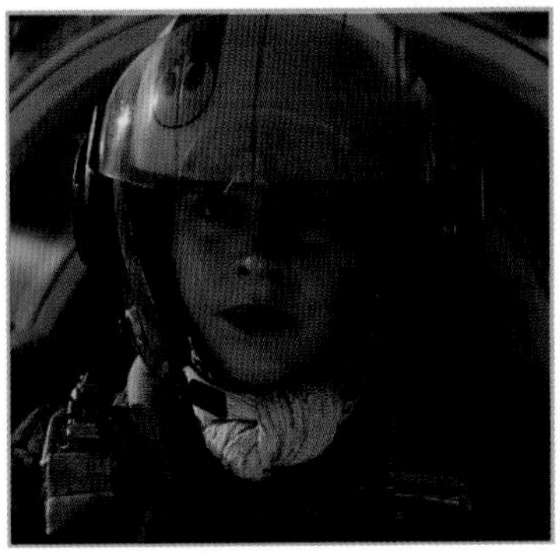

Tinted, retractable flight visor
Life-support activation switch
Reinforced gear terrets
"Interstellar orange" color
Vibro-knuckles concealed in boot for fisticuffs


Resistance starfighter squadrons are far more improvised than those of more formal military forces. Squadron names are simple and recyclable—a pilot who flew in Blue Squadron for one engagement may form part of Red Squadron in another.

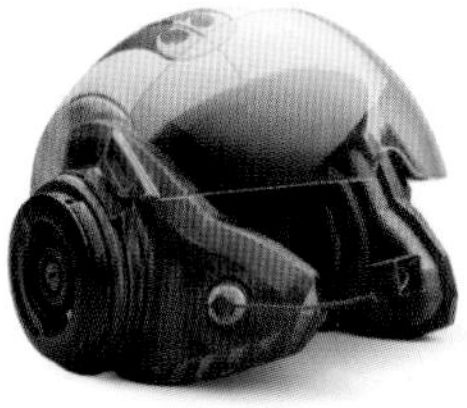

TALLIE'S HELMET

STARCK'S HELMET

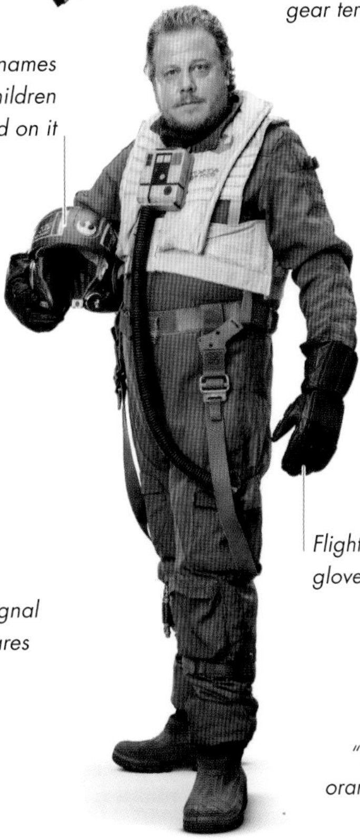

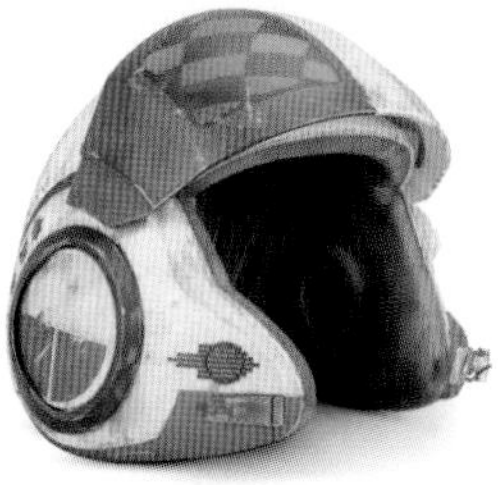

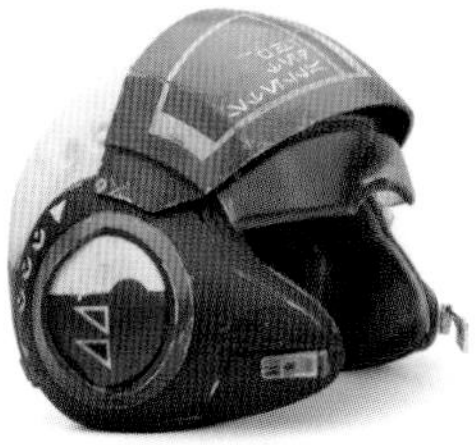

TUBBS' HELMET

Signal flares


STOMERONI STARCK

Helmet has names of Tubbs' children stenciled on it
Flight gloves


JAYCRIS TUBBS

### DATA FILE

> As was the case with the Rebellion, the Resistance has more pilots than it does craft. Pilots are often on standby, awaiting deployment.

> During the Resistance exodus from D'Qar, many fighter aces serve as lifeboat and transport pilots instead.

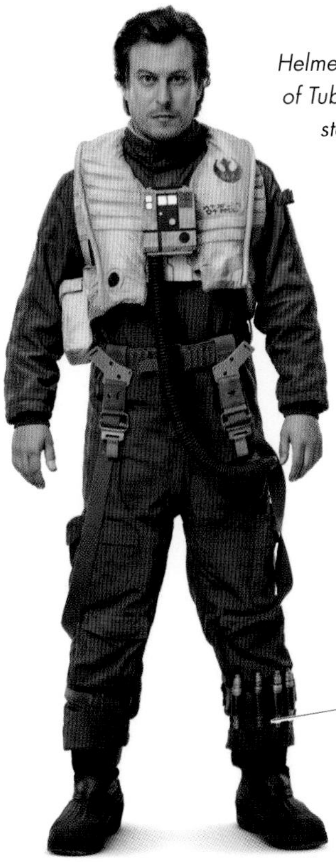

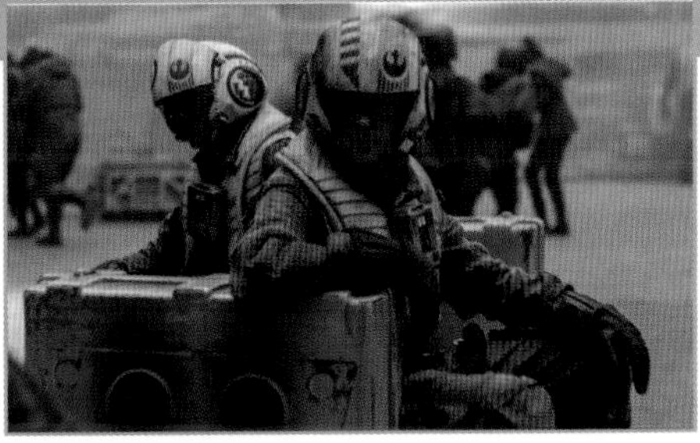

# RESISTANCE GROUND CREW

**THE RESISTANCE MAKES DO** with a small arsenal of upgraded starfighters, mostly of the X-wing variety. To keep these ships in fighting shape, the Resistance relies on tireless ground crews who recognize the enormous value these fighters contribute to the war effort. The Resistance has little in the way of capital ships, since Republic demilitarization efforts have made them difficult to obtain. As such, the fighters have to do the bulk of the work to defend worlds targeted by the First Order for expansion and colonization.

Sound-dampening work helmet

Static discharge prevention coveralls

**GOSS TOOWERS**

Controller Dand is a stickler for detail, and does not tolerate anyone operating out of protocol.

**ELECTROBINOCULARS**
Ground crew spotters monitor the arrival and departure of starship traffic with simple yet reliable instruments.

## COMMAND CENTER

The Resistance base on D'Qar was originally scouted as a potential rebel base by Corona Squadron during the Galactic Civil War. The Rebel Alliance established a short-lived outpost there just prior to the mop-up operations against the retreating Imperial forces. When the resource-strapped Resistance began operations, it relied on old Rebellion-era bases as starting points.

Comlink headset

GLD (Ground Logistics Division) controller's coat

**VOBER DAND**

# RESISTANCE DROIDS

Power droids, comms droids, astromechs, and loading droids all play their part in the Resistance ground crew. With only periodic recharge and maintenance breaks, they diligently work around the chrono to keep equipment operative or to monitor communications and sensor data.

*Hazard-painted ceramic armor plate*

**B-U4D'S PROGRAMMER**

*Durasteel shell*

*Internal fusion generator*

*Droid walks to where it is needed*

**4B-EG-6 GNK-SERIES POWER DROID**

*Hydraulic compressor claws*

**B-U4D "BUFORD" LOADING DROID**

**M9-G8 ASTROMECH**

# RESISTANCE TECHNICIANS

A generational divide exists within the assembled ranks of the Resistance command center. Older, graying officers who witnessed the destruction of the Galactic Empire lead inspiring younger volunteers who are barely in their twenties. Though the younger technicians have not witnessed the horrors of tyranny firsthand, they believe the words of their elders and diligently work to track and stop the covert activities of the First Order.

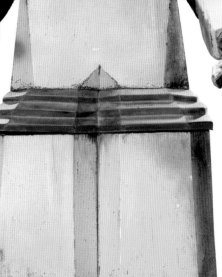

Resistance engineers use large scale yet portable generators to produce power with which to charge starships and weaponry.

The D'Qar Resistance base lies underneath foliage-covered mounds. A landing strip assists pilots in avoiding the towering vegetation.

*Shrouded repulsorlift generator*

*Control yoke*

*Armored hull*

*Defensive laser cannons*

**RESISTANCE BASE SPEEDER**

A battered Gian-211 patrol speeder serves as an example of the Resistance philosophy of using every asset possible. Technicians keep the antiquated repulsorlifts on the transport and recon vehicle working.

# ROSE TICO

**ROSE TICO IS** a hardworking member of the Resistance support crew, who has hated the First Order since she was a child. Rose grew up on the impoverished mining colony of Hays Minor, the smaller world in a double-planet configuration in the Otomok system, far beyond the scope of the New Republic's policing efforts. Unknown to the galaxy at large, the system fell under sway of the expanding First Order, which secretly tested its weapons on the populace and stole children to turn into stormtroopers. Rose is now finally able to fight back against her sworn enemy.

Dark hair common on Otomok worlds

Duty uniform identification plaque

Self-coded override data spikes

Adjustable utility belt with cargo loops

Rose, Finn, and BB-8 leave the fleet on an unsanctioned mission, sneaking off in a transport pod. The vessel is the smallest hyperspace-enabled ship capable of reaching Cantonica.

Charge electrode

Intensity dial below trigger button

## ELECTRO-SHOCK PROD

## FLIGHT TECHNICIAN

Rose is an imaginative mechanic. Her innovations include a baffle system that makes the Resistance's bombers harder to detect by enemy sensors. This modification is also rolled out into escape craft, which is unusual for such vessels. They ordinarily use powerful automatic distress beacons to alert anyone in the vicinity of a ship in crisis. However, the Resistance desperately needs to keep a low profile, even if that means hiding emergency craft from potential aid.

## ROSE'S MEDALLION

Rose's medallion is a stylized ensign of the Otomok system, representing Hays Minor. It is made of pure Haysian smelt, a transition metal with incredibly efficient conductive properties. It is the partner medallion of the one worn by Paige Tico.

# RESISTANCE FIGHTER

Rose gives her all during the fight against the First Order. Her parents, Hue and Thanya, raised her with a strong sense of right and wrong, and her elder sister also provided guidance. In more peaceful times, Rose and Paige would daydream about traveling the galaxy, but the evil of the First Order has now made that impossible. Though intensely focused, Rose must try not to let her temper get the better of her.

Wear and tear of adventure

During the Battle of Crait, Rose rams her ski speeder into Finn's, stopping him from flying into a First Order cannon. She is gravely injured in the process, but tells Finn that they must fight for what they love— not what they hate.

Salt dust from Crait

Stabilizer fin

## TRANSPORT POD

Rose's shuttle is the modified control pod of a Resistance transport, which began life as a B-wing Mark II cockpit. Its small size and Rose's skill at keeping engine flux below sensor thresholds allow her and Finn to depart the fleet without being detected. Though Rose doesn't consider herself a great pilot, she has more experience behind the controls than Finn.

Resistance all-weather poncho

Durasteel armored cockpit

Docking hatch

Canto Bight's opulence provokes very different reactions in Rose and Finn. While Finn is seduced by the resort's grandeur, Rose sees its guests for the war profiteers and criminals that they really are.

Alliance crest is usually concealed

## RESISTANCE RING

Rose's ring hides an Alliance crest. It is an antique from the Galactic Civil War, which was once used to show support for the Rebellion in the corridors of the Imperial Senate.

Pilfered First Order officer boots

# RESISTANCE DROIDS

**THE UNDERSTAFFED RESISTANCE** would not be able to operate without its extensive labor pool of droids. These tireless workers assist the flesh-and-blood personnel, and keep the weapons and starships functioning while asking for little in return. The Resistance, proudly honoring the egalitarian ideals of the Rebel Alliance and New Republic, treats these droids not as property but as sentient beings. Rather than restricting their access to escape vessels, the Resistance allows droids equal access to them. When the decision arises, however, most droids sacrifice themselves, giving up space aboard the emergency transports for their organic crewmates.

Replaced high-frequency receiver antenna

Primary photoreceptor

Articulated holoprojector array and worklight

Computer interface tool–bay disc

Bherring-24 blinkcode processing indicator

With so much happening in a short space of time, BB-8's processors work overtime to keep up. A byproduct of this increased activity is an amplified spirit of adventure within the little droid.

## BB-8

BB-8 frets over the wellbeing of his friends in the Resistance. The droid extracts an astromech-to-astromech promise from R2-D2 that R2 would watch over Rey when she travels to Ahch-To. BB-8 also keeps a concerned photoreceptor on Finn while he recovers from deadly injuries. The little droid has come to trust the former stormtrooper, but recognizes that Finn needs extra guardianship.

### DATA FILE

> Resistance droids often feature extended-usage power cells due to a lack of regular downtime for recharging.

> The Resistance spy droid network was ordered to lie low by C-3PO prior to the evacuation of D'Qar.

Tool-bay discs can be swapped for different functions

Surface sensor

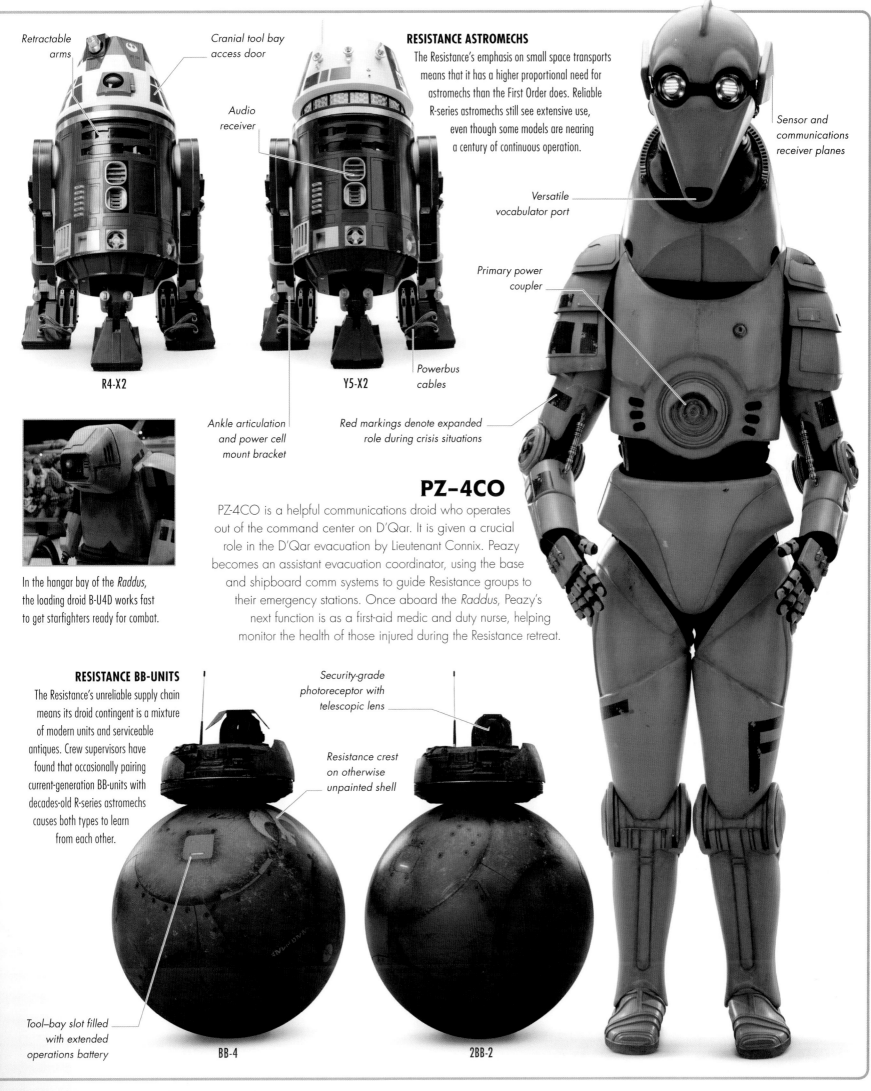

*Retractable arms*

*Cranial tool bay access door*

*Audio receiver*

## RESISTANCE ASTROMECHS

The Resistance's emphasis on small space transports means that it has a higher proportional need for astromechs than the First Order does. Reliable R-series astromechs still see extensive use, even though some models are nearing a century of continuous operation.

*Sensor and communications receiver planes*

*Versatile vocabulator port*

*Primary power coupler*

**R4-X2**

**Y5-X2**

*Ankle articulation and power cell mount bracket*

*Powerbus cables*

*Red markings denote expanded role during crisis situations*

In the hangar bay of the *Raddus*, the loading droid B-U4D works fast to get starfighters ready for combat.

## PZ-4CO

PZ-4CO is a helpful communications droid who operates out of the command center on D'Qar. It is given a crucial role in the D'Qar evacuation by Lieutenant Connix. Peazy becomes an assistant evacuation coordinator, using the base and shipboard comm systems to guide Resistance groups to their emergency stations. Once aboard the *Raddus*, Peazy's next function is as a first-aid medic and duty nurse, helping monitor the health of those injured during the Resistance retreat.

### RESISTANCE BB-UNITS

The Resistance's unreliable supply chain means its droid contingent is a mixture of modern units and serviceable antiques. Crew supervisors have found that occasionally pairing current-generation BB-units with decades-old R-series astromechs causes both types to learn from each other.

*Security-grade photoreceptor with telescopic lens*

*Resistance crest on otherwise unpainted shell*

*Tool-bay slot filled with extended operations battery*

**BB-4**

**2BB-2**

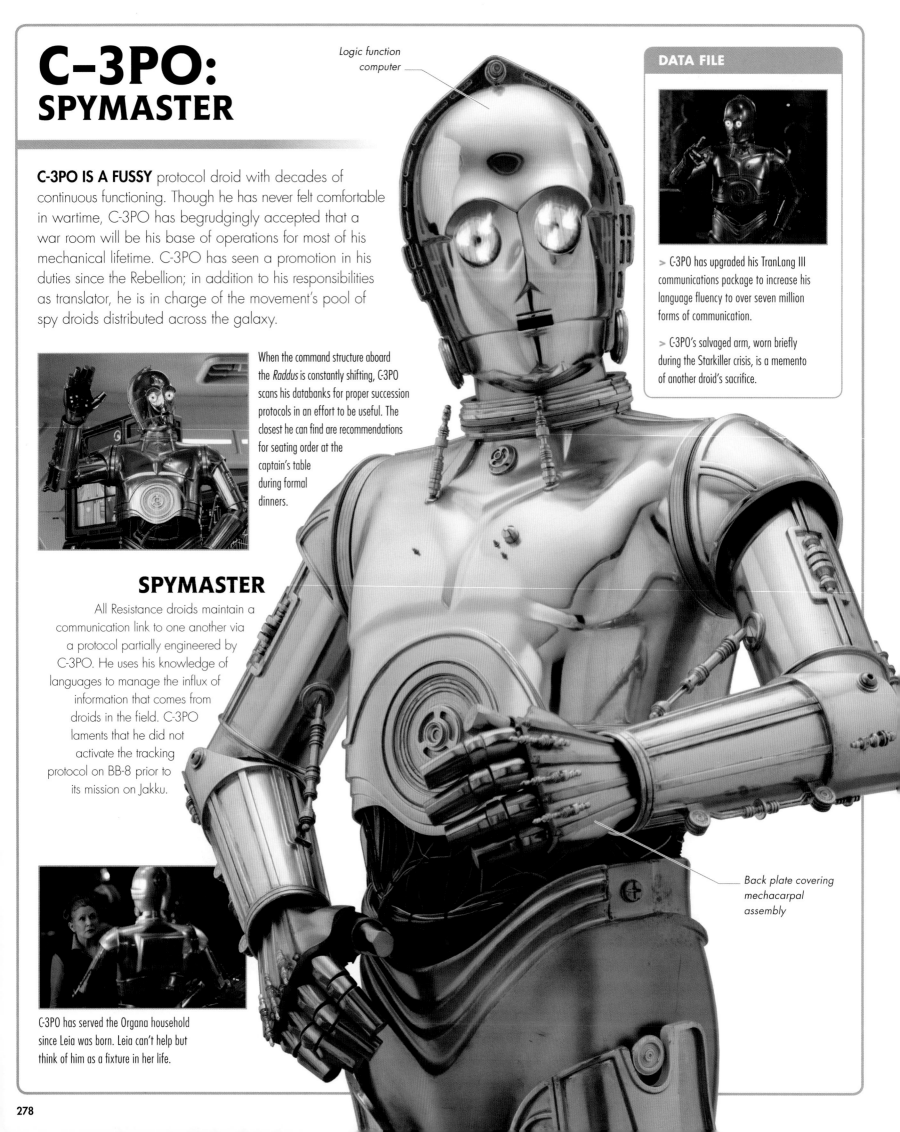

# C-3PO:
## SPYMASTER

**C-3PO IS A FUSSY** protocol droid with decades of continuous functioning. Though he has never felt comfortable in wartime, C-3PO has begrudgingly accepted that a war room will be his base of operations for most of his mechanical lifetime. C-3PO has seen a promotion in his duties since the Rebellion; in addition to his responsibilities as translator, he is in charge of the movement's pool of spy droids distributed across the galaxy.

Logic function computer

When the command structure aboard the *Raddus* is constantly shifting, C-3PO scans his databanks for proper succession protocols in an effort to be useful. The closest he can find are recommendations for seating order at the captain's table during formal dinners.

### SPYMASTER

All Resistance droids maintain a communication link to one another via a protocol partially engineered by C-3PO. He uses his knowledge of languages to manage the influx of information that comes from droids in the field. C-3PO laments that he did not activate the tracking protocol on BB-8 prior to its mission on Jakku.

C-3PO has served the Organa household since Leia was born. Leia can't help but think of him as a fixture in her life.

**DATA FILE**

> C-3PO has upgraded his TranLang III communications package to increase his language fluency to over seven million forms of communication.

> C-3PO's salvaged arm, worn briefly during the Starkiller crisis, is a memento of another droid's sacrifice.

Back plate covering mechacarpal assembly

# R2-D2:
## RESILIENT REBEL

R2-D2 is overjoyed to be reunited with Luke on Ahch-To. He longs for his master to return, and tries to stir Luke's memories of better days as best he can.

**AS NEWER AND MORE** advanced astromech droid models become the norm for starship support duty, R2-D2 begins to show his age. For several years now, he has not been operating at peak capacity. R2-D2's celebrated role in the Rebellion has afforded him semi-retirement, rather than the standard recycling the resource-strapped Resistance would normally employ.

R2-D2 keeps internal copies of much of the data he has accessed over the decades. He uses this data to help fellow droid BB-8 project a completed star map. The Resistance is able to use this to find Luke Skywalker.

*Acoustic signaler*

## STANDBY MODE

As R2-D2 recuperates in his self-imposed low power mode, his diagnostic systems attempt to organize the vast trove of information in his databanks from over seven decades of uninterrupted operation. The defragmenting of millions of exanodes within his memory is causing R2-D2 to "dream" many of his greatest adventures.

*Primary photoreceptor*

*Shoulder articulation joint*

*Actuating coupler*

**DATA PROBE**

**UTILITY ARM**

### DATA FILE

> R2-D2 was a constant companion to Luke Skywalker during his journeys across the galaxy following the Battle of Endor. The astromech has been witness to both triumph and tragedy, including the destruction of Luke's Jedi Temple.

*Third tread (retracted)*

*Ankle articulation servomotor*

*Motorized all-terrain treads*

*Powerbus cables connecting power cells*

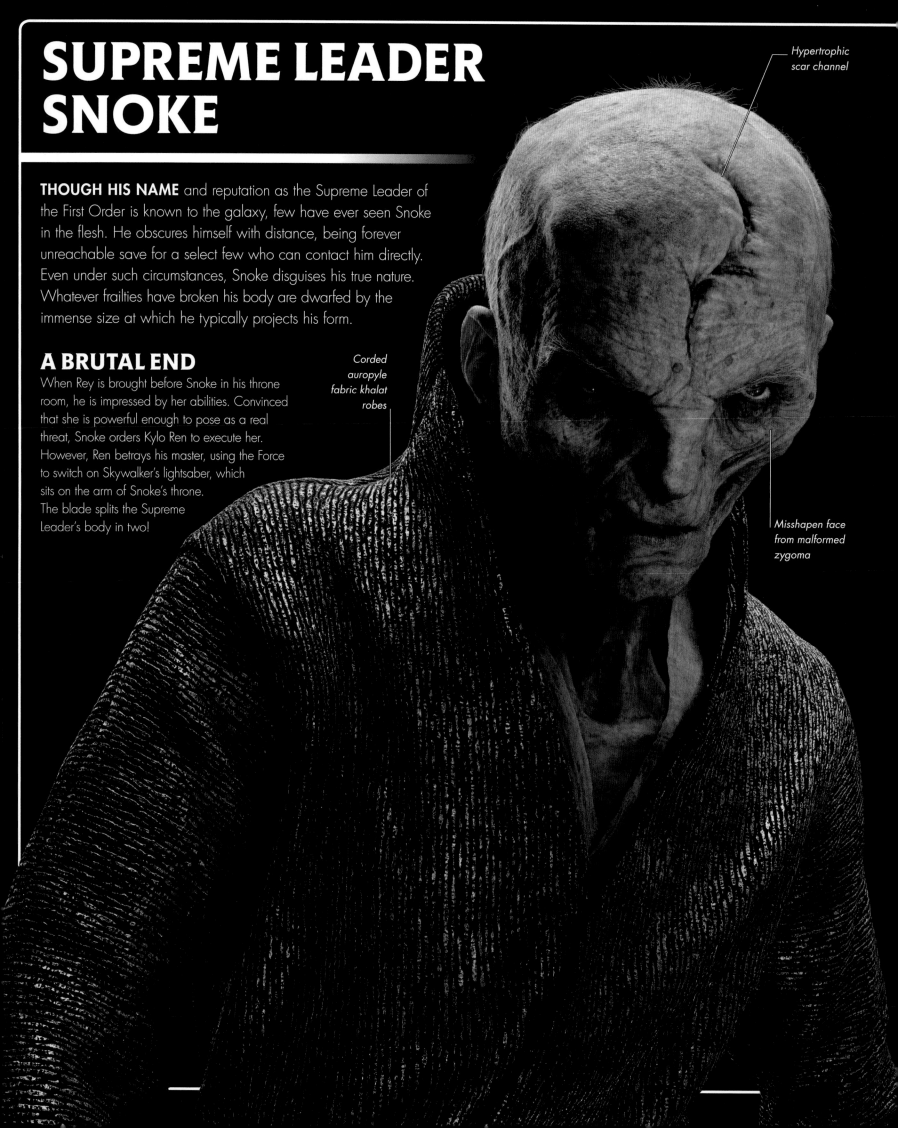

# SUPREME LEADER SNOKE

Hypertrophic
scar channel

**THOUGH HIS NAME** and reputation as the Supreme Leader of
the First Order is known to the galaxy, few have ever seen Snoke
in the flesh. He obscures himself with distance, being forever
unreachable save for a select few who can contact him directly.
Even under such circumstances, Snoke disguises his true nature.
Whatever frailties have broken his body are dwarfed by the
immense size at which he typically projects his form.

## A BRUTAL END

Corded
auropyle
fabric khalat
robes

When Rey is brought before Snoke in his throne
room, he is impressed by her abilities. Convinced
that she is powerful enough to pose as a real
threat, Snoke orders Kylo Ren to execute her.
However, Ren betrays his master, using the Force
to switch on Skywalker's lightsaber, which
sits on the arm of Snoke's throne.
The blade splits the Supreme
Leader's body in two!

Misshapen face
from malformed
zygoma

Snoke's painful stance has caused him to prioritize comfort

**SLIPPERS**

Obsidian from catacombs beneath Darth Vader's Mustafar castle

Gold etched with glyphs of the Dwartii

**RING**

Enlarged brains can process multidimensional calculations

Amplification lenses assist naturally weak eyes

## THRONE ROOM

Snoke's throne room aboard the *Supremacy* is an enormous chamber veiled by an opaque red curtain. It is from here that Snoke broadcasts his image, magnified into a towering giant, across the First Order's territories.

Dark purple robes, meant to evoke the royal hues of old Imperial advisors

## ATTENDANTS

Snoke's retinue includes mute alien navigators who originated in the Unknown Regions. Were it not for the ancient hyperspace trails blazed by these towering servants, the Imperial survivors who fled into this uncharted realm would certainly have perished. These navigators designed and operate the oculus viewing scope in Snoke's throne room.

Electro-blade filament runs parallel to vibro-voulge blade

Robes conceal segmented, chitinous plates

Symbolic red armorweave

## PRAETORIAN GUARD

Eight Praetorians flank Snoke's throne, their red armor blending into the curtain that surrounds the chamber. They stand as implacable, unmoving sentinels, but should any hostility surface from Snoke's rare invited guests, they snap instantly into combat stances.

## DATA FILE

> Snoke takes Ben Solo as his apprentice, as he believes only someone of the Skywalker bloodline could destroy the last Jedi.

> After Kylo Ren kills Snoke, he and Rey work together to defeat every member of the Praetorian Guard.

# PRAETORIAN GUARD

**THE PRAETORIAN GUARD** are a bold example of an Imperial symbol reimagined, distorted, and aggrandized by the First Order. These elite sentinels stand watch over Supreme Leader Snoke's throne room aboard his flagship. Their brilliant red uniforms are a deliberate echo of those worn by Emperor Palpatine's Royal Guard, but the pageantry of the robes has been swept aside to allow an unhindered view of precision-machined combat armor. The Praetorians are the ultimate close-circle guard, eschewing ranged weaponry. They are the last line of defense protecting Snoke, ready to destroy any threat that would dare penetrate so deeply into the First Order's heart.

## WARRIORS OF SNOKE

Supreme Leader Snoke's first line of defense is his reclusiveness. His reputation looms large over First Order territories, but he rarely makes public appearances, preferring instead to transmit his image across light years as a hologram. Very few ever see him in the flesh, and those that are afforded an audience with the Supreme Leader are kept within lethal distance of his ever-vigilant Praetorians. Snoke's Force abilities are strong, but his body is broken, his stride staggered, and his muscles weak. He relies instead on the combat prowess of his crimson protectors.

Scintillating
electro-plasma
blade

SEVENTH GUARD

Twin vibro-arbir blades in
connected configuration

Ultrasonic vibrational
blade cradle

Eight soldiers make up the Praetorian Guard. With their all-enveloping uniforms, their identities are completely concealed. The First Order aesthetic heavily favors symmetry ("What is past is future"), so they are actually four sets of pairs, with each pair brandishing the same weapons.

Tempered
micro-edge
carbonite blade

Electro-chain whip

Electro-bisento
tempered
blade surface

Large
pauldrons
to deflect
vertical
strikes

Segmented
plate armor
allows for
flexibility

Greaves
protect
lower legs

# ARMORED GUARDIANS

The layered armor of the Praetorian Guard is a high-tech onion-skin of laminate, impregnated with conductive wirepaths that, once powered, create an intense local magnetic field. Once this energy-intensive field activates, the powered plates can deflect blaster fire. Even a lightsaber will glance off, though a directed thrust will penetrate the shell. The mag-coils are costly, the plates heavy, and mag-field exposure is ultimately painful to the wearer, but such are the sacrifices of protecting the Supreme Leader. The Praetorians endure this out of unswerving loyalty and duty.

**THIRD GUARD**

**FIRST GUARD**

## PRAETORIAN WEAPONS

The Praetorians carry weapons that are high-tech versions of unpowered analogues found in primitive societies across the galaxy. Each tempered metal blade is connected to a compact ultrasonic generator that creates a high-frequency vibration across the cutting edge, increasing its lethality. Parallel to each cutting edge is an electro-plasma filament that creates an energized blade capable of parrying a lightsaber.

**BILARI ELECTRO-CHAIN WHIP
(ARTICULATED CONFIGURATION)**

Electro-plasma
filament

TWIN VIBRO-
ARBIR BLADES
(SEPARATED)

**VIBRO-VOULGE**

Power cell in hilt

Ultrasonic generator

**ELECTRO-BISENTO**

# KYLO REN

STRIDING ONTO BATTLEFIELDS with purpose, his robes whirling about his lean frame, is Kylo Ren. His body radiates with anger, a fiery temper honed to a deadly point. Ren's ability to use the Force grants him many impressive combat skills, but he is no Sith. He is the archetype of a new generation of dark side users—the Knights of Ren. Having studied both light and dark side lore, Ren is the embodiment of conflict, drawing upon contradictory teachings and deriving power from discord. Through his veins courses the bloodline of the most powerful Jedi and Sith, and Ren sees it as his birthright to rule the weaker beings in the galaxy.

*Unstable plasma blade matrix*

*Battered combat helmet*

*Crudely assembled hilt that mirrors ancient design*

Kylo Ren exists outside the command structure of the First Order, and has a direct link to Supreme Leader Snoke. In this way, Kylo's placement within the hieracy resembles that of Darth Vader in the old Galactic Empire. This is entirely by design.

## FALLEN SON

Kylo Ren once was Ben Solo—the son of Han Solo and General Leia Organa, and gifted Jedi apprentice of Luke Skywalker. Learning the truth about his grandfather, Darth Vader, causes him to turn against his family and fall to the dark side. Kylo betrays the other Jedi students studying with Skywalker, and is responsible for their destruction. This has earned him the nickname "Jedi Killer," which is whispered in the First Order ranks.

*Padded armor*

**Silver inlay radiates from the eyes as a symbol of power**

**Static discharge vane**

**Hinged mechanism seals tightly when shut**

**Wings are articulated to slant outward in flight configuration**

**Durasteel armor**

**Passenger compartment**

## KYLO REN'S HELMET

Patterned after the battle gear of the Knights of Ren, Kylo Ren's helmet conceals his identity and adds to his imposing demeanor. Servomotors drive articulated arms that separate the face mask from the helmet, letting Kylo remove the black form to stare down his opponents with uncontained malice.

**Articulated restraint plastron**

## INTERROGATION

To ensure the First Order remains unchallenged, Kylo Ren is tasked with hunting down any remnants of the Jedi. The dark warrior employs torture on his helpless captives, using a disturbing array of pain-inflicting devices. Beyond such tools, Kylo is a master of telepathic intrusion, using the Force to coerce or torment his prisoners into revealing secret information.

**Twin heavy laser cannon**

## REN'S SHUTTLE

The shuttle's enormous stabilizer wings serve as deflector shield projection and sensor surfaces, providing the ship with impressive data collection capabilities and resistance to incoming fire.

**Arm restraints**

### INTERROGATION CHAIR

Kylo Ren's interrogation chair is a collection of pain-causing implements distributed along a prisoner-confining frame. It is similar to devices developed by the Inquisitorius of the Galactic Empire.

**Electroshock conduit**

Kylo Ren is reunited with Han Solo on Starkiller Base. Solo begs his son to turn away from the dark side and come home with him, but it is too late. Ren ignites his lightsaber, piercing it through Solo's body, and watches as his father falls to his death.

# KYLO REN:
## SERVANT OF DARKNESS

*Lightsaber wounds typically cauterize, leaving dead scar tissue behind*

**KYLO REN'S HEINOUS ACTS** drive him deeper into the grip of the dark side. The personal pain caused by killing his father, Han Solo, makes him more conflicted and torn than ever, further destabilizing an already dangerous man. Kylo obediently carries out the Supreme Leader's orders to pursue and cripple the fleeing Resistance, but Snoke's berating punishments weigh on him, opening hidden emotional wounds just as his physical ones are healing. This pain leads Kylo to question his loyalty to the Supreme Leader, and to explore the connection he shares with Rey, his mysterious opponent on Starkiller Base.

*Delicate multiceps for injury treatment*

### MEDICAL DROID

After Kylo's lightsaber battle with Rey, an IT-S00.2 medical droid tends to the slashes across his chest and face, and the bowcaster wound to his abdomen. Although they are sealed with mechnosutures, bacta therapy is applied too late to prevent scarring.

*Kylo's dogged pursuit of the Resistance leads him to the abandoned world of Crait. It is here that he faces his old Jedi Master, Luke Skywalker, in lightsaber combat.*

*Partially exposed inner workings allow for easy modifications and upkeep*

*Static-damping fabric in cape grounds electrical interference*

### THIRST FOR POWER

Kylo has sacrificed everything in his commitment to the dark side, rejecting his family through his pledge of loyalty to Supreme Leader Snoke. But Han Solo's warning that Snoke is only using Kylo for his power echoes through Kylo's mind. Now that the First Order campaign to retake the galaxy is truly underway, Kylo plots his future through uncertain times. With ambition fueled by the dark side, Kylo prioritizes his own survival and ultimate ascension.

**KYLO REN'S LIGHTSABER**

*Ragged lightsaber blade leaves trail of embers with each swing*

*Built-in vocoder modulates voice*

*Shaft contains bifurcated kyber crystal*

## DARK DESTINY

Kylo has long been under the dark influence of Snoke, who has fanned the embers of resentment and isolation in Ben Solo into a white-hot anger. While Kylo projects the air of an obedient servant, he cleverly plots his own path to regain the status and power he has lost to Rey's blade. The fate of the scavenger from Jakku is inextricably connected to his, and Kylo cannot deny the bond they share in the Force.

**SHATTERED HELMET**

*Helmet smashed into shards in a fit of rage*

### KYLO'S CHAMBERS

After being rescued from the Starkiller disaster, Kylo returns to his quarters aboard the *Supremacy*, Supreme Leader Snoke's vast flagship. Here, Kylo's isolation allows him to meditate on the Force. He has left Darth Vader's charred helmet aboard the *Finalizer*, perhaps not ready to face that visage until he recovers from his failure.

*Heavy laser cannon*

*Shielded and armored cockpit*

*Transport Corps flight helmet*

**TIE SILENCER**

*Densely-layered solar collector surfaces*

# STARFIGHTER ASSAULT

Kylo inherits the amazing piloting skills of his father and grandfather, bolstered by his Force abilities. In pursuit of the Resistance fleet, Kylo leads Special Forces starfighters in his prototype TIE silencer. Kylo fires a volley of torpedoes that destroys the *Raddus*' hangar bay, but finds he cannot open fire on the warship's vulnerable bridge, as it holds his mother, General Organa. This decision is ultimately taken from him by a less-conflicted wingmate.

*Retractable ordnance bay in wing joint*

**LIEUTENANT JOBER TAVSON, KYLO'S SHUTTLE PILOT**

# CAPTAIN PHASMA

Brushed chromium crown with comlink transmission planes

Traditional cape of First Order command

Polarizing lenses with integral MFTAS (Multi-Frequency Targeting Acquisition System)

Vocodor speaker ports

Modified precision-crafted crush gauntlets

Mid-torso mounted ammunition holders

## CHARGED WITH COMMANDING

the stormtrooper forces of the First Order, Phasma's true rank is higher than the simplistic label "captain" would suggest. Although her position could easily afford her a well-appointed war room far from the battlefield, Phasma insists on seeing combat operations firsthand, and shuns any comfortable trappings of elevated rank. She wears distinctive chromed armor that broadcasts her authority, but also makes clear that she is a woman of action who fights alongside those under her command.

Phasma disagrees with General Hux over what it takes to make a soldier. The methodical Hux has developed automated training regimes that simulate battle situations. Phasma believes such programs don't test the true heart of a soldier: courage and tenacity.

## STORMTROOPER COMMANDER

Despite the intensely patriotic First Order records of the Empire's military effectiveness, Phasma privately concedes the shortcomings of its original stormtroopers. She believes it was the interference of politics—and shortsighted, ambitious Imperial officials—that led to soldiers of uneven skill and effectiveness. Phasma looks to guard against such meddling. She sees it as her duty to ensure that only the best soldiers wear the armor of the First Order, and that their numbers aren't wasted on trivial assignments.

Phasma's armor is coated in salvaged chromium from a Naboo yacht once owned by Emperor Palpatine. Its polished finish helps reflect harmful radiation, but it serves primarily as a symbol of past power.

> Phasma serves as the third partner in the unofficial command triumvirate of the Starkiller operation, alongside Kylo Ren and General Hux.

> Phasma takes it upon herself to memorize the serial numbers of all stormtroopers under her direct command.

## PHASMA IN COMBAT

Phasma has led from the front as the First Order expands into the wilderness of the Unknown Regions. Obsessed with physical perfection, she spends every waking hour honing her combat abilities. She is a qualified expert on all First Order small arms, and has also trained in vehicular and starfighter combat. She pays little heed to outdated notions of inequality between genders, an idea common on undeveloped worlds. To her thinking, a female stormtrooper is nothing new at all. The anonymity provided by their armor concealed the fact that both men and women served the Galactic Empire as stormtroopers.

Armorweave cape with First Order colors

Segmented sabatons

Chromium finish

PHASMA'S BLASTER RIFLE

Pistol grip

Macroscope sight gives eight-power magnification and low-light capability

Recurved trigger guard for two-handed grip

Extensible stabling grip for long range sniping

Finn, Han Solo, and Chewbacca take Phasma captive during their infiltration of Starkiller Base. They force her to lower the planetary shield, so that the Resistance can launch an attack. Furious that one of her former soldiers now has the upper hand, Phasma warns Finn that her troops will stop him and his friends.

# CAPTAIN PHASMA:
## RUTHLESS COMMANDER

The augmented sensors of Phasma's helmet penetrate the smoke of the *Supremacy*'s burning hangar bay. Her steely focus is on eliminating the Resistance infiltrators and finally correcting the anomaly that is FN-2187.

**PHASMA'S ULTIMATE LOYALTY** is to her own survival. This ethos has kept her alive and secured her elevated position as captain of the guard, overall commander of the First Order's stormtrooper forces. Within the First Order, she is used as a symbol of what the regime can offer— she was a native of a primitive world that was "tamed" and "civilized" with modern methods and technology. But behind that artificial polish, her treachery and craven selfishness are the true reflection of First Order principles. The fact that Finn, the most famous First Order turncoat, sees through her façade angers Phasma no end.

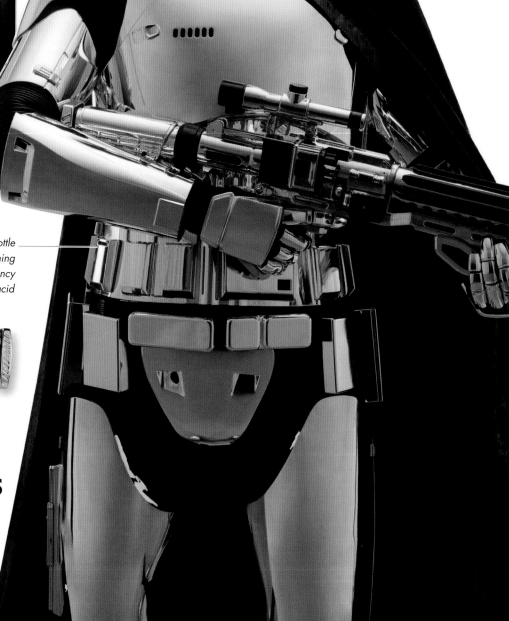

*Newly polished chromium finish*

*Grilled mesh serves as vocoder and breathing inlets*

A perfectionist, Phasma routinely patrols the areas under her command as a means of keeping her senses keen and her soldiers in line. Phasma makes most of these inspection rounds on foot, walking dozens of kilometers in a typical day.

*Magnetic bottle containing emergency cyrothoric acid*

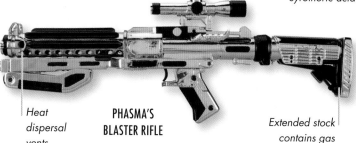

*Heat dispersal vents*

**PHASMA'S BLASTER RIFLE**

*Extended stock contains gas reservoir*

## SURVIVAL AT ALL COSTS

When Phasma escapes from a trash compactor into the chaos of the collapsing Starkiller Base, her first priority is clearing all record of her disastrous lowering of the station's shields. In a further effort to tie up loose ends, she goes to great pains to track down and eliminate Lieutenant Sol Rivas, a First Order officer who could have revealed her treason. This is not the first time Phasma secretly assassinated a troublesome ally.

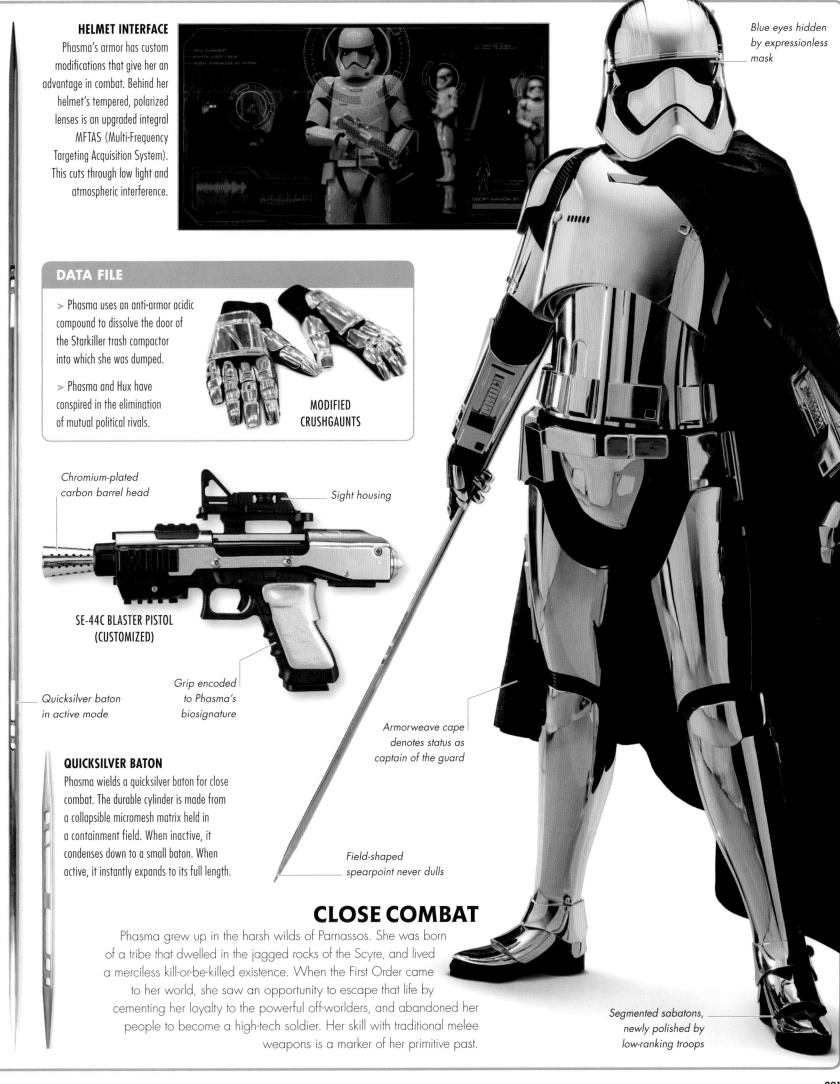

### HELMET INTERFACE

Phasma's armor has custom modifications that give her an advantage in combat. Behind her helmet's tempered, polarized lenses is an upgraded integral MFTAS (Multi-Frequency Targeting Acquisition System). This cuts through low light and atmospheric interference.

*Blue eyes hidden by expressionless mask*

### DATA FILE

> Phasma uses an anti-armor acidic compound to dissolve the door of the Starkiller trash compactor into which she was dumped.

> Phasma and Hux have conspired in the elimination of mutual political rivals.

**MODIFIED CRUSHGAUNTS**

*Chromium-plated carbon barrel head*

*Sight housing*

**SE-44C BLASTER PISTOL (CUSTOMIZED)**

*Grip encoded to Phasma's biosignature*

*Quicksilver baton in active mode*

*Armorweave cape denotes status as captain of the guard*

### QUICKSILVER BATON

Phasma wields a quicksilver baton for close combat. The durable cylinder is made from a collapsible micromesh matrix held in a containment field. When inactive, it condenses down to a small baton. When active, it instantly expands to its full length.

*Field-shaped spearpoint never dulls*

## CLOSE COMBAT

Phasma grew up in the harsh wilds of Parnassos. She was born of a tribe that dwelled in the jagged rocks of the Scyre, and lived a merciless kill-or-be-killed existence. When the First Order came to her world, she saw an opportunity to escape that life by cementing her loyalty to the powerful off-worlders, and abandoned her people to become a high-tech soldier. Her skill with traditional melee weapons is a marker of her primitive past.

*Segmented sabatons, newly polished by low-ranking troops*

# GENERAL HUX

**GENERAL HUX IS A** young, ruthless officer in the First Order, who has complete confidence in his troops, training methods, and weaponry. He has grown up celebrating his Imperial heritage—his father was a highly placed official in the Imperial Academy of old—and Hux feels it is a matter of destiny that he be given a chance to sit on the throne that rules the galaxy. Hux's experiences in warfare are entirely theoretical. Few would question the thoroughness or complexity of his simulations, but Kylo Ren has little respect for Hux as a warrior.

Pallor from time spent indoors

Charcoal gray general's uniform

Formal parade stance

A tense competitiveness exists between Kylo Ren and Hux. Both vie for the attention and approval of the First Order's mysterious commander, Supreme Leader Snoke.

Polished officer's buckle

## DATA FILE

> A man of science and technology, Hux has little understanding of or patience for the mystical side of the First Order that Kylo Ren represents.

> Hux's rank of general extends beyond the control of armies; he is the commander of the Starkiller operation, and able to order its use—pending Snoke's approval.

Traditional flared-hip breeches

## IMPERIOUS DESTINY

Hux was a child when the Empire surrendered to the New Republic with the signing of the Galactic Concordance. His father fled the Academy on Arkanis, and was one of the Imperials to make the exodus into the Unknown Regions, which the Empire had secretly been exploring. Hux grew up hearing legends of great Imperials, and how the Empire saved the galaxy from the violence of the Clone Wars. The young Hux firmly believed the galaxy needed to be saved from itself, as the New Republic was too weak to prevent the inevitable chaos.

Hux continues to use the stormtrooper training regimen pioneered by his father, based on ideas the elder Hux hatched as an Academy commandant. Hux has total confidence in his father's idea that stormtroopers trained through vivid simulations make the most loyal soldiers.

Insulated boots

## RANK INSIGINIA

The First Order uses a commemorative rank insignia system. It consists of armbands bearing the names of famous units and heroes of the Galactic Civil War.

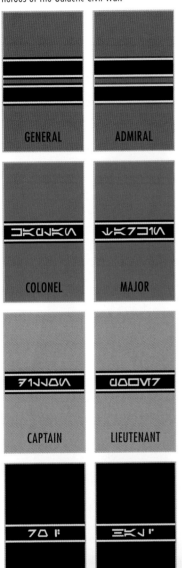

GENERAL

ADMIRAL

COLONEL

MAJOR

CAPTAIN

LIEUTENANT

SERGEANT

SQUAD LEADER

When chaos erupts in the hangar bay of the *Finalizer*, Hux oversees the attempts to capture the wayward TIE fighter that has caused the disruption.

GENERAL'S COMMAND CAP

*Crested command cap*

*Gaberwool officer's greatcoat*

*First Order insignia*

*Heat dispersing barrel head*

*Power cell*

*Lasing chamber access pins*

*Trigger is coded to Hux's fingerprint*

### HUX'S BLASTER

The officer's edition of the standard stormtrooper sidearm is cast in dark plasteel as opposed to the white body of the infantry version.

## WAR LEADER

When Hux stands upon the Starkiller superweapon, he can feel its destructive power coursing through the world. He knows it will signal the end of the illegitimate New Republic and cause the galaxy to bow to the power of the First Order. To Hux, the future of warfare is now—a war that can be won with a single shot.

Hux has always believed that appearances are vital for maintaining discipline, and wears a parade uniform designed to broadcast his authority as general.

*Ranks of TIE fighters*

*Base defense walker*

# GENERAL HUX:
## HIGH COMMAND LEADER

Remorseless gaze

Gaberwool expedition greatcoat

**ARMITAGE HUX IS BASKING** in his own glory. Under his command, the Starkiller weapon proved successful, despite its subsequent destruction. His vision of superior technology, precise conquest, and the methodical deployment of forces decimates the New Republic. Hux is responsible for the deaths of billions, but he feels no remorse. He has dispatched many enemies or would-be foes who became too dangerous a threat. This included quietly eliminating his own father, the elder General Brendol Hux. The young general is a man of no scruples, as he craves power above all.

Hux loathes Kylo Ren, and takes pleasure both in Kylo's failures and Snoke's anger with his apprentice. The fact that Kylo had to be rescued from Starkiller Base after being bested by a lightsaber novice delights the young general.

## RESISTANCE TRACKER

The next technological terror in Hux's arsenal is active hyperspace tracking. Originally explored in its infancy by the secret Imperial think tank known as the Tarkin Initiative, it has now evolved from theory into reality. Hux's engineers have perfected the system, creating a devastating countermeasure that tracks Resistance ships through hyperspace, making escape impossible.

Hux hides a monomolecular-blade dagger in his sleeve

Basic sight also serves as mount for custom scopes

**SE-44C OFFICER'S BLASTER PISTOL**

Encoded serial mark for security tracking

Replaceable perforated barrel head

The *Finalizer* is Hux's dedicated flagship. When it flies in formation with Snoke's *Supremacy*, Hux often transfers to the larger vessel, leaving Captain Peavey in command. Hux covets the *Supremacy*, but tries to hide such thoughts. He is aware that they may betray him to Kylo Ren and Supreme Leader Snoke.

*Volume control*

### CONTROLLER'S INTERCOM HEADSET

*Crested command cap with insignia*

*Fake code cylinder contains poison*

*Unit is mounted on bridge bulkhead*

*Tough plastoid shell*

*Primary holo-camera*

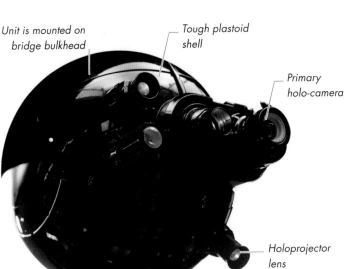

*Rank cylinder encoded with Hux's command clearance*

*First Order insignia*

*Holoprojector lens*

## HOLOPROJECTOR

Supreme Leader Snoke has eyes throughout the First Order fleet. Though he rarely ventures from the confines of his flagship, he can observe events and transmit his image through dedicated holoprojectors.

*Traditional flared-hip breeches*

*Often contains Hux's favorite beverage, bitter Tarine tea*

### OFFICER'S INSULATED DRINKING CUP

**PETTY OFFICER LANK PAZE**

## HUX'S STAFF

A team of officers keeps Hux's affairs in order, accompanying him as he travels between various ships and facilities. The stern Captain Tritt Opan has worked with Hux for years, and was a junior aide under Brendol Hux before him. Opan is skilled at carrying out Hux's dirty work, from assassination to sabotage, in order to ensure that no enemy can get the better of the general. Opan is tight-lipped about such duties, for he knows Hux could just as easily have him eliminated, if he so wished.

**CAPTAIN TRITT OPAN**

# STAR DESTROYER CREW

## LIEUTENANT MITAKA

Dopheld Mitaka graduated at the top of his Academy class, earning a prestigious placement aboard the *Finalizer*. He wears a commemorative armband that bears the name of a notable admiral of the Old Empire.

Rank cylinders

**THE GALACTIC CONCORDANCE** prevents the First Order from accessing the scattered Academies that had filled out the ranks of the Imperial Navy. Instead, the surviving Imperials create new Academies far from the prying eyes of the New Republic, situating them aboard Star Destroyers built in hidden shipyards on the far side of the galaxy. The young fleet officers produced by these shipboard schools often spend their entire lives aboard Star Destroyers, and many think of these giant warships as their homes.

Insulated helmet with integrated data displays

Flame-resistant duty uniform

## FIRST ORDER FLEET

Though too small to rival the navy of the Galactic Empire, the First Order fleet is nonetheless a formidable concentration of destructive power. The New Republic, with what First Order admirals mock as typical shortsightedness, was so thorough in its galactic disarmament that the First Order's secret fleet of Star Destroyers now stands almost unchallenged.

Lieutenant armband

Concealed tool pouches

Lieutenant Mitaka's impressive academic career proves to be inadequate when faced with the fierce temper of Kylo Ren.

## FLEET ENGINEER

Whether maintaining the power or weapon systems of the *Finalizer*, or operating its powerful turbolaser, tractor beam, or missile emplacements, engineers carry out their orders with precision.

With its immense hangar space, each *Resurgent*-class Star Destroyer carries with it the operational challenges of a bustling spaceport.

Stiff boots help in maintaining posture

# BRIDGE PERSONNEL

First Order starship crews work closely together to ensure the smooth operation of their massive vessels. Ever-mobile and immensely complex, Star Destroyers require constant attention from their personnel. As a result, each standard day is divided into six four–hour–long shifts, divided among three crew sections. Each section fosters a strong sense of unity and team identity.

The bridges of *Resurgent*-class Star Destroyers are much better protected than the exposed conning towers of old Imperial warships. The sunken work stations, a design that dates back to the Clone Wars-era Jedi cruisers, continue to be the preferred layout for architecturally denoting command hierarchy.

### BRIDGE SCREENS
Simplified bridge displays with limited colors allow for the rapid dissemination of complicated data.

## DATA FILE

> Access to command systems and certain areas of First Order vessels and installations is governed by coded rank cylinders worn by officers.

> The Resistance has limited intelligence of the First Order fleet, and many fear that the *Resurgent*-class is not the largest of the new Star Destroyer designs.

Intercom headset

Lighter fabric duty uniform

First Order insignia

Regulation spotless boots

Medical telemetry transmission array

**CHIEF PETTY OFFICER UNAMO**

**PETTY OFFICER THANISSON**

Command order tray (retracted)

Biological systems monitoring sensor

### INTERROGATION DROID
The new generation IT-000 is a corruption of medical droid tech. It is developed in violation of strict New Republic laws prohibiting torture.

### MOUSE DROID
A tireless mainstay from the days of the Old Republic, the skittish Rebaxan Columni MSE-series serves as a messenger, repair, and custodial droid aboard First Order starships and installations.

Stormtroopers follow their own chain of command while aboard fleet vessels, with a captain of the guard serving as ultimate authority over the troopers. However, during alerts, troopers will follow orders from any officer regardless of branch of service.

# STORMTROOPERS

**THE ARMORED SOLDIERS** of the First Order are the latest evolution of one of the galaxy's most distinctive symbols of military might: the stormtrooper. That the First Order had stormtroopers in its ranks was no secret to the New Republic, even though they were forbidden by the Galactic Concordance treaty. That they were more than a defense force and actually an invasion army is what few outside of the Resistance predicted. For the young men and women beneath the helmets, this is their moment in history. They have trained a lifetime to serve one purpose—using strength to bring order to chaos.

Helmet has integral polarized lenses

Filtration system with external tank hook-up

Web gear holds extra ammunition

Missions can turn into brutal bloodbaths. Kylo Ren leads stormtroopers into the village of Tuanul so that he can interrogate Lor San Tekka. He orders the troopers to burn the village to the ground and execute everyone living in it.

Sonn-Blas FWMB-10 repeating blaster—also known as a megablaster

## TRAINING REGIME

During the time of the Galactic Empire, inconsistent academy standards led to stormtroopers of varying skill and ability. The First Order enforces a more regimented approach to training, ensuring excellence across its reduced ranks. First Order stormtrooper training emphasizes improvisation and counter-insurgency operations. No longer tasked with ensuring loyalty to a galactic government, these soldiers instead need to know how to claw their way back into power.

### DATA FILE

> To keep the weight of their armor light, most stormtrooper helmets lack advanced imaging gear. Stormtroopers must use separate quadnoculars to provide them with enhanced imaging in the field.

Barrel cooling shroud

# CLOSE COMBAT

Worlds within First Order territory are ruled with cruel authority, and stormtroopers are the first line of punishment for anyone who needs to be reminded of this. To suppress unruly civilians, stormtroopers are trained in riot control tactics and assigned specialized equipment to beat their opponents into submission.

Lightweight composite betaplast ballistic riot shield

**Z6 RIOT CONTROL BATON**

Collapsible conductor contact vanes

Adhesion grip magnatomically pairs with trooper gloves

Spotlight

Cockpit

## TROOP TRANSPORTER

The Atmospheric Assault Lander (AAL) ferries up to 20 stormtroopers from an orbital carrier to a combat site quickly and precisely, avoiding anti-ship fire long enough to deploy its forces.

Landing gear

Disembarkation ramp

Lethal force used if riot situations escalate

# ADVANCED ARSENAL

To avoid the treaty restrictions that prevent galactic corporations from selling arms to the First Order, BlasTech Industries and Merr-Sonn Munitions spin off a subsidiary called Sonn-Blas Corporation, which operates within First Order space. This company manufacturers First Order weaponry, building on classic templates that date back to the Clone Wars. This weaponry boasts precision manufacture, rugged designs, and efficient energy cells for greater battlefield accuracy, ammunition yields, and operational lifespan.

Heat dispersing barrel head

Integrated sight and mounting bracket

**SONN-BLAS SE-44C BLASTER PISTOL**

Vibrating pulser warns of low ammunition

Adjustable J19 electroscope

**SONN-BLAS F-11D BLASTER RIFLE**

Power cell

Improved joint design allows greater flexibility than Imperial-era armor

Removable stock assembly

Magnatomic adhesion grip with integrated power feed indicator

Collapsible steadying grip

# STORMTROOPERS

*Sonn-Blas
F-11D rifle*

*Pauldron color
indicates rank*

*High-density
ammunition
power cells*

*Composite
betaplast
armor*

SQUAD LEADER

SERGEANT

*Utility
pouch*

OFFICER

## SECRETS UNCOVERED

Finn provides his newfound allies in the Resistance with valuable intelligence on the stormtrooper program. Finn's low rank limits the scope of his knowledge, but he is able to confirm a number of rumors. That the First Order draws stormtrooper cadets as children from conquered worlds is a firsthand experience for Finn. This strategy is an evolution of a training regimen originally devised by the late Imperial general Brendol Hux.

### HEAVY TROOPER

Specialist gear diversifies the stormtrooper ranks, giving commanding officers greater options when deploying forces. The heavy trooper specialist carries web gear loaded with extra ammunition. It is designed to power the megablaster squad assault weapon he or she carries.

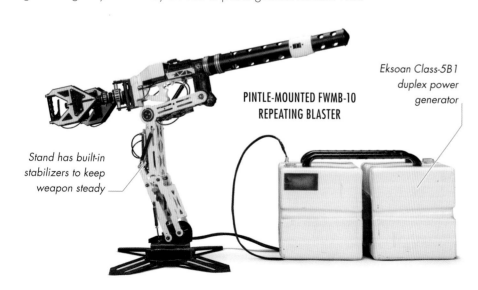

*Eksoan Class-5B1
duplex power
generator*

PINTLE-MOUNTED FWMB-10
REPEATING BLASTER

*Stand has built-in
stabilizers to keep
weapon steady*

The standard operational unit for stormtroopers is the squad, made up of ten troopers. It is common for squadmates to have trained together in large classes called batches—Finn trained under Batch Eight, which has graduates stationed aboard the *Supremacy*.

# EXECUTIONER TROOPER

The First Order shows its intolerance of disloyalty with public executions. Executioner troopers are not drawn from a specialist infantry unit. It is a role that any standard stormtrooper may find him or herself in, based on that day's assignments. Willingness to carry out capital punishment without hesitation is a mark of effective stormtrooper training.

Collimator sleeve

Polarized lenses with multi-frequency targeting and acquisition system (MFTAS)

Carbon-finish armor denotes executioner role

## LASER AX

Executioner troopers carry weapons that maximize the theatricality of First Order justice. The laser ax is a powered hand weapon with a quartet of collapsible claws, from which extend razor-sharp energy ribbons.

Emitter claws (in stowed configuration)

Monomolecular energy ribbon with cycling power

Temperature control body glove

Extended emitter claws

## EXECUTIONER HELMET

Executioner troopers wear custom-marked armor to denote their duty. Unlike standard armor, which broadcasts a trooper's serial number to their squadmates' helmet displays, executioner armor is silent in regards to identity, leaving the executioner anonymous to all but their commanding officer.

Vocodor can further disguise identity with voice modulation

Betaplast knee plate

Flexible weatherproof boots

# FLAMETROOPERS

**SPECIALIZED STORMTROOPERS** of the First Order, flametroopers carry incendiary weapons that can transform any battlefield into a blazing inferno. When strategically deployed, flametroopers can deprive the enemy of safe cover by torching it, while also supplying cover for friendly forces in the form of walls of fire that stormtrooper armor can withstand. In particularly dry and flammable environments, flametrooper deployment may lead to a quick and decisive victory, as the fires started by their weaponry grow to rapidly engulf any resistance.

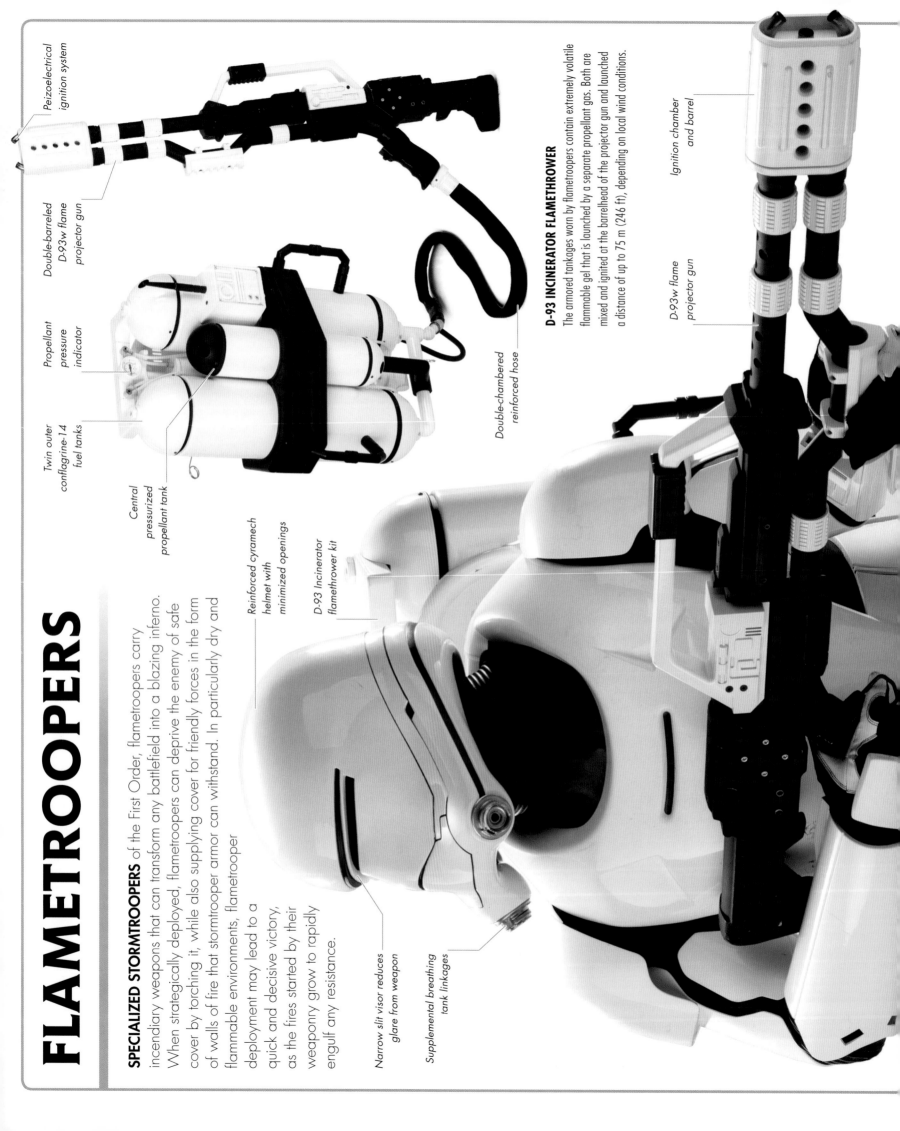

Peizoelectrical ignition system

Double-barreled D-93w flame projector gun

Propellant pressure indicator

Twin outer conflagrine-14 fuel tanks

Central pressurized propellant tank

Double-chambered reinforced hose

## D-93 INCINERATOR FLAMETHROWER

The armored tankages worn by flametroopers contain extremely volatile flammable gel that is launched by a separate propellant gas. Both are mixed and ignited at the barrelhead of the projector gun and launched a distance of up to 75 m (246 ft), depending on local wind conditions.

Ignition chamber and barrel

D-93w flame projector gun

Reinforced cyramech helmet with minimized openings

D-93 Incinerator flamethrower kit

Narrow slit visor reduces glare from weapon

Supplemental breathing tank linkages

Standard ten-soldier stormtrooper squads contain a slot for a single weapons specialist. Depending on mission profiles, that specialist may be a megablaster heavy assault trooper, a riot control trooper, or a flametrooper. The soldiers sent to raid Jakku consist of representatives of all of these types.

## DATA FILE

> Incendiary weapons are a millennia-old infantry mainstay, modernized by the Mandalorian supercommandos and the Republic clone troopers of the Clone Wars.

> Common Resistance nicknames for flametroopers include "roasters," "hotheads," and "burnouts."

*Heat deflecting armored gaiters*

*Articulated greaves allow for greater foot movement*

*Integrated knee cover*

*Temperature control body glove*

*Braced firing stance for maximum control*

*Positive grip boots*

## FLAMETHROWER TACTICS

Under most combat conditions, flametroopers are specialist units accompanied by standard stormtrooper infantry. The incendiary assault troopers are best deployed to flush out entrenched enemy positions, allowing the standard infantry to fire upon targets as they flee cover. The standard infantry also serves as protection, guarding the flametroopers. Flametroopers advance slowly and methodically, as it would be unwise to outrun the advance of the blaze unleashed by their flamethrower.

# SNOWTROOPERS

Betaplast helmet
with flared
neck shroud

**THE IMMENSE POWER** harnessed by the Starkiller requires technology that penetrates and spans an entire planet. This means the crew and support staff of the weapon must remain mobile, zipping across and through the snow-covered globe. For security and maintenance of the Starkiller's surface facilities, the First Order equips stormtroopers with cold weather gear that is an advancement of similar equipment worn by the shock troops of the Galactic Empire. The First Order also uses such gear in the conquest of low-temperature worlds in its growing territory of space.

Breather
tank inlets

Rank
pauldron

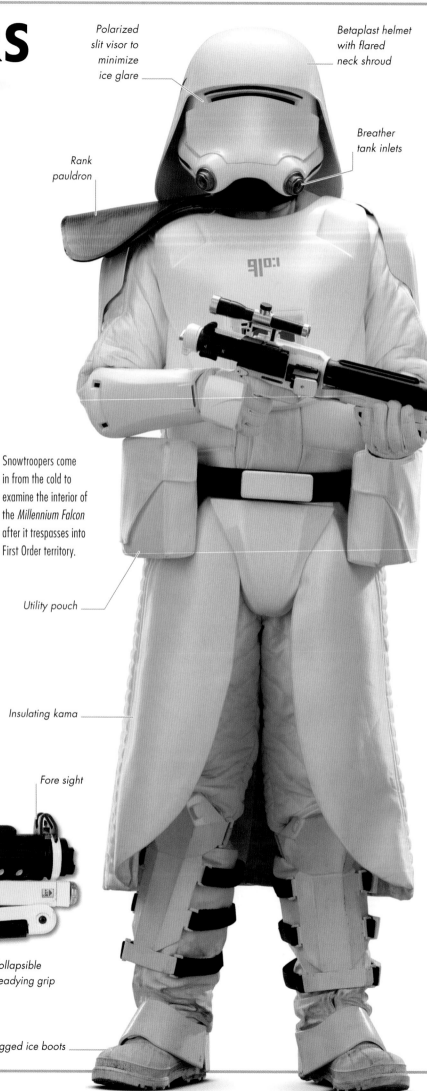

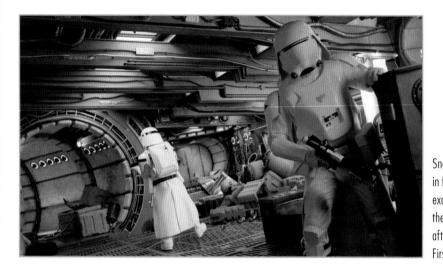

Snowtroopers come in from the cold to examine the interior of the *Millennium Falcon* after it trespasses into First Order territory.

## GUARDING THE STARKILLER

The result of decades of searching for a world in the Unknown Regions with exacting specifications, the Starkiller planet is destined to play a crucial role in the First Order's bid for galactic dominance. As such, it is very well protected. Snowtrooper teams were the first to scout the frozen world, eliminating any native life forms that could pose a threat to the colossal excavation and construction project. Snowtroopers now guard all access points to the control headquarters, supported by patrol droids.

Utility pouch

Insulating kama

Adjustable J19 electroscope with antifogging filaments

Cooling vanes with heat shunt

Fore sight

Blaster gas valve cap

Heated filament wraps around trigger

Collapsible steadying grip

Magnatomic adhesion grip

### SONN-BLAS F-11D BLASTER RIFLE
Snowtroopers carry standard stormtrooper weaponry, with slight modifications to shunt excess heat into the more sensitive interior mechanisms.

Rugged ice boots

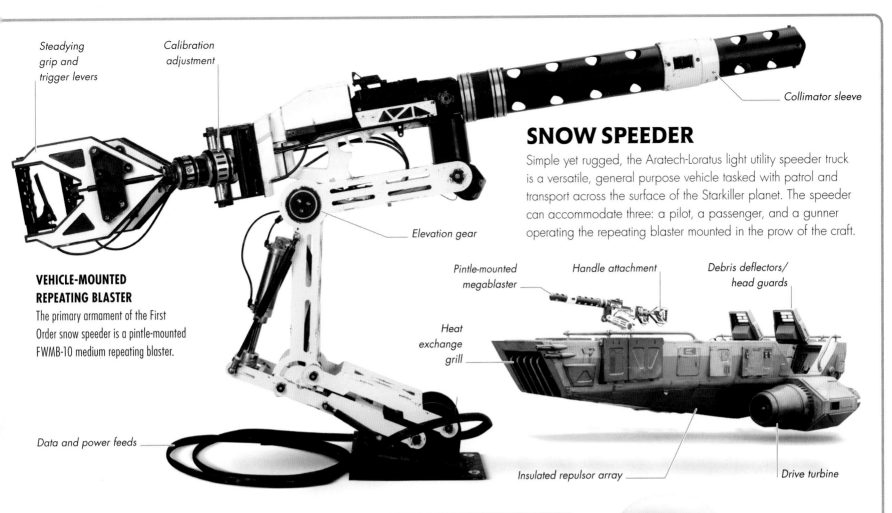

Steadying grip and trigger levers

Calibration adjustment

Collimator sleeve

Elevation gear

## SNOW SPEEDER

Simple yet rugged, the Aratech-Loratus light utility speeder truck is a versatile, general purpose vehicle tasked with patrol and transport across the surface of the Starkiller planet. The speeder can accommodate three: a pilot, a passenger, and a gunner operating the repeating blaster mounted in the prow of the craft.

## VEHICLE-MOUNTED REPEATING BLASTER

The primary armament of the First Order snow speeder is a pintle-mounted FWMB-10 medium repeating blaster.

Data and power feeds

Pintle-mounted megablaster

Handle attachment

Debris deflectors/ head guards

Heat exchange grill

Insulated repulsor array

Drive turbine

## BODY ARMOR

The snowtrooper chest plate is made of betaplast composite, with an icephobic coating that prevents the buildup of frost, even in humid conditions.

The deep mental conditioning that First Order stormtrooper recruits undergo helps eliminate weak-willed types likely to complain about cold conditions.

## COLD WEATHER GEAR

Snowtrooper armor consists of fewer plates than the standard stormtrooper kit, to permit increased movement in difficult snow or icy terrain. However, the whole suit is sealed in an insulated "envelope," consisting of wind- and water-resistant fabric worn over a dense, heat-retaining body glove. A powerful heating and personal environment unit worn as a backpack monitors and regulates body temperature.

Braced firing stance

Personal environment unit

Unit insignia

Insulated gloves with adjustable heating units

Greave adjust straps

Suit heater controls

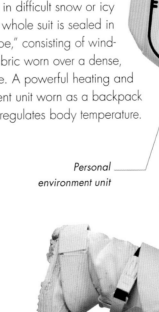

# STARKILLER BASE

**HIDDEN WITHIN THE** Unknown Regions that make up a vast swath of the galaxy westward of the Core is the true heart of the First Order. Concealed from the prying eyes of the New Republic and the questing probes of the Resistance, the descendants of the Galactic Empire have been amassing a power that violates the treaty restrictions of the armistice. But even their fleets of Star Destroyers and legions of stormtroopers pale in comparison to the destructive power of the First Order's newest superweapon: the sun-targeting Starkiller weapons platform.

## JOINT OPERATION

The Starkiller operation is an unprecedented undertaking, requiring the efforts of every service branch of the First Order. As it has the unique characteristic of being both a planet-based and interstellar weapon, the command and operations crew draws from both Navy and Army ranks, meaning admirals and generals, commanders and majors work side by side to prime the weapon for its devastating debut.

*Starkiller engineer duty uniform*

*Coded access cylinder*

*Static-grounded boots*

**TECHNICIAN MANDETAT**

**LIEUTENANT RODINON**

Starkiller Base is carved from the rock of an icy world, meaning that throughout the installation, mechanical surroundings give way to natural ones.

## BASE DEFENSES

Starkiller Base is the largest known deployment of First Order military forces. Legions of stormtroopers stand ready to defend the base, bolstered by TIE fighters, missile batteries, and powerful planetary shields that can deflect any bombardment.

*Stormtrooper executing a parade ground about-face*

*Enormous banner of the First Order*

### COLONEL DATOO

Colonel Datoo is a methodical officer in charge of the primary fire control room of Starkiller Base. He believes that such destructive power demands respect from all within the ranks of the First Order.

Crested command cap

## DATA FILE

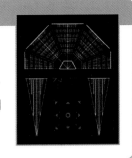

> The Starkiller is the culmination of Old Empire research into dark energy translations and hyperspace tunneling.

> The First Order selects the icy world for its unique energy-transmitting crystalline deposits.

The sheer size of the Starkiller operation means that the First Order must rely on droid workers. From the polished corridors to the frozen plains, droids carry out a wide variety of essential tasks.

## STARKILLER OFFICERS

The officers of the First Order military grow up shielded on the far side of the Unknown Regions. They are the first generation to grow up after the Galactic Civil War, and with an Imperially skewed version of galactic history. Under the guidance of Imperial veterans, they learn of a glorious past and the destiny that was stolen from them by terrorists who called themselves "rebels" and, later, the New Republic. These true believers see themselves as the only power capable of wresting the galaxy away from a path of chaos and corruption.

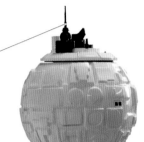

**SENTRY DROID**

Rolling casters for travel through base interior

Long-range communications antenna

**PATROL DROID**

Commemorative band identifying Kaplan, a historic Imperial warlord

Teal army uniform

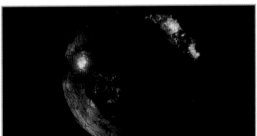

Han and Chewbacca plant explosives within the Starkiller Base to bring down the shield protecting the oscillator. Once they succeed in their mission and the oscillator is vulnerable, Resistance starfighters are used to destroy Starkiller Base.

## INFILTRATION

Han Solo and Chewbacca have made a decades-long career of infiltrating seemingly impenetrable fortresses. Starkiller Base is just the latest challenge in their path. Solo's foolhardy ingenuity lands a team of intruders into the heart of the First Order operation, but the sheer scale of the base is unlike anything they've ever faced.

# FIRST ORDER FLEET

**IN THE SHADOWY CORNERS** of uncharted space—and within the hidden ledgers of scheming weapons manufacturers—the First Order has been secretly building for war. When the New Republic fleet is vaporized by the Starkiller, it stands unopposed. The discovery of the Resistance base's location leads to the dramatic arrival of the First Order fleet at D'Qar. Spearheading the assault is the *Finalizer*, the *Resurgent*-class Star Destroyer under General Hux's command. Even this overwhelming force is merely the first wave of a larger offensive. The true scale of the First Order military is beyond even General Organa's worst-case projections.

Despite their impressive firepower, the First Order's capital ships fail to inflict critical damage on the *Raddus*. Instead, it is a squadron of tiny starfighters that lands the most devastating blow.

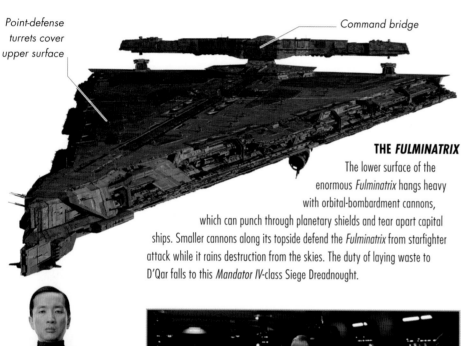

Point-defense turrets cover upper surface

Command bridge

### THE *FULMINATRIX*
The lower surface of the enormous *Fulminatrix* hangs heavy with orbital-bombardment cannons, which can punch through planetary shields and tear apart capital ships. Smaller cannons along its topside defend the *Fulminatrix* from starfighter attack while it rains destruction from the skies. The duty of laying waste to D'Qar falls to this *Mandator IV*-class Siege Dreadnought.

Worry lines publicly display private doubts

Officer rank cylinders

The command decks of the Dreadnought are bathed in dim red lighting. This helps maintain the gunnery crews' night vision as they switch between their targeting scopes and visual scans of the surrounding region of space.

## CAPTAIN CANADY
The commander of the *Fulminatrix*, Captain Moden Canady, served aboard the Star Destroyer *Solicitude* during the time of the Galactic Empire. Now in his 50s, he is surrounded by First Order personnel half his age and is dismayed by their youth. While he can appreciate and empathize with their zeal, their untested nature and failure to work effectively as a team chafes against his operational discipline. He is proud of his starship's power, but wishes it had a crew worthy of its destructive potential.

WARRANT OFFICER
SUDAY BASCUS

### TIE PILOT CORPS

The TIE fighter pilots of the First Order are particularly driven to destroy the Resistance. It was the failure of the Starkiller's TIE defenses that led to its loss, and now the surviving pilots are eager to prove their worth.

Ship-linked targeting sensors

Life-support unit

Faceted armored viewport

Solar collector array

First Order symbol

TIE/FO STARFIGHTER

TIE/SF STARFIGHTER

Heavy weapons turret

Lieutenant Poldin LeHuse, formerly part of the Starkiller aerial defense force, is newly reassigned to Kylo Ren's personal squadron. He holds nothing back in his desire to make the Resistance suffer.

**LIEUTENANT POLDIN LEHUSE**

### DATA FILE

> First Order crews develop intense loyalty to their starships, spending most of their time aboard a single vessel.

> The Resistance counts at least 30 Star Destroyers engaged in the pursuit of its fleet at D'Qar.

### THE *FINALIZER*

The *Finalizer* serves as General Hux's command ship. It leads the siege of D'Qar and coordinating the initial pursuit of the Resistance. With the arrival of Supreme Leader Snoke's enormous flagship, the *Finalizer* moves to a support role.

Primary command bridge

Heavy turbolaser batteries

Pursuit and combat command bridge

Much like the Empire, First Order design accentuates the idea of command hierarchies, with bridge officers literally afforded a higher platform than the noncommissioned crew working in sunken pits.

Upper deck superstructure

## CAPTAIN PEAVEY

Another Imperial veteran, Edrison Peavey is older than his commanding officer, Armitage Hux. He was a contemporary of Armitage's father, the late General Brendol Hux. Watching the younger Hux advance through scheming and nepotism has soured Peavey's view of the man, but he is professional enough an officer to keep his deep disrespect silent.

# TIE FIGHTER PILOTS

**ADVANCES IN TECHNOLOGY,** as well as the necessity that comes from no longer being the dominant galactic space force, have greatly benefited the latest generation of TIE fighter pilots. They are no longer callously treated as simply a line in a military ledger, and are given greater training and support in their missions. Their new generation fighter craft strongly resembles the TIEs of old, but they have a much greater survival rate than that suffered by the TIE pilots of the Galactic Empire.

The rudimentary deflector shields aboard new generation TIE fighters also smooth their passage through atmospheres, granting TIEs greater atmospheric control without needing streamlined modifications to the spaceframe.

## TIE PILOT CORPS

The new generation of TIE fighter pilots undergo rigorous training not unlike the dehumanizing drilling faced by stormtrooper cadets. They begin training at childhood, and grow up within the corridors of Star Destroyers, becoming intimately familiar with starship operations. The First Order maintains strict standards of reflexes, visual acuity, and hand-eye coordination. Those pilots who fail to measure up are transferred to other roles within the fleet.

Targeting sensors

Complete vac-seal helmet

Dark hull makes spacebound TIEs harder to target with visual scanning

Flight gloves and vambrace armor

Sienar-Jaemus Fleet Systems L-s9.6 laser cannon

## TIE FIGHTER

The standard fighter craft of the First Order fleet is the TIE/fo, an advanced version of the ubiquitous TIE/ln of the Galactic Civil War.

Weapon interface

Solar collector array wing

Left-hand control column

Right-hand control column and weapons trigger

Ejection harness

## FLIGHT CONTROLS

A sophisticated Torplex flight computer translates the movements of the pilot's two control columns into micro-adjustments to the twin ion streams that propel the craft.

Positive gravity pressure boots

## SF TIE FIGHTER

A more robust edition of the TIE fighter is the Special Forces variant, equipped with a heavy weapons turret (for a tailgunner), limited hyperdrive, and enhanced shield projectors.

Structural bracing

Pre-charged deuterium power cells

Heavy weapons turret

Special Forces unit marking

### DATA FILE

> Standard TIEs have finally been granted deflector shield technology—a profound change in philosophy from the days of the Galactic Empire.

> Aboard First Order Star Destroyers, TIEs are deployed from hangar conveyor mechanisms that carry them up from deeper storage decks.

TIE fighters engage the *Millennium Falcon* over the junk-strewn dunes of Jakku.

Red markings indicate Special Forces status

Ship-linked communications

SE-44C officer's pistol

Targeting node connects to external targeting sensors

Targeting interface projector

"Target acquired"

Padding

Life support gear

Detachable chin unit

Flexible vac-suit

Pilot comlink

Atmosphere hose

**SPECIAL FORCES PILOT HELMET**

A particularly stubborn Special Forces pilot pursues his prey through the inner workings of the derelict Super Star Destroyer *Ravager*.

# SPECIAL FORCES

Some TIE fighters and their pilots have distinctive flashes of red that stand out from their all-black armor. They are the mark of the Special Forces—elite starfighter pilots answerable directly to the upper command levels of the Starkiller operation. The markings date back to the decorated flight barons of the Old Empire.

# THE *SUPREMACY*

**EMERGING FROM HYPERSPACE** to eclipse the First Order fleet is the flagship of Supreme Leader Snoke, the *Supremacy*. The only *Mega*-class Star Destroyer in existence, the *Supremacy* is the command headquarters of the fleet. It is a giant wing, 60 km (37 miles) wide, which blurs the line between capital ship and mobile space station. The *Supremacy*'s interior not only carries entire armies into battle, but also serves as an industrial complex on a vast scale. Its enormous shipyards and manufacturing facilities can assemble and repair vehicles ranging in size from scout walkers to Star Destroyers.

**COMMAND BRIDGE**
The primary command bridge is found within the tower that caps the huge terraced structure at the center of the ship. From here, wraparound viewports provide a sweeping vista of the city-like structures that line the wing.

## SNOKE'S HEADQUARTERS

Snoke has no throne world, and has not rooted the First Order to a single planet that serves as its capital. Instead, he prefers to rule from within the safety of the *Supremacy*, staying ever mobile and maneuvering First Order agents onto countless worlds. Though Starkiller Base represented a sizable concentration of First Order power, Snoke's preparations meant that its destruction did not set back the regime's invasion plans.

Shielded bridge tower

Throne room

Engines line rear edge of wing

Forward artillery escarpment and docking bay band

Habitable "city" sprawl

Targeting data is projected onto visor

### FLEET GUNNERS
Lining the *Supremacy*'s surface are artillery emplacements that can lob devastating plasma volleys at any target foolish enough to come too close. First Order gunners fire at the retreating Resistance fleet, keeping up a steady barrage that pummels any fleeing ships that stray within cannon range.

Multi-spectrum photoreceptor with telescoping lens

### FIRST ORDER DROIDS
Unlike the Resistance, which values the individuality of droids, the First Order treats its machines as machines, resulting in cold personalities. Even the normally friendly BB-unit model has taken a sinister turn. BB-9E, for example, seems downright malicious when reporting transgressions.

Grilled openings permit ventilation and enhanced sensor transparency

**BB-9E**

### TRACKING ROOM
At the heart of the *Supremacy*'s advanced hyperspace tracker is a complex static hyperspace field generator. This envelops arrays of databanks and computers in a localized hyperspace field that accelerates their calculation speeds to unimaginable rates.

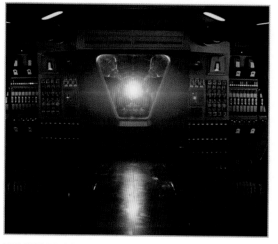

**GUNNER BRUN OBATSUN**

Star Destroyer docking bays

The communications complex monitors the galaxy's holonet traffic, identifying trends and weaknesses the First Order can exploit. Orders are dispatched to agents operating in New Republic and independent space.

Indicators show crate contains foodstuffs

Magnetic seal keeps contents fresh

**SUPPLY CRATE**

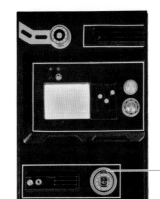

Code cylinder port

**FIRST ORDER ENCODER DATAPAD**

# WAR MACHINE

The *Supremacy*'s crew numbers in the millions, all carrying out Supreme Leader Snoke's escalating plan of conquest. On the operations decks, floors of open workstations bustle with efficient controllers. Many of the crew are subadults—too young for active combat deployment—and are among the First Order's most loyal servants. These personnel have been fully indoctrinated into First Order mythology—the idea of a chaotic galaxy requiring strong, unflinching order to bring it under control.

**LIEUTENANT LUSICA STYNNIX**

Work gloves have electro-sensitive fingertips that permit touch-screen access

Operations division status datapad

Rank sash commemorating Imperial Admiral Clyss Power

## JUNIOR OFFICERS

Whereas Imperial youth brigades were largely symbolic pledges of patriotism, the First Order puts its youth into actual military service. Raised since birth in the First Order fold, these subadults have a natural competitive streak that drives them to excel.

**GUNNERY CHIEF PEERA MASO**

**SCAN-OPS PETTY OFFICER RUMITAR SHAY**

# THE SENATE

**SINCE THE SIGNING** of the Galactic Concordance between the New Republic and the defeated Empire, the preservation of peace in the galaxy has been the dominant focus of the newly restored Galactic Senate. Convincing a war-weary galaxy that this period of renewal would be different proves challenging, as similar promises had been made during the rise of the Empire. As a bold demonstration of the government's dedication to break with historical precedent, the New Republic does not settle on Coruscant. Instead, its capital shifts across member worlds by a process of election.

Hosnian Prime serves as the current New Republic capital. Moving the Senate from Coruscant did much to convince the many disaffected systems that had tried to withdraw from the Republic prior to the Clone Wars.

Simple, modest robes of office

Signs of age respected in Tarsunt culture

Regent's turban

Surcoat of office

Robe of assembly

**BRASMON KEE OF ABEDNEDO**

**THANLIS DEPALLO OF COMMENOR**

## CHANCELLOR VILLECHAM

Lanever Villecham is a delegate from the Mid Rim Tarsunt system, and is in the second year of his first term of office as Chancellor of the New Republic Senate (the word "Supreme" has been eliminated from the title). Villecham's principal concerns in office include forging more agreeable trade relations with the neutral systems of the Trans-Hydian Borderlands. He is not worried about the First Order, as long as the former Imperials are contained within their borders and are following the dictates of the Galactic Concordance.

**NAHANI GILLEN OF UYTER**

Traditional Ubardiani headdress

Sash of agreement

GADDE
NESHURRION OF UBARDIA

DATA FILE

> Despite operating with the begrudging acknowledgment of the Senate, General Leia Organa's Resistance movement is a wholly independent body. Its actions are not sanctioned by the New Republic.

> The New Republic fleet is the largest defense force in the galaxy. Nevertheless it is a fraction of what it was during the Clone Wars.

Faced with concrete evidence of the First Order's march to war, Leia dispatches Korr Sella to the Senate, in hope of securing military assistance from the New Republic.

# KORR SELLA

Leia has come to realize that her reputation has been twisted by corrupt politicians, and the power of her voice has been weakened by personal attacks and rumors of delusion. She therefore relies on Korr Sella, a young envoy, to make her case for the Senate to take direct action against the First Order.

Studied diplomatic demeanor

Rank of commander

Resistance command uniform

No-nonsense stance exudes authority

Military cut boots

Tarisian colors of administration

ANDRITHAL ROBB-VOTI
OF TARIS

Formal Naboo coif

Frock of the Theed reforms

THADLÉ BERENKO
OF NABOO

Ultraviolet vision

ZYGLI BRUSS
OF CANDOVANT

# GUAVIAN DEATH GANG

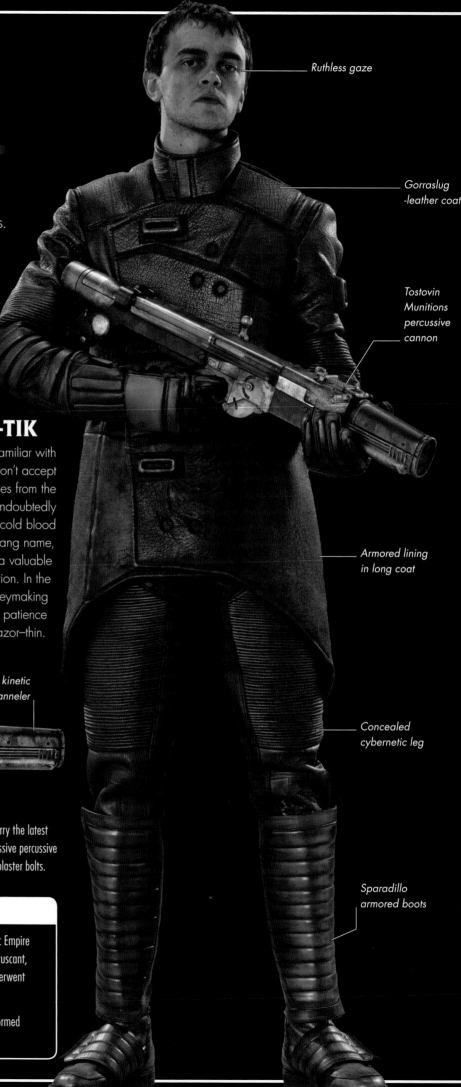

Ruthless gaze

Gorraslug -leather coat

Tostovin Munitions percussive cannon

Armored lining in long coat

Concealed cybernetic leg

Sparadillo armored boots

**TO BANKROLL HIS HAUL** for King Prana, Han Solo foolishly borrows 50,000 credits from the Guavian Death Gang, a criminal organization formerly based out of the Core Worlds. With the Guavian bosses tired of his excuses and delays, soldiers of the organization shadow Solo's freighter from his departure point on Nantoon. They seek to collect on Solo's overdue loan, and also make clear that a criminal organization with the words "Death Gang" in its name is not to be taken lightly. The security soldiers of the Guavian Death Gang wear high-impact armor that makes them stand out among other deadly criminals.

## BALA-TIK

Guavian frontman Bala-Tik is familiar with Solo's silver tongue, and won't accept another catalog of excuses from the Corellian. Although it would undoubtedly be easy to gun Solo down in cold blood and thus live up to the Death Gang name, Bala-Tik knows Solo to be a valuable source of profitable information. In the past, Bala-Tik has shaken moneymaking leads out of Solo, though his patience with the pilot grows razor–thin.

Bala-Tik speaks with the clipped tones of the Core Worlds, but with a harsher edge.

Targeting sight somewhat unnecessary, given weapon's blast radius

Reinforced kinetic channeler

Recoil counterweight calibrator

### PERCUSSIVE CANNON

Bala-Tik and the rest of the Guavians carry the latest in black market technology, such as massive percussive cannons that fire particularly explosive blaster bolts.

### DATA FILE

> Following the collapse of the Galactic Empire and the transfer of the capital off of Coruscant, the Core World criminal underworld underwent massive changes.

> The Guavians were displaced and reformed in the Inner Rim and Colonies regions.

### MASKS

Guavian security soldiers communicate via high frequency data streams transmitted from the central disk in their faceplates. They are otherwise expressionless, giving them an even greater air of menace.

### DEADLY WEAPONRY

The Guavians have contacts throughout the armament industry and pay a steep price for the latest weapon prototypes to go "missing" and end up in their hands.

Fore sight

Serial numbers completely obliterated

"Sawed-off" percussive cannon

Recoil compensator

Stabilizing grip

Tostovin Munitions micro-grenade launcher

Magazine drum

Central sensor and broadcasting dish

Arterial chemical shunt

Ablative gorget armor

Flexible armor shin guard

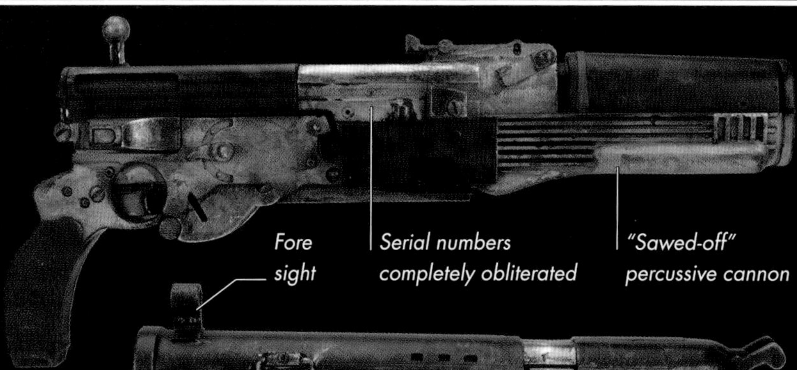

### SECURITY SOLDIERS

The Guavian Death Gang's red-armored foot soldiers are faceless killers who have sworn loyalty in exchange for cybernetic augmentation. A mechanical reservoir pump acts as a second heart, injecting a secret concoction of chemicals directly into the bloodstream, boosting a Guavian soldier's speed and aggression to deadly levels. Everything about them is inhuman and highly illegal.

Reactant emitter barrels

Segmented gauntlets

Utility belt

Bala-Tik is wary enough of Han Solo and Chewbacca to bring with him an armored contingent of security soldiers. He suspects Solo will be crazy enough to start a gunfight near an airlock.

# KANJIKLUB

**AN OUTER RIM GANG** of ruffians known as Kanjiklub often comes into the conflict with the Guavian Death Gang. Kanjiklub find common ground with their rivals in the form of a mutual hatred of Han Solo. The sly Corellian smuggler has borrowed money from both outfits to complete his risky cargo haul, and neither organization cares for Solo taking such risks with their capital. Added to that, Solo has twice left Kanjiklub empty-handed after failures to deliver cargo.

*Unkempt, feral appearance*

*Plastoid blast jerkin*

*Narglatch tusk vibro-spike*

*Hand-assembled blaster body*

**TASU LEECH'S "HUTTSPLITTER" BLASTER RIFLE**

*Gundark bone grip*

## TASU LEECH

Tasu Leech is the nominal leader of the scruffy Kanjiklub gang. Unlike their more organized and polished Guavian rivals, Kanjiklub resembles an unruly group of streetfighters and weapon-wielding thugs who dabble in extortion and piracy. Leech is not one for elaborate plans and rarely thinks beyond the next raid. Traditional to his frontier roots, he refuses to speak a word of Basic. He deems it a "soft language for soft people," though he can understand it well enough.

*Bell-mouthed blaster increases bolt spread*

**DONDERBUS BLASTER**

*Oversized amplifiers increase blaster bolt charge within barrel*

*Flexorcord-fastened assembly*

*Kintan strider ulna handle*

*Lightweight armor does not impede agility*

In accordance with Kanjiklub tradition, the leader of the gang may be challenged to combat by his underlings at any time. Tasu Leech has defeated many would-be usurpers to his command.

# KANJIKLUB MEMBERS

During their long enslavement by the Hutts, the human colonists of Nar Kanji developed fighting styles that incorporated improvised weaponry, both melee and ranged. The modern Kanjiklubbers celebrate the ingenuity that kept their ancestors alive, and typically equip themselves with intimidating patchwork armor, jury-rigged rifles, blades, and clubs.

Flame-retardant uniform

Tibanna-jacked boiler rifle

Braced firing stance for intense recoil

**VOLZANG LI-THRULL**

The raucous nature of Kanjiklub and the constant vying for dominance within the ranks means the ragtag group rarely operates well as a team, unless Tasu Leech is directly in command.

Pit-fighting injuries

Roggwart-bone rifle butt

Cybernetic leg rigged for fierce kicks

**CROKIND SHAND**

Zygerrian-style faux crests

Homemade explosive cylinders

Insulated palm sparring gloves

Scope largely for show on short-range weapon

Extended recoil-absorbing stalk

**LI-THRULL'S BOILER RIFLE**

Spin-sealed Tibanna bottle

Pump action gas compression

External accelerator barrel cage

**QIN-FEE'S "WASP" BLASTER RIFLE**

Reinforced galven circuit barrel

**SHAND'S HEAVY BORE RIFLE**

# RAZOO QIN-FEE

Razoo Qin-Fee is a lieutenant to Tasu Leech. He was banned from the underworld Zygerrian fighting circuit for suspected cheating—a remarkable feat in a sport that has no rules. A pyromaniac and tech expert, Razoo maintains the hodgepodge weaponry and explosives favored by the wild Kanjiklubbers, frequently upgrading and modifying their deadly tools of the trade to sinister specifications.

# RATHTARS

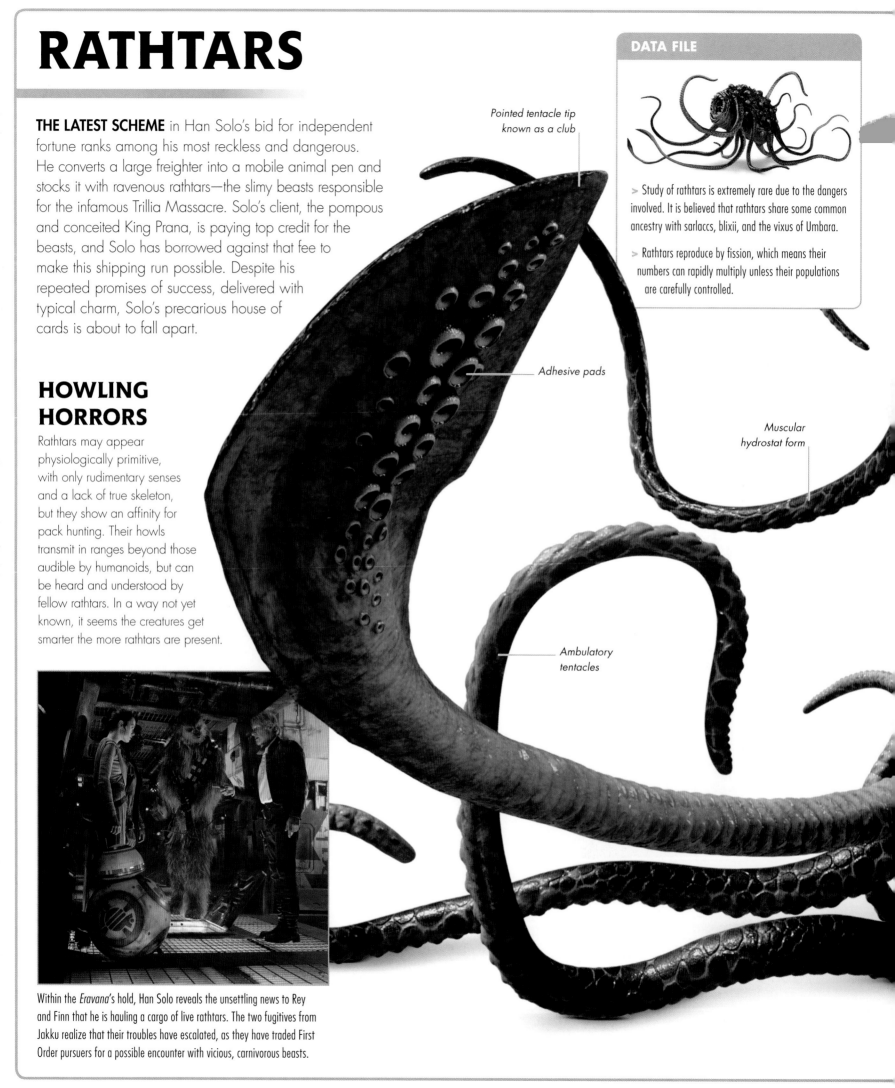

**THE LATEST SCHEME** in Han Solo's bid for independent fortune ranks among his most reckless and dangerous. He converts a large freighter into a mobile animal pen and stocks it with ravenous rathtars—the slimy beasts responsible for the infamous Trillia Massacre. Solo's client, the pompous and conceited King Prana, is paying top credit for the beasts, and Solo has borrowed against that fee to make this shipping run possible. Despite his repeated promises of success, delivered with typical charm, Solo's precarious house of cards is about to fall apart.

## HOWLING HORRORS

Rathtars may appear physiologically primitive, with only rudimentary senses and a lack of true skeleton, but they show an affinity for pack hunting. Their howls transmit in ranges beyond those audible by humanoids, but can be heard and understood by fellow rathtars. In a way not yet known, it seems the creatures get smarter the more rathtars are present.

Pointed tentacle tip known as a club

Adhesive pads

Muscular hydrostat form

Ambulatory tentacles

Within the *Eravana*'s hold, Han Solo reveals the unsettling news to Rey and Finn that he is hauling a cargo of live rathtars. The two fugitives from Jakku realize that their troubles have escalated, as they have traded First Order pursuers for a possible encounter with vicious, carnivorous beasts.

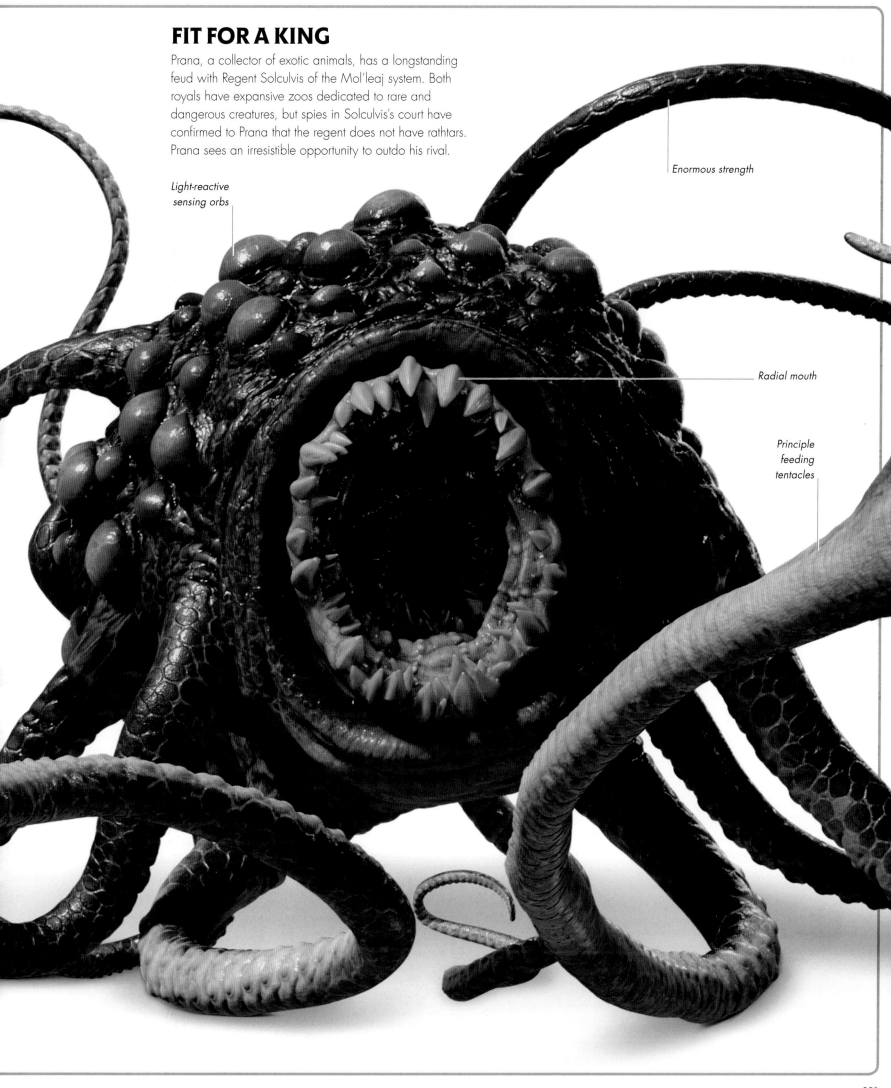

# FIT FOR A KING

Prana, a collector of exotic animals, has a longstanding feud with Regent Solculvis of the Mol'leaj system. Both royals have expansive zoos dedicated to rare and dangerous creatures, but spies in Solculvis's court have confirmed to Prana that the regent does not have rathtars. Prana sees an irresistible opportunity to outdo his rival.

*Enormous strength*

*Light-reactive sensing orbs*

*Radial mouth*

*Principle feeding tentacles*

# MAZ KANATA

**THE ECCENTRIC MAZ KANATA** has carved herself a safe haven on the fringe of the galaxy, where she holds court in an ancient castle as the preeminent font of smuggler wisdom. Kanata has gotten many a young brigand started in the freebooting trade, and has a preternatural gift for sensing the shifting tides of fortune in the galaxy. She has weathered many regime changes in her long life, and has not only survived, but found ways to thrive.

*Compact weapon fits Maz's small hands*

*Power setting adjust*

**MAZ'S BLASTER**

Rey is compelled to explore the deeper recesses of Maz's castle. There, she experiences an overwhelming vision brought on by the power of the Force.

*Statue of an ancient Jedi Master*

**BUST OF MASTER CHERFF MAOTA**

*Variable lens corrective goggles*

## PIRATE LEGEND

Maz's small form seems at odds with her legendary exploits, though her larger-than-life personality bridges these extremes. Affable and wise, she has seen much in her centuries of life and can quickly take stock of new acquaintances. In recent decades, Maz has concealed one of her greatest strengths—an affinity for the Force. Though she has encountered many Jedi, she never walked that path herself. Instead, she relies on her connection to the Force to keep out of danger.

**FUSION CUTTER HEAD**

**DIATIUM POWER CORE**

*Four-thousand-year-old hyperspace sextant*

*Bracelet of the Sutro*

*Ancient wroshyr wood*

**MAZ'S CURIO BOX**

### MAZ'S TREASURES
Maz has collected countless trinkets and treasures on her travels, including Luke Skywalker's old lightsaber. She has seen the tide of dark and light ebb and flow across the galaxy, and believes that this relic from the past may someday make a difference in the future.

*Maz keeps the box unlocked*

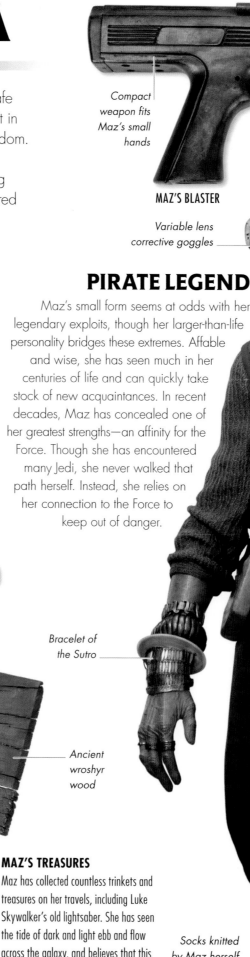

*Socks knitted by Maz herself*

Disfigured
Artiodac face

Kitchen
vibro-knife

Stained leather
apron

## STRONO "COOKIE" TUGGS

Tuggs is a centuries-old fixture within the castle. He has a surly attitude that is the subject of good-natured ribbing by those who eat his cooking in the dining hall.

CHADIAN AND UBESE
DRESSINGS

GORNT MEAT

BAKED CUSHNIPS WITH FRAL

MEAT TENDERIZER

FRESH FRUIT PLATTER

Thromba and Laparo are Frigosian cryptosurgeons who offer cosmetic alterations for those looking to disappear.

## MAZ'S CASTLE

Maz extends a warm hospitality to those who abide by the rules of her castle. Though the occasional scuffle inevitably erupts from so many spacers and pirates mingling in a small area, matters of politics and warfare must be left outside. Government emissaries are not given special treatment, and business trumps all matters of diplomacy and protocol.

Upon arrival at the castle, Finn, Rey, Han, and BB-8 pass by a jovial loadlifter droid named HURID-327.

### DATA FILE

> Services available at Maz's castle include appraisals, loans, medical assistance, food, room and board, games of chance, navigational updates, and basic repairs.

> Maz has only felt comfortable openly acknowledging her Force abilities since the death of the Emperor.

Witherstring
topboard

fingerboard
and nut

SEVEN-STRING HALLIKSET

Bodhar-bone
tone bars

Hypolliope
horn cluster

XYLOXAN

KASTA DRUM

TAYBIN RALORSA

INFRABLUE
ZEDBEDDY COGGINS

UBERT "STICKS" QUARIL

SUDSWATER
DILLIFAY GLON

## ENTERTAINMENT

Maz is a poet and painter. She delights in all forms of art, as it provides a way to discover new wonders. She offers board to traveling musicians in exchange for their performances, and aspiring and occasionally desperate bands brave the cutthroat-filled castle. Some are thrill-seekers; others are looking to line their coffers in ventures that have little to do with music.

# MAZ'S CASTLE

**MAZ KANATA'S CASTLE** has stood at the shore of a freshwater lake for millennia, and is a peculiar blend of ancient and current. Sensor arrays and communications gear help keep Maz connected to the wider galaxy, but a short walk from the castle plunges visitors into a primordial forest seemingly never touched by technology. Maz enjoys this contrast. To her, it is yet another manifestation of a cosmic balance. The relaxed formality of the castle attracts a motley assortment of outlanders from all across the galaxy.

The castle stands on what was once a battle site between the Sith and the Jedi.

## GRUMMGAR AND BAZINE

Grummgar is a big game hunter and gun-for-hire. He is obsessed with trophies, whether of the animal kind illegally poached in the wilds of distant worlds, or of the head-turning female variety attracted by his brute magnetism. Grummgar is too self-centered to consider anybody else's agenda, and does not realize that the woman he has attracted, Bazine Netal, is in fact a spy with a direct line to the First Order.

*Complex pattern is sensor-jamming baffleweave*

*Remote trigger interface*

*Sniper barrel flash suppressor*

**GRUMMGAR'S HUNTING RIFLE**

*Tough, puncture-resistant skin*

*Plastoid armor plate*

*Fierce Dowutin features include chin horns*

*Dagger coated with neurotoxic kouhun venom*

**GRUMMGAR**

**BAZINE NETAL**

*Sharp claws*

## WOLLIVAN

The inquisitive Wollivan is an interstellar scout and hyperspace trailblazer. He sells—or gambles away—valuable astrogational data and scavenged trinkets to smugglers and traders.

*Spacer's gloves*

*Blarina vac-suit*

It is hard for outsiders to tell members of the Blarina species apart. Wollivan has a large family, and when in trouble, he has more than once claimed to be the victim of mistaken identity.

*Kaleesh helmet conceals Delphidian heritage*

**CAPTAIN ITHANO**

*Armorweave-lined cape*

### CAPTAIN ITHANO'S BLASTER RIFLE

*Proudly captured from a Kanjiklubber*

Finn is desperate to find a new path in life. He seeks to depart Takodana with Captain Ithano and First Mate Quiggold, a pair of smugglers and pirates recommended by Maz.

*Gabdorin species*

**QUIGGOLD**

*Made from hyperdrive plotter pins*

*Power plant contained in chest*

### QUIGGOLD'S PRAYER BEADS

*Hydraulic line*

### GA-97
Unassuming servant droid GA-97 is aligned with the Resistance, and plugged into their intelligence network.

*Replacement leg made from fuel funnel*

*Collapsible legs for compact stowage*

# PIRATE CREW

"Lower ye shields and come about!"—these are the terrifying orders no starship crew wants to hear over their comm. They signal the arrival of Captain Sidon Ithano, also known as the Crimson Corsair, the Blood Buccaneer, or the Red Raider. He lets his reputation, and his First Mate Quiggold, do the talking for him. They travel the starlanes in their modified freighter, the *Meson Martinet*.

# CASTLE GUESTS

**TAKODANA IS A POPULAR** departure point for star travelers of every type. Its location in the Tashtor sector offers access to major trade routes that connect the Inner and Outer Rim. For those willing to brave the lawlessness of the Outer Rim or Western Reaches, Maz's castle is often the last taste of civilization. For those heading Coreward, it's a last gasp of frontier living. Fugitives avoiding law enforcement have their pick of escape routes, provided they have the credits to pay for transit and the skill to negotiate proper terms.

### PRU SWEEVANT'S BLASTER PISTOL

*Amplified galven chamber for intense blasts*

*Blue color is camouflage in Narq's fungus forests*

### PRU SWEEVANT

A blue-faced Narquois bandit, Pru uses contacts within the Mining Guild to find out the schedules of vulnerable convoys.

## DIVERSE CROWD

Many different reasons brings people to Maz's castle. A reformed criminal named Praster Ommlen, offers spiritual guidance to other criminals. Pru Sweevant robs commerce ships, while Sonsigo and Munduri are gemologists who appraise precious stones harvested on newly cataloged worlds. As different as they all may be, these beings connect, each offering something of value to another.

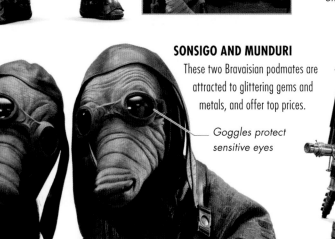

Takodana holds a host of new experiences for Rey. She has never seen a world so lush, so humid, and with such a diverse population.

### PRASTER OMMLEN

Ommlen is a devotee of the Sacred Ramulus, an Ithorian sect of worship. This Ottegan former gunrunner has put his life of crime behind him.

*Ottegan physiology similar to Ithorian*

*Faded ascetic robes offer little comfort*

### SONSIGO AND MUNDURI

These two Bravaisian podmates are attracted to glittering gems and metals, and offer top prices.

*Goggles protect sensitive eyes*

*Measures the angle of light within gem types*

**ELECTRO REFRACTOMETER**

**PRASHEE AND CRATINUS**

Prashee and Cratinus are Ubdurian brothers who love a good game of chance. They take advantage of their identical appearance to swap identities in profitable swindles.

*Aurodium belt buckle*

*Matching Ubdurian travel smocks*

## JASHCO PHURUS

When away from Maz's castle, Jashco is a pirate who prowls the Arrowhead Region east of Coruscant.

*Field-accelerated blaster rifle*

*Tricorraan raider robes*

## HASSK TRIPLETS

Near-feral subhumanoids, these Hassk thugs are frequently itching for trouble in the main hall of Maz's castle, but other, larger beings keep the peace.

## GWELLIS BAGNORO

Gwellis is an expert forger who specializes in transit documents. This mysterious Onodone doesn't talk about his past.

*Izby, a pet barghest and loyal protector*

*Battered VT-33d blaster pistol*

**SABACC CARDS**

*Coded value only redeemable at Maz's*

**GAMBLING CHITS**

*Large eyes offer keen night vision*

*Sensitive hearing*

**CHANCE CUBES AND FIGHTING DROIDS**

*Contains valuable technology*

**PRIZE BOX**

*Flesh-tearing fangs*

# GAMBLING DEN

Games of chance are a popular pastime in Maz's castle, as they provide a non-violent way for competitive cutthroats to prove their mettle. There are many casino classics like sabacc, pazaak, and dejarik. Other popular games include Deia's Dream, a board game favored by the insectoid Dengue sisters, and droid ball fighting, wherein spheroid droids bash against each other in an arena table. Droids of the same color are able to clump together to form more formidable fighters.

# CANTO BIGHT

**AS THE REST** of the galaxy falls into conflict, the planet Cantonica and its resort city of Canto Bight remain insulated from the chaos. This does not mean its citizens are unaware of the turmoil gripping the galaxy—rather, these rich barons of industry and commerce see it as an opportunity for immense profit. They have already made fortunes secretly supplying First Order armories. Now that open warfare creates a need for ammunition, technology, and other equipment, these profiteers eagerly foresee the wealth that it will bring.

The Old Town avenues that surround the casino complex are lined with luxury shops that promise a wide variety of rare and bespoke creations. The Raduli café and patisserie on Cabranga Street is a popular eatery.

### LUXURY SPEEDERS

Speeder corporations like Astikan Gridworx, SoroSuub Corporation, and Narglatch AirTech make their high-end luxury models available to Cantonica's rich and famous, in hopes of celebrities becoming living advertisements for their products. It's no small irony that those able to afford such speeders rarely need to pay for them.

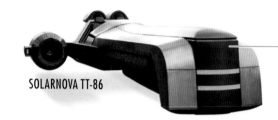

**SOLARNOVA TT-86**

**STREETBOSS 50-50**

**GROWLER-556**

Discreetly armored power plant

Ventilation airscoop grill

Formal pointed chauffeur's hat

**THOMKINS WATAM, CHAUFFEUR**

### ARRIVING IN STYLE

Guests to the opulent Canto Casino and Racetrack are greeted by valets and hosts who direct them inside without delay. Most guests do not pilot themselves, relying instead on organic chauffeurs who represent a greater status symbol than droid-operated or driverless vehicles. Immense underground parking zones make discreet meeting places for shadowy deals and information exchanges, away from prying eyes.

Glove fitted with concealed pocket to deliver bribes

### CASINO ENTRANCE

The tree-lined entryway to the Canto Casino was landscaped at great expense, with rare Alderaanian chinar trees engineered from a private seed bank.

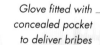

Ostentatious vessels such as the *Undisputed Victor*—captained by the tyrannical Baron Yasto Attsmun—voyage across the resort's artificial sea. The baron's attempts to woo nightclub owner Ubialla Gheal meet with little success.

**BRONZIUM MINERAL-OIL PITCHER**

**FATHIER-BRISTLE SKIN BRUSH**

**RINSING BOWL**

**DATA FILE**

> The casino and racetrack are the newest additions to what was once an ancient desert city.

> Canto Bight's responsive police department keeps tabs on trouble with datapads devoted to filing incident reports.

Canto Bight local Slowen Lo has made a fortune selling driftwood sculptures, and now owns a beachside residence. He is concerned about a shuttle seemingly abandoned on the beach, and reports it to the Canto Bight Police Department.

*Surgical implant lenses amplify failing eyesight*

**SLOWEN LO**

Kedpin Shoklop has been looking forward to a relaxing massage at Zord's. Lucky Shoklop won a two-week trip to Canto Bight.

## SPA TREATMENTS

The city's visitors and residents treat themselves to indulgent spa sessions in order to offset the "stresses" of their wealth and power. Zord's Spa and Bathhouse in Old Town offers a wide assortment of pampering amenities, including zero-gravity massagers, ozone chambers, medicated rinses, mud tanks, and gill-flushes. Zord's Spa leaves its customers in the capable hands of skilled specialists rather than entrusting them to impersonal droids.

*Chemically sensitive receptors can detect lactic acid in body tissue*

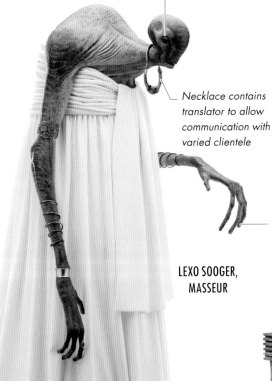

*Necklace contains translator to allow communication with varied clientele*

*Fingertips can create soothing vibrations*

**LEXO SOOGER, MASSEUR**

**STURG GANNA**

*Ticklish tail end, considered off-limits*

*Heat-retaining stone plinth*

# CANTO BIGHT POLICE

Holographic department
letters can reverse for
rearview mirror legibility

OFFICER
SOMMEL
ATANDU

High-impact betaplast
flexible neck guard

**PUBLIC SAFETY IS** taken seriously in Canto Bight, for secure visitors are generous visitors. Society is tiered here, with the wealthiest having the greatest sense of security and immediate access to justice—a flexible concept in Canto Bight. Every law and regulation in this city is negotiable, depending on the wealth of the suspect or accuser. Corruption is rampant in law enforcement, and as long as transgressions do not disrupt the resort's relaxing atmosphere, much can be ignored. Nonetheless, there are unspoken rules, and lines that should not be crossed.

The veneer of this coastal city is carefully and expensively maintained. Property crime is not tolerated here, and offenses such as vandalism or even littering are punished with greater severity on Cantonica than on most other planets.

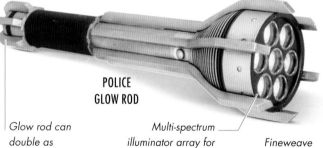

**POLICE
GLOW ROD**

Glow rod can
double as
crude baton

Multi-spectrum
illuminator array for
crime scene investigation

Fineweave
cape

## PATROL COPS

The most visible members of the Canto Bight Police Department (CBPD) are the Uniformed Branch. These officers patrol the Old Town and casino grounds looking for troublemakers and projecting a general air of order. Hospitality training is part of the CBPD academy curriculum, as keeping guests content is the key to keeping them docile. The police headquarters is also the site of the largest jail on Cantonica.

### POLICE SPEEDER

Anyone attempting to evade the law in Canto Bight had best move fast, as police employ swift, lightweight GB-134 pursuit craft, also known as jet-sticks. The nimble craft are well suited to navigating the narrow roadways of the Old Town.

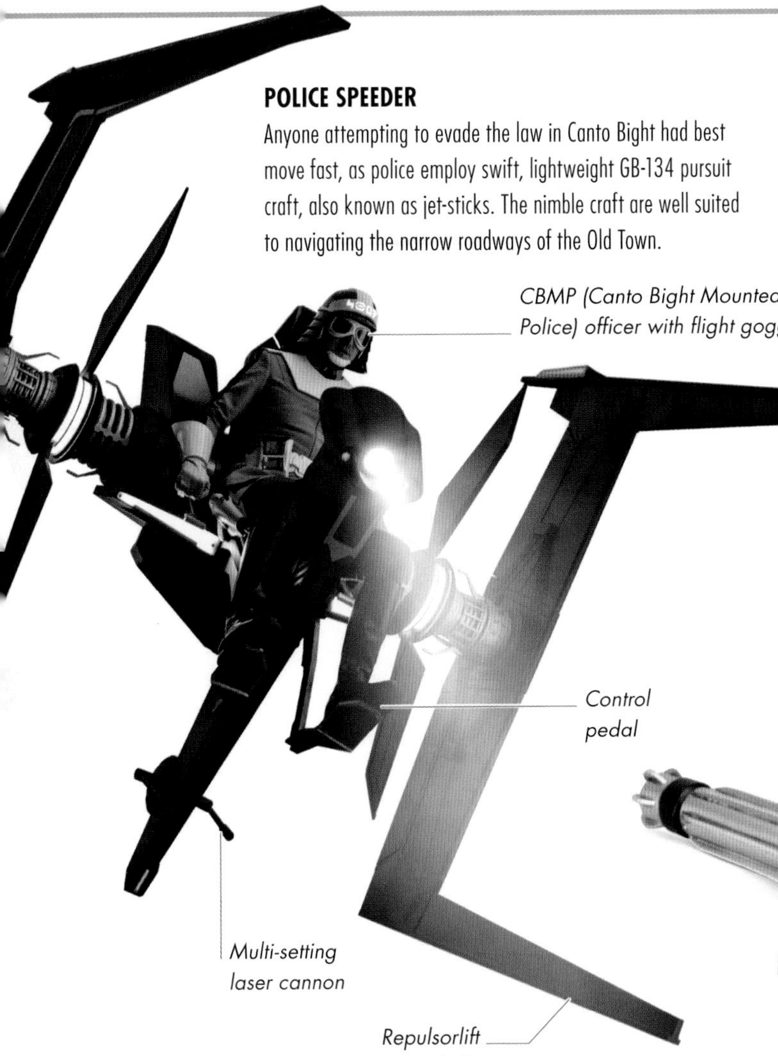

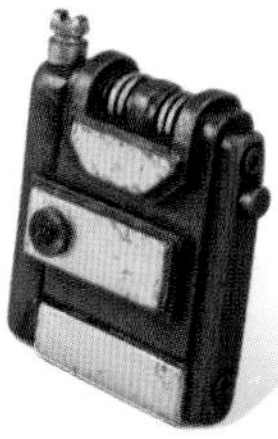

*CBMP (Canto Bight Mounted Police) officer with flight goggles*
*Control pedal*
*Multi-setting laser cannon*
*Repulsorlift generator forks*


SCRAMBLED LONG-RANGE COMLINK

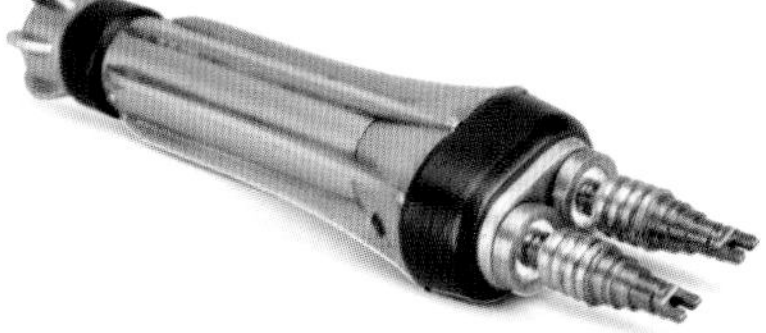

ELECTRO-SHOCK STUN PROD

*Noise suppression and range-extending barrel attachment*
*Rank insignia*
*Betaplast armored collar*
*Short-range wrist comlink*
*High-polish synth-hide officer's boots*


OFFICER STEPHEDEN THALDREE

## NON-LETHAL FORCE

The police are trained to subdue and arrest without resorting to lethal force, in an effort to maintain the confidence and comfort of the public. Even the slightest injury suffered by a bystander or a suspect could have costly legal and public-relations consequences. Officers' blaster weaponry is set to stun by default, and patrols carry electro-shock stun prods to deal with tough targets. Since weapons are prohibited in public areas, firefights in Canto Bight are rare.

**DATA FILE**

> The Canto Bight police headquarters stands on a hill above the Old Town, giving the officers in its surveillance center a clear view of events unfolding in the streets below.

*Additional ammunition reservoir in stock*
*Attached glow rod*


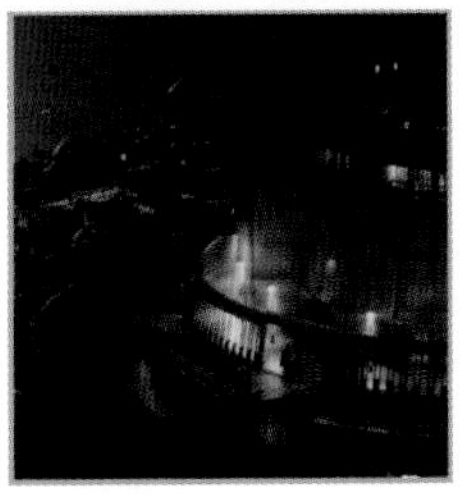

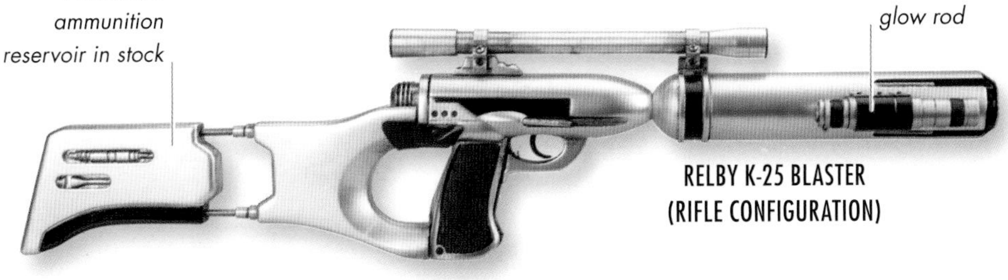

RELBY K-25 BLASTER (RIFLE CONFIGURATION)

RELBY K-25 BLASTER (DEFAULT CONFIGURATION)

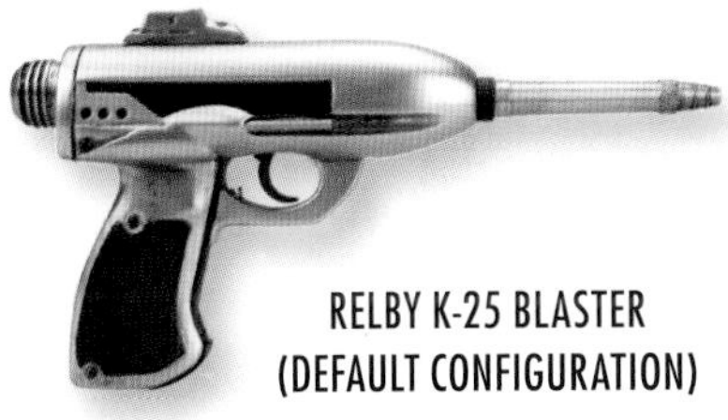

*Long-range macroscope*


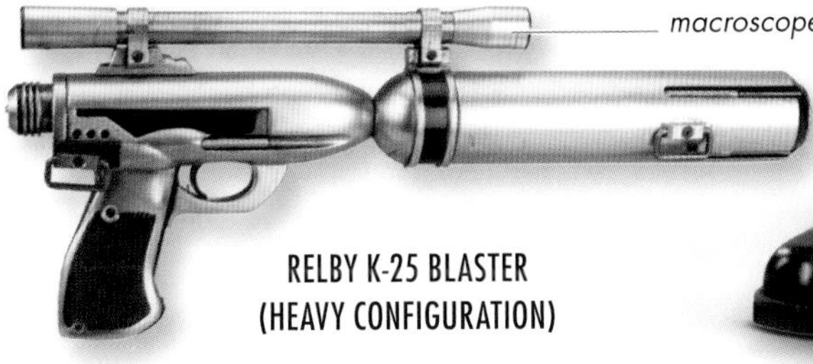

RELBY K-25 BLASTER (HEAVY CONFIGURATION)

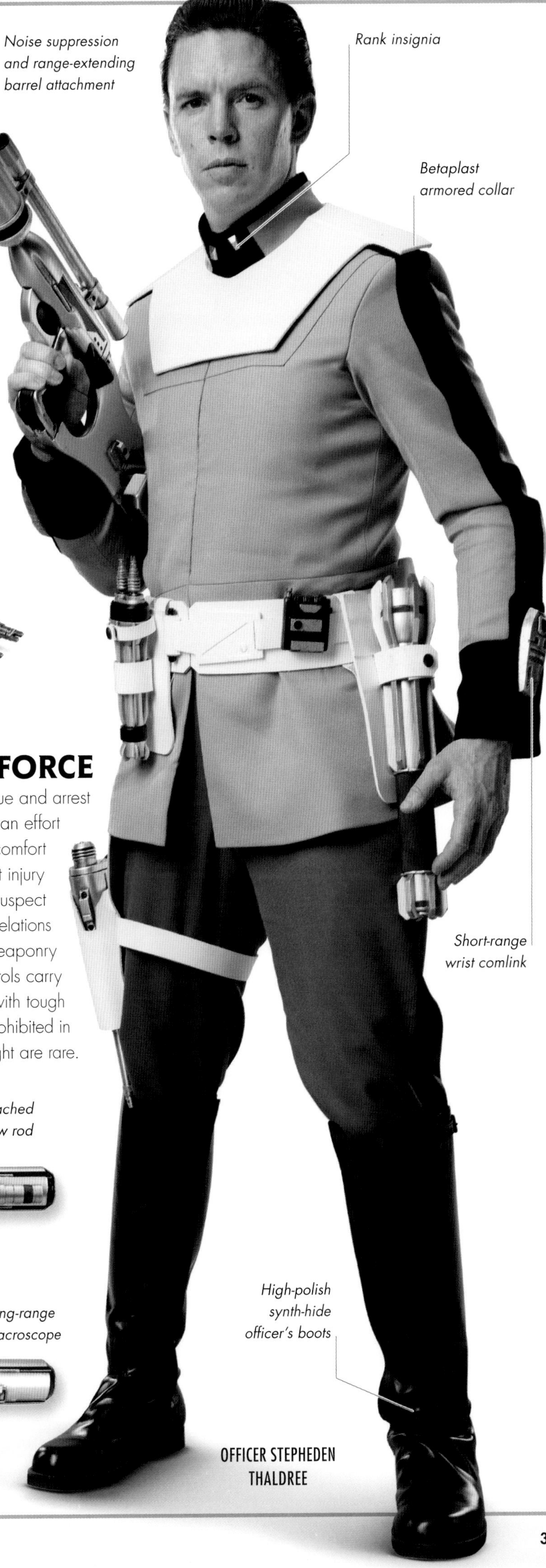

# THE CASINO

**THE ACTIVITIES OF** the Canto Casino and Racetrack dominate the days and nights of Canto Bight. This massive structure separates central Old Town from the artificial coastline. It includes a luxury hotel, top-rated restaurants, a shopping concourse, and bustling game rooms that overlook the fathier racetrack. Cantonica favors its own currency, made from precious aurodium, rather than relying on the volatile value of New Republic credits. Visitors looking to spend money in the casino must exchange their funds for the resort standard.

The casino's interiors match the sandy hue of the planet's original desert environment. Sweeping curved walls and ceilings are adorned with gleaming fixtures and stained glass windows.

## AT THE TABLES

The games of chance at the Canto Casino are more upscale than common amusements found in spaceport cantinas. Sabacc, binspo, and dejarik are frowned upon in favor of "gentlebeing's games," such as Savareen Whist, Zinbiddle, Uvide, and the ever-popular Hazard Toss, which is sure to draw a crowd when a gambler hits a winning streak.

**SOBURI HANNEMTIN, CROUPIER**

*Vest in casino livery*

*Hand signals let bouncers communicate silently*

*Fierce expression; the only casino employees permitted to scowl*

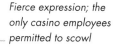

*Smartly tailored jacket conceals stun baton*

**PEMMIN BRUNCE**

**KUARI ZINBIDDLE CARDS**

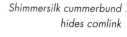

*A Vermilion Six is needed for an "Ion Barrage" hand*

*Shimmersilk cummerbund hides comlink*

**ROLLING CUP**

**HAZARD TOSS DICE**

*Polished dress shoes*

## CASINO SECURITY
While the CBPD can be called in to handle major disturbances in the casino, the everyday guarding of the venue is carried out by plainclothed bouncers who report to head of security, Pemmin Brunce.

The audience cheers as Sosear Latta, a lesser count, scores a perfect cross-cap in Hazard Toss. The table's croupier, Karlus Stee, keeps a sharp eye open for any cheating, but so far everything seems clean.

## GAMING MACHINES

For those looking to gamble at their own pace, the casino has carousels of floating slot machines. Gamers feed coins into the slots, causing the trio of reels to spin, and hope that they display a row of matching symbols once they come to a stop.

Coin input slot

Center symbol reel

Bonus and game status display

Payout tray

Repulsorlifts in base

Quantum-layered carbonite shell prevents tampering

## THAMM

Thamm is currently the most popular croupier on the gambling hall floor. His boisterous demeanor is encouraging to nervous gamblers, while his consoling nature helps cushion devastating losses. The tiny quadruped exudes an oddly pleasing aroma that helps put patrons at ease.

## CROUPIER STICK

Illuminated indicators change color to denote drink specials

## PRECIOUS METAL CANTOCOINS

Inner edge has magnetic strips to better gather coins

Tentacular embouchure

HHEX

Wide-set eyes

F'nonc horn gas bag

Traditional yekermo outer robes

Industrial Automaton SE8 servant droids shuffle across the casino, weaving their way through crowds to deliver refreshments to discerning customers.

## SE8 WAITER DROID

## THE BAND

Jhat, Dhuz, and Hhex are wind instrument players from a naturally musical species, the Palandags, who communicate through musical sounds of different pitches. Their powerful exolungs make them the galaxy's leading f'nonc horn performers.

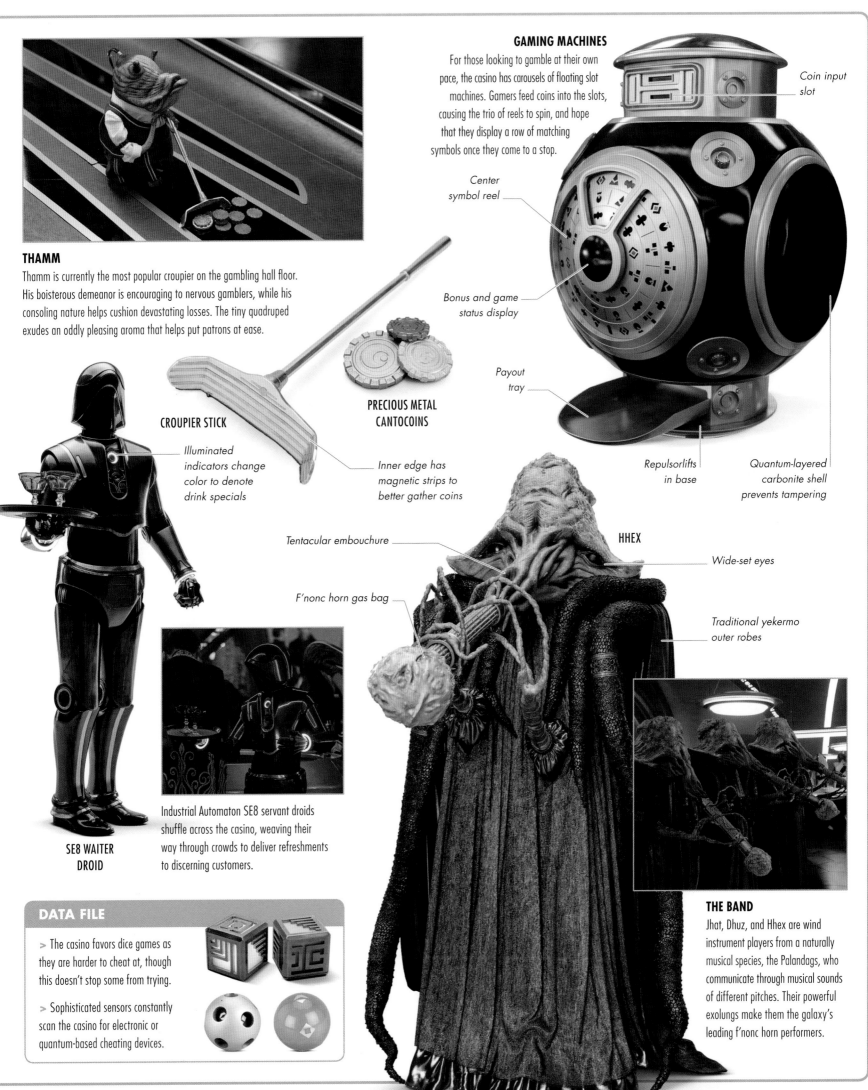

# CASINO GUESTS

**THE CANTO CASINO CLIENTELE** is a mixture of many kinds of beings, all with one thing in common—they have the money necessary to play the high-stakes games. Politicians, celebrities, and above all, business magnates gather to play and make deals away from public scrutiny. These revelers are insulated from the daily lives of other galactic citizens by their unfathomable wealth. That their profit-making may cause suffering to others is of no interest to the galaxy's elite.

Distinctive white streak (artificial)

Gaberwool tuxedo coat

Dress shoes have hidden compartments

### WINNING THREE

The trio of Wodibin, Thodibin, and Dodibin belong to an eerily lucky species, the Suertons, who appear to have the ability to subconsciously affect probability. They are closely monitored by casino security, but the "Winning Three" seem devoid of malevolence. These light-hearted beings care more about having fun than wealth.

Stellabora lapel bloom

Formal coat

**DODIBIN**

**CODEBREAKER'S PLATINUM RING**

Nova Sundari-style hairdo

Serendibite earrings

Fitted lattice dress with low clarion skirt

**"LOVEY"**

Matching Master Codebreaker's level of secrecy, his companion refuses to tell him her real name—so he simply calls her "Lovey."

## MASTER CODEBREAKER

Known only by his intriguing title, Master Codebreaker keeps his real identity a secret. He has posted his personal data in a public network node, wrapped in quantum-spread biohexacrypt code. It is an open invitation: Anyone who can crack his code is welcome to take over the mantle of Master Codebreaker. To date, no one has come close. The Canto Casino only lets the Codebreaker play dice games, and forbids him from any electronic forms of entertainment.

# THE ELITE

It is a mark of special social status to enter the exclusive, innermost clubs within the Canto Casino. Annual private parties stir up heated demand to get on the guest list, and past guests make exceptional efforts to remain relevant each passing year. Baroness Tagge-Simoni, for instance, is too frail and aged to attend in person, but appears as a young holographic head projected from a droid body.

Holographic head and neck

Medicated aerosol inhaler

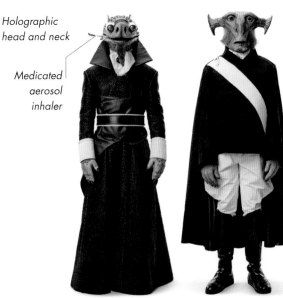

**EDMO ECTACLE**　　**SOSEAR LATTA**　　**DEFANCIO STORSILT**　　**CENTADA RESSAD**

## RHOMBY AND PARALLELA GRAMMUS

Wealth attracts eccentrics, and the Grammus sisters are among the most striking in the city. These identical performance artists claim to be from another dimension, and sometimes speak in a seemingly invented language.

**BARONESS WAYULIA TAGGE-SIMONI**

Thick, puncture-proof outer skin

The Onyx Bands of Cato Neimoidia

**TRYPTO BUBALL**

BUBALL'S CANE

Contessa Alissyndrex delga Cantonica Provincion (or more simply, the Countess of Canto Bight) is of royal blood and nominally presides over the city. Her husband, the Count, is rarely seen in public.

**THE COUNTESS**

Freshly exfoliated face

Self-spun web-chiffon drape

Engorged egg sac

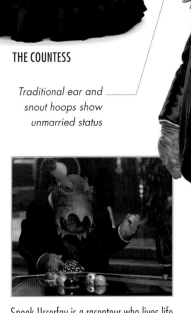
**NEEPERS PANPICK**

Traditional ear and snout hoops show unmarried status

## UBBLA MOLLBRO

Disdainfully called "new money" by the ultra wealthy, Ubbla Mollbro doesn't let that stop her making an entrance. This boisterous, egg-laden Xi'Dec opera singer is eager to find a hatching partner.

Snook Uccorfay is a raconteur who lives life to the fullest, in order to build a catalog of outlandish tales. He is drawn like a tractor beam to wealthy females, and dazzles them all with his exceptional dancing.

**SNOOK UCCORFAY**

# FATHIERS

**FORTUNES ARE WON** and lost on the backs of the racing fathiers of Canto Bight. These graceful steeds are bred and trained to maximize their speed and power, to the delight of their wealthy spectators. The pageantry and raw power of the sport conceals an unpleasant reality—these majestic animals are penned in tight quarters, frequently beaten, and are pushed to the limits of their endurance in the name of entertainment. Attempts to regulate or outright ban the sport have failed. There is simply too much greed involved to stop the races.

On Cantonica, a fathier's miserable and monotonous life spans only the distance from the track to the nearby stables. The pens within are so small that the animals must stay standing even while sleeping, leaving them exhausted and irritable.

*Identification chevron*

*Sponsor logo emblazoned on helmet*

**PINRADO NOZA**

**SHUMA KALAMO**

**ARCA YROCA**

*Padded wrist guards*

## BRED FOR SPEED

Fathiers are found across the galaxy, although their planet of origin remains a mystery. The ones found on Cantonica are bred specifically for speed and endurance. Their builds are lean, and their metabolisms are high and hot-blooded. Their powerful legs propel the massive animals to speeds upwards of 75 kph (46mph), while their long, wing-like ears help dissipate excess body heat and act as air-steering rudders.

*High cantle holds jockey in position*

**RACING SADDLE**

*Shape minimizes air resistance*

**HIGH-IMPACT HELMET**

*Hock joint undergoes immense strain when running or jumping*

## FATHIER JOCKEYS

The skill of the jockeys separates prize-winners from also-rans, but it is a risky profession: Falls are often fatal. Most races in Canto Bight are flat races—without jumps—meaning that raw speed is the ultimate factor in victories. Fathiers do not have the endurance to run at full speed across the entire race, so jockeys must apply force for bursts of speed when it can be most impactful.

**ELECTROCROP**

### JOCKEY EQUIPMENT

Fathier jockey gear is built to reduce weight and air drag. Sleek lycresh fabric envelopes the rider in a comfortable fit, usually finished with bright, attention-grabbing colors.

### DATA FILE

> Those who have never seen a fathier in person are often shocked by their true size. The average fathier stands 3 m (10 ft) high at the shoulder.

Ears have dense blood vessels near surface to assist in cooling

Wide binocular field of vision

Nose length can be deciding factor in close races

Looped dressage whip

Four dexterous arms typical of Cloddograns

BARGWILL TOMDER

Infected ingrown nose tendrils

Powerful forearm muscles

## THE STABLES

Managing the fathiers is the surly groom Bargwill Tomder. He oversees a small team of urchins—children abandoned on Cantonica by losing gamblers—whose small size assists in navigating the cramped confines of the stables. Tomder is ill-tempered, and his default approach to solving problems is simply to crack his whip.

As children do all across the galaxy, the stable hands engage in imaginative play to fill their downtime. Travelers from distant worlds bring them fragmented tales of adventure that excite their young imaginations.

**FATHIER BRUSH**

Unlock switch

**STABLE DOOR CONTROL**

Serrated hoof pick

Farrier rasp

Collapsible glow rod

**JEDI DOLL**

**WALKER TOY**

Rough work boots

Keratinized hoof absorbs gallop impact

**ARASHELL SAR**

**TEMIRI BLAGG**

**ONIHO ZAYA**

**GANGSTER DOLL**

# DJ

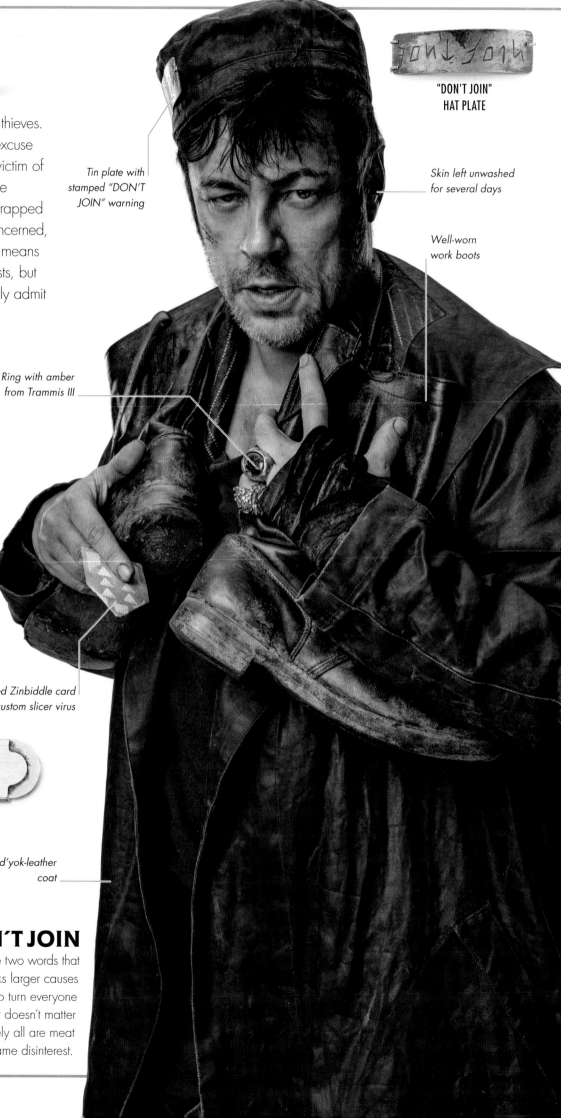

"DON'T JOIN"
HAT PLATE

**EVEN IN THE MOST** luxurious heights dwell lowly thieves. On the rare occasion that he feels compelled to excuse his actions, the man known as DJ claims to be a victim of society's imbalance, which tips all odds toward the wealthy. Although DJ prides himself on not being trapped by riches, he does covet money. As far as he's concerned, getting your hands on currency—no matter how—means you've earned it. The galaxy is filled with con artists, but DJ insists he's the only one honest enough to openly admit what he wants, and just how far he'll go to get it.

Tin plate with stamped "DON'T JOIN" warning

Skin left unwashed for several days

Well-worn work boots

Ring with amber from Trammis III

DJ has won and lost countless credits, but he weathers his constantly changing fortunes with an armor of cynicism. He is an opportunistic survivor, who will do or say anything to con another day.

Modified Zinbiddle card infected with custom slicer virus

Liquid-metal teeth automatically change shape to match lock

## SKELETON KEY

DJ has incredible technical aptitude and a knack for cryptography. He handcrafts his own computer spikes and bypass keys capable of temporarily befuddling even bio-hexacrypt-protected data networks. If he had the discipline, he could excel in the information security industries.

Kod'yok-leather coat

## DON'T JOIN

DJ has little that passes as a personal ethos, save for the two words that are the source of his nickname: DON'T JOIN. He thinks larger causes are for fools, since society is just a machine looking to turn everyone into a cog. First Order, Resistance, or New Republic—it doesn't matter where on the spectrum such a cause may lie, ultimately all are meat grinders that chew up their followers with the same disinterest.

338

## THE *LIBERTINE*

DJ steals the *Libertine* in order to depart from Cantonica. The sleek star yacht belongs to a manager with the Sienar-Jaemus corporation, who has been making a tidy profit selling surplus starfighters to independent worlds nervously expecting a new galactic war. DJ feels no qualms stealing such a prize, as he figures its original owner is just as corrupt as he is.

Recessed sublight drive

Communications spine

Repulsorlift generator plane

DJ finds comfort in the *Libertine*'s luxurious interior. He quickly bypasses locks granting him access to the ship's safe, liquor cabinet, and computer systems. Inside its databanks, he finds a catalog of starfighters for sale.

## CANTO BIGHT JAIL

Already known to local authorities, DJ purposely arranges his own arrest for a petty crime. The jail is the only place he can grab some sleep with the assurance that he won't be pestered by the Canto Bight Police Department.

Illegal x-ray monocle

JIO LOSTER

Guavian Death Gang jacket

Airspeeder jacket

Data goggles

Helmet with tracking sensors

Welding tank (empty)

OLVIN TEEPS

TORREB SAVATO

WOLFID DORNA

DAXO "ODDS" ECLOSS

## OTHER PRISONERS

The free-flowing wealth in Canto Bight attracts all manner of thieves and pickpockets, who find to their dismay that the locals pay well for security. Those who underestimate the CBPD will find themselves cooling down in the local prison. Criminals are able to work off their fines and sentences through menial labor in Cantonica's industrial and infrastructure services.

# INFILTRATION

**ONE OF THE MOST** significant Resistance missions is the infiltration of the Mega-Destroyer, when Finn and Rose take advantage of DJ's code-cracking skills to sneak onto Snoke's flagship. Disguised as First Order officers, their objective is to disable the hyperspace tracker long enough to allow the Resistance fleet a single, unmonitored lightspeed jump. Hurriedly navigating the enormous interior of the *Supremacy* while remaining inconspicuous proves to be a challenge. Finn's inside knowledge of the flagship's layout is invaluable, but vigilant troopers, officers, and droids await at every turn.

**SECURITY-SEALED OFFICER'S DATAPAD**

## TRAITOR'S RETURN

Finn is more than passingly familiar with Snoke's immense warship. As part of his service aboard the *Finalizer*, he spent several brief stints on the *Supremacy* as his Star Destroyer underwent servicing within the Mega-Destroyer's enormous docks. This included uneventful rotation through shifts of guard, inspection, sanitation, and gunnery duties. Finn returns, fearing that his reputation as the only stormtrooper to break ranks may precede him. He raids a laundry room, and dons the uniform of a nameless captain.

### DATA FILE

> DJ's code creates a gap in the *Supremacy*'s sensor perimeter. This lets the *Libertine* land in a heat-sink structure hidden in the glow of an immense engine.

> Unable to procure working code cylinders in the laundry room, Finn has to guide the team on a path to the tracking room that bypasses major security checkpoints.

**FIRST ORDER BINDERS**

### LAUNDRY DROID

Thousands of Serv-O-Droid SO-1P autovalet droids tend the uniforms of the First Order aboard the *Supremacy*. These menial, fifth-degree automatons have little personality programming, and are solely dedicated to the washing, folding, and upkeep of military linens.

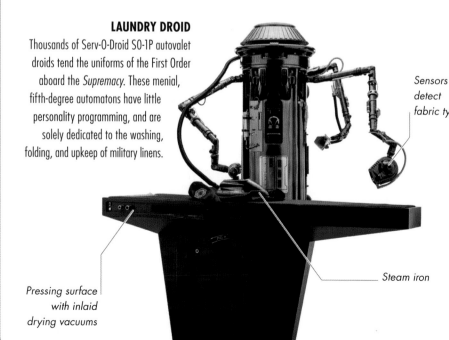

Sensors detect fabric type

Steam iron

Pressing surface with inlaid drying vacuums

Crested officer's cap with First Order emblem

Rank cylinders (blank and unregistered)

*Officer's cap in major's colors*

*Rose has bypassed the security locks on her blaster pistol*

### DROID IN DISGUISE
BB-8 is hard to hide in the open. A crude but effective disguise is improvised by emptying a garbage can, inverting it, and using it to cover the little droid.

*High-security access keys*

*Quick-draw shoulder holster*

### FIRST ORDER SECURITY BUREAU
The First Order Security Bureau ensures that loyalty to the First Order is drummed into personnel throughout their lives. Agents, observers, and loyalty officers closely watch the crews for any transgressions, hoping to prevent another desertion with disastrous consequences like FN-2187's infamous betrayal.

Tipped off by BB-9E, Colonel Garmuth gathers stormtroopers and alerts Captain Phasma of the infiltration. Garmuth intends to make a very public display of capturing and eliminating the traitor and his ally.

## INSIDE THE MONSTER'S DEN
In other circumstances, Rose would marvel at the technological advancements on display all around her, but her focus on her mission is unbreakable. She is not used to the pressed major's uniform, preferring the more comfortable baggy work coveralls of a Resistance technician. However, she plays the role well enough that a junior officer seeks her approval, little suspecting that Rose is not what she seems.

**COLONEL ANSIV GARMUTH**

*Ill-fitting, uncomfortable boots*

*Crates filled with payoff money on repulsor pallet*

### BLOOD MONEY
The First Order's plunder of worlds in its domain has filled its coffers with local currencies minted from precious metals. These peggats, aurei, and zemids have universal value as they can be melted down.

# CRAIT

**THE UNINVITING MINERAL PLANET** of Crait is tucked in a remote sector of the Outer Rim Territories. It is Leia Organa and Amilyn Holdo's secret endgame to bunker down on this former rebel world that had fallen off most modern starcharts. The Resistance's penchant for using old rebel-era caches and facilities is part of Leia's strategy, for she alone has a store of navigational information from the early days of the Rebellion that she has never shared.

Resistance U-55 loadlifter evacuation transports crowd into the gloom of the abandoned mine. The number of surviving personnel steadily dwindles as they rush out to repel the First Order's assault.

Transparisteel windows offer panoramic views

### RESISTANCE TRANSPORTS

Sienar Fleet Systems U-55 loadlifters, outdated yet still functional craft, are versatile orbital ferries designed for a variety of functions. These transports are commonly known as lifeboats to the Resistance personnel that crowd aboard them, and that is indeed their function during the dramatic escape to Crait's surface.

BlasTech hepta-mag ammunition carrier belt

Duty uniform identification plaque

Rank markings on helmet

Lenses filter out atmospheric dust and haze

**NEURO-SAAV ND.621 RANGEFINDER**

**KOO MILLHAM, GROUND LOGISTICS DIVISION**

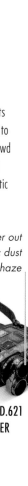

Flame-resistant material

## FINAL EVACUATION

With the fleet exhausted of fuel by the lengthy pursuit, the surviving Resistance crew brave the landing on Crait with the First Order still at their heels. Now numbering only in the dozens, the evacuees must bravely stage a holding action long enough for Leia Organa's distress call to be answered. Though their position is fortified, it is clear this may be their last stand.

**COVA NELL, TRANSPORT PILOT**

**SERGEANT "SALTY" SHARP**

## DATA FILE

> Crait's day lasts 27 standard hours. It orbits its star (also named Crait) in 525 standard days.

> Crait's breathable atmosphere comes from the slow dissolving of subterranean solid oxygen and nitrogen-suspending crystalline compounds.

# DESOLATE WORLD

Crait is a moonless, highly reflective planet. Its surface is covered in barren salt flats, with steppes of halite breaking up the terrain. Just beneath the salt is a thick crust of red crystalline rhodochrosite— a moderately valuable commodity. An underground briny ocean seeps through the softer minerals, creating an enormous cave network.

*The Nupayuni salt flats, named after the original mining charter*

## MINE BASE

The Nupayuni Mining Consortium charted Crait decades ago for potential excavation. The enterprise was abandoned, but early construction efforts erected an enormous blast door to withstand crystalstorms as well as wildlife. The Mining Guild abandoned its equipment rather than pay for its salvage, and rebel engineers made further modifications, adding a localized bombardment shield.

## BASE DEFENSES

The Rebellion hastily abandoned Crait during the base's construction when a traitorous ally alerted an elite Imperial unit, SCAR Squadron, to their location. The rebels left behind their Spiezoc v-120 and v-232 artillery emplacements.

*Keen eyesight adapted to low light conditions*

*Sharp crystalline "fur" evolved as a defense mechanism*

*Whiskers help a vulptex navigate darkened tunnels*

**BLASTER RIFLE RECHARGING BACKPACK**

**HORIZON-RANGE COMMS ANTENNA**

*Targeting data input*

## VULPTEX

Since its abandonment, the mine base has become home to a skulk of vulptices—fox-like creatures with crystalline features. The curious vulptices have explored the deepest depths of the caverns, finding pathways that only they can traverse.

**PORTABLE BATTLE ANALYSIS COMPUTER**

# FIRST ORDER INVASION

Ultra-dense matrixed composite armor

MegaCaliber Six turbolaser cannon

Armored crew cabin

Heavy fire-linked dual laser cannons

Reinforced forward leg armor

Capitate drum joint

Upscaled AT-AT rotating knee joint

Mecha-carpal foot structure

WHEN IT COMES TO fighting the Resistance, the First Order's armored forces are just as intimidating in ground combat as they are in intersteller battles. Proving the cyclical nature of history, the Battle of Crait recasts ancient siege tactics with modern battlefield technology. Newly designed colossal combat walkers plod overland to root out the entrenched Resistance.

## AT-M6

The All Terrain MegaCaliber Six (AT-M6) walker is effectively a towering mobile artillery cannon. Over 36 m (118 ft) tall, it has a hunched build and a knuckle-walking gait similar to that seen in simians. The heavy legs and finger-like structures are designed to secure purchase and stabilize the massively powerful turbolaser on its back.

Rank pauldron

Anti-glare slit visor

When the Crait defenses are cracked, First Order snowtroopers storm the breach and enter the darkened tunnels.

## SNOWTROOPERS

Although Crait superficially resembles an ice planet, it is a temperate world. The salt coating and crystalline structure have enough in common with subzero environments— intense surface glare and low skid resistance—that the First Order deploys its snowtrooper forces as infantry. The heating units that line their armor and gear are deactivated for this particular assignment.

The First Order walkers assemble in classic Veers Formation. In this attack strategy, the AT-M6s are tasked with the destruction of the enemy base's artillery defenses.

### AT-ST

The First Order's scout walkers are built upon the classic All Terrain Scout Transport design, with some modest updates. Improved gyroscopic systems have stabilized the walker's balance, and the armored shell has been upgraded following new breakthroughs in lightweight materials.

Unit marking

Shin strut

Reinforced cockpit armor

Layered body armor

Cockpit entry ramp for docking (retracted)

### AT-AT

The venerable All Terrain Armored Transport dates back to the Clone Wars, and has seen some upgrades for its latest First Order iteration. Lighter armor materials can now be layered, providing even more protection without increasing weight.

Weight-distributing footpad

Directed repulsorlift recoil buffer

Comms antenna

Defense turret

Armored kyber breech and fueling port

Retractable stabilization outriggers

### SUPERLASER SIEGE CANNON

The 200 m (656 ft) long superlaser siege cannon is a piece of miniaturized Death Star technology. A fiery tracer beam creates a path along which a devastating pulse travels toward the target, detonating with terrifying impact. However, the cannon requires time to charge up between blasts, during which time it needs escort walkers and air support to protect it. The First Order airlifts one of these enormous weapons to Crait's surface, hoping to penetrate the Resistance's defenses.

Forcing cone barrel head

Flashback suppressor field generators

Rotating rifled collimator assembly

Bundled strand made of 27,572 steelton wires

### AT-HH

All Terrain Heavy Haulers (AT-HH walkers) pull the siege cannon across the battlefield on ultra-dense cables. These crustacean-like tug walkers have legs that are a complex arrangement of crowded, redundant limbs. This greatly increases their resistance to battle damage.

# RESISTANCE GROUND FORCES

THE RELENTLESS FIRST ORDER pursuit forces the Resistance to land on Crait, and the conflict must be decided by a surface assault. Although the Resistance has the advantage of defending a fortified position, it is hopelessly outnumbered. Every capable Resistance fighter must pick up a blaster rifle, and try to hold back the First Order long enough for a distress signal to reach anyone capable of mounting a rescue. The abandoned rebel outpost's energy shield prevents orbital bombardmentt while its trench network and artillery emplacements transform Crait into a formidable, if desperate, bulwark.

Trenches carved into the crystalline rock of Crait form frontline and reserve positions for infantry defenders, supported by heavy artillery pieces and anti-armor cannons. The troops can retreat back into the base through underground tunnels.

Vo-pickup

**WRIST-MOUNTED COMM**

## GENERAL EMATT

Major Caluan Ematt is a veteran of the Galactic Civil War, having served in the Rebel Alliance since its earliest days. He is among the first of the former rebels to answer Leia Organa's call to form the Resistance. Ematt also accompanies Leia during her recruitment of Poe Dameron, and watches the young pilot's career with great admiration. The dwindling roster of Resistance leadership leads to Ematt taking on the rank of general, as he organizes and leads the exterior defense of the Crait outpost.

### DATA FILE

> Image-intensifying quadnoculars employ digital filters to reduce the blinding glare of Crait's salt flats.

> The Resistance is forced to use small arms fire to hold off TIE fighter strafing runs, a desperate move that requires pinpoint accuracy.

Multi-mag tactical ammunition pouch harness

Weatherproof insulated jacket

Neuro-Saav TE4.4 field quadnoculars

BlasTech EL-16 blaster rifle

Officer's boots are soon salt encrusted

# RESISTANCE TROOPS

The Resistance doesn't have dedicated infantry units. The soldiers defending Crait are technicians, pilots, and security sentries. Regular combat drills and clear lines of command prepare these improvised soldiers for the worst, and they put up a tenacious defense against the inexorable First Order advance. They retreat only when all other options have been exhausted. Many do not survive the onslaught.

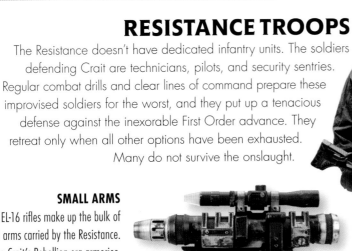

Bunched collar opens up to become hood

Protective antiglare visor

### SMALL ARMS

Outdated EL-16 rifles make up the bulk of the small arms carried by the Resistance. Breaking into Crait's Rebellion-era armories, the troops power up their weapons with old rebel cartridges. As a result, their blaster bolts change color from blue to red.

**BLASTECH DT-15 BLASTER PISTOL**

**BLASTECH EL-16HFE (HEAVY FIELD EDITION) RIFLE**

Power setting adjust

SERGEANT COBEL TANSIRCH

### TROOPER HELMET

Like most Resistance equipment, the helmets worn on Crait date back to before the mass disarmament that occurred at the end of the Galactic Civil War. They are no longer manufactured, but come to Leia via a "misdirected" shipment from a friendly senator.

# SKI SPEEDERS

Crait's discarded technology includes a few barely functional V-4X-D ski speeders. These ultra-light, low-altitude repulsorcraft actually predate the Rebel Alliance, and employ a ventral halofoil for stabilization and maneuverability. The rebels of yesteryear outfitted these one-time civilian sporting vehicles with a light coating of armor and outrigger laser cannons. During the Battle of Crait, Poe Dameron leads a frenzied defense of the entrenched Resistance with a squadron of hastily assembled ski speeders.

NODIN CHAVDRI

Emergency flight vest

Shuttle and transport pilot livery

The speeder cockpit, nicknamed the "tub" by Resistance personnel, is open to the air, with a reinforced windshield to protect the pilot. The Rebellion did at least see fit to place extra armor along the cockpit module's nose.

Cooling vents

Pilot's seat

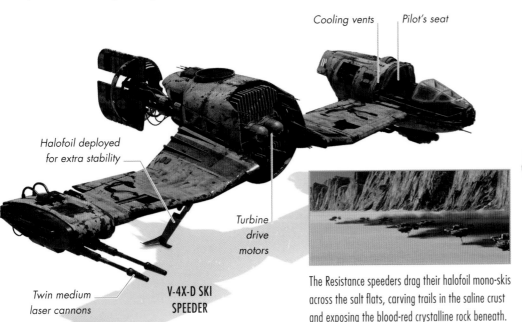

Halofoil deployed for extra stability

Turbine drive motors

**V-4X-D SKI SPEEDER**

Twin medium laser cannons

The Resistance speeders drag their halofoil mono-skis across the salt flats, carving trails in the saline crust and exposing the blood-red crystalline rock beneath.

# INDEX

Page numbers in **bold** refer to main entries

**C1-10P "CHOPPER"**

Strong but delicate clamps

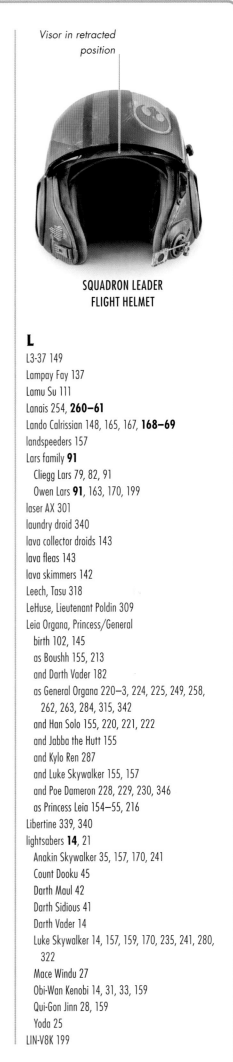

Visor in retracted position

**SQUADRON LEADER
FLIGHT HELMET**

*Swiveling cannon mounting*

**RZ-2 A-WING INTERCEPTOR**